W9-ACL-894

F
D36s

12532

DATE DUE			
GAYLORD M-2			PRINTED IN U.S.A.

SMITH

SMITH

WARWICK DEEPING

Lenoir Rhyne College
LIBRARY

19  32

ALFRED·A·KNOPF·NEW YORK

Copyright 1932 by Warwick Deeping
All rights reserved. No part of this book may be reprinted
in any form without permission in writing from the publisher.

Published October 1, 1932
Second Printing October, 1932
Third Printing October, 1932

823.9
D36s
12532

Manufactured in the United States of America

D365

SMITH

Chapter One

1

FOUR men were at work in the carpenter's shop.

Two large windows facing south let the sunlight in upon the benches and the shavings littering the floor. In a corner four coats hung upon pegs.

The windows of the shop looked out upon the yard of Messrs. Samson & Hoad, Builders, of Kingham, and this yard was full of building material: yellow bricks, red bricks, flettons, tiles, drain-pipes, sand, ballast. An old blue door, taken from some dismantled house, stood leaning against a black tarred fence.

The names of the four men were Tower, Smith, Woodward, and Scudder. Tower and Smith were busy at the benches. Woodward, a sallow man, baldish and with a sneering nose, was honing a chisel. Young Scudder, the shop's lout, had got hold of a broom and was preparing to sweep up the shavings. Both he and Woodward, while ostensibly at work, were waiting for the hooter of Royal's Carriage Works to set them free.

It was a Saturday in May, and above the tarred fence enclosing the yard a lilac showed its purple spikes. Tower, the foreman, would pause in the cutting of his mortise holes and look at the lilac bush. At sixty-five he liked to look at such things with some of the gentleness of a man who realized that life did not last for ever. Keir Smith, with his dark head bent over a piece of oak, might glance occasionally at the lilac bush, but his gaze was different. It was swift and cursory like that of a man lifting his head

[3]

momentarily to look at a flame, something that was both near and far, like a sunset beyond a factory chimney. His work absorbed him. For the moment his consciousness was constrained to follow the grain of the oak, and the purple flame of the flower belonged to tomorrow.

The facetious lad with the broom, finding himself close to the man who was sharpening the chisel, nudged him and then levelled the broom handle at the worker in oak. Their glances were pointed at the other man's figure, with its rather rounded shoulders and thin neck. It was an unusual figure both in its concentration and in its colour. It wore grey flannel trousers and a blue pull-over with a pattern of yellow zigzags. Its hair had a black intensity. The glances of the broom-squire and the chisel-sharpener met and mingled in a little sneer.

The lad winked. He resumed his sweeping, pushing the broom under the oak-worker's bench. It played challengingly round Keir Smith's feet.

"Don't mind me, old lad."

And then, since no notice was taken of the playful provocation, he clipped Keir's ankle with the head of the broom.

Keir turned his head sharply. He smiled, but the smile was willed, and at the back of his eyes other scorns were concealed. He knew that it was easier to shrug off the provocation than to challenge it.

"Doing the job thoroughly—aren't you, Scudder?"

He moved to one side so that the broom's progress should not be impeded, but he had been guilty of irony, and the delicate flavour of the product may not mingle with the smell of sawdust. The head of the broom was proposing to try a second flick at Keir's ankles, but at that moment Royal's hooter blew. The broom was pitched into a corner. The man with the chisel tossed it up, caught it deftly by the handle, and began to whistle.

They went to the corner of the shop where their coats

and hats hung. Keir was at work again on his oak door, and old Tower was looking at the lilac bush, but he had not put down his tools. Hooter or no hooter, he would finish cutting that mortise, but old Tower was grey-headed and beyond redemption. He did not matter. Keir did matter.

As they passed down the shop, he of the broom addressed the worker in oak. He too could be ironical.

"Haven't you heard the — hooter—Mr.—Smith?"

Yes, Keir had heard it, but being of a different fibre from those others, he did not regard it as the voice of his god. If he dreamed dreams—and he did dream them—they were not the negation of all ardour and all effort. If he had visions of some magic beanstalk up which he would clamber, he had cause to know that there were other men who would rush to catch him by the legs and pull him down. He did not turn his head to answer the broomster, and had he listened to the two voices in the doorway, he might have heard the sallow fellow with the sneering nose refer to him as a sulky swine.

Mr. Tower had laid down his chisel and mallet and was wiping his hands on the swell of his apron. It was a characteristic gesture. Old Tower's hands were always clean. He turned to look at Keir, and his look at him was kindly. He could have said: "You're not on the jump for the whistle. You haven't got a girl or a garden waiting for you." But, being wise in his generation, he understood the unusualness of Keir.

He said: "I'm going to stick a row of peas," and with a last glance at the lilac bush he took off his apron and hung it up, then put on his coat and his old grey felt hat, and somehow the brim of it fitted his round, mild face like a halo.

Keir straightened his back and smiled at Mr. Tower.

"That doesn't go on the time-sheet, Tom."

[5]

Old Tom let out a faint belch.

"Life isn't all time-sheet, my lad."

But Keir knew that as well as old Tom di

With the shop to himself, he went and ex
parcel of sandwiches from his coat pocket,
one of the benches, he made his meal and
lilac bush flagging him over the top of th
Tomorrow—Sunday—would be his lilac tim
and thought of the downs above the Shere V
whitethorns in flower, and the windings of
Way. He would be out on his bicycle at nin
a haversack on the handlebars, and in it a
day's rations.

Someone had come to the door of the s
watching him, an old man with the head of a
Samson of Samson & Hoad. His hair, like a b
cap, made his high colour seem all the mo
looked at Keir as though the young man's f
provocative as his name, for an unusual fat
glorying in the undistinguished name of Smi
tened the boy Keir Hardie.

Mr. Samson gazed and reflected. The origin
been a bit of a character, one of those intense
swarthy men who must preach, and wear with
either a red tie or a white one. The origina
preferred the red. He had been a firebrand,
with windy woe. But the boy was different. W
of very black hair and the smoulder of his eyes h
have worn a red tie and the aggressive glow of a
But Keir—Keir's urge was somehow separati
sonal. It set out and climbed the hills instead o
the soap-box. Its ambition was not to count h
transcend them.

Mr. Samson had very bright, dark eyes an
jocund vigour. There was very little that he

[6]

and hats hung. Keir was at work again on his oak door, and old Tower was looking at the lilac bush, but he had not put down his tools. Hooter or no hooter, he would finish cutting that mortise, but old Tower was grey-headed and beyond redemption. He did not matter. Keir did matter.

As they passed down the shop, he of the broom addressed the worker in oak. He too could be ironical.

"Haven't you heard the — hooter—Mr.—Smith?"

Yes, Keir had heard it, but being of a different fibre from those others, he did not regard it as the voice of his god. If he dreamed dreams—and he did dream them—they were not the negation of all ardour and all effort. If he had visions of some magic beanstalk up which he would clamber, he had cause to know that there were other men who would rush to catch him by the legs and pull him down. He did not turn his head to answer the broomster, and had he listened to the two voices in the doorway, he might have heard the sallow fellow with the sneering nose refer to him as a sulky swine.

Mr. Tower had laid down his chisel and mallet and was wiping his hands on the swell of his apron. It was a characteristic gesture. Old Tower's hands were always clean. He turned to look at Keir, and his look at him was kindly. He could have said: "You're not on the jump for the whistle. You haven't got a girl or a garden waiting for you." But, being wise in his generation, he understood the unusualness of Keir.

He said: "I'm going to stick a row of peas," and with a last glance at the lilac bush he took off his apron and hung it up, then put on his coat and his old grey felt hat, and somehow the brim of it fitted his round, mild face like a halo.

Keir straightened his back and smiled at Mr. Tower.

"That doesn't go on the time-sheet, Tom."

[5]

Old Tom let out a faint belch.

"Life isn't all time-sheet, my lad."

But Keir knew that as well as old Tom did.

With the shop to himself, he went and extracted a small parcel of sandwiches from his coat pocket, and, sitting on one of the benches, he made his meal and looked at the lilac bush flagging him over the top of the black fence. Tomorrow—Sunday—would be his lilac time, and he sat and thought of the downs above the Shere valley with the whitethorns in flower, and the windings of the Pilgrims' Way. He would be out on his bicycle at nine o'clock with a haversack on the handlebars, and in it a book and the day's rations.

Someone had come to the door of the shop and was watching him. an old man with the head of a Roman, Mr. Samson of Samson & Hoad. His hair, like a brilliant white cap, made his high colour seem all the more vivid. He looked at Keir as though the young man's figure was as provocative as his name, for an unusual father somehow glorying in the undistinguished name of Smith had christened the boy Keir Hardie.

Mr. Samson gazed and reflected. The original Smith had been a bit of a character, one of those intense and fervidly swarthy men who must preach, and wear with their oratory either a red tie or a white one. The original Smith had preferred the red. He had been a firebrand, spluttering with windy woe. But the boy was different. With that ruff of very black hair and the smoulder of his eyes he too should have worn a red tie and the aggressive glow of a Glaswegian. But Keir—Keir's urge was somehow separative and personal. It set out and climbed the hills instead of mounting the soap-box. Its ambition was not to count heads, but to transcend them.

Mr. Samson had very bright, dark eyes and an air of jocund vigour. There was very little that he missed, nor had he missed his opportunities. He knew that old Tower would soon be on the shelf, and that as a foreman old Tom was too mild and easy. Inevitably, Keir was the man for the job, but Keir would never be popular. He set too hot a pace. He was unusual, and the world distrusts the unusual, for it casts a shadow over the plains.

Mr. Samson walked into the shop. Kingham knew him without a hat in all weather and in all places, and said that old Samson was foolishly proud of his white hair and boyish skin, and that the old rascal still had an eye for the women. It was possible, for his handsome head and jocund eyes were very noticeable, even in a crowd. But if Mr. Samson had looks, Keir had manners. He got off the bench and stood, not like an employee on parade, but because there was that in him which respected the older man. Mr. Samson noticed the act. He knew that most men would have remained perched and munching, not necessarily to show their independence, but because they were made that way.

He nodded at Keir.

"Taking it out of me in overtime, what?"

It was their joke, like some facetious reference to the English weather, but if Keir took time and a quarter or time and a half out of Samson & Hoad, he was worth it.

"Get on with your lunch, lad."

Mr. Samson crossed to the bench by the window and, putting out two large hands, lifted down the door that Keir had left leaning against the wall. He held it to the light and looked at the fine texture of the wood. Being English, he loved the stark simplicity of oak. Walnut was all very well, but too mottled and tricky. As for mahogany, Mr. Samson loathed it.

He laid the door on the bench and ran the tips of his fingers over it.

"She won't shrink, Keir."

"No, sir."

"Been in store five years. That's one of the things you can't hurry even in these cut-and-come-quick days."

Keir stood looking at his work, and his dark face seemed to catch the diffused sunlight.

"That's the last but one of the six. They're up to the Darvels standard. Couldn't put cheap stuff in a house like that. Mr. Lugard understands."

Mr. Samson raised his white eyebrows, and for the moment his expression was whimsical. Mr. Lugard was a difficult man to please, and Mr. Samson had assured him that he had one craftsman in his shop.

"Well, you haven't let me down, Keir."

Keir looked thoughtful.

"Mr. Lugard knows what he wants. Well, that's all right. It's—beauty."

Mr. Samson, out again in the sunlight, wondered not so much at those words as at their implication. Keir's father would have grown furious over a thing of beauty produced for the benefit of the idle rich, but Keir did not react in the same way. He saw further than his father. Possibly he understood that beauty is an abstraction and not to be contained in wranglings upon surplus value. Because a thing was beautiful and belonged to some other man Keir did not want to smash it.

Mr. Samson chuckled.

"Idle rich? What rot!"

2

Keir, being an orphan, lodged with Mrs. Marter of Mulberry Row, and Mrs. Marter was sixty and a widow. She was a round and comfortable woman whose figure was divided into two bulges by her apron strings, and she was a great talker, but she fed Keir well and charged him only

[8]

twenty-five shillings a week for his board and lodging.

Occasionally she gave him good advice.

"Never you have anything to do with the skinny sort, or a woman with a beady black eye, or a girl as gets chilblains and a red nose."

Most of her advice was superfluous, for Keir seemed proof against petticoats or shy of them, though his finances might have justified little adventures. He was paid one and fivepence an hour, and with overtime he could make his four pounds a week. His National Health and Unemployment Insurance payments totalled one and fourpence a week. He did not drink and his cigarette bill was negligible.

As a worker young Keir was a warm man. He was putting by two pounds a week, and his spare cash went mostly on books. He picked them up second-hand at a shabby old shop in Church Lane or indulged himself in one of a series on economics and industrialism. He held certificates from the secondary school for building construction and drawing and the trade course. His bed-sitting-room was full of books. He had made himself a bookcase with glass doors, and Mrs. Marter, when she was doing his room, would shake her head at all this literature.

For Keir was such a serious young man, and though no lodger could have given Mrs. Marter less trouble, she would have preferred a youngster who was less worthy, less silently intense. Mrs. Marter "my deared" everything and everybody, and she even managed to "my dear" her lodger, but without that satisfying sense of motherliness that swelled in her like a loaf in an oven. Mrs. Marter believed that boys should be boys, and young men—just a little hearty, and it wasn't as though Keir hadn't looks and a sense of colour. He owned a pair of brown plus-fours and a tight blue pull-over which he put on when he went cycling on Sundays.

On that particular Saturday in May, Keir returned to

Mulberry Row at five o'clock. Mrs. Marter had his tea ready and was waiting to go out for her Saturday shopping. He hung up his hat in the narrow passage and went into the scullery to wash.

Mrs. Marter was filling the tea-pot. She proposed to allow herself a ninepenny seat in the Kingham Picture House. Keir never went to the pictures. She heard him busy at the roller towel, and his voice came to her from the scullery.

"Oh—I shall be out tomorrow."

Well, that wasn't unusual, but why didn't he take a girl with him? There was young Ida Thomas at No. 5, a nice girl if ever there was one, and quite ready to be interested in Keir.

"Wanting sandwiches, my dear?"

"Just some bread and cheese, and a slice of cake."

The usual celibate meal! Keir was no more interested in food than he was in girls. He seemed to browse upon books. Well, some day perhaps he would get it badly and with the wrong sort of girl. Mrs. Marter was inclined to regard him as dreadfully innocent. And she did enjoy cooking a good Sunday dinner and eating it and going to sleep afterwards.

"Have a little bit of ham, my dear. I can get you a couple of slices at the International."

But Keir did not react to the crude colour of ham. He said that bread and cheese would do, but Mrs. Marter might buy him two apples.

So Keir sat down to his tea, and Mrs. Marter put on her best hat and collected a string-bag and went out to shop. Apples—indeed! Well, there ought to be an Eve in the picture. She supposed that Keir would go and fiddle with his bicycle, which he kept in a little shed in the garden, and then disappear upstairs and pick up some book; and that was exactly what he did do.

He had an old basket chair in his bed-sitting-room. He

[10]

pushed it close to the open window and sat down with the poems of Keats. He had discovered Keats only two months ago. "Windows opening upon foam!" And his particular window opened upon Mrs. Marter's one apple tree, an old Blenheim Orange. It was in full flower, and the flowers were full of bees.

3

Mrs. Marter could say of him: "If it rains or it snows, he'll be off on that bike of his. And what do you think he takes with him? A flapper? Oh, no. A book. I see'd the title of the last one. 'A Text-book of Gee-ology.' Yes, you can believe me or not—but that's what it was. Gee-ology. Somethin' to do with how the earth came to be made. It doesn't seem quite natural—somehow."

On that Sunday in May, Keir got his bicycle out of the shed before nine and, wheeling it into the passage at the back of Mulberry Row, fastened a haversack and a mackintosh to the handlebars. The cold snap of early May had passed, and in the garden next to Mrs. Marter's a bed of blood-red wallflowers scented the air. At a bedroom window of No. 5 a girl was powdering her nose, and if she was aware of Keir's blue pull-over and hatless head, his senses were not responsive. She watched him wheel his bicycle along the passage, and when he had disappeared she gave a little toss of the head and laughed.

Keir liked to leave Kingham early, before the world upon wheels could drive him into the gutter. Usually he took the Esher, Cobham, Ripley, Guildford road, and turning off towards West Clandon, he would walk his machine up the long hill to Newlands Corner and the Albury Downs. This rolling country of chalk and of sand lying between the Leatherhead-Guildford road on the north and Ewhurst on the south had an eternal fascination for him. He loved its great grassy slopes, its yews and beeches, the high dark pinewoods, the deep and mysterious valleys. He knew it in spring, summer, autumn, and winter. In one of his note-books he had drawn a rough contour map of its geological formation, and from the Thames towards the sea the rhythm ran:

Alluvium. London Clay Downs Gault. Greensand, Weald. South Downs.
Tertiaries Chalk.
Bagshot Sands.

At the top of the hill Keir took to the turf, for the world on wheels had overtaken him, and in those days Newlands Corner was an abomination. The crowd had not been coerced into cleanliness by the courage of a certain great gentleman now dead. Keir wheeled his bicycle along the broad, grassy way that led eastwards just below the brow of the chalk ridge. The beech trees were coming into leaf, and the old yews looked very black against the marvel of all this greenness. The thorns were in flower, and in the more secret places the bluebells had been left to bloom. Keir fled from the crowd and its cars and motor-bikes. He wanted to be alone, and this passion for separativeness was to make life poignant for him, for in the world of today only the fortunate few can afford to be alone.

But he knew all this piece of country like the pages of a book, how to avoid the beaten track and to gain places to which cars and motor-bikes did not penetrate. He had one particular haunt close to a group of beech trees, and leaving the grass, he pushed through a thicket towards the place, but on this Sunday in May someone had forestalled him. A party of young men and women had spread itself on the grass between the beech trees and a group of old thorns. The young women were unpacking baskets, and one of the young men kneeling on the turf was opening bottles of beer. It was a happy and a noisy party, and Keir paused with his bicycle under the lee of a big yew.

"What do we do with the bottles, Bert?"

"Buzz 'em away, old lad."

And Keir watched three black bottles go hurtling one after another into the heart of an old thorn tree.

He withdrew. In those early days his separative self was moved too easily to scorn. He was too conscious of the crowd's crudities and not sufficiently wise as to its kindness. He did not realize that the world was full of childishness, that it did not think or understand, and that his own sensitiveness might possess the superciliousness of the prig. He went elsewhere, pushing his bike along the hillside until he came to another of his sanctuaries. It was a little green recess on the sunny side of the woods shut in by thorn trees, an elder, and two hazels. It was wholly and serenely his. He unfastened his belongings from the bicycle, and pushing the machine into the undergrowth, he spread his mackintosh and lay down.

In that green nook the turf was stippled with flowers, blue bugle, a tiny wild forget-me-not, dog-violets. He could smell the mayflower. The hillside fell away steeply to a barrier of old yews, and beyond and below them the deep valley was full of sunlight. On the farther slope spread a wood of wonderful and varied greenness, fields, oaks and elms, and the grassy spaces and the domed trees of a park. Beyond it rose a wooded ridge, and beyond it yet another ridge serrate with dark pines against the sky-line. The hills were blue and black and green and grey, for the day was a day of moods and of cloud masses that drifted. Away to the west he could see the silver smoke haze over Guildford.

Keir left his book unread and lay and looked and dreamed.

The dreams of a young man with a smoulder of ambition

in his eyes, and a head of hair that was somehow turbulent.

Part of the crowd—not he! A wage slave doomed to a silly sameness by the very fools who preached the solidity of that sameness? He belonged to no union. Blind idiots, complaining that all opportunity was denied to the worker, and by their very regulations making opportunity more and more impossible! A stultifying tyranny. The expert and the fool shackled together.

His dreams mingled the ideal and the material, for he saw what his father had not seen, that the ideal is founded on the material. Bricks and mortar—yes, creation upon creation, not a peevish pulling down, but a passionate building up.

The people who threw beer bottles at beauty!

Work? He was going to work like the devil. He was not going to stay for ever in a carpenter's shop with men who skrimshanked and shilly-shallied and thought it clever to cheat. Wasn't it true that the average man loathed work? He was a lazy creature wriggling on the horns of necessity and always accusing those horns of exploiting him.

He was going to save money. He was going to do what old Samson had done, though he might do it rather differently. A business of his own? Oh, perhaps. Or the firm might gather yet another S and become in due season, Samson, Hoad & Smith.

4

He did not see the girl coming along the path; nor did she see him. It was her dog, a wire-haired terrier, who discovered Keir, and the dog protested. Maybe he felt himself responsible, as dogs do.

"Peter, come here."

But Peter still growled and objected to the fortuitous male.

"Peter, you silly ass."

She appeared before him suddenly, a creature of beautiful fairness, slim and self-sure in her short brown skirt and knitted coat of apple-green. Her skin had the perfect texture of her golden youth, and her hair was like honey. She apologized to Keir. She bent down and took the dog by the collar.

"Sorry. Peter's so self-important."

Keir had been lying prone with a book under his chin. He sat up. He was aware of her blue eyes appraising him and his clothes. His clothes were passable, and though his hair might be a little tumultuous, the cult was prevalent.

"Quite all right. I must have startled him."

His voice betrayed him to her. Being what she was, she knew at once that he did not belong to her world, and though her world was far less distant than it had been, he became for her at once one of the casual crowd. Keir was just a young man with an untidy head and a bicycle, and an environment that was not hers. Less than half a century ago at Cambridge her father and his fellows had cheerfully spoken of all shopmen as cads. Cads on casters.

"Come on, Peter. Sorry he was rude to you."

Her cold and casual courtesy had other implications. She had slipped a leash through the dog's collar, and she swept him off, passing away along the grass path to disappear beyond one of the green and white may trees. And Keir sat there with a little, wincing smile upon his face. To her he had been a stranger, but more than a mere stranger, and her dog had growled at him.

Chapter Two

1

Now, it happened in June that a patch of tiles came adrift on Mr. Lugard's house of Darvels and betrayed to Mr. Samson's bricklayer and tiler the rottenness of things within. Parsons, the bricklayer, and his mate had put their ladders up, but when Parsons examined the scar on the Darvels roof, the battening crumbled in his hand. Parsons was a red-haired man whose language was apt to be as colourful as his hair. He put a big hand into the hole, got hold of something, and gave it a twist, and part of a rafter came away in his fingers.

"Well—I'm blowed!"

The piece of timber was peppered and tunnelled with worm holes. Portions of it looked like yellow parchment, and when Parsons tapped it on the ladder, fragments broke away and powder flew. Parsons tossed the thing down to his mate.

"Look at that, Bill. — worm."

He put his hands again into the cavity, groped, and, finding more rotten timber, tore it out.

"Gosh, she's eaten to bits."

The business was too serious for patching. Mr. Samson was sent for, and when Mr. Samson had been up the ladder and had investigated, he knew that Mr. Lugard would have to find much money.

"It's the big worm, Jim. Old Scotch fir, and not squared up properly. Here's a bit with the bark on it."

Mr. Lugard was at home, and he and Mr. Samson and

the bricklayer ascended to the attics. The roof of the particular wing was sealed in with lath and plaster, but there was a wooden panel in one attic that gave access to the eaves. Mr. Samson, bent double and carrying a torch, went in to explore. He came out looking rather dusty and with cobwebs adhering to his hair.

"Absolutely eaten to pieces, sir."

Mr. Lugard looked glum.

"That means a new roof. Good Lord! Wait a bit, I happen to know that this wing was re-roofed forty years or so ago."

Mr. Samson showed him a piece of timber.

"Perhaps it was, sir. And I guess I know who did it. Oh, yes, they're with the worms too—now. Look at that. Green Scotch fir with the bark on it."

Mr. Lugard examined the crumbling yellow fragment.

"The damned scoundrels!"

So it became evident that the roof of that particular wing would have to be stripped. The job would take at least a month even if Mr. Samson put every available man on to it. The old tiles would have to be taken down carefully and stacked. Luckily the trouble was confined to this one wing.

"It's a most infernal nuisance, Samson. What will it cost me?"

"Roughly—three hundred pounds, sir. I'll measure up and get out an estimate."

"We had better clear out. Dust and noise."

"Yes, you wouldn't like it much, sir. But it's the right time for the job. You were lucky not to have the roof in on you last time it snowed."

So Mr. Lugard and his wife packed themselves into two cars and drove off to Scotland. They left the maids in the house, and the firm of Samson & Hoad took possession of Darvels.

Darvels was Queen Anne. It stood about a mile from Kingham Bridge, and its garden was protected by the river and an old red brick hipped wall. The house itself had the beautiful proportions of its period and reminded Keir of some of the old houses that he had seen in the Close of Salisbury during one of his bicycling holidays. The garden was famous for its trees, especially two very old cedars, a tulip tree, and a catalpa, and Mr. Lugard, being a man of understanding, had swept away certain Victorian adornments that had spoilt the completeness of the place, and had restored all the sweeping turf and the stately separativeness of the trees. The garden of Darvels was an eighteenth-century garden, save that Mr. Lugard and his wife allowed themselves masses of colour. As at Hampton, the red brick walls were covered with every sort of creeper, and the walls themselves seemed to rise from the flowery foam of the great borders.

Keir understood that Mr. Lugard resented being exiled from this garden just when it was coming into summer flower. Mr. Samson had put all his carpenters on the job, the two outdoor men and the four who worked in the shop. Old Tower was in charge, but he was growing too old for roof work, and much of the laying out and supervising fell to Keir. Moreover, the restoration had been complicated by the discovery that the joists of the attic floors were badly worm-eaten and that the floors and ceilings of the rooms below would have to be replaced.

Keir, up in the roof, had the Darvels garden spread below him, and the garden had a life of its own. Mr. Lugard's two gardeners, and especially the elder man, regarded the activities of Messrs. Samson & Hoad with no friendly eyes. The house had a broad, paved walk surrounding it, and on the west—under the library windows—a bed of polyantha roses was coming into flower. Mr. Samson's men had instructions to shoot all the rotten old timber into the yard at the back of the house.

Keir had young Scudder working with him up above, he of the irresponsible blue eyes and the playful broom, and on the second morning Mr. Sydney Scudder allowed a length of rotten rafter to crash on the bed of dwarf roses. Cant, the head gardener, was mowing grass. He saw the thing crash, and there was trouble.

He stood below, a broad, brown, angry man and shouted.

"Hi, you blasted fools up there!"

Young Scudder leaned over the wall and cheeked him.

" 'Allo, Whiskers, what's wrong?"

"Who dropped that bit of timber on my roses?"

Scudder grinned.

"I did. It just slipped out of my hands."

Mr. Cant was not accepting sauce.

"You — young fool! Hi, Mr. Foreman."

Old Tower happened to be away in the timber store, and the business fell to Keir. He walked across the ends of the old joists and looked down at Mr. Cant and the smashed roses.

He was in complete agreement with Mr. Cant.

"Sorry. Shouldn't have happened. It won't happen again."

He turned on Scudder.

"What did you do a damned silly thing like that for?"

Young Scudder flared.

"And what the — is it to do with you? You ain't the — boss."

"I'm in charge when Tom's away."

"Well, you're not coming it over me."

"Supposing we put it to the boss?"

"Yes, you — sneak."

Keir had a temper, and Scudder's red face was a rag to him.

"Look here—you cut that out, or I'll have you stood off."

Young Scudder did cut it out, but sullenly so, and there was to be another clash between him and Keir, but that was not yet.

The Darvels garden had something else to display to the men working on the roof. Each morning a girl would come out and play with Mr. Lugard's dog—an Aberdeen—on one of the lawns. Apparently, she had been made responsible for the dog and his recreation, and she would throw a ball for him and run races. She was the under-housemaid, one Sybil Kelsey, a slim, dark creature with long legs and very white skin. Her movements suggested the fluttering of a bird, a certain happy breathlessness, and it seemed to Keir that she played with the dog without any thought of showing off. He noticed that she looked but rarely at the men up above. She seemed shy of them.

She was a graceful thing and her almost childish movements intrigued him. He found himself waiting for her to appear, and watching her when she came. She was so light on her feet, so irresponsible without being hoydenish. Sometimes the ball would vanish under the spreading branches of one of the cedars, and she and the dog would dive for it together. Sometimes she retrieved it; sometimes the dog was too quick for her.

Nor was she always in movement. She had her moments of stillness, of absorbed staring. He gathered that she loved flowers. He would see her go to one of the borders and stand there and look. Sometimes she touched, or put her face down to smell. Her touch had the deliberate tenderness of a caress.

He heard one of the other maids come out and call to her. "Sybil—Syb, cocoa's on."

The Sybil remained with him. He repressed the Syb and the cocoa.

[20]

Later Keir discovered that young Scudder was always
sneaking down the ladder and hanging outside the kitchen
windows. He had further glimpses of young Scudder half
in and half out of a ground-floor window, and of young
Scudder being repulsed by a short-tempered and elderly
cook. The young man reappeared on the roof, smoking a
cigarette and looking sly. Keir heard him telling one of
the other men that the old cook was jealous because he had
been palavering with the girl. Yes, she was a bit of all right,
and pretending to be shy, but he—Sydney—knew something
about girls. They didn't stay shy long when you got 'em
alone in the dark.

The Darvels gardeners finished work at five, and since
overtime was being worked on the new roof, some of Mr.
Samson's men were left on the premises after the gardeners
had left. A couple of tarpaulins had to be spread each night
in case of rain, and Mr. Samson would come along himself
to see that the thing was done, for however clear the sky
might be, he was taking no risks with Darvels and the
English weather.

Young Scudder, normally shy of overtime, was display-
ing a peculiar enthusiasm in the matter of late hours. He
had discovered that Sybil Kelsey sometimes appeared in the
garden after tea to pick flowers, for Mr. Cant was an autocrat and would allow none of the women to touch his
beloved borders. Keir was not blind to the lout's loafing,
and in a measure he felt responsible for it, for Mr. Samson
had given Keir orders to see everybody off the place.

It was on a Thursday, and the men had left and Keir was
putting in a last ten minutes sharpening a saw. He had the
saw clasped in the vice of the carpenter's bench that stood
on the terrace, and as he drew the file over the saw's teeth
he was aware of Sybil Kelsey crossing the grass. She did not

look in his direction. She disappeared beyond the yew hedge of the rose garden that lay beyond the cedars, and Keir, with a curious little smile, filed away at the saw's teeth. A pair of blackbirds were feeding their youngsters on the lawn, and it occurred to Keir that a cock blackbird —considered as an artist—might resent the metallic squawkings of a file.

Suddenly he heard a scream. It came from beyond the yew hedge, and Keir's back straightened. He stood and listened, and then he saw Sybil Kelsey come running from behind the yew hedge. She had two or three roses in one hand and she seemed to clutch them. The tumult of her panic was no rehearsed provocation; she was in flight like a frightened child.

Keir threw the file down on the bench and went quickly across to intercept her.

"Who's frightened you?"

She was breathless. Her very dark eyes had a kind of blindness. She seemed to hover for a moment in front of him.

"Oh, let me go, please."

He stood aside.

"It's all right. What's frightened you, kid? Tell me."

He noticed the trembling of her long, sensitive lips. Almost she stammered and was incoherent. A man had sprung out at her. He had been hiding in a recess in the yew hedge where the stone seat stood. Yes, one of the workmen, the young one.

Keir understood.

"Run along, kid. I'll settle that."

On the other side of the yew hedge he found young Scudder looking sheepish and lighting a cigarette, and young Scudder glared at Keir with eyes that were like the eyes of an angry dog.

"Hallo. What are you butting in for?"

Keir was very pale.

"You know."

"— sneak"

It was Keir's one and only fight before his marriage, and Keir could box. There were no preliminaries. They fell on each other like a couple of dogs. Young Scudder was two stone heavier than Keir, a husky young lout, but he was not so quick on his feet or so coldly furious. Keir got a bloody mouth, but he knocked out young Scudder in the first half minute.

He stood over him.

"Now—you clear. I'll have you put off this job tomorrow."

The lout hadn't the guts for a second assault. He could be noisy and truculent till someone licked him. And Keir, with a splodge of blood on his chin, and a face that was still dead white, shepherded Scudder across the lawn and round to the back of the house and saw him out by the door of the little courtyard into the lane.

It was then that he discovered three women in the kitchen doorway, the cook, the housemaid, and Sybil. The cook had her arm round Sybil. And Keir was annoyed. He was aware of his bleeding lip.

"That's all right. I've—settled him. Sorry it happened."

All three of them appeared interested in Keir's bleeding lip. The cook wanted to bathe it for him.

"Young blackguard— You ought to have that seen to."

Keir shrugged off this sympathy. Young Scudder had a worse lip, and an eye that would close before nightfall.

"Nothing to fuss about. Thanks all the same."

He was aware of Sybil Kelsey still holding those roses and looking at him with large eyes from the half shadow of the doorway. She seemed to have shrunk back behind the others.

And suddenly she smiled at him, and her face had for him

a swift fragrance. Her lips trembled, but no word passed from her to Keir.

3

That was the beginning of it, Keir's first straggling on the line of march, his surrender to a situation that could not be sustained by mere enlightened selfishness.

Sybil was an orphan like himself, and her childhood had not been of the happiest. She was a sensitive and a lovable thing, quick in her colour and her movements and quite unable to resist the appeal of a dog or a flower. She had moments of utter absent-mindedness and was always getting into trouble with the domestic world of Darvels because of it. She would go off into dreams and leave dusters about and suddenly forget such things as early morning tea and the proper place for a chair or an ornament. She had broken one of Mr. Lugard's *famille rose* bowls, and had wept over it and had pleaded to be allowed to pay for the damage.

No one ever succeeded in being seriously angry with Sybil. The quality of her gaze was so transparent, her emotional quality so generous. Animals were devoted to her. Mr. Lugard, reflecting upon the girl's forgetfulness and omissions, forgave her for them and was wise.

"Not quite responsible? Oh, yes, she is—when things matter."

For Mrs. Lugard herself was a sensitive, and a semi-invalid, and when she was in pain she was glad to have Sybil to do things for her. The girl could be kind and gentle and full of understanding. She never came noisily into a room or stayed too long in it. She was at her best when you were feeling sorry for yourself.

For two creatures who belonged to the mundane workaday world, their coming together was gradual and almost secret. Keir remained late each evening, and for two evenings he saw nothing of Sybil. She was like a timid bird hiding in a hedgerow.

It was the cook who suggested that Mr. Smith might not quarrel with a cup of tea. The cook was beyond adventure, and the housemaid had a friend of her own, so obviously the adventure was Sybil's.

"Go and ask him, Syb."

"No—I couldn't."

"Don't be silly. He won't eat you."

Sybil went. She found Keir at work with mallet and chisel.

"Cook wonders whether you would like a cup of tea."

Keir looked at the girl's short-sighted brown eyes. What the devil had she to be afraid of? But almost his shyness equalled hers.

"Very kind of her. Yes—I should, if I can have it here."

She disappeared and returned with a large blue and white breakfast cup, and in the saucer a slice of plum cake.

"Shall I put it on the bench?"

"Please."

"Oh—I've slopped some into the saucer."

Her hand was shaking, and her trembling had a strange effect on Keir. Perhaps he fell in love with that which trembled in her and with the gentle poignancy of her mouth and eyes.

"No harm done."

"But—the cake!"

"It won't be any the worse. How's the dog?"

For she was on the edge of flight and he did not want her to go. She had become part of the Darvels garden, and more than that.

"Poor Mac. He hasn't been very well."

"Bad luck. You're fond of dogs, aren't you?"

"Oh, very."

[25]

"Same here. But I haven't got one."

"Haven't you?"

"Well—I live in lodgings. And I don't get much time to give to a dog. Wouldn't be fair, would it?"

He found an odd piece of clean floor-board and, putting the cake on it, used it as a plate. And she remarked on her lack of foresight.

"How silly! I ought to have brought you a plate. I've got such a head."

He looked at her with sudden intentness.

"Have you?—Well—I don't see anything to quarrel with."

"How?"

But she understood him. She coloured up. She became confused.

"I'll just wait and take the cup back. You know—I've—I've not thanked you—"

"What for?"

"About the other evening."

She was looking at his lip.

"Oh—that! You needn't worry. The young blighter isn't coming here again."

She leaned against the bench, and the fingers of her right hand played with some chips that littered it.

"You must be stronger—"

"Than I look!"

His smile had a tinge of irony, and she winced.

"Oh, no—I didn't mean that."

"I can box a bit."

"You—were—angry."

"Did I look it?"

"Yes."

He had finished the tea, and he put the cup down on the bench. He saw her hand move towards it, and his inspiration came to him.

"I say, you are shy of me."

"Am I?"

"Almost as shy of me—as I am of you."

That seemed to surprise her. Also, it seemed to please her.

"But isn't that funny? Why—are you shy?"

"I can't quite say.—Well, I had better get on with the job."

"Yes, of course."

And he noticed that same trembling of her hand as she picked up the cup.

But in a week she had ceased to tremble, or she trembled differently. Her tremor was towards him—not away. Each evening she brought him out a cup and a plate. She perched, and sat on the bench, and she let him come quite near her. The cook and the housemaid—good creatures—spying from an upper window—saw that the affair was going admirably.

The cook was just a little troubled.

"Do you think he's the chap for her? Seems to me she wants one of the big—easy sort."

The housemaid had social ambitions.

"He's quite the gent. She wouldn't mix well with the rough kind. Besides, you couldn't be unkind to the kid."

"I don't know. The thin, dark, busy chaps grow irritable. And he's got a temper."

The housemaid asserted that she wouldn't look twice at a man who hadn't some of the hot stuff in him. And that was that.

4

On the last Sunday before the Lugard family returned, Keir asked Sybil to spend it with him. She possessed a bicycle, and he suggested that they should start very early and camp out for the day on the hills above Shere. Had she seen the Silent Pool? No. And could she ride forty miles

a day with a long rest between the outward and the home-
ward journeys?

"Oh, yes—but I ought to ask cook."

"Why?"

"She's in charge. And it's her Sunday. She might change
with me."

The cook said that she would like to have a few words
with Keir, and she had them and was satisfied. She was
ready to give up the day to Sybil, and on the morning of
that particular Sunday Sybil woke at five and ran to her
window, for she had been terribly afraid of the day turning
out badly, but she saw the Darvels garden lying still and
secret in the haze of a perfect dawn. Her brown eyes were
tender. Her impulse towards loving and being loved was
like wind upon water, an innocent yet passionate urge.
She was more consciously in love with Keir than he was
with her, but the day was to prove Keir human.

They started soon after eight. Keir had gone shopping
the night before, and had a special picnic basket on the
luggage-carrier, and much of its contents owed nothing to
Mrs. Marter. Both of them took mackintoshes, Sybil's a
blue one. She was wearing a light blue frock and a little
black hat. Keir rode on the off side between her and any
passing traffic, and by ten o'clock they had dismounted and
were climbing the long hill to Newlands Corner.

Keir wheeled both machines.

"Tired?"

No, she wasn't tired, but the day was a day of summer
heat, and Sybil found a blue handkerchief and arranged it
under her hat.

"The sun's so hot on my neck."

She laughed over it. She had a pretty neck, creamy and
soft, and she had let her hair grow.

"We'll find plenty of shade up there."

Their mutual urge was to get away from the crowd, and

[28]

when they came to the grassy spaces and the shadowy woods and thickets of the downs, they seemed to draw more close to each other. Sybil took charge of her own machine. They found themselves holding hands.

Her face grew dreamy.

"Oh, isn't it lovely, Keir?"

He looked at her with the eyes of a lover.

"Yes, it's just made for you."

She gave a little laugh, and her cheek seemed to approach his shoulder. She was not afraid of him now.

"Let's find a wild place all to ourselves."

There was a kind of happy wildness in her eyes.

They found their sanctuary, a grassy hollow close to some beech trees and sheltered by thorns, and they parked their bicycles against a tree and unpacked. The day was still young, so they spread their mackintoshes on the turf and sat down close together, and suddenly Keir was shy. He had become acutely conscious of the exquisite strangeness of this girl, of her slim hands and dark eyes and poignant mouth and of that fragrant, creamy skin. He was in love with her, and all of her was wonderful.

He said: "What small hands you've got, kid!"

She hid them for a moment under her knees.

"They get so rough."

"Nonsense. Let's see."

She allowed him to take one of her hands and to reassure her. She had spent half an hour manicuring her hands the night before.

"Like pink shells, your nails."

She looked confused and happy.

For there was a gentle seductiveness about Sybil, and all through the sunlight and the shadow and the sleepy heat of that summer day her youth and its wonder grew upon Keir. They ate their lunch, and there were cherries and jam tarts. The lemonade was rather rebellious, and it made them laugh. Sybil confessed that she felt sleepy, and actually she fell asleep with Keir's jacket rolled up under her head. He sat and dreamed and watched her, and felt the desire of her stirring in his blood. How very innocent she looked! The soft shadows of those long, dark lashes!

And suddenly she was awake. She sat up with an air of confusion and shook her hair.

"Haven't you been asleep too?"

"No."

He had been watching her, and she knew it.

Later they left their bicycles hidden in a thicket and went down that steep yew-shaded tunnel to the Silent Pool. The water had a tinge of blue in it, and fish were swimming. The sunlight hung in the tree-tops, but there were too many people here, and the pool had lost its silence. They clambered along the little steep paths where the wild box trees were fragrant in the summer heat. They looked at the water and the fish.

But they could not hold hands here or let their bodies touch, for their mutual sensitiveness was confused by the crowd. Children were chasing each other and shouting. Two small boys were searching for stones to throw at the fish.

"Look at that big un, Bert."

"Slosh him."

There was a sudden almost irritable fierceness in Keir's eyes.

"Why can't people teach their damned kids—"

She looked poignant. Quickly compassionate and suddenly courageous, she went and spoke to the boys.

"You mustn't throw stones at the fish."

The boys scorned her.

"Don't you take no notice of her, Bert. She can't do nothing to you."

Keir rescued her from the impasse, slipping a hand

under her arm.

"Let's get away, Sybil. I might feel like chucking one of those kids into the water."

They wandered away, returning to the steep hillside and the shadows of the yews, and the wilderness was theirs once more.

Keir had brought a thermos with him and a couple of cups, and they spread themselves again in that green nook among the thorn trees. They could hear the Sunday traffic passing in the valley along the Guildford-Dorking road, but on this wooded bluff they felt themselves far from the world. Now and again they heard the voices and the laughter of people passing along the Pilgrims' Way, but no other lovers disturbed them. Keir found a packet of cigarettes and offered Sybil one.

"I've never smoked."

"Never!"

She nodded at him. It was true.

"Well—I shouldn't begin now. Believe you feel sleepy again, kid?"

"No, just dreamy."

He rolled up his coat and put it under her head, and as he did so, he realized that he had not kissed her yet. He wanted to kiss her, but he was afraid, most strangely afraid of the mystery of her beauty. Keir had read his war books, and he knew that in them sex could not be accused of a sensitive diffidence. In them love did not look and marvel and hold back, but sprang like an animal upon its prey. Yet his feeling towards Sybil was tinged with compassion, a tenderness that was ever present when beauty moved him.

He sat staring at the greenness of one of the thorn trees, his arms clasping his knees.

"You do look serious, Keir."

Her eyes were half-closed. The soft, virginal curves of her breasts showed as she lay. One black leg was crossed over

[31]

the other.

"I—am—serious, kid."

She put out a hand, palm upwards, and suddenly he turned and, bending, put his lips into the hollow of that hand.

"Oh—Keir."

Her other hand touched his head. Her face was a blur of soft desire. She was far less complex than he was.

He knelt and looked at her, and she smiled at him, and her arms seemed to open.

"Keir—"

They lay close, face to face, and body to body. He felt the soft pressure of her breasts. She clung to him exquisitely.

"Oh, Keir—"

Chapter Three

1

THE Borough of Kingham was becoming suburban, though there were a few green fields left between it and the flux of London. It had the river flung across its loins like a silver girdle of chastity, and the turf and the bracken and the trees of Richmond were still near and green and inviolate. Westwards there were other notable and stately spaces, relics of regal days, refusing to be swallowed up by new little cardboard suburbs. Kingham had a market of its own, and an Assize Court, and a High Street that was crowded with people whose need was cheapness. It had a Woolworth's Store, and obsolete trams, and incessant traffic, and two very considerable picture-houses, one of which had christened itself "The Elite." Kingham could provide you with anything from a Morris Cowley to a penny packet of nasturtium seed, but in the matter of houses it was a little cramped.

As for the new houses, they had sprung up on one or two estates, and they had cost anything from eight hundred to two thousand pounds to build. They were sold or let to city workers or local tradesmen or elderly people who had retired. These new estates represented a middle-class community. Certainly the Borough of Kingham had a housing-scheme of its own, cottages that let at from twelve to eighteen shillings a week with the rates included, but the prospective tenants formed a long waiting list. There would be as many as ten applicants for each new cottage, and preference was given to people with children.

This problem of a house was both tantalizing and unexpected. Keir had helped to erect quite a number of houses, but he had not proposed to inhabit one. He had regarded marriage as a state that might be contemplated in the far future when his position in the social scheme should be more what he intended it to be. Marriage might be a spur, but more often it was a rope round a man's legs. His urge had been to save money, to get his hands on the rungs and climb.

But the sacrament of marriage was being forced upon him by the gentle seductiveness of Sybil and by the enthusiasms and the ardour of Sybil. She was a creature to whom it was not easy to refuse things, and a creature whom Keir would have found it impossible to betray. He was very much in love with her, or as much in love as a self-centred young man could be. Her dark-eyed, poignant eagerness enveloped him. The locks of the young Samson were to lose some of their sanctity.

Sybil wanted a house and she wanted children. Keir was to be astonished by the eagerness with which she desired a child, and he was not attracted by children. Moreover, she assumed that he desired a house and children as ardently as she did. She saw him as a dear fellow conspirator.

"Oh, Keir, won't it be lovely!"

She was such a warm-blooded and pretty creature that he was seduced by her domestic enthusiasms even as he had been persuaded by her poignant mouth and clinging hands. The workshop was growing facetious at his expense, though lout Scudder had been extruded from it.

"Bought a pram yet, Smithie?"

Keir was not one of those who could be easily facetious. He did not encourage confidences; he was apt to resent them, and his young, dark reticence was misunderstood. There were times when other men spoke of him as a sidey young swine. Keir had a lot to learn. A girl and a pram would teach him something.

[34]

Mrs. Lugard was being kind to Sybil. She allowed her two evenings off a week, and Keir would put on his Sunday clothes and go house-hunting with his future wife. They explored every corner of Kingham, but every niche in the borough appeared to be occupied.

Keir suggested lodgings.

"We might manage for a year and put our names down for one of the borough houses."

Sybil looked poignant.

"Oh—Keir, not lodgings. I don't mind how tiny the place is."

"All right, kid."

"Couldn't we get a cottage built? Mr. Samson might help us."

Keir had to repress that suggestion. You might be a good employee, but Mr. Samson was not to be antagonized by being pushed into too much altruism. Mr. Samson was not the man who believed in lifting young people over gates. Let them climb their own gate. Nor did Keir want to sink his savings in a house and be beholden to some building society at the rate of six per cent on borrowed money.

He said: "There's the furniture. That will be as much as I can manage for the present."

Sybil was twenty-three and she had been in service for five years, but she had not saved a sixpence, and if she had she would not have been Sybil.

It was Mr. Samson himself who directed Keir to Paragon Place. One of his bricklayers, Tom Santer, had occupied No. 3 Paragon Place, and after twenty years of thrift had bought a cottage of his own. Keir might be able to snaffle No. 3. Keir gave up half of one dinner-hour in order to go and survey Paragon Place, and when he had seen it he loathed it.

Paragon Place belonged to Victorian Kingham. It was a strand in a spider's web of obscure and ugly little streets. It was built of yellow brick, and every cottage had the same flat, bilious face, the same two windows at the front and back. Each door was artificially grained and had a top-light of cheap blue and yellow stained glass. A brick wall, with cast-iron railings perched on it, ran the whole length of the row. There were iron gates and minute front gardens.

But the place had a kind of tired squalor. It suggested casual labour and casual ladies in caps, and when Keir found a passage and explored the hinterland of Paragon Place he discovered just what he had expected, little back gardens decorated with every sort of improvisation in the way of wireless poles and sheds, fences that were made up of old egg-boxes and bedstead frames, iron advertisement plates, and discarded galvanized sheeting. There were clothes lines, and tin baths hanging up on nails. At the back of No. 4 a fat woman was banging a frowsy doormat against a wall. Some of the gardens possessed flowers, dahlias and autumn asters, or perhaps a row of runner beans, but the general atmosphere was squalid.

Paragon Place symbolized all those mean makeshifts from which Keir was passionately determined to escape. It was not that Paragon Place was impossible merely because of its ugliness; it was impossible to Keir because it had been built by a man without vision, for people who had not been taught to see. Keir was under no illusions as to the kind of neighbours he might expect to have in Paragon Place. Thirty years ago it had been inhabited by better-class working people, but now it was a corner to which the casual and the careless tended to drift.

He did not see himself and Sybil in No. 3 next to the frowsy woman with the doormat, but he did tell Sybil that there was a house available.

"Not the place for you, kid."

But Sybil asked him to take her to see Paragon Place, and she was far less conscious of its ugliness than he was. The tenant of No. 3 allowed them to go over the house. It had a front parlour and a kitchen and three small bedrooms, and it had been kept in good condition by Santer and his wife. They were decent, quiet, and rather old-fashioned people.

Sybil's enthusiasm was already active in the house. Her short-sighted eyes were less restive than Keir's and were not so aware of the nearness of all those neighbours. The Santer's back garden was one of the few flowery and self-respecting plots in the place, and Sybil thought the view from the kitchen window quite pretty. Both the Santers were slightly deaf and, having lived for twenty years or so in Paragon Place, were inclined to be lenient towards noise.

Mrs. Santer gave them tea.

"We shouldn't be moving, my dear, but Tom does want a bit more garden. We've got a bit more ground at the new place."

Keir was reticent and guarded. He could not very well tell these good people just what he thought of the place they had lived in all these years. They were used to it. They belonged to a previous generation. But when he closed the iron gate he was aware of Sybil looking quite possessively at No. 3.

"It's not such a bad little place, Keir. I don't see why it shouldn't do to begin with."

"Like it?"

"Well, of course—it's not like one of the new cottages, but it would be—ours, wouldn't it?"

Ours! Yes, that was the magic word, but in those early days Keir was not fully wise to the child behind the brown eyes of Sybil. Life to her was a kind of playground, and perhaps all the toys in her particular playbox would appear wonderful. She had not the urge that obsessed him, or her urges were different. She was quite uncritical. She would stand in front of a shop-window and think the furniture was lovely, furniture that Keir suspected of being trash.

He was troubled.

"I can't say I like the neighbourhood."

"But where else can we go?"

She had him there; not triumphantly so, but with a kind of seductive, intimate innocence. Certainly she was not a snob, and assuredly she was easy to please. And perhaps her vivid eagerness cast a glamour over the place for Keir. In one of those little rooms he and Sybil would sleep together. Those other poignant intimacies would be made possible. He wanted Sybil, and he knew that she wanted him.

"Well, it's going to be your house, kid. Call it the half-way house, if you like. I've got other ideas for the future."

She pressed his arm. Of course he had, and so had she, but perhaps—like many a girl before her—she was moved by the lore of Eve—to make sure of her man.

2

When Keir began to explore the financial aspect of the adventure he realized that the cheapness of Paragon Place was in its favour. No. 3 was rented at 10/6 a week, with the rates included, and he supposed that it would be sufficient for them to furnish the kitchen and parlour and one bedroom.

He spent an evening in his bed-sitting-room working out a budget, though its details were somewhat theoretical. He had had very little experience of domestic ways and means. His weekly budget ran as follows:

Rent and rates	. . . .	10	6
Clothing. Self	. . . .	2	6
Sybil	. . . .	3	6
Insurances	. . . .	1	4
Housekeeping—at 15 -each . . .	1 10	0
Gas	. . . . . .	1	6
Coal. 1 cwt.	. . . .	2	0

Holidays	.	.	.	.	.	.	1	6
Tobacco	.	.	.	.	.	.	1	0
Sundries	.	.	.	.	.	.	2	6

$$2 \quad 16 \quad 4$$

There were many omissions in this budget, but he was not aware of them at the time. He had allowed nothing for soap and cleaning materials, for repairs to shoes and boots, for matches and firewood, for the possible advent of children. He had estimated the housekeeping costs at fifteen shillings a head without considering the multifarious details, or the muddle Sybil would make of them to begin with. His earnings totalled some four pounds a week, and he could place his savings at a pound a week. Certainly, he would have to spend less on books, but in Sybil he would have a book more enthralling than a whole circulating library.

It was not that Keir was mean. He was adding to his responsibilities, but he had not renounced his ambition, that urge towards separativeness and independence. He had his vision. He saw no reason why he should not become a member of the firm or the master of a business of his own. He was not a union man. He knew that if he saved money and gained in experience and grip, he might make himself somehow inevitable. Mr. Samson had no children, and Mr. Hoad—Sneak Hoad, as the men called him—had one small daughter, and the firm was prosperous, and since it employed no union labour, it was not obstructed by having to haggle with local trade secretaries. Certainly, there had been attempts to rope the men in, but old Samson was still John Bull.

Actually, Keir did sound Mr. Samson on the subject. He said that he was saving money, and that he was ready to serve his term and gather experience—but would there be any chance—? Old **Samson** eyed him with quizzical gravity.

"Want to be one of the exploiters, Keir?"

"I'm not afraid of responsibility, sir."

"Ah, that's it—that's the whole thing in a nutshell. A man's got to make himself fit to give orders. Most men only make themselves fit to take them. Well, yes—I've got it in mind."

Keir's dark eyes smouldered.

"That means a lot to me, sir. I'd make it my business not to let the firm down. I shall have seen the inside of things."

Mr. Samson smiled down his nose.

"Getting married, aren't you?"

"Yes. But I don't think that will make any difference."

"Perhaps not—Keir. A working man's—job—is so much tied up with his wife. More so—these days—I think—. Is she—?"

"She's been in service. She's keen."

"Not a shop girl. Well, that's all to the good. She ought to know how to manage.—Just one thing, Keir. Don't think I'm meddling—but if a chap's going to rise—"

He looked at Keir kindly, and Keir understood.

He said: "She's one of the gentle sort, and quick—sensitive—you know. She'd like things nice—but I think she'd always be ready to work for them."

Mr. Samson said: "Well, that's the stuff."

Keir arranged to take over No. 3 Paragon Place from the Santers, who were moving into the new cottage on the 1st of October, and Sybil and Keir fixed their wedding for the first Saturday in October. It was to be a very quiet and inexpensive affair at St. John's Church, Kingham. An uncle of Sybil's who was door-porter at one of the big London stores had promised to come down and give her away. Keir had trouble in finding a best man, but he persuaded one of Mr. Samson's painters to act for him. He would have been quite satisfied if the ceremony had been performed at a register office, but Sybil wanted to be married in a church.

Meanwhile there was the furniture to be bought. The honeymoon was to be limited to a long week-end at Hastings, and Sybil and Keir had decided that No. 3 should be furnished and ready to receive them on their return.

Sybil was full of ideas on furnishing—or, rather, she had absorbed her ideas from the windows of Messrs. Bond & Beaverbrook, Kingham's universal providers. She dreamed in suites. She wanted mahogany for the parlour, yes, and a Chesterfield sofa, and painted wood for one bedroom. Messrs. Bond & Beaverbrook stocked a series of standardized suites at standardized prices, though they labelled them with various names—"The Hampton," "The Richmond," "The Twickenham." Sybil led Keir to the slaughter. Her enthusiasm was a little flushed and self-important.

"Of course—we could do it on the instalment system. Isn't 'The Richmond' just sweet?"

Keir had visualized their operations as a careful selection of specimens purchased at various less impressive shops. Bargains? Well, not exactly that, perhaps. He had supposed that some of the necessities could be purchased second-hand. A bedstead might be just as good a bedstead even though somebody else had slept on it, and an hour or two's work with a brush and a pot of enamel would put the thing right. But Sybil's naïve enthusiasm for the new home was—like her person—innocently seductive.

"No, cash down, kid. No instalment business. Besides— we should get a discount for cash."

She had an arm linked in his, and she held him to the window.

"It does seem a lot of money, Keir, doesn't it? But, after all, it's common sense to buy good things. They'll last us a lifetime."

"Yes, that's true."

"And we've got to think of having a better cottage. Oh—I

[41]

do want you to have a glass-fronted bookcase for your books."

"I can do with something simple. I can make it myself, if it comes to that."

She squeezed his arm.

"So you could, Keir. Aren't you clever?"

The furnishing of No. 3 Paragon Place cost Keir some ninety pounds. Sybil had her "Richmond" suite for the bedroom, at the price of £12.13.6. The parlour, with a Chesterfield sofa, and two easy chairs at two guineas each, proved more expensive than the bedroom. The kitchen furniture was of white wood and included a cupboarded dresser at £2.11.6, a table, three Windsor chairs, and an additional cupboard. But, as in public finance, it was the supplementary estimates that upset the balance of Keir's budget. It had never occurred to him that a small house could develop such a capacity for assimilating inorganic matter. There were carpets, linoleum, curtains, yards and yards of cretonne; linen, some of it in threes, some of it in sixes; bedroom crockery, fenders, kitchen utensils. The kitchen was an absolute ogre in its appetite; there were articles that Keir had never seen before and did not know the use of.

"What the dickens is that?"

"A whisk."

Then there was the china and the cutlery and the silver.

"We must have a clock, Keir."

"What for? Won't our watches do?"

"Everybody has a clock."

"For the kitchen. All right."

"We ought to have one in the—the drawing-room, too, really."

"That can wait a bit."

"Oh, yes. Let me look at my list again. Mats, a doormat, two doormats. Let's see—we have done the blankets, haven't we?"

"Blessed if I can remember. Anyway, we shall want them."

"And a small mangle or wringer."

Keir was getting tired. He had said yes to so many things with a sense of their inevitableness, but when Sybil was tempted by the serpent to covet a mahogany gramophone cabinet, Keir stood firm. In his case the serpent had taken the shape of a most persuasive and talkative young salesman whose motto was: "You find the girl, sir; we find everything else." Almost Keir came to hate that young man with his facile smile and his infernal catalogue.

"I think that's about our limit, Syb."

It was, and sensing a vague restiveness in her Adam, Sybil refrained.

"You—have—been good to me, Keir. Won't it be lovely arranging all the things? Our things."

She was such a happy, seductive creature.

3

Keir had been saving money for the last five years, and when he had to cash a wad of Savings Certificates to pay for the furnished felicities of the new home, he understood that it would take him at least two years to make the damage good. But he was not in a mood to regret it. After all, the act was very much to his credit. He had been able to walk into Messrs. Bond & Beaverbrook's and behave like a man of property. He had laid the foundations of a home, both sentimentally and in reality.

He was very much in love with Sybil, and Sybil was very much in love with him. Her enthusiasms could be personal. She thought Keir a rather wonderful person, and she showed it, and no man quarrels with a plumed hat when it is placed on his head by such eager hands. Keir felt pleasantly self-important, and Sybil was so sure that she could make life pleasant for him.

She was impulsive and affectionate. She told him that cook was giving her lessons in the Darvels kitchen, and that she was making famous progress, though her first cake had had to be smuggled into the Darvels dustbin.

"I do want you to be comfortable, Keir. I'm going to be so busy."

His vision of her active in No. 3 Paragon Place was a happy one. Every evening he would come home to Sybil. He saw himself sitting in one of those two-guinea chairs, smoking a pipe and reading, while Sybil sewed. He supposed that all women sewed. And they would have their bicycles, and on Sundays they could set out together on those pleasant pilgrimages into the country, and it seemed to him that every Sunday would be like that wonderful Sunday on the hills above Shere.

Meanwhile the old Santers had decided to vacate No. 3 and to move into their new cottage at an earlier date, and Sybil discovered that she would like the little parlour and the best bedroom repapered. Keir interviewed his new landlord, a retired ironmonger, who had found to his cost that cottage property could be more bother than it was worth. He owned six of the cottages in Paragon Place and was always trying to sell them. He was curt with Keir.

"What! New wallpaper! I did the cottage up inside three years ago, and it's in good order."

Keir said that his wife wanted new paper, and that if the landlord would provide the paper, he would get the hanging done.

"Expect me to waste money, do you, just because a young woman's got ideas? Nothing doing. I don't get three per cent on those damned cottages."

So, Keir agreeing with Sybil that the wallpaper previously selected by the old Santers was utterly hideous, bought new paper himself from Samson & Hoad and paid one of Mr. Samson's painters and paperhangers to hang the paper for him. He decided to do the painting himself on Saturday afternoon. Sybil had been allowed to choose the paper, and she had selected a flower pattern that was rather highly coloured. Keir would have preferred a plain buff or pale lemon lining paper, but he allowed Sybil her *couleur de rose*.

Going round one Saturday afternoon to Paragon Place, two days after the Santers had moved out, and carrying a four-pound pot of cream paint and an old attaché case that contained brushes, an apron, a putty-knife, sandpaper, and other accessories, a coincidence introduced him to one of his next-door neighbours. Happening to look out of the kitchen window, he saw a man in what was now his—Keir's —back garden. The man had a spade and was digging up something. Keir watched him for a moment. The man was removing one of the rhubarb stools that the Santers had left in a corner near an old shed at the end of the garden.

Keir opened the back door and challenged the stranger.

"Hallo—what's the idea?"

The man swung round rather like some large beast, and to Keir his appearance suggested a rogue elephant. Even his trousered legs were like the legs of an elephant. He had little, evil eyes, a vastness of shoulder and of belly, a nose that was both long and flattened and red at the tip.

The man stared at Keir. He was one Mr. William Block, a casual labourer, and very casual at that, and the husband of the frowsy lady whom Keir had seen banging a mat against the wall. He appeared quite unabashed by Keir's challenge. In fact he met it with a suggestion of truculence.

"Takin' somethin' what's mine—that's all."

Keir walked down the path.

"How's that? I've taken on this place."

[45]

Quite deliberately the man resumed his disinterring of the rhubarb root.

"Old Tom gave it t'me."

It was a lie, but Keir could not nail it as such. Mr. Block got hold of the stool by the stalks, lifted it, dropped it over the fence, wiped a hand on the seat of his trousers, and spat. Then he looked at Keir in a particular sort of way. The other tenants of Paragon Place were wise as to that look.

"Any complaints?"

Keir flushed slightly. He was beginning to feel more than unfriendly to this great sodden, swaggering hulk.

"Well, you'll keep out of here in the future."

The man showed him an assortment of very rotten teeth.

"Bit cocky, aren't you? You keep yer sauce to yerself."

He swung one large leg over the improvisation that was a fence. It was his fence, and he said so. The second leg followed the first, but he had left his spade behind. He told Keir to remedy the omission.

"Chuck it over, Mr. Little-un."

Keir chucked it over and went back to No. 3.

Chapter Four

1

A SOCIOLOGIST might have found much to interest him in Paragon Place, and Keir, who had to live in Paragon Place without studying it impartially and objectively, was open to prejudice, but since all active living is prejudiced, Keir's fundamental fastidiousness reacted to reality. He was to suffer in Paragon Place because of his fellow human beings. They disliked the smoulder and the separateness of him, and he could not help being what he was.

A sweep named Moore lived at No. 1, and the name was apposite, for Mr. Moore was perennially black, but when he washed and appeared in his back garden, he was very much white. In fact Keir and Mr. Moore were never in conflict. Contact with soot appeared to have made the man more sensitive to other cleanliness. He had a decent little round robin of a wife, and no children.

Jervis, a jobbing gardener, inhabited No. 2, a man who put on a sly civility when he went out to work, and took it off again directly he reached home.

No. 4 was Block, William and Bertha, with two tow-haired boys.

A municipal dustman occupied No. 5, a lorry-driver No. 6.

No. 7, significantly seven, was the hot-spot of Paragon Place. Here lived a Mrs. Job and her two daughters, strapping young wenches who sometimes worked in a laundry and were also public property as ladies of the town. No. 7 was referred to by the local wits as "Job Lot."

[47]

No. 8 was inhabited by a painter, one Phelps, who had at one time worked for Messrs. Samson & Hoad, until his political proclivities had made him a sore spot in the firm's affairs. Phelps was a communist.

The remaining cottages, numbered nine to twenty-five, housed no fewer than five workers who were on the dole. Keir never came into active contact with any of their occupants, but he was known to them and to Mr. Phelps as a blackleg.

Paragon Place began to become seriously interested in Keir and Sybil when a green van arrived from Messrs. Bond & Beaverbrook's with the young people's furniture. Sybil had been given a free day, and Keir had knocked off work at one o'clock, for this was a very great occasion. They were to be married on the Saturday, and they wanted to put No. 3 in order so that it should be ready for them after a four days' honeymoon. The neighbours were provoked by the appearance of the green van. Mrs. Jervis's little black head could be seen at her parlour window. Mrs. Block was more bovine and less in ambush. She came and stood at her front door and watched the operations and was inclined to be friendly.

She nodded her frowsy head at Sybil, who was flushed and excited.

"All new."

Yes, it was all very new.

"Got a pee-anno, I suppose?"

"Not yet."

"You'll be kep' busy paying th' instalments."

Sybil, anxiously watching the men inserting a new oak wardrobe through the front entrance, remarked rather casually to Mrs. Block that all the furniture was paid for, and Mrs. Block misunderstood the casualness of Sybil. Stuck-up young bit of goods. And all this swanky new furniture! Mrs. Block's sandy head was apt to be irritable. She scratched it and went to the back of No. 4 to exchange confidences with the lady of No. 5.

"Seen all the new furniture coming in?"

No. 5 had not. She was a tired little woman who had borne many children, and she lived in awe of Mrs. Block.

"Reg'lar fancy show. Quite—the lidy. Sort that says: 'Mind the paint, please.' They're a couple."

No. 5 blinked faded eyes.

"Oh, yes, I dare say they feel as fresh as paint. Let 'em wait till they have a few kids kicking the chair legs."

Mrs. Block laughed. She had a very loud laugh.

"Well, if you ask me—I'm not so pleased to 'ave them for neighbours. And what did they want to come 'ere for? A van-load of swanky new furniture. So refained!"

No. 5 supposed that it was not easy for a young couple to find a vacant cottage in Kingham, and Mrs. Block was still scratching her head. She said: "Mrs. Santer was a decent body. You could borrow 'alf a loaf from 'er—at a pinch. Give me folk you can be neighbourly with."

But Keir and Sybil were two innocents, so whole-heartedly absorbed in the business of dressing the new home that it occurred to neither of them that their affairs could be of any serious significance to the people next door. They were not conscious of having neighbours. Keir had been laying carpets in the parlour and the front bedroom so that the furniture could be carried in and placed just where Sybil wanted it. She fluttered about, directing operations and getting in the way, but the two men from Messrs. Bond & Beaverbrook's were as fatherly as the firm.

"Shall we put the bed up for you, miss?"

Sybil blushed.

"We shan't want it till next week, you know. We are to be married on Saturday."

The men thought Keir a lucky fellow, going to bed with a pretty thing like that.

[49]

"Best of luck, miss."

Sybil was calling down the stairs to Keir, who was carrying a roll of linoleum into the kitchen.

"Keir, the gentlemen have offered to put up the bed. Shall they?"

"Well, yes. I want to get this linoleum down before the kitchen things come in."

By five o'clock the men were bundling the wrappings back into the van, and Keir and Sybil were alone together in No. 3.

Said one of the men, with a knowing look at his mate: "Well, if I was that chap—I'd christen that bed—straight off," and he closed the green doors of the van with a bang.

Sybil had brought a small suitcase with her to No. 3, and the suitcase contained a thermos, some sandwiches, and two slices of Darvels cake. She was the happy mistress of the occasion.

"Let's have tea in the parlour, Keir."

She collected some of the new china, and sitting on the Chesterfield sofa, they christened the parlour of No. 3. It was very full of the new furniture, so full that there was very little room to move. In fact, one of the two-guinea armchairs had had to be exiled temporarily to the kitchen.

But Sybil was full of enthusiasm and ideas.

"We can have it in the bedroom, Keir."

Keir laughed.

"The congestion's pretty serious up there. It's a good thing you're not stout, kid, or you'd get caught between the bed and the dressing-table."

Sybil refilled his cup from the thermos.

"But isn't it lovely, Keir? And it's all ours."

2

Three golden days in October. They could not have been

more fortunate in the weather or in their lodgings, and when Keir slipped out of bed on that Sunday morning and pulled up the blind, he found that the sea was visible, a pearly, flickering sea. A friend of his at Kingham who had recommended him these lodgings had assured him that the landlady was not a liar. Keir stood there for a moment with an untidy head of hair, and his eyes at gaze.

"Fine day, kid."

He was conscious of Sybil stirring in the bed, and both sound and movement were seductive.

"What's the time, Keir?"

He looked at his watch on the dressing-table.

"Just after seven."

"We needn't get up yet. Come back, Keir."

He was aware of her smiling at him, and of her hand turning the bed-clothes back. The whiteness of it seemed to open like the petals of a flower. He lowered the blind and slipped into the bed. Her warm, soft body pressed itself against his.

"Oh, Keir."

"You'll be tired."

"Oh, no, I shan't. Besides, does it matter?"

When the little struggle was over, they fell asleep again.

They spent the morning wandering along the sea-front and sitting on the beach. It was an idle, happy, desultory day, with the sea in an innocent mood, and Keir picked up flat pebbles and played at ducks and drakes. He made one stone leap seven times on the surface of that calm sea, but when Sybil tried her hand at the game, her stones plunged and sank.

"They won't skidder for me, Keir."

He looked at her with the benevolence of the young male.

"It's not your job."

He was happily obsessed by the youth and the sex and

[51]

the silk of her. She was still so fresh and strange to him; she had both roused and assuaged the sweet anguish of sex. The illusion of her strangeness lasted for him through those three October days, and remembering them in later years, he would wonder at the thing called love. It was like a plant from which the beautiful petals suddenly fell, but if you had patience and pity, it would put forth other flowers that were less vivid, but more deeply scented and enduring.

"Come on, can't loaf all day."

He dragged her up, feeling himself very much man and her man.

"Where are we going?"

"To see the old town."

They discovered that part of Hastings that still fished and smelt of tar and spread nets on the shingle and hung its tackle in queer black wooden towers. They explored the old town, and Keir was interested in the timber-work of some of the old houses. They climbed up to High Wickham and wandered over the grassy slopes and sat down close to the cliff.

"Funny to think that France is over there."

He sat with an arm round her.

"Perhaps we'll travel some day, kid. I don't see life as all Kingham. How do you say: 'I love you' in French?"

Sybil didn't know, so he kissed her.

On the Monday they took seats in a motor-coach and drove to Winchelsea and Rye, returning by the upland road past Brede Broad Oak. Sussex was deeply green and preparing for the golden festival of her oaks. They had glimpses of the blue sea, and Keir sat with his arm round his young wife. It was the end of the season, and they had the back seat of the coach to themselves.

He said: "I shall remember all this, Syb. It's been wonderful, hasn't it?"

She snuggled up against him, and her face had a dreamy,

tender tranquillity.

"Wonderful, Keir; I'm so happy."

"Same here."

3

On their first Saturday in No. 3 Paragon Place Keir knocked off work at one, for No. 3 and Sybil needed him. There was a new plate-rack to be fixed in the scullery. Also, the little shed at the end of the garden, taken over at a price from old Santer, was to hold their bicycles, but it had a leaky roof, and Keir had bought six yards of rubberoid to re-cover the roof.

October was still giving the world a little summer, and when Keir went out with the roll of rubberoid, a hammer, and a packet of galvanized nails, he was not the only Adam in that multiple paradise. Mr. Moore was out with a white face and busy with a fork, lifting the last two rows of a potato crop. At No. 6 the lorry-driver was erecting a minute hutch sufficiently large to house a motor-bike.

The garden of No. 4 was empty, and Keir, placing the roll of rubberoid on the roof, went back for a kitchen chair to be used as a stepping-block. He climbed up on the roof of the shed and became busy, and since his back was turned towards the cottages, he did not see the two Block children come out into the next garden. Their ages were ten and eight, their names Sydney and Harold. Both of them had tow hair and little, hard, red faces, blue eyes, and depressed noses.

How it was that these children divined the fact that in Keir they had a victim might be put forward as a problem in elementary psychology. As children they were elementals. Any cat that ventured within a stone's throw of them had cause to regret it, but if any local cat sighted the two boys, it—if it had been educated—vanished over the nearest

[53]

fence or disappeared into its own back door.

These children had Keir marked. He was a new animal in the way of a neighbour, and, as such, fair game. Moreover, the Block boys enjoyed a certain immunity by reason of their father, with whom milder men had found it unadvisable to quarrel. The elder of the two, picking up a stone, took aim and hit the closed door of the shed just below Keir's right foot.

Keir, turning sharply, discovered the two urchins, who, with eyes like blue pebbles, stood to brazen the act out.

"Hallo—which of you two threw that?"

This was the kind of situation which the Block children loved to create.

"Threw what?"

"A stone."

The elder of the two had modelled himself upon his father.

"Who are you speaking to? I never threw no stone."

Keir looked at the younger brother.

"Was it you?"

"Me?"

"Yes—you."

"I never threw no stone."

"One of you did."

The elder boy took up the argument.

" 'Ere, mister, you keep your 'air on. You never saw either on us throw a stone."

"I heard it."

"Call us liars. You be careful or I'll fetch my dad."

Keir went on with his work. He was sufficiently sensitive to size up a ridiculous situation and to know that such situations are best dealt with by a show of indifference. He ignored the Block children, but for some ten minutes they remained in the back garden, watching Keir at work and making comments. Their remarks were personal and can

[54]

did. They giggled. Their inspiration was to stir up the man creature until he lost his temper and made some unadvised and tumultuous attack. Then, of course, they would bolt incontinently for the Block back door, shouting loudly for their parents.

"Watch 'im 'it 'is finger, 'arold."

"Gosh, if 'e ain't got a 'ole in the seat of 'is trousers."

"Mister, y'shirt's showin'."

Keir continued to ignore them, until Mrs. Block, suddenly appearing with a grievance against life in general and a husband who hadn't brought the weekly money home, found herself articulate.

"Syd—. 'arold. Come in at once. Leave—the gen'leman —alone."

The Block children went. They were wise as to this other situation. Dad had not come home, which meant Dad had gone on the booze, and at such times their mother could become a frowsy-headed fury.

Keir completed the re-roofing of the shed, and as his hammer drove home the nails, he found himself supposing that the garden of No. 3 was not a place in which he would ever take his pleasure. It was too elementally situated. It was not a piece of God's earth upon which you could cultivate peace, potatoes, and philosophy. It was too public, too much like a pen with other cattle-pens crowded up against it. Raw, sour earth, and little cruel faces growing up out of the black soil.

Sybil, who had been busy altering the curtains in the front bedroom, and hanging some pictures in the parlour, knew nothing of Keir's adventure with the Block children, but at tea he appeared to have something on his mind. He sat and stared at the loaf of bread, but not as though he saw it as bread. His face made Sybil think of someone looking out of a dark window, and in the future she was to come to know this look so well and to fear it, while finding in her fear a strange and elemental pity. The perplexities and secret grievings that were to trouble her love for this intense and smouldering creature who was her husband were to grow at last into an understanding of him, but that was not yet.

"Got a headache, Keir?"

He came out of his dark mood to speak to her.

"No. I was just thinking that the back garden is not going to be much use to us."

"Oh—why?"

"No decent fences."

She was a little puzzled. She was not wise as yet to the passionate separatist in Keir, nor did she understand his sensitiveness to people, and especially to ugly people. She was much more a social creature than he was.

"Well—you won't have much time, Keir."

Her face brightened.

"I want to grow flowers. I'll be gardener. I wonder if we could get a few wallflowers to put in. Yes, and some forget-me-nots and red daisies."

Keir said that at Kingham market all sorts of plants could be bought quite cheaply. The front garden certainly needed dressing, but as it was no larger than a good-sized table-cloth, it could be dealt with at no great expense.

"I'll raise all my own plants next year, Keir."

He did not damp her enthusiasm, but he did say that when they moved into a better cottage, the garden of that cottage should have proper defence against too much neighbourliness.

This was their first Saturday night in No. 3 Paragon Place, and Paragon Place was to impress upon them other exhibitions of neighbourliness. The cottages had been built for cheapness, and the dividing walls were only one brick thick. Mr. Jervis next door was a wireless enthusiast, and on Saturday nights he allowed himself a special occasion with

[56]

the apparatus at full blast. The Santers had both been slightly deaf, and the bellowings and crashings had not worried them. Sybil had lit a fire in the sitting-room, and Keir had got out a book.

Mr. Jervis had put himself in touch with some prize brass band, and his speaker was of the loudest.

Keir, irritated, tried to appear whimsical.

"I say, that fellow next door—"

"It is rather noisy, isn't it?"

"One might be living next door to a steam roundabout."

Sybil was reading the domestic notes in a popular weekly paper.

"Oh, I believe he only turns it on like that on Saturdays. He can't afford it every night."

"Thank God," said Keir.

At ten o'clock Mr. Jervis switched off, and No. 3 enjoyed a transient and fallacious peace. Keir and Sybil had locked up and were going to bed when Mr. Block came home after a festive evening and began by kicking his own front door. His remarks were very audible to Sybil and Keir.

"Op'n th' — door—you ol' bitch. Op'n the — door."

Apparently there were parleyings between the lady and her husband.

"You'll stay outside till you're sober, you drunken swine."

She was as much a creature of violence as her mate and almost as strong as he was, and when he kicked the door in, she did not wait upon compassion, but attacked. The row could be heard through the flimsy wall, bangings and cursings, and the squeals of the two small boys. It was a savage and a dishevelled show, and Keir, with a face of dark disgust, stood unbuttoning his braces.

"Nice lot of animals next door."

Sybil was frightened.

"Keir, oughtn't we to do something? It sounds as though

[57]

somebody was being murdered."

"Well, I shouldn't grieve if there were. People like that—better dead."

"I can't turn out the light Keir, till that noise has stopped."

In bed she lay and clung to him; she was trembling, but presently the savagery next door wore itself out. The lady had clubbed her mate with a rolling-pin, and then thrown a bucket of water over him, and presently Paragon Place slept.

Chapter Five

1

KEIR's mistrust of Paragon Place was quickly justified, but when he came to analyse Paragon Place and its organic life, he found himself confronted with a curious anomaly. There were in Kingham many other terraces of working-class cottages which, while appearing to resemble Paragon Place, did not produce its particular atmosphere. Nor could the differences be just a question of coincidence. A silly brute like Block was not a coincidence; he was a universal, a type, just as much a type as Keir himself, or Mr. Samson, or Mr. Lugard, who loved beauty. Each little house and each little street might assume an appearance of likeness, but in each house there were fundamental contrasts.

Keir would say to himself that the standardization of modern life tricked one into assuming that the heads under the hats were as like as the hats. But were they? Obviously not. Society had graded itself. The reformers would have it that inequalities had arisen because the masterful and the selfish had made footstools of their less aggressive brethren. But was it so, or was it always so? To declare that Paragon Place was solely the product of the capitalist system was rather like accusing biology of being responsible for the unlikeness of the ape and the ass.

The more Keir thought about the problem, the more convinced he was that life was a study in differences instead of an assumption of sameness.

"From each according to his powers, to each according to his needs."

"Remove the exploiter, and society will perfect itself."

"Educate—educate."

Keir did not believe in these sanguine solutions. It seemed to him that when the crowd man accused society of exploiting him, he was inventing a cock-shy. The crowd was exploited by its own limitations. It was being taught to deny these limitations and to howl down anyone who suggested that social values differed, the social values of the expert and the fool.

Later, patiently and poignantly, in another community he was to watch life grading itself, man becoming the artist, man remaining a creature just capable of hammering in nails; but in Paragon Place he could contrast Sybil with the frowsy virago who lived next door. Nor did he see himself as the loving comrade of a silly brute like Block. Even Darvels had its significance, a beautiful personality, a little aloof and secret. He suspected that—relatively to Darvels— society would always possess a Paragon Place. It was waste of time to argue about it; the thing was to get busy as an individual and escape.

Keir left the garden to Sybil, for she had much more time to deal with it than he had, nor did she appear to excite those little sadists next door. Their mother came out to gossip with Sybil. She was interested in Sybil as a neighbour from whom it might be possible to borrow things, for Mrs. Block was Paragon Place's most blatant borrower, and she had exhausted its possibilities. Her neighbours were shy of Mrs. Block's sudden shortages.

"You ought to get your man to do that digging."

For Sybil was busy with a spade, and enjoying it, and since Keir was working overtime, why shouldn't she dig?

"It's not the job for a slip of a girl like you."

To have Mrs. Block hanging over that disreputable fence and exuding sophisticated sympathy was worrying to Sybil.

"Mr. Smith is so busy."

Mr. Smith indeed! Mrs. Block referred to her husband as Bill, save on those special occasions when she was upon her dignity with the rent collector or the milkman.

"Well, if I was yer 'usband, I wouldn't like to see yer slavin' like that."

Sybil turned on Mrs. Block a sudden, innocent smile.

"But I like it."

Peculiar people, these Smiths! No doubt the fellow was mean, one of those nasty little chaps who were always sweating on a job and who kept a P.O. savings book. But Mrs. Block proceeded to exploit Sybil and borrowed on various occasions loaves of bread, oddments of butter, and half-pints of milk, nor was any restitution made. Mrs. Block blamed her memory.

"Oh, my poor 'ead! Yes, you shall 'ave that loaf back tomorrow," but Mrs. Block's tomorrow never came.

Mrs. Moore, who was a clean, decent, quiet little body, warned Sybil against the lady of No. 4.

"Don't you lend that woman anything, my dear; she's a sponge."

Even the impulsive and generous Sybil became recalcitrant when Mrs. Block borrowed her frying-pan and forgot to return it. Sybil had to go to the door of No. 4 and claim the article. Mrs. Block produced the frying-pan and once more blamed her head.

"I've been so worried. Mr. B.'s bin stood off."

But when Sybil took the frying-pan back with her, she found it in such a state of filthiness that she had to spend half an hour cleaning it with soda and hot water. Keir came in and surprised her at the sink, nor had all the grease been dealt with.

"What's the trouble, kid?"

"Oh—I lent it to the woman next door. I had to fetch it, and it was filthy."

Keir had had his suspicions.

"Been cadging from you, have they?"

"Yes. But I'm not going to lend her anything again."

Keir wondered if Sybil was afraid of Mrs. Block. Yes, it was more than possible. Sybil's timidity could be exploited.

"You can put it down to me, kid. Tell her I found out and made a row."

Sybil might be sensitive, but she had more moral courage than Keir suspected. She was not going to have Mrs. Block telling all Paragon Place that Keir was both mean and masterful.

So, in the main, and perhaps inevitably so, the Smiths were not popular in Paragon Place. Keir was working overtime all through the winter, for Samson & Hoad had secured several good contracts, including the fitting up of a large new shop. Keir would come in for his tea at half past five and then go back to work, and there were evenings when he worked till ten. The majority of Keir's neighbours disapproved of such strenuous industry.

Mr. Block said of Keir: "The — young — will kill 'imself, and a good job too."

Phelps, the communist, had bitter things to say of Keir. He was a blackleg, a greedy swine who guzzled on other fellows' jobs, a — — to old Samson. It was chaps like Keir who kept the capitalist system on its legs.

Keir and Sybil, two young things newly mated and still very full of each other and their affairs, kept very much to themselves. No. 3 was blockaded by Nos. 2 and 4 and not feeling neighbourly to either household, particularly on Saturday nights. Mrs. Block, denied further borrowings and treated by Sybil with a timid hauteur, was on her dignity, referring to Keir and Sybil as "Lord and Lady Smiff."

2

But as the winter progressed, Keir began to experience

the little moods of matrimony and to gather worries of his own.

Sybil was seeing very little of her husband. Even Saturdays were working days, and Sunday was the only day that was wholly theirs together. Keir would come home tired. He had what Sybil had begun to know as his working face, and often he would bring that face home with him and sit with it.

She was an affectionate and sweet-tempered creature, but she did ask of life that it should amuse her sometimes. For the first two months of their marriage she was happily absorbed in the new life of No. 3, but when she had all her curtains up and the furniture in order and had planted the little front garden and a strip of the back garden, she found herself wedded to routine. After one or two disasters she had made herself a fairly efficient cook, and when some of the polish had worn off the new adventure, she found that her domestic duties did not fill her day.

They were very long days. Keir disappeared on his bicycle at a quarter to eight, and he took his lunch with him. She did not see him again until half past five, and overtime took him away from her at half past six. He might return at half past eight or nine, tired and in no mood to play with a creature who was little more than a grown-up child.

She spoke to him a little hesitatingly about his work.

"You never seem to get any time off, Keir."

He sat down with a book.

"Well, we're lucky, kid."

"I think you do too much. I don't see much of you."

He did put the book away and talk to her. He explained to her his theory of life from an ambitious working man's point of view. He said that if you were keen to climb the ladder, you had to be pretty quick on the rungs, but that when you arrived at the top of the ladder, life might be easier.

[63]

"I want to get you out of this back alley."

She understood.

"Yes, Keir, but I wish you didn't have to work quite so hard. Supposing—"

She hesitated, and his eyes watched her.

"Supposing—what?"

"You got ill."

He scoffed at the idea.

"I'm one of the wiry sort, kid. Work never killed anybody. It's the loafers who rot. Finding the days a bit long?"

Yes, she confessed that she was. She was a sociable creature.

"You go out for walks, don't you?"

"Yes."

"Do you go and see the women at Darvels?"

"Yes."

"Why shouldn't we keep a dog? You could take the dog out."

Yes, she could do that. But Keir seemed to forget about the dog, and it did not occur to him that she might like him to take her to the "pictures" once a week. Paragon Place went to the pictures even when it was on the dole. Certainly, she had her shopping to do, but her shopping was as domestic as her routine, and she had nothing supremely exciting to buy. The house was dressed, and so was she as a staid little housewife. But is any woman satisfied with sameness, especially in the matter of clothes? Sybil would find herself in Kingham High Street, and looking at hats and frocks and jumpers and all the cheap prettiness of those exciting windows. They were like a garden to her, and her own garden was not in flower. She had a passion for colour, and a woman's tenderness for flowery things. She may have desired them as a child desires to rush in among bluebells and pick, but she was a good child, a sensitive child, and she was finding the finances of No. 3 a perpetual problem.

[64]

But one Saturday afternoon she fell, and so innocently. She came home feeling flushed and guilty and excited with a brown paper parcel, and in it a pretty, cheap, cretonne frock. It had cost her seven and sixpence, and she had paid for it out of the housekeeping money. Incidentally, the settlement of the grocer's bill had had to be postponed.

She put on the frock and looked at herself in her mirror. What would Keir think of it? And wouldn't she have to confess to Keir? And suddenly she was frightened, for hadn't Keir said: "We shan't have to spend much on clothes, Syb, for a year. We started as fresh as the house." She took off the frock and hid it away in her wardrobe. She felt guilty.

Which—of course, was absurd, and a condemnation of Keir's blindness, in that he was traversing the present with his attention fixed upon a hypothetical future. There were plenty of other men who would be ready to take his wife from him, or at least to enjoy her at the price of a few frocks. Other men turned to look at Sybil in the streets, and sometimes she was followed. Moreover, even her friends at Darvels—the cook and the parlour-maid—would have sympathized with and admonished Sybil.

"What, worried about a seven-and-sixpenny frock, and your chap working overtime! You're being a bit too easy with him, my dear."

Yet Sybil was worried about that frock, for the extravagance hastened the development of a financial crisis. Keir handed over thirty shillings a week for the housekeeping, and also the three and sixpence which was Sybil's personal allowance, but as a manager Sybil was something of a dear muddler, and to balance her accounts she had had to throw her three and sixpence into the domestic scales. For a while the sacrifice had retrieved the situation, but in January Sybil found herself seriously in debt.

The deficit amounted to less than three pounds, but,

being Sybil, she accused herself of being responsible. She had allowed Christmas to persuade her to very natural generosities, a new pipe for Keir, crackers, fruit, holly and mistletoe, and a very small turkey. Keir had given her a winter coat with a fur collar and cuffs, and she had felt both delighted and distressed over that coat. It was an accusation. And they had eaten turkey in various disguises for four days.

It somehow did not occur to Sybil that she should have confessed to Keir that she could not manage on thirty shillings a week. It was a confession of failure. Nine girls out of ten would have seized the situation by the horns and assumed the offensive.

"You'll have to let me have another five shillings. What —I'm wasting money? Well, I like that!"

Nor was this Sybil's only trouble. A far more dear and serious situation was developing, and Keir was curiously blind.

Inevitably, one or two of the tradesmen began to suggest that she should settle these outstanding accounts, and Sybil became frightened. What if Keir found out that she was in debt and did not find it out from her? And so she told him the truth.

"Keir, I'm so sorry. I haven't been able to manage."

She did not tell him that she had been eating bread and butter for her lunch for three weeks. Had she told him that at once and confessed to the other secret, Keir might not have behaved like the rather severe young husband. He was taking off his boots in front of the parlour fire, and it was a very small fire, just as Sybil's offence was a very small one.

"What's the matter, kid?"

"I find I can't manage on thirty shillings."

"Not in debt, are you?"

"Yes. Nearly three pounds. I'm so sorry."

Keir happened to be very tired, and there had been a silly squabble in the workshop to irritate him.

"Three pounds on the wrong side?"

"Yes."

She saw that he was annoyed, and instead of being easy with her he behaved rather like the severe Victorian husband. He told her to get out her books and demonstrate to him just where and how she had failed to make ends meet. He was coldly practical. He did not light a pipe and make her join him in front of the fire. He went and sat at the table and proceeded to hold an audit. He began to go into details.

"Butter. A pound of butter—twice—here—"

Looking rather pale and poignant, she tried to explain that she used a lot of butter in her cooking, and she had butter for lunch. She did not accuse Keir of being fond of butter, which he was.

"And tea. A pound of tea at two and eight. That seems—"

And suddenly she was in tears. She let herself go.

"I—I've only had bread and butter—for my lunch— And I've spent all my dress-money on the housekeeping. I know I'm—I'm rather new to it, but I do think it's unkind of you—"

He sat and looked at her in shocked silence. Tears! And he was only trying to help her, to point this out.

"All right, Syb—all right."

But to her his face still appeared severe and accusing, and abruptly she pushed back her chair and fled. She rushed up the stairs, still sobbing, leaving Keir to confront this emotional crisis.

If he was shocked, he had the sensitiveness to be shocked at himself. Could he claim to a complete authority on housekeeping? And she had been spending her own money, and starving herself in the middle of the day! Probably

[67]

that damned woman next door had been sponging.

He rushed upstairs after her. He found the room in darkness. She was lying on the bed, weeping, as though the little heart of No. 3 was broken.

He knelt down by the bed. He was very much moved.

"Don't, kid, don't. I didn't mean to be nasty. I know much less about the job than you do."

He got his arms round her and drew her to him.

"I'm not a mean devil. Perhaps I've been a bit too keen on saving. It's all right. I'll give you a bit more."

She clung to him. She put her wet face against his.

"Oh—Keir—there's something else."

"What? Tell me."

"I think I'm going to have a baby. Things have stopped —and I'm feeling so sick in the morning."

"My dear—!"

He was shocked—but chiefly because he somehow hadn't noticed— Serious? Yes, this was serious. The shadow of his share in life seemed to deepen, and with it his compassion for this creature who clung to him and who was so easily hurt.

"You ought to have told me, kid. Or—I ought to have guessed. Good Lord, one can be damned selfish in trying to be too careful. Kiss me, Syb. I'm sorry."

She held off for a moment.

"Sorry—because—"

"My dear, not that.—Because—I've hurt you—"

"Oh—Keir."

Chapter Six

1

KEIR insisted upon Sybil's going to see a doctor, and not as a mere panel patient. In fact he took her himself to be examined by the physician who attended at Darvels, and it appeared that Sybil was three months pregnant. She was a healthy young woman with a normal pelvis, and the doctor reassured Keir, while warning him that he himself had ceased to attend maternity cases. He left the midwifery to his two junior partners.

Keir understood. The doctor who attended the Lugards was a man of five-and-fifty who would sacrifice his sleep only for exceptional cases, and Sybil's was not an exceptional case; so Sybil was transferred to one of the junior partners.

"Dr. Richards will look after you just as well as I should," which was true, and when Keir had seen Dr. Richards, he gathered that Sybil would be in good hands.

Keir's financial responsibilities enlarged themselves. No longer was it a question of considering a pound of tea or half a pound of butter. A new life had to be prepared for, and as yet the State does not provide free baby-linen and bassinets! Sybil was to be her own seamstress in the matter of the little creature's wardrobe, but when she and Keir came to investigate the problem, they were shocked at the amount of money they would have to spend. What with one thing and another, the trousseau of the hypothetical small Smith would cost them nearly twenty pounds.

"It does seem an awful lot, Keir."

Keir was being very gentle with her.

"No use doing the thing by halves, Syb."

"Of course—if it happens again, it won't be quite so expensive."

Keir did not say that it was essential that such a luxury should be curtailed, but he was thinking of it. Too many children could be a curse to a crowded community, whose urge was to escape from the crowd. One child would be sufficient, or at all events for the time being. These domestic etceteras would keep him marking time on the ladder.

But he did not present his views to Sybil, for he was realizing the limitations of Sybil. She might be a lovable creature, but she was no pioneer or social climber. He had begun to see his wife as a dear and rather unpractical person, or so confusedly practical that she might involve herself and him in a little world of social compromises. She was more content with elementary things than he was. Her short-sighted brown eyes did not look very far ahead.

His urge was to work more furiously, but so far as work was concerned, Keir was fully exploiting his present possibilities. Also, Sybil and the moods of the young mother were in conflict with too much overtime, and Keir gave up working late. Sybil disliked being alone. She was ready to be considered and caressed. She had moments when she was afraid of the ordeal ahead of her, and she liked to have Keir there by the fire while she sewed at those baby garments.

He cleared away the tea-things and washed up for her, and sometimes he would sit on the hearth-rug at her feet and she would pass her fingers through his insurgent hair.

"Which do you want, Keir?"

Keir had no prejudice in favour of either sex. If he asked anything of fate, it was that Sybil should come safely through the crisis, though both of them were pretending that the bearing of a child was hardly more alarming than getting married.

"Well—I suppose I ought to want a girl."

"Let's imagine it's a girl. We ought each to choose a name. You think of one."

Keir was staring at the fire, and a name seemed to rise like a flame.

"Joanna."

"Joanna! What an unusual name, Keir! Where did you get it?"

He remembered that the name had been that of a heroine in a book that had impressed him considerably.

"Out of a book, Syb."

"I suppose we should shorten it to Jo. My name's much more simple. Mary."

He repeated the names—"Mary Joanna Smith," and the rhythm of them pleased him. It was good English.

"Where did you get your name, Syb?"

She laughed.

"Why, silly boy, it's my other name."

"Of course. But I always think of you as Sybil."

Yet if she was Sybil, she was so much else, and the secret self of Keir was following the implications of this present and this future. Inevitably he saw himself with far less freedom than a year ago, and if he regretted it, he did so with compassionate resignation. Yes, this was life, a far more complex affair than the filling in of a time-sheet. The path would be a little more circuitous and full of hazards, the old, well-worn path of the multitude, trodden by generations of men and of women. You could not take a comrade and then quarrel with her because your effort was for two or three instead of one. Your courage and your power might be enlarged by the duality if you were rightly man.

Also, he had the courage to confront this increasing complexity. That which he had dreamed of was a little farther off. He might have to tramp ten miles instead of five. His savings would be less; he would be more involved in the present while still pressing steadily towards the future. He was not afraid. As yet life had not infected him with its dreadful and elemental fear.

Working at his bench in the carpenter's shop, with old Tower beside him, he would look through the window at the yard with its building material and high black fence. The lilac bush had shed its leaves, but the ghosts of its flower spikes were visible. Less than a year ago—spring and the lilac blossom and the solitude of his dreams upon the downs! Now a builder's yard and bricks and drain-pipes and the limitations of that little hutch in Paragon Place. Sometimes he had a feeling that the exquisite virtue of youth had gone from him. The flower of the lilac had fallen. He was just a little fellow working in a shop.

He would glance at Thomas Tower and reflect upon the old man's gentle absorption in his work. It was a kind of ritual, patient and predestined, and for old Tower that lilac might flower once or twice or thrice. But in his youth had this docile and rather inarticulate craftsman felt—as he —Keir—felt? Had Tower conceived some dream edifice of his own and lived to find it—Babel?

One afternoon, when the yard was growing dim, Keir asked his neighbour at the bench a question.

"How long have you been in this shop, Tom?"

Old Tower's large, mild face was turned to the sky.

"How long? Oh, a matter of thirty years. We'd better have the lights on. My eyes aren't what they were."

Thirty years at the same bench in the same shop!

2

In winter Paragon Place was less communal than in summer, for most of the gardens were dirty brown blankets tucked up under the grey sky, and citizens did not linger at their doors. Debates and arguments removed themselves to the bar of the "George," a somewhat slovenly pub in Richmond Road where the sociable members of both sexes warmed themselves both within and without.

It might be said that the population of Paragon Place could be divided into those who pubbed and those who did not, the abstainers being in a serious minority and regarded as socially smug. Paragon Place had its own hatred of high-brows, for the paunch of the low-brow and the pate of the high-brow do not mingle over the pots.

Yet Keir was not cut off completely from members of the other clique. He met some of them during his comings and goings, and the cheery salutation was not passed to him: "Hallo, Bob"—or "Morning, Jim." He was under suspicion; he never stood a chap a drink or became sociably and reassuringly silly.

Coming home late one February evening, he met under the street lamp at the end of the road the two Job girls, very much dressed up and with somewhere to go. They were in spirits, two mischievous young wenches out upon adventure, and when they and Keir met by the street lamp, he stepped off the pavement to let them pass. He did not look at them, and to the Misses Job he was both dull dog and little Pharisee. There was no "Hallo, Gertie!" about Keir.

They broke into giggles at the confrontation and at his abrupt divergence. The occasion had its humour. The elder of the two girls seized her inspiration.

"Hallo, darling."

They passed on with sudden laughter, and Keir, suddenly hot about the ears, stepped back on to the pavement. Damned young—! They were still laughing, and a valediction was cast back to him.

"Wifie's waiting, dear. Get busy."

[73]

Yes, he was not *persona grata* to Paragon Place, and he was misliking Paragon Place more and more. Like sex, it involved you and submerged you, and it was the sweet seductiveness of sex that had hurried him into this back street. It would have been so much better if he and Sybil had waited for a year. Meanwhile his urge to escape from certain environments crystallized upon the little, sordid thread that was Paragon Place. It was like some sinister and suggestive fate, slowly spreading its shadow over the world of his endeavour, darkening it, obscuring it. Almost Paragon Place propounded to him the old metaphysical problem of "Free Will and Fatalism."

On yet another night, when the street lamps were blurred by fog, Keir came suddenly upon two shapes blocking the little iron gateway of No. 3, Mr. Block and Mr. Phelps, both in drink and on the dole. Mr. Block had mistaken the gateway of No. 3 for that of No. 4, and the coming of Keir added to the complication, for Mr. Block remained in the gateway, but he was not so drunk that he did not recognize his neighbour.

"What d'yer want 'ere?"

Keir explained curtly that he wanted to reach his own door, and Mr. Block was suddenly and grossly amused.

"Don't know his own gate, Syd! The little blighter's boozed."

It was a huge joke, and Mr. Block enjoyed it.

"You go in there, Mr. Smiff, and see what my old woman gives yer. She won't hang round your neck, my lad."

Keir, who was tired and irritable, did not deign to argue the point. He slipped over the iron rail on the top of the wall, putting a foot on one of Sybil's wallflowers.

He said: "Start at the end and count and you'll find yourself one short of four."

He had reached the door, but Phelps, the communist, who was less and differently drunk from his comrade, became suddenly eloquent. He had the gift of language, especially when in liquor. His bitterness would blaze into furious, cold invective.

"Here, 'alf a mo. I've got something to say to you, Mr. Smith."

He entered the gangway of No. 4 and, leaning over the dividing fence, pointed a long first finger at Keir as though menacing him with a pistol.

"— little blackleg.—Overtime, overtime, — old Samson's —, with other fellahs starving. Yes, you — little skunk. I'd have you shot and shoved underground. Yes, you think you're going to be an employer, a — boss, climbing on the backs of your betters. Overtime, overtime! What you want is—"

Keir, astonished by the other man's fury, stood there holding the handle of his front door.

"Seem a bit excited, Phelps."

"By God, don't you give me any of your lip or I'll come over the fence at you. If I had my way, I'd have every man out of that — business. A lot of blacklegs, that's what you are, and we know it, and we're not going to forget it. You wait till the next general strike comes along, and we'll show you something."

Keir opened the door of No. 3.

"That's all right—then. How to get everybody down in the gutter, I suppose?"

He went in, closing the door. He locked it, and in the passage he found Sybil frightened and trembling.

"What is it, Keir?"

He was white and scornful.

"Only two of our nice neighbours—rather drunk and seeing red. Nothing to worry about. Just Paragon Place."

In April Sybil's small garden came into flower, wall-flowers and forget-me-nots and a few early tulips, and since she was growing big with child, she was obliged to content herself with looking at her flowers. She had a passion for being out of doors, and Keir bought her a two-and-six-penny deck-chair for use in the garden. There was no room for the chair in the minute patch in front of No. 3, and when Sybil sat out at the back, she was at the mercy of her neighbours. Paragon Place had no privacy. Mrs. Block would appear and force her familiarities upon Sybil, and since Sybil had refused her the loan of domestic articles, Mrs. Block retaliated by compelling Sybil to lend her ears.

Mrs. Block described vividly and in detail her two child-births and sundry miscarriages, and the "labours" of various friends. She referred to all the terrible things that might happen, and which she had known to happen. There was Gertie Parsons, who had lived at No. 7, and whose first pregnancy had been a horrible affair.

"They 'ad to put the instruments in her. She was torn to bits, she was, and the child was born dead. Its 'ead was all—"

Sybil fled into the house, and when Keir came home, he found her in tears. What was it? She confessed that the woman next door had been telling her things.

Keir was furious, and his fury translated itself into eighteen feet of deal fencing erected on the Block side in the form of a recess so that the lady should be excluded. He had managed to pick up some old posts and rails cheaply from a dump in the Samson & Hoad yard, for the fence—like their sojourn in No. 3—was not planned for permanence. This piece of fencing shut out Mrs. Block, but it was an added affront to the occupants of No. 4. The Block children hammered upon it; their mother said things over it.

Mrs. Jervis at No. 2 was less obvious than Mrs. B., and being upon her dignity, she had persuaded Mr. Jervis to erect a panel of trellis between No. 3 and No. 2. It was possible to look through the trellis, but Mrs. Jervis had become blind of eye towards No. 3. Her husband was to plant runner beans at the foot of this screen, and in the summer Mrs. Jervis would find herself almost as select as the Smiths.

Keir, appreciating Sybil's loneliness and their isolation, was worried by it. He had to leave her so much alone, and Sybil was showing signs of becoming emotional and introspective. She had too much time to think about her ordeal, poor kid. He made a point now of coming back in the middle of the day to dinner, and one morning he met Mrs. Moore of No. 1 coming out of his gate.

She was a little, bright brown bird of a woman, sensible and kind, and she told Keir that she had been helping his wife.

"I just dropped in. She gets upset so easily about things."

Keir thanked her. He was glad of those friendly brown eyes.

"I'd be glad for you to drop in any time, Mrs. Moore. I don't like leaving the kid so much."

Mrs. Moore had her own views upon Keir as a husband. He was rather too serious and strenuous a young man, but he would learn, and Mrs. Moore knew how much husbands had to learn, but if a chap was kind and kept off the drink, all things were possible. She could refer to her own husband as a man of few words, but one of the best.

"I'll come in each day, Mr. Smith. I suppose you've arranged for the nurse."

Keir had, but a nurse is not as valuable as a friendly neighbour when a baby comes into the world, and the home is disorganized.

"I'll give her a hand when the baby comes. She's a sweet thing, Mr. Smith, and I think you're lucky."

Keir agreed with her, and he was to become more and more glad of Mrs. Moore. She could be kind and practical without fussing; she had a soothing and a happy effect upon Sybil. Moreover, she was quietly but decisively anti-Block and not afraid of saying so. Like many small women she was a creature of great courage, and she had fought her battle with Mrs. B. and won it.

She said: "I'd be a socialist, Mr. Smith, if I thought the socialists could get rid of people like that, but I can't say I see how they can. It's in the blood. Look at their children. Block goes on being Block. That's what I say."

Meanwhile the back garden of No. 3 was asking to be cultivated, and since Sybil could not give herself to it, the challenge was Keir's. She persuaded him to it, not foreseeing a certain incident that was to make that garden Eden after the Fall. She wanted Keir to grow potatoes and lettuces and peas and greens and to sow some annuals to make a summer show outside the kitchen window. If time was precious, she would be satisfied with dwarf nasturtiums, but she did ask for the faces of flowers.

Keir agreed. He began to give up his Saturday afternoons to the garden, in spite of the possible proximity of William Block and the Block small boys. He would go out with spade and hoe and rake as though the disreputable fence was five miles high or the next garden a rolling wilderness. Keir put in two rows of peas and six rows of early potatoes and pricked out a hundred or so lettuce seedlings presented to him by Mr. Moore. He had decided that Sybil should have her flowers, and he spent ten shillings on plants at Kingham market, French marigolds, snap-dragons, asters, and ten-week stocks. The strip of ground fronting the kitchen window promised to be gay, but one night the Smith garden was raided and half the plants were torn up and thrown over into the Jervises' garden next door.

Keir suspected the Block children. There were foot-marks in the soil that had not been planted there by the boots of adults, but he could not prove his suspicions. The damage had been done after he and Sybil had gone to bed in the front bedroom.

But he mentioned the matter over the fence. He assumed that the Block children had been responsible for the out-rage.

"I'll trouble you to keep your kids out of my garden."

The challenge was caught up and tossed back. Keir was accused of making unsubstantiated allegations against those innocents. He was told to mind his own business. He did mind it, while becoming increasingly aware of the active and jubilant hostility next door. Strange objects appeared in Sybil's secret enclosure, discarded tins, and a paper parcel full of fishy remnants, an old bicycle tire. No. 4 was out for provocation.

The climax arrived one Saturday afternoon. Sybil did not witness the gathering of the storm. The boys invaded Keir's garden, were chased, and the elder of the two received a box on the ear as he was scrambling over the ragged fence. He went in roaring to his parents, and the Block world erupted.

Sybil had just made tea and had gone to the kitchen window to call her husband. She stood there with a kind of stillness of shocked horror. She saw Keir prone among the young potatoes with that hulk of a man on top of him. Mr. Block was rubbing Keir's face in the soil, while the two children hung over the fence and exulted.

Sybil's impulse was to rush out and rescue Keir from that final humiliation, but something seemed to give way in her. Her eyes were dark and blind. She groped for a chair and sat down.

And suddenly she was aware of Keir in the doorway.

[79]

His face was filthy. It had blood on it, and more than blood, a kind of soiled shame. His eyes avoided hers. He seemed to know that she had seen him squashed and vanquished by the strength of the silly brute next door.

She heard him hurry up the stairs. He was going to try and wash away that shame, but some shames are ineffaceable.

She wanted to rush up after him and take his soiled pride in her arms.

"Keir—oh, Keir, don't look like that."

But an elemental pang smote her. Her own crisis was at hand.

Chapter Seven

1

JOANNA was born at about five o'clock the following morning, a premature child, but viable, and Keir, who had been walking up and down Paragon Place and watching the dawn come up over those slated roofs, heard for the first time the voice of his small daughter.

He stood at the gate, a bare-headed and somewhat dishevelled young man with a bruised lip and an eye that was swollen. Almost he had forgotten the affair of the potato patch. The night had held other emotions. He remembered going round for Mrs. Moore, a Mrs. Moore who, in a moment of understanding, had refused to see the wounds—both physical and spiritual—upon his face.

"I'll come at once."

He had had cause to bless that quiet, capable little woman who had taken charge and brought with her a sense of sweet sanity into the outraged heart of No. 3.

"You had better go for the nurse and the doctor, yes, at once."

Mrs. Moore had got Sybil to bed, and Keir had rushed off on his bicycle. There had been a bright full moon. He had spent half the night with that moon, for, with all those other people in his small house, he had felt himself a superfluous creature and most strangely and restlessly alone. He had tried sitting in the parlour, only to hear in the room above a kind of moaning and the voices of women.

Mrs. Moore had come below and spoken to him.

"Nurse says everything's all right. You'd better go round

and smoke a pipe with my man."

Keir had sat for an hour with Mr. Moore, a white Mr. Moore who in some strange way had ceased to be a stranger. They had said things to each other, simple and obvious things that seemed to grow out of the soil of their common humanity. And Keir had wondered at life and at some of his own crude impressions and prejudices. The soul of a sweep! Mr. Moore had made him a cup of tea.

But principally Keir appeared to have spent the night walking up and down Paragon Place, while the moonlight played upon the slated roofs. He had come to other conclusions with regard to Paragon Place. It had held one particular window for him, and he had both avoided and sought that window. It had been the only lighted window in the row, and occasionally a shadow had shown upon the blind. Life had become both poignant and shadowy. A sudden cry of pain!

When would it be over?

He had not been very conscious of the passing hours, for time had been measured by that prodigy of nature. It had both exasperated and touched him, and the exasperation had been a part of the pain. Why should Sybil have to suffer? Why had he no bed to go to? But how absurd! The crisis had caught him in a moment of raw humiliation. He had gone up and down, up and down, avoiding that window and yet being drawn to it.

And then, just after the dawn, the small voice of the child, an infantile protest against the newness of things and the process of being born! A thin, strange puling, and suddenly he had felt infinitely grateful and reassured. He had gone in with a kind of surreptitious haste, crept up the stairs, and knocked at the door.

It had been opened three inches. He had seen the face of the nurse.

"Is it all right?"

"Quite."

She had closed the door on him, and he had gone silently down the stairs and out into the little front garden.

Well, thank God, that was over! He went in to find Mrs. Moore busy in the kitchen, and realizing that she must have been up all night, he wondered at her good nature. Why should she bother about a couple of young people who a few weeks ago had been strangers? What did Mrs. Moore get out of it? Did she expect to get anything out of it? For, though Keir had read many books, he was very ignorant of life's elementals. He had views upon sociology, and, like many of his more learned betters with a passion for theory, he might despise the crowd, while remaining blind to the crowd's sanity. Having dissected society, he might sit perched on a stool, perplexed by his own cleverness and still in search for the strange force or substance that holds society together. What was the mysterious matrix? Just humanity's simple good nature, an urge towards kindness? That seemed too simple.

Mrs. Moore was filling a kettle. She looked tired, but contentedly so, and her voice was gentle.

"Well, feeling proud, my dear?"

Keir was not feeling anything of the kind. He was hungry, and he wanted to shave.

"I'm jolly glad it's over. Did she have a very bad time?"

"More or less. The first, you know. But she's got more pluck than you'd think. I've heard some girls—well—never mind. I've got to go round presently and get my man his breakfast. You come along and have your breakfast with us."

Keir went and looked at himself in the little mirror that hung on the wall beside the scullery door.

"I'll have a shave and a brush up. I don't know why you are being so good to us, Mrs. Moore."

"No more don't I. It's just neighbourliness."

[83]

Keir smiled at the reflection of his own rather haggard face. Yes, unquestionably he would have to show the world a black eye.

"Perhaps there are some people one can't help being kind to. She's that sort—my wife, I mean."

Mrs. Moore did not contradict him. She was not there to explore or to discuss human motives. She herself was a motive. She had the day's work on her hands.

And then she surprised both herself and Keir.

"Bless me—if it isn't Sunday morning! I was thinking it was Monday, with Jim having to be out at six."

Keir too had forgotten that it was Sunday, though the Sabbath's peculiar significance was confined to the fact that he would not have to go to work. He could stay at home with Sybil and the new prodigy and conceal his bruises from his neighbours, for the smart of that shame was reviving now that the night's ordeal was over. He had had his face rubbed in the dirt by that sodden chunk of flesh next door.

"Can you spare me a little hot water, Mrs. Moore?"

Yes, she could spare it. She was about to make Sybil and the nurse an early cup of tea. The nurse would be leaving in half an hour, and if Sybil could be persuaded to fall asleep after her cup of tea, the rest of the world could attend to its own affairs for an hour.

"I'll just see she's comfortable."

Keir shaved himself in the scullery. He heard the nurse and Mrs. Moore come down the stairs, and he was given to understand that his wife and child were to be left undisturbed.

"She wants to see you, Mr. Smith, but I told her you'd come up presently. She's so sleepy, poor dear."

Keir accepted the situation. He went out into the back garden and walked down the path to the place where too sensitive a self-regard had received chastisement. He sup-

[84]

posed that it was just as well that he should confront both the reality and his neighbours' back windows, but since it was Sunday, Paragon Place still slumbered. He stood and looked at a patch of disorder where the young haulms of half a dozen potato plants had suffered violence—even as he did. Silly, brute strength! But it had got him down in the dirt— He turned quickly and walked back to the cottage, for sudden ugly anger flared in him, and ugliness and anger were not good on a morning such as this.

He had breakfast with the Moores, and Mr. Moore was jocular and fatherly, and Keir, who was waiting for one of them to remark upon his face and the fracas of the previous evening, was surprised and comforted by a nice reticence. It was as unexpected and as pleasant as Mr. Moore's white face, his Sunday face, and Keir felt touched. These good people could hold their tongues, which was more than some of the world's wise men have been able to do.

At the end of the meal he lit a pipe and went and stood by the Moores' kitchen window. He wanted to thank the sweep and his wife.

He said: "I would never have thought people could be so kind. I shan't forget it."

Mr. Moore struck a match on his boot and smiled at his wife.

"That's her. I don't take no credit. And besides—if there weren't a little neighbourliness, where would the world be?"

Keir took that fragment of philosophy back with him to No. 3. No. 4 was out of bed and vocal. The two small boys with the hard red faces were out in their back garden, waiting for a possible victim. They began to hammer on the boards of Sybil's sanctuary. Keir stood for a moment in the kitchen, conscious of the white squall ready to rage within him, and trying to restrain it. Then he heard a voice, the voice of Mrs. Block.

[85]

"Stop that—or I'll knock your 'eads together."

The hammering ceased, and Keir supposed that even Mrs. Block might on occasions attain to some sense of neighbourliness. Or did the banging on those boards annoy her?

The storm mood passed from him. He smiled, and without realizing the quality of his smile and its whimsical irony, he went softly up the stairs and stood outside his wife's door.

2

She was awake and she had heard those careful footsteps.

"Keir, is that you?"

He opened the door and went in. The blind was down, and in the subdued light he saw Sybil's face. It had a kind of tranquil pallor. The large, dark eyes looked at him.

"Oh—Keir—"

He closed the door very gently. He was down on his knees beside the bed, conscious somehow of the tired and serene fragility of that face. He was deeply moved; his chin quivered.

"Glad it's over, kid.—I—"

His eyes felt hot and suffused, and the face of his wife became blurred to him. He was aware of her putting out a hand and touching his cheek.

"Dear Keir—I'm so happy— Look—"

He had forgotten that small piece of new life, and he got up and, going round to the other side of the bed, bent over the bassinet. He saw a funny little withered face, two little puds of hands. The baby's eyes were closed.

He wanted to say something, and no words came. He stood hesitant and smiling.

"Pretty marvellous, isn't it?"

"Ours— Oh—Keir—"

He was back again, on his knees by the bed.

"Seems worth while, kid, doesn't it?"

She held fast to one of his hands.

"Joanna Mary."

"No, Mary Joanna. You came first."

She smiled at him, and then a sudden shadow of intense seriousness spread swiftly over her face.

"Keir—I—I don't want her to grow up here, not near those other children—"

He understood. It was perhaps the most complete refutation of communism that he was ever likely to hear. He bent down and kissed his wife's forehead.

"That's all right, Syb. We'll get out of this place—even if I have to build. That's a promise.

The shadow passed. She lay and looked at him with eyes that were both tired and bright, and it seemed to Keir that his wife's face had a new, strange beauty.

"You are good to me, Keir."

"Well—I couldn't be anything else, could I, Syb, with you being you?"

3

Keir did not know it then, but his wife—being woman —carried with her through the months that were to follow, an unconfessed and secret fear. Joanna Mary had been brought into the world prematurely by the emotional shock that her mother had suffered, and Sybil's dread was that the child might not be normal. Probably the thing was purely coincidental, but Joanna Mary did exhibit in later years a slight disharmony. She did not stammer, but was curiously hesitant in uttering the first two words of any sentence. It was a kind of fumbling of the lips, rather appealing and attractive. Or, at least, her father found it so.

Meanwhile the present was proving so much more

persuasive than the future that Keir accepted the immediate adventure. In deciding to build a cottage of his own his inspiration was a miscellany. There was a little vanity in it, a snapping of the fingers under the nose of Paragon Place, a touch of swagger. The ideal home that was to be would contain more than emotion in its foundations. He persuaded himself that the investment would be reasonable and sound. He could put the rest of his savings into the small house and obtain the balance of the capital required from a building society. A mortgage, yes, but he would be able to pay off the mortgage in five or six years and then—if he should need capital for a venture on his own, he could raise it by mortgaging his house.

Moreover, the urge to escape from Paragon Place was as passionate as his pride. He might confront Paragon Place with an air of stiff-lipped nonchalance, but, being the sensitive creature that he was, he would be too much at the mercy of his reactions. You might despise things that were brutish and blatant, but when in contact with them, it was you who would suffer, not they.

"Hallo, old dirty face!"

The hard-eyed children next door were always ready to utter that salutation, and behind their little gloating faces loomed the bulk of that silly brute—their father.

Possibly the Block man symbolized for Keir the stupid strength of the herd, the menace of a crowd community that may stampede in a moment of panic and crash through the flimsy fences of convention. Hoofs and not intelligence may count in such a crisis. The ark of Noah was built to confound a cataclysm of nature, but to Keir the cataclysm to be feared was some upheaval of the crowd community. A few snarling creatures like Phelps leading some howling and hungry pack! For Keir was an individualist. Paragon Place had taught him that it might not be possible to love your neighbour; you might fear and hate him, and hate

[88]

yourself for that fear. Paragon Place and a police force confessed to a dual inevitableness, and Keir was on the side of the police. Cheerfully would he have watched all that was Block in the world clubbed to extinction. The separative creature may have to fly or fight, and fight with a ferocity that disguises itself in creative cunning, and Keir had a wife and a child.

It so happened that an estate had come into the market that winter. The place, known as Abbey Lands, had comprised a large garden, a small park, and several meadows. A syndicate was developing the estate and turning the park into a residential quarter for middle-class people, and the meadows were being sold off in lots for cottages and bungalows. Keir knew the estate. It lay on the outskirts of Kingham and not far from the river, a pleasant property rising to a slight plateau and well treed.

Having to go out on a job near Abbey Lands, he called at the estate office, a white wooden hut surrounded by posts and chains. He interviewed a clerk and was told that plots could be had at prices ranging from a hundred and twenty to a hundred and fifty pounds. There were certain restrictions. No bungalow to be erected should cost less than six hundred pounds, and a two-storied cottage, seven hundred pounds. Roads, water, gas, main drains, and electric light were to be arranged for by the company.

Keir went to look at the land. Some of it had been pegged out into plots, and these plots fronted upon a lane. The old thorn hedges were still standing, and a particular corner plot attracted Keir, for on it grew a big beech tree, a green and stately fountain of a tree. Already two or three bungalows were being erected, but compared with Paragon Place, this new little world was sweet and peaceful.

Keir walked over the plot and stood under the tree. The day was hot and sunny, and the shade of the tree made him think of a large, cool, gentle hand. He had a vision of a little white bungalow standing well back from the lane, with a grassy space and flower-beds in front of it. Certainly that tree would possess a large part of the garden, but how could you grudge space to so stately and proud a neighbour? A little white bungalow with a brown pantiled roof, a home for Keir, Sybil, and Joanna Mary.

Keir said nothing to Sybil. Also, Sybil was so full of Joanna Mary. It was really amazing how eight or ten pounds of young flesh complicated the domestic symphony. No. 3 seemed to be all Joanna Mary, towels and diapers and sudden tantrums and enthusiasms and the feeding of the small creature. Alarums and excursions at night, swift maternal panic in the heart of Sybil, sustained and tolerant resignation on the part of Keir.

"Oh, Keir—she's been sick. I wonder if the milk—?"

To Keir it appeared evident that a baby's normal state was one of lively incontinence at both ends.

"Sick? Well, I don't think it's much to worry about."

"Do you think we ought to have the doctor?"

"Go and ask Mrs. Moore."

Mrs. Moore was an incredibly wise woman and quite indispensable.

Keir spoke to Mr. Samson about the bungalow, and it so happened that Messrs. Samson & Hoad had secured a contract to build four cottages on the Abbey Lands estate nor was Mr. Samson surprised by Keir's passion to escape from Paragon Place. Also, Mr. Samson had good cause to know that when a firm had a man like Keir in its employ he might be worth hundreds a year to it. Mr. Samson always asserted that a good man need never be out of a job in the south. The north appeared to be a different proposition, for the individual was more coerced by massed Trade Unionism. He wanted to keep Keir. He was interested personally in the career of Keir Hardie Smith.

"What's it going to cost you?"

"One hundred and fifty for the land, and six hundred for the bungalow."

"How much can you put down?"

"About two hundred, sir. I can go to a building society for the rest."

Keir and Mr. Samson were alone together in the firm's office, and Mr. Samson picked up a paper from the desk. His fresh-coloured face had a jocund slyness. Business might be something of a dog-fight in these crowded days, but there were occasions when it was pleasant to spring a surprise upon life.

"Six and a half per cent, my lad."

"Yes, I suppose so."

Mr. Samson played with the piece of paper.

"Look here, Keir, we have a contract to build four cottages on the estate at seven hundred and fifty pounds apiece. We shall have all our stuff and our staff out there. I'll put you up a bungalow at cost price."

Keir went white.

"I don't know why you should, sir— I'm—"

"A matter of business—perhaps, what! One may get more out of a man than the return for the wages you pay him. Besides—"

He chuckled.

"One doesn't talk like this to everybody. Keep it quiet. And about a mortgage. I'm what they call a warm man. I'll let you have a mortgage at five per cent."

Keir sat down rather suddenly on one of the office chairs.

"It's extraordinarily good of you, sir."

"Why? I'm not losing money on it. Or put it another way, my lad, I'm backing my fancy. One may put money on a man as well as on a gee-gee. Old Tom is leaving us at the end of the year, and you'll be our foreman carpenter. Besides, you remember that little conversation we had?"

Keir's hands were clasping his soft hat and spoiling the

[91]

shape of it.

"I'm not likely to forget it. But I shall be saving to pay off the mortgage. I shan't have any capital to put into—"

Mr. Samson looked amused.

"Possibly—we can do without that. I might get a silly pup with a gold dog-collar. I might prefer a chap without the dog-collar. You carry on for another year or two, my lad."

Keir got up from his chair, still looking rather white.

"You know what you are offering me, sir, my chance."

Mr. Samson laid a large hand on his shoulder.

"Just so. Someone gave me a chance once. I suppose they thought I was worth it. Go ahead."

"Then—I can close with them for the land?"

"Yes, go ahead."

Keir sacrificed the day's dinner-hour and, cycling over to Abbey Lands, found a clerk lunching on sandwiches in the white hut. The clerk was a phlegmatic young man, and this other fellow appeared a little excited and breathless.

"Is Plot 29 still open?"

The clerk turned to look at an estate map hanging on the wall.

"Plot 29?"

"Yes, the one at the corner, with the beech tree."

The clerk's consciousness was un-treed. He was an urban soul.

"Yes, 29's not taken up yet."

"I'll take it."

The other man looked with bored blue eyes at Keir The fellow seemed in a hell of a hurry.

"All right. But there are restrictions, you know."

"Yes, you told me all about that. I was in here two o three days ago."

"So you were. Get a lot of people buzzing in and out When can you put the money down?"

[92]

"Tomorrow—if necessary."

The clerk selected another sandwich from the tin box. It was a cheese sandwich.

"Right-o. Better give me the details and sign a form. We shall have to get the conveyancing put through."

"Freehold—of course. No ground-rent—or anything like that?"

"No. The whole happy home is yours."

Keir scorched back to Paragon Place, where Sybil met him with a face of reproachful relief.

"Oh, Keir—I thought you'd had a smash. I've kept your dinner."

It was ten minutes to two, and Keir was too full of other food to trouble about dinner.

"Give me a piece of bread and cheese, Syb. I say—I shall have something to show you after tea. Can you get Mrs. Moore to take charge of Joanna?"

Sybil caught his vibrant enthusiasm.

"Oh, what is it, Keir?"

"I've bought a bit of land. Yes, just the spot for us. Samson's going to put us up a bungalow."

Sybil's eyes seemed to catch the light. Then she rushed at him, put her arms round his neck, and kissed him.

"Oh, Keir, how lovely!"

Chapter Eight

1

KEIR's predestined plot of ground had a frontage of fifty feet and a depth of a hundred and fifty. He had brought with him half a dozen rough wooden pegs cut from the lid of a box, and when he and Sybil wheeled their bicycles through a gap in the thorn hedge and saw what to them was green and unvexed country, they experienced one of those moments of pure happiness that remain like the memory of some exquisite afterglow.

"Oh—Keir!"

She stood holding her bicycle and looking out over the meadows towards the trees of the Abbey Lands park, elms, chestnuts, and three very old cedars with the evening light upon them, and to Keir his wife's face was like the face of the woman bending over Joanna Mary, faintly smiling, tender, vaguely wistful. Her lashes seemed to quiver. There was something melting in the lines of lips and chin.

"Like it, kid?"

"Are we really going to live here?"

"Well, of course there will be a lot of houses later on."

"Yes, but I shan't mind them, somehow."

Then she discovered the beech tree, and when Keir told her that it would be their tree, she uttered a little cry of delight. She was a simple creature both in her joys and in her sorrows, and she would give to life that which was lovable and lasting in herself. She put her bicycle against the hedge and, going to the tree, touched the smooth trunk with her fingers and then stood looking up into the green foliage. The half-light under the tree seemed to make her face appear paler and more mystical.

"Isn't it beautiful! I can put Joanna here in hot weather."

Keir had left his bicycle beside her and taken the wooden pegs. His eyes were smiling.

"Now, then, where shall we have the house?"

They paced out the plot and, standing side by side, discussed the sitting of the house. They agreed that it should be set well back from the road and with a view of the beech tree, and that the thorn hedge should be left as it was. Sybil was for having the flower garden in front of the house. She wanted a small lawn. Joanna could play on that sacred plot of grass.

"How big will it be, Keir?"

"Oh, about thirty feet by twenty, I expect. Yes, roughly that."

He began putting in his pegs, and Sybil followed him from corner to corner, while he described the building to her. He visualized a little white bungalow with a brown roof, a green front door, and green window frames. Yes, and brown chimney-pots. All the windows were to look to the front or to the back so that they should see as much garden as was possible. A home should not stare at fences, or the walls and roofs of other people's houses.

"You shall have a real up-to-date kitchen, Syb. What I mean is—all the rough work can be done in the scullery, and we can use the kitchen as a living-room. In the scullery a gas cooker and a gas copper, and everything to hand. Save time and tissue."

"Shall we have a bath, Keir?"

"Of course. A 'Cook & Heat' in the kitchen with a hot-water boiler fixed there will do us proud."

"And I should like a good larder, Keir. Something that isn't like a black hole and yet keeps things fresh and cool."

"Not like No. 3, kid. That's the idea."

Returning to the beech tree they sat down on the grass. There were still innumerable details to be discussed, the advantages of stained doors and skirting-boards over painted ones, the question of cupboards, whether they should choose paper or distemper, the position of the front gate, and of the shed for bicycles, tools, and etceteras. Sybil, finding herself referring to the dream house as "It," realized that it needed naming.

"What shall we call it, Keir?"

"Well, it isn't born yet."

"But we christened Joanna, didn't we—?"

"That's so. Any ideas?"

She sat and gazed at the stretch of grass where the little white building was to stand, and her thoughts went back a year to that lovers' day upon the downs.

"Let's call it 'Merrow,' Keir."

He understood her, and he let an arm lie across her shoulders.

"Good idea. Yes, that was a day, wasn't it? Merrow. Yes, we'll call it 'Merrow.' "

Having walked once more over the land that was to be theirs, they wheeled their bicycles out into the lane and returned to Paragon Place, and Joanna Mary. Mrs. Moore, when told the news, looked just a little sad. "Well, that will be nice for you, won't it? I'd like a little place like that myself." She delivered up Joanna Mary and tried not to feel jealous of Sybil or to say that life seemed so much easier for the younger generation.

"A bungalow? No stairs? And a bath?"

"Yes, not like Paragon Place."

"Well, it's lucky for you that your man's got such a good job."

When Joanna Mary had been put to bed, Keir and Sybil sat down at the kitchen table, and Keir drew plans of the bungalow that was to be, but the first plan that he produced allowed for no bath-room. Sybil called his attention to the omission, and he ran his fingers through his hair.

"Well, I'm blessed! Must squeeze it in somewhere. Let's see. Kitchen—living-room, parlour, two bedrooms, scullery, bath-room."

"And a hall and passage, Keir."

"It will have to be all passage. Getting everything in on the ground floor without spreading your foundations all over the earth—! Wait a bit—I have it."

He was a good draughtsman, and his final plan—though it was only roughed in—brought the right exclamation from Sybil.

"You are clever, Keir. Could we have taps that don't need too much cleaning? Not brass taps."

"Rather. And I'd have liked glass handles on the doors, but they cost too much."

2

Since the building of "Merrow" was to be a somewhat secret affair, Mr. Samson suggested that Keir should draw out his own plans and do his own measuring up and estimating. It would be good experience for him, and Mr. Samson was interested to see how Keir would handle his first house. A man may be a certificated craftsman and yet prove incapable of confronting reality and of budgeting for all the etceteras that control profit and loss. Keir spent seven evenings on materials, ballast and cement, bricks, timber, tiles, drain-pipes, plastering, fire-grates, and fittings. These were calculable details, while labour and the time-costs of labour were more hypothetical. But Keir had kept his eyes wide open during his years with Messrs. Samson & Hoad, and he had a fairly accurate knowledge of what the brick-layer, the plasterer, and the carpenter should do in a day.

His estimate worked out at £470. He had gone into every

detail, and the document that he handed to Mr. Samson was a complete schedule. He had borrowed various trade-lists from the office, and the prices that he quoted for the various fittings were up to date.

Mr. Samson, having examined Keir's figures, found them substantially accurate. The estimate was for a sound and solid little place, honest work everywhere.

Mr. Samson was pleased. Keir had a head on his shoulders. Here was a youngster who had not been content to live merely amid shavings and sawdust. He had ideas and the technical knowledge to put those ideas into practice. An architect might be a very cultured gentleman, and sometimes incredibly fussy, but so often he was blind to the blood and sinew of reality. He might raise hell and heaven over a mantelpiece or a chimney-flue and be quite unable to tell you whether a particular man was slacking or when there was too much sand in the cement. The architect might say that these commonplaces did not concern him, but Mr. Samson knew that the business of building houses is as personal as the rearing of a baby. You may possess plenty of theory and yet misunderstand and mishandle the poor little beast's metabolism. Mr. Samson loathed theorists. They belonged to the great hierarchy of high-brow hoodlums. He classed them with district visitors, extension lecturers, and all government officials.

"That's quite a good bit of work, Keir. You've allowed the men a margin. Then—there's the weather."

Mr. Samson had to have his little joke.

"Seems to me the gentleman who draws out the weather reports don't understand plain language. When it rains, it's unsettled; when the sun shines, it's settled. Much better if they changed the words over. Settled and rainy. Another depression from the Atlantic. I'd like to see some good foul language in those weather reports."

"Occasional showers, sir."

Mr. Samson smiled one of his crooked, sly smiles.

"Well, couldn't they call it a damned deluge—on occasions? But—just a moment. This bungalow of yours—I regard it as a piece of secret diplomacy. I don't want it gossiped about. You take me? Besides, we shall have to put the figure at six hundred to satisfy the Abbey Lands people."

Keir said: "Quite so. I like minding my own business."

Keir's plans were passed by the Borough Surveyor of Kingham and approved by the Abbey Lands Building Estate, but though Keir's world did not know of the understanding between Keir and Mr. Samson, it soon discovered that he was building a house. The Moores knew, and soon all Paragon Place had heard of the Smiths' adventure in bricks and mortar. Phelps, who was painting one of the new houses on the Abbey Lands estate, had nothing but bitter things to say of the people who were going to inhabit those houses. Private property, villas for the middle classes, comfortable homes for the swine who sold you things and sold you in the selling of them. The house upon which Phelps was working was the property of a successful ironmonger.

He had bitter things to say about all tradesmen and lawyers and estate agents. They did not produce. They just sat on the stuff that the workers produced, and hatched out a profit. He had bitter things to say about Keir and Keir's bungalow. He would stroll along the lane during the dinner-hour and observe the growth of the Smiths' new home. He called it another incubating box for little profiteers.

"You mark my words. That chap Smith will soon be putting his tools away and getting into a black coat to live on the fellows who are doing the job. You can smell a capitalist a mile away. Dirty little shark."

Paragon Place might agree with Mr. Phelps in regarding the Smiths as unsuitable neighbours, but it did not share Mr. Phelps's scorn of property. Paragon Place purchased sweepstake tickets or portions of tickets and dreamed dreams, and those dreams confounded the communist. The lorry-driver would confess in his expansive moments that if the luck ever came his way, he would buy a Rolls-Royce. Mr. William Block's fancy was a prosperous pub within half a mile of Hurst Park or Sandown. Mrs. Jervis sometimes dreamed of a nice villa in Surbiton, with two maids and a conservatory and a daily dinner that should suggest an eternal and glorified Sabbath, asparagus and strawberries, and a glass of port when you felt like it. Possibly Paragon Place was grossly material in its ideals, but it preferred the worldly substance to the product of Mr. Phelps's social gasometer.

It was Mr. Moore who—upon an occasion—asked Mr. Phelps to explain to him how Mr. Everyman was to live like a lord on three hours' work a day. Would the product of such enlightened ease be sufficient to maintain the world in a state of material bliss? It didn't seem sense somehow to Mr. Moore. Oh, machines were to do everything, were they? Machines to sweep chimneys? Oh, there wouldn't be any chimneys. And everyone would be wafted about in beautiful communal motor-coaches. The English artisan would "fly" to China, and the Chinese coolie would be seen spending the week-end at Hampton Court. There would be no bossy brains, or was it that braininess would be the prerogative of Mr. Phelps?

The communist would get excited in the face of opposition, and his language lapse into the vernacular.

"Oh, you — are all blind. Can't you see that if we get rid of the exploiters and agree that no man's to make a — profit out of his neighbour—?"

"Well, aren't you playing the prophet, old lad?"

"I said proff-it. Selling some silly muck that's worth tuppence to some boob—for sixpence."

"Then—I'd be sweeping your chimneys for nothing, and you'd be painting my house—free—and when my old woman asks me for the weekly money, what about it?"

"Can't you see—that there won't be any — money?"

"What about the groceries, and my pint of beer?"

"There will be communal allowances."

"Rations?"

"Well, in a sense—yes."

"And what if the rations get short—with all of us being so easy-osy? I might object to sweeping chimneys; I might find it beneath m'dignity to sweep chimneys."

"We'd cut off your rations."

Mr. Moore reflected.

"Well, there doesn't seem much difference in it after all, but I have a sort of notion that under your scheme there'd be more hard biscuit than good bread."

Keir and Sybil, cycling over every summer evening to exult over the growth of "Merrow," were troubled by none of these disharmonies, and Joanna Mary, left in the lap of Mrs. Moore, chuckled and crowed and cared not a jot for the hard things Mr. Phelps might say of her. "I'm a little blackleg. I was born a little blackleg, oh—dear, oh—dear!" She was a healthy and a happy infant who caused her elders to perform innumerable useless acts. She enslaved them and exploited them, and Sybil was a willing slave. She talked elemental nonsense to Joanna Mary, and possibly the noises they exchanged would have attracted more attention from the world than the debates in the House of Commons.

Life was all so very new to Sybil. She was enjoying her youth. She could be eternally surprised at life. She was very much surprised at the apparent smallness of "Merrow's" foundations when first she saw them.

"Oh, Keir, haven't they made a mistake?"

He assured her that they had not. Foundations always looked like that. Let her preserve her soul in patience until the walls were ten feet high.

[109]

Lenoir Rhyne College
LIBRARY

The weather was kind, and very little rain fell before "Merrow" had its roof on, a roof of soft brown pantiles. With the doors and windows in and the walls whitened Keir was able to look upon the completeness of his creation, and it pleased him. The little place was admirably proportioned, simple, and its very simplicity naïvely dignified. It was like a perfect frock cut by an expert, and yet Keir was a novice save in his inward vision.

Mr. Samson, standing under the beech tree with Keir one wet afternoon in September, said exactly what he thought.

"That's the prettiest little place I have seen round Kingham, and it isn't a question of cash."

Keir was a little flushed.

"I just saw it—in my mind. How have the costs worked out?"

"Ten pounds or so under the estimate. We've had good weather. Well, you've got the stuff in you, Keir."

On another day Keir had been hanging doors. He was the only man at work in the bungalow, and when he had locked up and was wheeling his bicycle out into the lane, he came upon a man looking at "Merrow" through a thin place in the thorn hedge. It was Phelps, the communist. There was a little snicker of a sneer on his face, and Keir, preparing to mount his bicycle and having ceased to be on speaking terms with Phelps, was conscious of that sneer.

Phelps addressed him.

"Who prigged the plan of that for you?"

Keir paused with a foot on the pedal.

"As a matter of fact, I prigged it out of my own head."

Phelps wagged an ironical head at him.

"Well, that's marvellous, isn't it? A bit of inspiration. Would you like me to find you a name for it?"

Keir gave Phelps one sharp, combative look and mounted

on his bicycle.

"Don't trouble. I have a name for it, and it's neither red nor black."

The walls had dried out well, and the Smiths moved into "Merrow" on the 15th of October, and Paragon Place was to see them no more, for in the middle of November the Moores were to transfer themselves to a new cottage. October 15th was a Saturday, and Mrs. Moore came to help Keir and Sybil in and to give some of her attention to Joanna Mary. The weather was perfect, golden and still, and the big beech tree was beginning to colour.

The Smith furniture had had no opportunity to show itself to advantage in No. 3 Paragon Place, but in "Merrow" it looked quite rich and important. Sybil thought so. She was delighted with everything. She stood and looked at her small parlour garnished with carpet, Chesterfield sofa, armchairs, and bureau, and it seemed to her that her parlour would not have been ashamed of itself at Darvels. She was going to give a party next week and show off her new home to cook and Russell and one or two acquaintances. She went about touching things tenderly.

Keir was lighting the kitchen fire.

"We'll christen the bath, kid."

Yes, it was an amazing little place, and when Mrs. Moore had gone, Keir and Sybil went into every room and were full of the pride of possession. Joanna Mary was peacefully asleep in her cot.

"She's taken to the house at once, Keir."

Keir stood and looked at his small daughter.

"Seems so. Funny little beggar, isn't she?"

"Oh, Keir! She's just like you."

He laughed, tickled his wife's neck, and went to see that the kitchen fire was burning as it should do. It was, and he called to Sybil.

"Like to try the taps, Syb?"

She ran into the scullery and turned on the hot tap.

"It's quite warm already, Keir. Isn't that splendid?"

"Not so bad."

It was not till they were going to bed that Keir reacted to "Merrow's" most significant virtue. He stood by the window, unfastening his braces, and the whole of him seemed to listen.

"Syb, what night is it?"

Sybil was sitting on the bed, removing her stockings. She glanced warningly at Joanna Mary's cot.

"Why, don't you know? It's Saturday."

She caught Keir smiling at her whimsically.

"But not the ordinary sort of Saturday. Don't you miss something?"

She did.

"It's so quiet—so peaceful."

Keir tossed his braces over his shoulders.

"Yes, thank God! No Jervis loud-speaker; no silly brute coming home boozed. That's what's wrong with our world, Syb. We're too much on top of each other. And when the crowd takes a fancy to a thing, it kills it by crowding it. Like the bluebells on Whit Monday."

Sybil hung her stockings over the end of the bed.

"Yes, it's lovely to know that you can go straight to sleep. Who's going to have the bath first?"

"You—of course. I'll do a little reading, or watch the kid. Don't pinch all the hot water."

"Of course I shan't."

Chapter Nine

1

WHEN Keir had put a wire fence round his plot—he could not afford a boarded one—and planted a young thorn and privet hedge, the separativeness and singularity of "Merrow" were complete. Keir had insured the little house against fire, and he had insured his own life at so much a week, though at Keir's age a man is not much concerned with the problem of dying. Death was not even a shadow to Keir. He had yet to conquer Canaan.

But, as a man successfully immured in the little house of marriage, Keir began to look about him at certain realities. He had escaped from Paragon Place; he had a house and a wife and a baby and a future that appeared to be assured, and suddenly the domestic serenity of his small success was invaded by a feeling of vague restlessness. It was like a little, plaintive, disturbing wind blowing through a keyhole while he sat with Sybil in front of his fire. It seemed to pipe to him like the Pied Piper. "Come, rise, follow."

His books were dusty. Yes, even in this new little house. He and his books had been strangers since the coming of Sybil and of Joanna Mary. In fact his books had been banished to a painted deal bookcase in the spare bedroom.

Keats, Swinburne, Rupert Brooke!

One November evening he went and rummaged among his books. Poetry. Why this urge towards poetry? He looked for his copy of Keats and found it jammed away between a cheap dictionary and a book on economics. Keats was dusty. He opened the book. Endymion! He stood very still, staring at a page as though some sweet strange voice had found him out in that little, empty room.

He heard another voice, his wife's voice.

"Keir."

He did not answer her at once.

"Keir, what are you doing?"

He smiled, but there was a twinge of irony in his smile.

"Looking out a book."

He switched off the light and carried Keats with him into the sitting-room kitchen. Joanna Mary had been put to bed. He saw his wife sitting at the table with a pencil and a catalogue. It struck him that her hair was not so well cared for as it had been. Almost, there was a suggestion of an incipient stoutness about Sybil, a domestic solidity.

"Keir, I want to do the seeds."

"Seeds?"

"Yes, it's best to get one's order in early."

He sat down in a chair by the fire and he did not open his book, for his consciousness was confronted by Sybil and the social orthodoxy of Sybil. She was the enthusiast in the garden. He had been surprised at the way in which she had tackled the garden; she was much stronger than she appeared. But it was Sybil as a person and not merely Sybil as an active young organism that was making Keir look at her as though he had discovered unexpected possibilities in his wife. There was a persistence in Sybil, a kind of gentle obstinacy. She was no longer the seductive girl, or the dear neophyte at the altar. She was developing a quiet solidity.

Almost, as the house-mother, she showed signs of dominating him. "Now, father, get out the wheelbarrow." She had a little air of pleasant authority.

"Let's go through the list."

She did not say: "Put your silly old book away," but Keats remained unread, and Keir resigned himself to the seed-list and next year's floral display. He was aware of Sybil suck ing a pencil and frowning slightly, as she read out a series of names and made ticks against them with the pencil.

"Yes, we must have larkspurs."

She was very much in charge of the catalogue, and though Keir made no single suggestion, his muteness did not matter. She assumed that he was there to play a game with her, though the game might be of her own choosing. Besides—it was his garden as well as hers.

"Virginia stock. Oh, wait a bit, we must have something to smell nice. Mignonette."

Presently she was busy adding up her score. The catalogue was a cheap one, but Keir's bill for flower seeds promised to surmount twenty shillings. Then, there would be the vegetable seeds; Sybil wanted peas, and peas were expensive.

Keir waggled a foot. His inclination was to remind Sybil of the economies and to tell her that he was saving only a few shillings a week. He wasn't Crœsus, but then Sybil had never heard of the Lydian king.

"Seems rather a lot, kid."

"But think of all the nice fresh vegetables. We must have our own lettuces. The greengrocer's bill—"

He smiled at her intent and pretty head. After all she was a very good kid about clothes. She seemed more concerned about Joanna Mary's wardrobe than her own. Even the frock she was wearing was a little tashed and domesticated. He hadn't the heart to oppose her and her horticultural enthusiasms. He remembered that the Sybil of Darvels had dawned on him in a world of flowers.

"All right."

"Won't it be lovely?"

He saw her suddenly as a simple and happy creature wholly involved in flowers and Joanna Mary and other wholesome activities. Was she happier than he was? Poetry? No little twinges of restlessness, no divine discontent, no passion for gadding about. Queer! He had always been told that the modern girl— But what would life be like with a little cinema fan—? Yes, there was a curious, sweet solidity about Sybil. She seemed to have planted herself like the beech tree in the front garden. Well, according to the wisdom of the elect, he should consider himself lucky.

"Oh, Keir, there's one thing."

"More seeds."

"No, we really shall have to buy a lawn-mower."

"A lawn-mower?"

"Yes. Of course I could cut the little front lawn with shears, but it would take hours and hours. Perhaps we can pick up a cheap American one second-hand. And I do want a piece of grass for Joanna. Besides—without grass—flowers don't get a chance to look their best."

Keir might be able to make many things, but a lawn-mower was beyond him.

"I'll look round."

"Try Tashleys. It's simply a marvellous place."

Tashleys was Kingham's universal junk-shop.

During those winter days Keir left "Merrow" at a quarter to eight each morning and returned at six. It was a raw and a foggy winter, especially so in the Thames valley, and the Abbey Lands lane was full of puddles. The wheels of his bicycle went squelching through these puddles, and one January morning when the fog was a grey blanket, it occurred to Keir that he might expect to ride to and fro up this lane for the rest of his life. The prospect shocked him, though as a man with a house and a family he had no right to be shocked. He had settled down. It was one's social duty to settle down. And yet—? Restless devils, men. He supposed that it was not that man loathed work as work so much as the sameness of his employment.

But his prospects were more pleasant than those of thousands. He had been Messrs. Samson & Hoad's foreman carpenter since the beginning of the year, and he had discovered— Yes, just what? A kind of dumb hostility in some of the men whose work he had to supervise. He had become the creature of the boss. Yes, even a little responsibility and authority made you unpopular. He could remember how the men had jeered at other supervisors, and thought it part of the game to fool them. Social discipline. He was one of those upon whom success would bind the burden of exercising authority in an age when the world was resenting the reality of the superior man.

He remembered that Mr. Samson had said to him: "Keir, you'll find out a good deal about human nature when you begin to give orders. Awkward beasts—men, and yet you'll do better with them by being a bit of an autocrat. You have got to make 'em accept you. Human nature's such a queer mixture, like streaky bacon, but it's good bacon on the whole."

He had to swing over to avoid a carelessly driven car. He gave the driver a fierce look.

The incident reminded him of something that Sybil had said last Sunday morning.

"Keir, there'd be room for a drive, wouldn't there?"

"A drive?"

"Well, we may have a little car some day. If Mr. Samson takes you into the business, we shall have to have a little car."

He had been surprised by Sybil's precocity as a prophet.

"Oh, possibly. But don't gossip about—that, kid."

"You would rather I didn't?"

"Well, yes, one might look such a silly fool if it didn't come off."

But Keir fully expected that it would come off.

Sybil was suggesting something much more serious than the purchase of a second-hand lawn-mower. She was saying that Joanna Mary ought to have a little brother, and she was proposing to give her one.

Keir had come home very tired. It had been one of those exasperating days when braces-buttons fail and your bicycle skids on a tramline, and the firm's passive-resisters indulge in ca' canny. Keir had had words with one of the men. "For God's sake, George, get on with it, or I'll buy you a manicure set."

On that evening he had words with Sybil. They did not quarrel, but there was a poignant argument between them, and a little lecture by Keir on finance and birth-control, and Sybil, with her new air of solidity, sat and sewed on some garment as though she meant to sew all night.

"Just think a moment, Syb. We have had new furniture, a new house, and a baby in twelve months. That's about the limit, my dear."

Sybil sat and sewed, and to his logic she opposed the elemental urge of her instinct.

"But I want another baby, Keir. An only child gets spoilt."

Keir ran a hand over his insurgent hair.

"Well, it's out of the question—at present. I expect to be able to save a little, and I'm saving practically nothing. We can't afford it."

"But other people—"

"Rot! Only the irresponsible and the social-problem class breed like that in these days. Good God, we're overcrowded as it is."

"There is the other bedroom, Keir."

He stared at her.

"For me—you mean?"

"Oh, no, Keir. I mean— Oh, don't be so cross and rude."

He was sorry to have spoken to her so roughly. He went and stood beside her chair and watched her hands at work.

"Sorry, kid, but don't you understand that I feel responsible? I don't want to be submerged. There's nothing between you and Joanna Mary and—the world—but my health. A man thinks about these things—sometimes."

She let her hands rest on the table.

"Yes, Keir—but when you're in the firm."

"I'm not in it yet, my dear. Yes, that might make a difference. You'll have to wait, Syb. I mean it."

She seemed to sit and reflect, and then she put up one of her hands.

"You've been very good to me, Keir. I'll wait."

"Wise kid."

He bent down and kissed her.

But Keir found it a difficult winter. In fact it was the first winter that made him conscious of the weather, of its raw drabness, its sordid monotony. There was no beauty, no sting in it, no frost or snow, just a congealed and foggy rawness. Never before had he caught himself fussing about his health, or feeling worried when he got wet. He was a married man with a family and a new accumulation of responsibilities, prospective lawn-mowers, prospective children, interest on a mortgage, insurance contributions, gas bills, electric light bills. He was sure that Sybil was careless about the electric light. A new bulb needed in the living-room? Why, the previous one had survived less than five months. He had had to buy a pram for Joanna Mary. He was much more careful about turning up his coat collar when he cycled home.

Also, Messrs. Samson & Hoad were building a new house in the Abbey Lands Park for an impatient and rather wealthy client, a Mr. Gibson, who had engaged an architect with ideas. The house was to be unusual, and the architect's

[111]

ideas upon this particular house's roof were more than unusual, and when Keir was shown the plan, he rumpled up
his hair.

"It won't work, sir."

He and Mr. Samson had an argument with the architect,
who was a self-assertive theorist. When it was suggested to
him that the roof was not practical, he became throaty and
superior.

"Of course, if you and your carpenter aren't up to the
job— The specifications are perfectly plain."

Keir intercepted a glance from Mr. Samson.

"If your client wants a roof like that—we can do it—at a
price, but if you could cut out—those valleys and gables."

The architect would cut out nothing, and his client
seconded him. Keir spent hours wrestling with the problem
of that roof. It was a silly, ostentatious, high-brow affair,
like the product of the new art that is in a hurry to create
an effect without learning to draw. Keir had a feeling that
Mr. Hoad, a rather smeary man with pince-nez who checked
all the plans and specifications, was sniggering over his—
Keir's dilemma. Mr. Hoad was polite, soft soap, to everybody, and nobody liked him.

"This roof, Smith—rather—subtle—what?"

But Keir did put the pieces of the puzzle together, though
the timber-work would be quite unorthodox. It was a silly,
tricky job, and it worried him for weeks and made him a
little irritable when Joanna Mary was in a protesting mood.

"Oh, can't you shut the kid up?"

Sybil was shocked.

"Don't be so—touchy."

"Sorry, Syb. I've been worried today."

He was thinking that he would like to take Mr. Gibson's
architect and hang him by the seat of his trousers to one of
those eccentric gables.

In February, Joanna Mary stirred up a panic at "Mer-

[112]

row" by developing bronchitis. Her little chest was full of wheezings and bubblings, and the doctor came twice a day, and Sybil insisted on sitting up with Joanna. She seemed to regard the child's illness as a personal challenge, a bitter accusation, and on the third night she looked so tired and tragic that Keir insisted upon her going to bed. He said that he would sit up with Joanna, but Sybil would not easily be persuaded.

"I feel it's my fault, Keir."

"How can it be your fault? Now, you go to bed, kid. You're just about all in."

He was so determined that Sybil should get some sleep that he stood over her while she undressed.

"I'm sure it's no use, Keir. I shan't sleep."

But sleep she did, and Joanna Mary, as though she had been playing off a joke upon her mother, ceased to produce infantile wet noises and became as mild as milk. She too slept, and Keir, reading a book by the light of a shaded candle, listened to the small creature's quiet breathing; and wondered at it. Joanna had given them a devil of a fright, and now her two small fists seemed to clutch and possess the jest. Ultimately Keir lay down on the floor with a cushion under his head, and the candle burned itself out.

In the darkness of a winter morning he was roused by Sybil putting a naked foot upon his shoulder.

"Oh—Keir!"

He sat up, feeling abashed and a little bewildered.

"Hallo—I must have dropped off. She was sleeping like—like—"

There was a scratching of a match, and by its momentary light he saw Sybil leaning over Joanna Mary's cot. Joanna Mary opened her eyes and greeted her mother with a toothless smile. The match flickered out, and in the darkness Keir groped for the electric switch.

"She's all right, Syb."

But he felt that Sybil would hold him guilty of sleeping at his post. Her voice reproved him in the darkness.

"Oh, do turn on the light."

Had Keir been told two years ago that he would be involved in all these domesticities, he would have been more doubting than a doubting Thomas. Like the ironic young Frenchman who was a rationalist in the matter of sex, he would have exclaimed on seeing a man loaded up with parcels: *"Voilà le mari!"* Keir was well and truly loaded, and if he sometimes regretted the bondage, he could cry to his insurgent self: "Get thee behind me, Satan." Yet, being the child of his generation, he understood his generation's challenging of the old landmarks and boundaries, its urge to kick down fences or leap over them. It was an experimental age. It smiled ironically in the face of tradition. Its world was the world of the moment, not some hypothetical heaven to be attained by climbing the Scala Sancta of negation. This young world asked for more money, more movement, more self-assertion. Life was to be a playing-field, not a factory.

But with a wife and a child and a mortgage on your house it is not very easy to conduct experiments, and with such a boat-load of merchandise in his charge Keir understood that it was his business to keep in mid-stream and look out for notices that shouted "Danger." He could not risk his human cargo at the weir's edge or dare a ducking. He had become careful, or carefulness had been forced upon him. He knew the cave-man's fear of things that prowled in the night. It was new to him—this fear. It was like some blackmailing rogue who had waited for Keir to commit himself and now followed him about. Cycling home on those winter nights, and especially when the roads were befogged, he found himself dismounting at dangerous corners like some careful old gentleman. No longer did he dare the traffic with the confidence of some irresponsible, vainglorious boy.

But he had other moods. There were days when the Cain in him lusted to turn upon and slay the dutiful Abel, the dull good fellow who sacrificed to the conventions. In seducing him Sybil had somehow taught him to look at other women. They were part of his restlessness, coming and going in the dim or brilliant streets, creatures of mystery, provoking his sense of beauty. Strange women! And sometimes he would resent the finality of marriage because it symbolized a little world in which the adventures were so small and calculable. He may have suffered from the illusion which fools most men, that other women are different from the wife at home.

It happened in February that Mr. Lugard of Darvels sent to Mr. Samson to borrow Keir for an hour. The door of a Jacobean cupboard in the Darvels library needed rehanging, and Mr. Lugard could be content with nothing but an expert. The day was gloomy and dim, and at four o'clock Keir had to turn on the lights in that very beautiful room. He was at work in the cupboard when Mr. Lugard came in to look for a book.

Mr. Lugard belonged to another world, a world that should have been Keir's world and was not. His appearance always suggested to Keir one of the old Norse vikings, but a gentle viking, whose hands handled books instead of a sword.

He spoke to Keir as one lover of craftsmanship speaks to another. He used Keir's Christian name. He ran his fingers over the oak.

"Some patina—there. You know, Keir, I can't swallow the new furniture."

Keir understood him.

"Yes, I know what you mean, sir. What I call polished sugar-boxes."

Mr. Lugard laughed and showed Keir his book.

[115]

"Benvenuto Cellini. Yes, we're off to Italy for six weeks."

Keir's eyes rested for a moment on the book, and it occurred to Mr. Lugard that Keir might well have lived his life in Renaissance Florence with a Medici as his patron. Yes, Keir should have belonged to the colour and the passion and the pride of that Italian city. And he divined in Keir a little bitterness, a flame that was concealed, a something that was unsatisfied.

Keir found himself in Kingham High Street. A drizzle had set in, and the roadway was so greasy and the High Street such a tangle of traffic that Keir dismounted and wheeled his bike. He could assert that the only way to transcend modern traffic was to be part of it in a car. Also the pavements were as congested as the roadway. The world seemed full of women and girls who had nothing to do but loiter and look at the shop-windows, and yet Keir understood that to the crowd Kingham High Street was a picture-show. On so dismal a night these bright windows were pleasant, especially to those who escaped for an hour from some melancholy back street. Pictures, colour, light, Italy! Over the way he saw a white building like a large lady wearing all her jewelry, red lights, and green lights, and orange lights, rubies, emeralds, topaz. A transparency blazing across the façade announced: "Serena Segovia. *The Lamp of Love.*" Keir, pausing to contemplate all this seductive glare, was wise as to its significance. Women and girls were pouring into the place to share Serena's luscious love-affair and to escape for a little while from the gas-cooker and the sink. Well, it was understandable. Had he no hunger for other worlds, Italy, blue distances of sea and sky and mountain?

Two young men paused close to him on the edge of the pavement.

"Going in, Bert?"

He who was questioned laughed.

"Serena—the world's prize tart! No, I've got something of my own to play with when the shops shut."

Keir and his bicycle moved themselves on.

The familiar puddles of the Abbey Lands lane waited for his tires to squelch through them. He came to the little white gate in the thorn hedge and saw the yellow curtains of "Merrow's" living-room lit up from within. Too much electric light for which you had to pay, and not sufficient sunlight that was gratis. Irritably he thrust the front wheel of his bicycle against the gate, but the gate was latched and it snubbed his impatience.

"Damn you!"

Yes, he was tired. The zest and the adventure seemed to have gone from life. He went and put his bicycle away in the small shed at the back of the bungalow. He remembered that the back wheel of Sybil's machine was punctured, and that she had asked him to mend it.

As he opened the back door, Joanna Mary discovered something in life to arouse her young indignation. She protested, and so did her father's tired temper.

"That kid always seems to be squalling. What's the matter now?"

Sybil was gathering Joanna Mary to her bosom.

"She can't help it. Didn't you ever cry when you were a child?"

Keir flung his hat into a chair.

"Oh, probably. I don't remember. We seem born to teeth and trouble. Tea ready?"

She gave him a poignant look. She had discovered that when Keir had a certain dark mood on him, it was better to keep the curtains drawn.

A week later he was down with influenza, and Sybil was nursing him, and he was made to realize that his wife could be a very unselfish and consoling creature. She was responsible for all the housework and Joanna Mary and a man who had to have his meals carried to him. Also, he discovered that Sybil's sympathy was very much a thing of the heart. She was troubled for his sake. She would get up in the middle of the night and bring him hot milk.

Serena Segovia!

Sybil's eyes were compassionate and gentle.

"Drink it down, Keir."

He was glad of her gentleness. He began to understand that there was a quality in Sybil's love that could confound the restlessness of the bitter streets. It lasted. It seemed to grow out of the ground and to put forth foliage and flowers.

"Get back into bed, kid; you'll catch cold."

"I'm all right, Keir."

And in the darkness he felt comforted by the nearness of Sybil.

Chapter Ten

1

BUT if Keir's passion to express that which was Keir transcended the little white walls of "Merrow," the small house was no egg-shell. Its new solidity symbolized the new solidity of Sybil, a young woman to whom life had become amazingly static because of the amazing aliveness of Joanna Mary. A contemporary flippancy might have accused Sybil of being a hopeless primitive whose sense of adventure was satisfied by mere domesticities. She did the same silly things every day in company with Joanna Mary, and she appeared to find in them complete satisfaction.

There were moments when Keir wondered at his wife. She was not topical. She did not seem to belong to a generation that had attained to the social singularities of the tennis-court, the motor-coach, and the picture-house. She was much less interested in the world's shop-window. She wheeled Joanna Mary out in her pram, and if she sometimes dusted Keir's books, she did it without regarding them as serious contributions to man's ascent into the self-conscious. Her environment and her reactions to it were both simple and very limited. "Merrow" did not allow itself the luxury of a daily paper, but Keir did buy one of the best of the Sunday journals, and when he had read it, it was pounced upon by Sybil and reduced to domestic uses. She wanted it for lighting the fires.

Nor did the Sabbath bulk suffice her. Always she was short of paper, and her criticism, ignoring leaders and articles upon finance and the international situation, centred upon the inadequacy of those crumpled sheets. India was nothing to her, the bankruptcy of the National Insurance Fund less than a dream. It seemed to her absurd that with a prodigal and prolific press a little house such as "Merrow" should be short of waste-paper.

"I can't get enough of it, Keir, no, not in the winter."

She never read the paper as its editor presumed it should be read; she burned it.

"You'll have to save up during the summer, kid."

Yes, that was all very well, but what about February, March, and April?

"Couldn't you get me some shavings? Your workshop must be full of shavings."

It was, and twice a week Keir stuffed shavings into a sack and carried the kindling home on the handles of his bike. It became known in the shop he made off with this plunder, and his traditional carefulness became even more of an offence to his fellows. He never stood a chap a drink and he scraped up the shop's shavings! But Sybil was delighted. Canadian wood-pulp that had been digested and transformed into journalistic cerebrations was supplemented by the products of the chisel and the plane. Sybil had her boiler nicely heated, while India sizzled unheard. She knew nothing of Gandhi, or of self-determination, or of Russia's Five Year Plan. She needed hot water for the house and for Joanna Mary, and she had it.

Inevitably, Keir's periods of restlessness were not appeased by the simplicities of Sybil. He was interested in things of which she knew nothing. She could not and perhaps would not emerge from the little world that was "Merrow." He did not realize it, but he was talking less and less to Sybil, for on one of those rare occasions when he had tried to persuade her to be a listener, he had watched her short-sighted brown eyes grow inattentive. A man may like to show off his cleverness, and Keir was human. He was telling Sybil that the chalk hills from which "Merrow" had taken its name had once been under the sea, and Sybil laughed.

"I'm not quite so silly as that."

"But it's a fact. Those hills were built up by the bodies of millions upon millions of minute sea-creatures—"

But if Sybil believed him she was not interested. She was not to be lured upon excursions into any of the ologies. Invariably her perceptions, momentarily distracted, reverted to the familiar objects of her little world.

"Oh—Keir—I forgot to tell you they're just coming up."

"That leaves me guessing."

"I mean—the broad beans."

Mentally she was no companion for a young man whose curiosity—diverted for a year towards sex and marriage, —had re-emerged and with a restlessness that promised perils of its own. Sybil could talk about nothing but Joanna Mary and all the multitudinous trivialities of a small and semi-suburban home. If Keir tried to plunge into other waters, she would sit down and wait for him on the bank, and when—perforce—he returned from an element in which she could not express herself, she would join the interrupted ends of her conversation and happily continue it.

"Did you notice—the milk, Keir? I'm sure it's watered. I'm going to change and try Higson's. It says on their van that they keep their own cows."

Keir gave it up. There was something of the gentle Jersey cow in Sybil. Even her eyes— And he supposed that his wife was a creature to whom you made the simplest of noises. Certainly, she and Joanna Mary understood each other better than did Keir and his small daughter. But there were moments when he was conscious of an increasing loneliness. He knew moods of impatience, of secret resentment. Mere physical contact could not satisfy him. It might be as cloying as sugar and the scent of roses when the crave in you was

[121]

for strong wine. Moreover, Sybil was sweet-tempered, and if she was aware of his deep, dark moods, they were no more to her than transient puddles.

"You dear, utter idiot!"

He caught himself using those words in secret, and he was shocked by them. Did she suspect? Did she ever realize that she bored him, and that the simple notes that were within her compass made him feel that he was listening to some child learning to play upon the piano? Always those same trite sweet notes, a little trivial melody, no wrath, no striving towards the inexpressible, no deep and crashing chords.

2

Early in April Sybil gave Keir a piece of information that was not news to him.

"Oh, Keir, they're going to build on the next plot. Isn't it a pity?"

She explained to him that while she had been at work in the "Merrow" garden, two men had arrived and had started to cut a gap in the thorn hedge separating the adjoining plot from the lane, and later in the day a lorry had driven in with a load of building material, and the two men had proceeded to erect a temporary shed.

"That was one of our lorries, kid. We are putting up a bungalow for a woman who runs a shop in Kingham."

"Then you know, Keir?"

"Oh, I heard about it a week or two ago. We didn't buy the whole landscape, Syb. And, after all, this isn't Paragon Place."

The new bungalow came into being on the adjoining plot, and Sybil realized that it was to be a much larger and more important product than "Merrow." There was no architect in charge of the work, for Mrs. Challis, who—

under the name of "Fifine"—supplied Kingham with all the latest models in the way of hats and frocks, was a woman of very definite ideas and a nice sense of the value of money. She knew what she wanted. She was an emphatic person both physically and mentally. If she ran her establishment very successfully under a French name, she too was somewhat French in her composition and her capacity. She was a confection, as suggestive as one of those exquisite products that can be purchased at a Parisian shop and just as hard as the bottle.

Sybil, very much at work in the "Merrow" garden, while keeping an eye on Joanna Mary, who was asleep in her pram under the beech tree, had her first glimpse of Mrs. Bertha Challis. Sybil's hands were dirty, for she was planting out clarkia and godetia seedlings and puddling them in with water from a can. Also she was wearing a utility frock, and it had split under one arm, and it showed the stains of many hours of housework. Moreover, it happened to be one of those warm spring evenings when midges arrive and bite viciously, and in making a dab at her forehead Sybil had left a streak of dirt above one eyebrow.

Mrs. Challis was immaculate and cool. She arrived in a small and highly coloured car—cream and apple-green. She banged the door of the car and passed through the gap in the thorn hedge. The shape of her was a slim black spathe topped by a very yellow head to which was attached one of the little black knitted caps which happened to be fashionable. Her mouth was a vivid streak. In age she might have been anything between thirty and forty-five, but she had one of those thick white skins that retain a perfect texture. Her poise, the product of vital self-assurance and the seductive cynicism of the successful saleswoman, linked Shaftesbury Avenue to Ascot.

Mrs. Challis had brought her little yellow bag with her, and in it her cigarette-case, but she had forgotten her matches. The lapse was exceptional. With the cigarette stuck in her red mouth she explored the interior of the yellow bag. One of the damned girls must have been at her bag! She snapped the catch of the bag, glanced sharply in the direction of the intervening fence, and discovered Sybil.

Sybil had been observing her, and the concentrated stare of Sybil's brown eyes may have caused Mrs. Challis to react to that almost childish scrutiny. But she wanted a match, and this rather untidy young person might provide one.

She approached the fence, picking her way between a stack of bricks and a squdge of mortar.

"Excuse me, could you let me have a match?"

Being what she was, the daughter of a suburban trades-man with business in her blood, and modernity and modes part of her texture, she saw Sybil both as a prospective neighbour and an untidy and over-domesticated creature. Yes, that pram! God bless our happy home! And the girl's frock had once been a cheap reach-me-down.

Sybil, reacting in her own fashion both to the request and to the refined flippancy of "Madame," put down her basket of seedlings.

"Of course."

She went for a box of matches, but not with any feeling of friendliness, for to the Sybils of this world Mrs. Challis was somehow a fiery cross. Her eyes were the eyes of the huntress.

"Excuse my hands being so dirty."

The match-box was passed across the wire fence, and Mrs. Challis lit her cigarette. The state of Sybil's hands was no concern of hers. This neighbour was a young woman who gardened and produced babies, and whose hair had not been attended to professionally for at least a month.

"Thanks. Just looked in to see how the men are getting on."

Her glance rested for a moment on Joanna Mary's pram. Did that infant grow vocal?

Sybil, suddenly and acutely self-conscious and resenting it, waited for the return of the match-box. For she would have said that Mrs. Challis when considered objectively was just like some of the smart women who had lunched and tea'd at Darvels, but yet not quite so. The child in Sybil was intuitively destructive so far as Mrs. Challis's culture was concerned.

The match-box was returned to her by a nicely manicured hand with nails tinted a deep rose.

"Thanks—so much. You garden—I see. Marvellous!"

She looked at the smudge of dirt above Sybil's eyebrow, nodded casually, and moved away, leaving Sybil holding the match-box as though Mrs. Challis's touch had contaminated it.

Yet it was no more than a clash of types, the brass pot and white china, and Sybil, reabsorbed in the garden and Joanna Mary, forgot all about Mrs. Bertha Challis. She inferred that there would be no neighbourliness between "Merrow" and the more pretentious person next door. "Fifine's" establishment was a luxury-shop, and a very successful one in spite of depressed trade and unlimited competition, for Mrs. Challis was not just lipstick and yellow head and self-assurance. She was a woman of ideas. She relished life and its adventure, and as a hedonist she had a philosophy of her own. She might be interested in men and money, but she was interested in other things. The war had left her a young widow, and she had found the post-war world and its business full of banditry.

It was not till the walls were up that Sybil realized Keir's involvement in the erection of the bungalow next door. He was to be responsible for Mrs. Challis's roof and floors and for more than these conventional necessities, for Mrs. Challis was nothing if not up to date. She read D. H. Lawrence and saw significance in Epstein. Her bungalow was to possess radiators and running water in the bedrooms, a refrigerator, and various labour-saving devices, but Keir was concerned in her craze for built-in cupboards. They were to be recessed wardrobes with polished walnut doors, and if the walnut was only veneer, it was all the more serious a challenge to craftsmanship.

Mrs. Challis had been frank with Mr. Samson.

"Can you people do it, or shall I have to get somebody down from town?"

Mr. Samson had assured her that his foreman carpenter was capable of carrying out the work—at a price, of course.

"All right, chuck me in an additional estimate. I am drawing my own designs. You had better send your man along to see me."

Both Keir and Mrs. Challis discovered at that first interview a mutual unexpectedness, for Mrs. Challis was more sympathetic to men than she was to women. She might dress for her own sex. Her more subtle nudities were reserved for the male. She and Keir met in her office behind "Fifine's" showroom. She sat at her desk and smoked a cigarette and pushed a set of drawings at him.

"That's the sort of thing I want. Tumble to it?"

While Keir was examining her sketches, she endorsed cheques and between the signatures examined Keir. The dark intelligent insurgence of him struck her as unusual. There was colour in Keir. He was both sharp edge and shadow, and most maleness was so flat.

He passed the pieces of paper from one hand to the other.

"I see. Flush with the wall. You want us to use the recesses between the chimneys and—"

"Quite."

"This one shows the doors open. Fittings. Plenty of hanging space."

She said: "Most wardrobes and cupboards are fool prod-

[126]

ucts. Mine have got to be two feet deep. A dozen frocks have to hang—"

He nodded.

"Mirrors? On the insides of the doors?"

That was quick of him.

"Of course."

"Two—I suppose?"

"You've got it."

He said: "I see you've sketched in a lot of things like pigeonholes. Much better have trays, something to slide out and show you at once what's there. Cost more—naturally."

She pressed the black end of her fountain pen against a full lower lip and considered him.

"Yes, naturally, provided the trays don't stick. I'm an impatient sort of person. I like things—oiled."

He glanced at her and smiled, and when she returned his smile, something linked them together.

"Yes, cheap inefficiency that sticks makes one furious."

She tapped her red mouth with the pen.

"But you'll be responsible—I understand? Well, things will be O.K."

3

In order to arrive at his day's work Keir only had to pass out of the gate of "Merrow," walk some ten paces along the lane, and turn to the left through the gap in the thorn hedge, and, to begin with, the simplicity of the ritual pleased Sybil. It was easy for Keir, and it was easy for the housewife. She had her man back straightway to his meals, and it was possible to suggest that Keir might help her in the garden, for June and its weeds and its multifarious activities were of serious moment.

"You might put out those young lettuces for me, Keir."

He did help her in the garden, but there were other

evenings when he told her that he would have to ride into Kingham. He needed certain things from the shop or from the "stores," or he had to see and discuss points with Mr. Samson. She let him go. In fact she was quite happy about Keir so long as he was at work upon the joists and rafters of the new bungalow. Once or twice a week the Challis woman appeared in her salad and cream car and observed how matters were progressing, but to Sybil she was no Serena Segovia, no modish Circe with a cigarette. For to Sybil Mrs. Challis belonged to another world. It was as though she stepped out of *Vogue* or *Britannia & Eve,* and though Sybil may sometimes have dipped into these journals during her Darvels days, they were to her almost as fabulous as Paris and Dinard and Cannes. She could not imagine Keir becoming translated into that sort of language.

But when the brown tiled roof went on next door, and the place became hooded and concealed, a little cloud-shadow seemed to arrive and remain above the building. At least, that was its effect upon Sybil. That which had been visible became shut up in a cabinet.

The plasterers had been in, and for some days Keir's daily work had taken him either to the shop or to other contracts, but when the ceilings and wall surfaces were complete, he returned to the house of Mrs. Challis. He let it be known that he would be working overtime on the job, but that it was no great hardship when nothing but a wire fence divided him from his labour and his bed.

He and Sybil had never discussed Mrs. Challis, but on this particular evening Sybil let fall a remark.

"She looks a funny sort of woman."

Keir's face expressed a kind of wooden obscurity.

"Funny! How do you mean?"

"Oh—just funny. What I'd call an amateur lady, Keir."

Keir went into the spare bedroom and squatted down

in front of the bookcase to look for a particular book, and Sybil's voice followed him.

"There must be money in hats."

His reply was that it depended upon the hats and how you sold them. He came back with his book and appeared rather ostentatiously interested in it. He was going out into the garden to read for half an hour.

Sybil was folding up the supper cloth. She said: "I shouldn't care to be that woman's maid. She's got one of those nasty mouths.—Why's she in such a hurry?"

"Mrs. Challis wants to get into the house, that's all. I suppose it's natural. I can remember you cycling over here every evening and feeling the walls."

Sybil held the cloth for a moment against her bosom.

"Well, yes, I did, but that was different."

Keir's overtime continued, and on those summer evenings he would be the only man at work in the new bungalow, fixing skirting-boards and hanging doors. Those special cupboards of Mrs. Challis's were being roughed out in the shop and sent on to Keir to assemble and fit. The firm had been put to some trouble in procuring walnut veneer, and the first consignment had proved unsatisfactory. It would appear from the frequency of her visits that Mrs. Challis was growing impatient, but Keir was not finding her impatient. She came to the bungalow nearly every evening.

He had begun to listen for the sound of her car. Not that he broke off work when he heard it. In fact he might appear more intensely absorbed, bending over the bench that had been installed in one of the rooms. And yet— inwardly—he would be acutely conscious of an approach, a nearness, a sudden presence, the drift of a perfume. In their mutual interplay they had reached a stage where the obvious salutation had become superfluous. She was not there—and she was there. That sheath-like figure of hers might have slipped in on a beam of light.

[129]

On this evening she paused in the doorway. She saw Keir's head in a streak of sunlight. He was bending over the bench under a window, and the window looked towards the sunset. He appeared to be unaware of her presence. but she was wise as to his awareness.

"Lend me a foot-rule, will you? I've come to measure for curtains."

He passed her a boxwood rule. He seemed to look up at her from under dark eyebrows. Her blue eyes were more level and direct.

"Thanks. It's a little quiet at the shop, and I'm turning one of the girls on to making frillies for the windows."

She understood his dark aloofness. It both interested and provoked her. She divined the smoulder in him. The sex of her was like a lamp which she flashed on him in the soft gloom of their apartness. A carpenter, a working man! But what was she but a working woman dressed to the part. The lure was so various, and he had beautifully shaped ears, clever hands, and a sensitive skin.

"I ought to have a box or something."

He found a step-ladder and placed it by the window. She climbed two steps, and her body shut off the light from him. Its blackness took to itself a golden aura.

She measured the window.

"Five foot six. Jot it down for me, will you? Yes, on any odd piece of wood."

She climbed to the top of the steps and sat there, and her downward glance was both intimate and amused.

"What was your father, my dear?"

His head rose to her and the sunlight.

"A clerk in a coal-merchant's office."

"Mine was a butcher. Our friend D. H. had a miner for his dad. Have you read that book I lent you?"

"Yes."

"Any reactions?"

His hands rested on the bench. He looked out and past her through the window.

"Yes, one of surprise that a book like that—"

"Should be read in Kingham High Street and by a woman who looks like a mannequin?"

"Yes."

She laughed.

"Oh, yes, one's uniform, one's pose! But we people who have to scuffle out a career throw off a damned lot of humbug. A fellow like D. H. may be fanatically candid, but I don't follow him everywhere."

He glanced up at her obliquely.

"Where and where not?"

"Well, socialist slop. When you have to run a show with half a dozen young wenches in it—you learn a few things about life. What about my mouth?"

He looked at her mouth and seemed to flinch like Adam in the presence of the forbidden fruit.

"You could say things."

"Quite. If some of those slopmongers—the social idealists —would say to the public—what I say to my girls—! You know, D. H. is lovely on paper, but I'm sure he would have made a devil of a mess of running a Lyons tea-shop. There are two kinds of realists, my dear, the theoretical and the practical."

He turned sideways against the bench. He seemed shy of observing her directly.

"I have to look after men. Yes, human nature gets your theory and blows it like froth off a pint of beer."

"Do you drink beer?"

"No."

"Ever been to Sicily?"

"No."

"I went there last year for a fortnight. Saved up for it. Yes, saw old D. H.'s villa. You'll go there—some day."

The little white box that was "Merrow" could not be seen from that particular window, but from the set of Keir's head she divined the direction of his inward glance. He go to Sicily with a wife and Joanna Mary? Moreover, he was not crying for Sicily at that moment. Sex sat upon a stepladder against a Homeric sky, and the apples of the Hesperides gleamed under that very new ceiling.

She came down the steps and became interested in the work he had been setting out on the bench. She stood very close to him.

"What's that? One of my cupboard doors?"

"Yes."

She ran a finger over the walnut.

"Almost as smooth—as—skin."

Chapter Eleven

1

THE affair of Mrs. Challis provided Keir with what the lady herself would have described as unexpected reactions.

It made him feel furtive, and in feeling furtive he was angry with himself and with Bertha Challis, but he was not angry with Sybil. He found himself slinking back to "Merrow" and putting on an air of extreme cheerfulness as he entered the little white gate. He was more openly affectionate to Sybil.

The sweet anguish of sex unsatisfied! He would fool himself with the assurance that he had found a woman with a mind and a personality, a woman who understood him, a woman to whom he could talk. Poor Sybil hadn't an idea in her head. She was like the little white pot that was kept filled with jam, plum and apple or raspberry, and was there ready for the domestic spoon. She suspected nothing, divined nothing; at least—he supposed so.

"I suppose you will soon have finished next door, Keir?"

Finished—when the perfumed person of Mrs. Challis was still a flower that had not been plucked! He did not know that his carefully cheerful face betrayed a little secret smile, and that Sybil, collecting articles on a tray with eyes that seemed downcast and unsuspecting, knew and was afraid. For that was part of the strangeness of Sybil; she both knew and carried that knowledge within her like an unborn child. She did not cry out or accuse. There was a stillness about her. It seemed so incredible that Keir—

She had seen— But what had she seen?

[133]

The thing had shocked her. She wanted to close a door gently and slip silently away to sit beside Joanna Mary and wonder— Yes, that world-wise cook at Darvels had assured her that all men were fools. But Keir—! Something in her crouched like a hare, with brown eyes big and frightened. Perhaps she had a feeling that the thing would not happen because she refused to believe that it could happen.

Keir was so difficult.

She understood that there were deeps in Keir that reminded her of a well in a cottage garden she had known as a child. You lifted the timber trap-door and saw a mysterious circle of gloom, moist bricks, perhaps slimy things. She had been fascinated and frightened by that well.

Sometimes she felt a sudden rage against Mrs. Challis. She would pick up Joanna Mary and walk up and down, up and down.

That other woman ruffling her husband's hair!

2

The bungalow next door had its gates in place, and on one of them was painted "My Cot."

Mrs. Challis should have been above and beyond such a convention, but when her dear "D. H." was subtracted from the lady, she was as much like a yellow cat as her less curious contemporaries. She had over-emphasized a topical flippancy. She could smoke her cigarette in a long black holder and confound the natural with the decadent. She covered her primitiveness with so much paint that when the paint was removed, your romanticist would be confounded by the rawness of the substructure.

Her furniture had arrived. It too was topical, flippant, and flimsy. She was the sort of woman who would be satisfied with a car, an ash-tray, and a divan-bed. Keir, as the

[134]

interesting and intense young ouvrier, had been extruded. All the walnut doors were hung—and he still supposed—

But there was no yesterday in the Challis calendar. She was poised on the present with her toes touching tomorrow. She was consumed by the insensate restlessness of a period. What you did yesterday was dead. When you had experienced a particular thing or person, you reached out a hand to the next dish.

Keir was not made for a Juan. He was too difficult, too intense. He had not the easy smirk that said: "Well, that's that, old thing. Thanks awfully. It's been simply marvellous. Cheeri-o." He both wanted to be the complete and passionate fool, and yet was full of dark qualms and hesitations. He both seized and let go and in the midst of a climax stood shaking. Like a very sensitive man who had received no education from sisters, he somehow imagined that there was a sacred something in woman, but he misconstrued his Bertha Challis. She wanted to play, she wanted to suck this particular orange, but she believed that for all sucked oranges there should be dustbins.

"Oh, beloved!"

Keir had ventured on some such language, and she had looked at him out of half-shut eyes and grimaced as though that sort of sweet stuff could be sour. No, certainly it wasn't modern and promiscuous and sufficiently casual. Well, really! Homespun! Yes, rather like his shirts, which that dowdy little person next door washed once a week and hung up on a line. A particular man might be intense and interesting and a novelty for the period of a month or so, but when he was apt to be as serious as his shirts—

She had satisfied herself with Keir.

And he, trembling disillusioned, somehow ashamed, and yet feeling a little vainglorious and triumphant, went away to brood over the experience. She had giggled, yes—actually giggled. He had been a little clumsy and apologetic, both

passionate and diffident. He had imagined— Well, what?
—A kind of submergence in rhapsody, two sun-warmed
bunches of grapes in contact, utter self-forgetfulness in the
sacred and exquisite rite. And she had said: "Wait a bit—
you're—" There had been a twinge of annoyance on her
face. And somehow he had a feeling that he had bungled
the business, and not for a moment had he been able to
forget himself in it. He had a suspicion that he had failed
to satisfy her.

She had laughed, and managed the inevitable anticlimax
with capable casualness, but behind her laughter he had
fancied that there was a touch of sulkiness, of balked dis-
satisfaction.

It was a wet evening, and he was glad of the rain, for
it covered his retreat. He picked his bicycle out of the
back of Mrs. Challis's hedge and wheeled it out of her gate
and in at the gate of "Merrow." He felt most horribly furtive during the next sixty seconds. Supposing Sybil—? But
he found her in the living-room with a pile of black currants on a sheet of newspaper spread upon the table, preparing the fruit for jam, and dropping it into a white china
bowl.

She raised her eyes and looked at him, and her eyes were
as dark as the fruit. Her fingers were stained with its juices,
and suddenly he was ashamed.

"Hallo, Syb, I'm late."

Her glance was steady and a little strange. It did not accuse. It had for him the quality of innocence.

"Wet, Keir?"

"Oh, nothing to speak of."

He kissed her and knew it to be a Judas kiss.

"Hallo, jam! I'll give you a hand."

He sat down and shredded the fruit with her, and once
or twice their hands touched over the pile of currants. And
she was silent. She looked at him occasionally in that mute,

[136]

strange way as though his shrouded face was a wound, and hers the pain. Did she suspect? And, feeling furtive in her presence, he loathed himself. That affair should cease. It was abominable, treacherous.

Yet next day and during the days that followed he was made to realize how subtly such a sex infection permeates the blood. His own imagination importuned him like a procuress. It even played upon his vanity. He was obsessed by a sense of failure, by the incompleteness of that previous occasion, by a sense of boyish bungling. He had been too shy, too much in a hurry. He had not behaved as the triumphantly passionate and consoling male. He— Yes, he must attain finality and, having attained it, retrieve himself and safety.

He would say: "This can't go on, Bert, you know. It's just our fate. I've got to think of my kid."

He was full of cowardice and confusion, consumed by a miserable restlessness that exhausted him like a fever. He could not concentrate upon his work, for his essential self seemed to be slipping away round some secret corner. And then in a moment of clumsy abstraction he cut himself badly with a chisel.

The blood spurted, and suddenly and instantly he was thinking of Sybil. He wanted to run to Sybil, the inevitable and assuaging Sybil.

Someone knotted a handkerchief round his arm, and the red spurt at the wrist ceased.

"That's a job for the doctor, my lad."

It was.

That evening Sybil was very gentle to him. She carried two chairs out to the shade of the beech tree. She sat by him and sewed. Joanna Mary had been put to bed.

"Does it hurt much, Keir?"

He was remembering her shocked face when he had appeared with that bandaged arm.

[137]

"Just smarts a bit, that's all."

"You mustn't go to work for a day or two. A cut like that's serious."

3

The salving of their mutual sanity was Sybil's.

She could have said to him: "My dear, if only you knew that I know all that there is to be known about loving. And if I could tell you all that I know about—her, what you have not seen—"

But she did not tell him. She did not blurt out her knowledge. There was that in her which flinched with an intuitive, childish sensitiveness from a trust torn to tatters. She lay awake beside him at night wondering. Her hands went on touching the intimate simple objects of the home as though in them she experienced security, reassurance. She tied up her flowers, washed and fed Joanna Mary, and waited.

In her simple wisdom she waited for Keir to find out who was the fool. If it was to be discovered, it was better that he should discover it for himself. Had she been more of the egoist and less the mother of Joanna Mary, she might have blazed at him. All this shame and humiliation, this secret fear!

She said to herself: "I suppose a man's not quite himself when a woman like that gets hold of him. But he'll find out. I hate her for the way she's hurting him."

One evening she heard the front door of "Merrow" open. Keir had been working late. It was a sultry night, and a heavy cloud canopy had brought down a deep and premature dusk. Sybil had been in to look at Joanna Mary, who was restless with the heat. She came out into the dark passage as Keir closed the door. The switch of the electric light was close to her hand, and she turned it on.

She saw her husband's face.

Her instant impulse was to bring back the darkness. She did so. They stood within six feet of each other in that narrow passage, and the darkness seemed to join them together.

She spoke very gently.

"Your supper's ready, Keir."

"I don't want any supper, kid."

"It's so hot in the house. Jo has been a little fretful. There must be thunder about."

She was aware of a movement at the other end of the passage. Keir had reopened the door.

"Yes—I think so. It's been working up all day."

"Let's go and sit outside, Keir, under the tree."

"Right-o."

"I left the chairs there."

In crossing the grass Keir stumbled over some object lying in the darkness, a small wooden box half full of weeds that Sybil had left there, but there was no responsive flare of impatience or of anger. He emitted a little sound that was like a sigh. His suddenly deflated self was unresisting.

"Sorry, Keir. How silly of me!"

There was no need for her to feel sorry, and he said so. He was aware of the cool, dark mass of the tree. He waited for her to sit down in one of the deck-chairs. He stood a moment, feeling inarticulate and awkward. Then he too sat down.

"Seems cooler here, Syb."

"Much cooler."

He felt her hand touching his knee. It was tentative and timid, and suddenly he was on the edge of things. He got hold of her hand in the darkness. He was aware of her fingers contracting on his.

"Syb—I've—I've been such a — fool."

"Have you, Keir?"

"Yes. Don't ask me about it. I'm—I'm—sorry."

There was a little sound from his wife. He sat up in the chair and realized that she was weeping, but her hand held fast to his.

"Oh—Keir—I knew you'd find out.—I knew somehow it wouldn't really—happen—that you—"

He sat turned to her in the darkness.

"Syb, do you mean—you knew?"

"Yes, Keir."

"Good God!"

He let her hand drop and, getting up, walked a little way off in the darkness. He felt both hot and icy. What could he say to her? What was there to say?

Her voice came to him.

"Keir."

He did not answer.

"Keir, come here. I'm—I'm not—"

He turned abruptly. He seemed to crumple at her knees.

"Syb—I'm sorry. I must have been mad—somehow. But it won't happen again. I'm—sorry."

She held his head in her hands.

"It did hurt me—Keir. Yes. But then—I had a feeling— Oh, my dear—there's no one who loves you as I do. I know I'm not clever. I'm such an idiot in some ways."

He drew her two hands against his face.

"You're not. You're nothing of the kind. You're clean and sweet. Oh, my God, what a damned fool—!"

Her tears had ceased. She gave a little exquisite shudder and caught her breath.

"Keir, come and sit here. Let's hold hands. Oh, did you see the lightning?"

He slipped into the chair; he edged it close to hers. He was in love with her differently, but supremely, and between them the sacrament of compassion had been consummated.

"Syb, you don't hate me?"

"No."

"That's so strange. Hallo—thunder. It's going to pour in a minute."

"I don't mind."

She snuggled up against him, her cheek against his shoulder.

"Nothing matters, does it? I was—so miserable, but now—"

"Syb, you've got something in you that I haven't—or hadn't. But it has come. Hallo—that was a big flash! I say, dear, what about Jo? She'll—"

His wife started up, and his figure rose with hers as though their twoness had become inexorably one.

"Oh, yes, Jo! Come."

They went in together to watch over Joanna Mary.

4

Mr. Samson called Keir into the office. Mr. Hoad was there, sitting at his desk and jotting down figures on a writing-pad. He looked at Keir through the upper halves of his pince-nez lenses and smiled, and Keir had never liked Mr. Hoad's smile. It suggested a snake poised on the tip of its tail, with its body arranged in slimy spirals. Mr. Hoad was one of those men who wear a neat grey felt hat with a black band set with precision upon his head, as though he had it adjusted with a spirit-level. There was nothing cocked or gaillard about Hoad. He carried an umbrella whenever an umbrella was likely to be necessary. He did not stride. He took short, prim steps with legs that were encased in rather meagre grey trousers that looked like a couple of zinc tubes.

Keir understood that Hoad was a useful supplement to

Samson. He was a sedulous sitter, a hunter of halfpennies, a born bureaucrat, a preparer of estimates and contracts, a checker of accounts. While Mr. Samson went out sailing in search of business, Mr. Hoad stayed at home in the office and presided over the pay-sheets and accounts. He was the firm's costing-department, its ready reckoner. He knew to a farthing how much a glass door-knob differed from a brass one.

Mr. Samson said: "Shut the door, Keir. I've just been talking to Mr. Hoad about that idea of mine."

Mr. Hoad sat, but Mr. Samson walked up and down as though he liked to traverse his subject actively. He would talk while going up and down a ladder. He liked to feel life moving under him. He was ruddy.

"Fact is, I'm not so young as I was, Keir. I'm not so quick on my legs or so early up in the morning. Young blood—what!"

Mr. Hoad was smirking over his figures. His thin, suave lips were pressed together. He wanted to say in his own particular manner: "Precisely—so. But why—why a fellow with no capital, and a rather uppish young fellow?" But there was a clause in the partnership agreement between himself and Mr. Samson that gave Mr. Samson the prerogative of behaving like John Bull, and Hoad had always eluded Mr. Samson's frontal attacks. Damned old autocrat!

He said: "A question of getting business—and supervising it. I suppose Mr. Smith understands—"

Keir intercepted Mr. Hoad's upward and oblique glance. He too understood that Hoad was not Samson.

"Get work and see that it's done."

Mr. Samson's ruddy face caught the light from the window.

"That's it, absolutely. I want a chap with the stuff in him and the knowledge. Some mawk of a mutt who'd have every man's tongue in his cheek! No, thank you. I want

[142]

bricks and mortar."

Mr. Hoad nodded and produced a platitude. He kept a number of tame platitudes like white mice in a cage.

"The early bird, sir. Attention to business is—"

Mr. Samson ignored him. He had never liked Hoad, but the fellow was supremely useful, though he suggested the smell of mice.

"Look here, Keir—I suggest next January 1st.—You'll come in—of course—without bringing any capital into the firm, but I count on your bringing in something more important than pounds, shillings, and pence. Guts and the knowledge of how to look after men. That takes some doing. I'm not sure that it's not nine-tenths of the business in these days."

Mr. Hoad pencilled in a very round O.

"The human cipher, Smith."

But Keir was looking towards Mr. Samson. He said: "There's nothing to be said, sir, except that I shall be all in on the job. I don't think I'm the sort of man to chuck a chance away. I'm—"

Mr. Samson nodded at him.

"All right. No need for soft soap. I want a man who will deliver the goods. I think you will. Let's go out and have a drink."

Mr. Samson, being John Bull, liked to raise a tankard.

"Coming, Hoad?"

Mr. Hoad excused himself. He had his figures to finish, and he was not the shape of a tankard.

"I have to get this estimate out."

Mr. Samson put out an arm across Keir's shoulder and swept him out of the office. There was something in Keir that warmed him. Hoad was such a stick of celery, bleached and crisp no doubt, but like a cold fish supper on a Sunday in December.

"Come on, lad, another S to the firm."

[143]

He gave Keir a jocund grin.

"I didn't make my business grow on tap-water. Yes, but I'm not saying that a cold-storage fellow isn't useful. Well, that's that."

Keir, opening the white gate of "Merrow," and wheeling his bicycle in between post and gate, surprised his very small daughter on the grass. Joanna Mary, emerging from the crawling stage, was beginning to stagger on two very fat legs. She was supremely solemn over it, and when she subsided rather abruptly, which was often, she said "Goo!" an exclamation that possessed a philological universality and yet was acutely personal. Keir paused at the gate to watch those two serious brown legs amble away from him towards the beech tree. Joanna had not seen her father, and Keir continued to watch her for a few seconds. He had yet to learn that a man's attitudes to life are as various as his moods. They may be flippant or ironic, serious or sentimental. But this product of the eggs and the sperm, this brown-legged young entity, his and yet not his—! He had not willed Joanna Mary; she had just happened.

And then Joanna Mary fell forward upon her tummy, and Sybil dashed out from the beech tree, solicitous and sudden.

"Oh, Jo—!"

But Joanna was neither hurt nor discouraged. She clutched her mother's frock and helped herself up. She stared hard at the grass as though accusing it of rising up and hitting her.

Keir wheeled his bicycle over to them.

"Hallo. She's getting her sea-legs."

He put his bicycle against the trunk of the tree and, squatting down, held out his hands to Joanna.

"Come on, young woman."

Joanna tried a spurt, toppled, and was caught by her father. He tossed her up, and she chuckled. He was feeling

[144]

rather full of himself both as man and as father.

"News, Syb. Give you three guesses."

She guessed it at once.

"Mr. Samson has asked you—"

"You're too quick. I'm to come in on January 1st."

"Oh, Keir!"

She was overjoyed and proud of his success, and Keir had yet to learn how very few people are pleased when life hands you a laurel wreath.

"I get a sixth to begin with."

"Only a sixth!"

"Well, that's pretty generous, my dear. It comes out of the old man's share. What do you think the profits were last year?"

"I couldn't say."

"Just over three thousand. That means five hundred for us."

"Oh, Keir, we'll be quite rich."

He rather thought so too, and when Joanna had gone to bed, and Sybil was washing up the supper things, he walked up and down his small grass plot. It was very much an estate, and so far as Keir's mood was concerned, it might have extended nearly as far as the mountains of the moon. Samson, Hoad & Smith! Five hundred a year! His vision enlarged itself. It took to itself spacious vistas as he patrolled his small garden. He found himself standing beside Sybil's row of runner beans. Jack and the Beanstalk!

A gramophone struck up next door. He heard Mrs. Challis's brassy and cultured voice.

"Little drinks—outside, I think."

The facetious voice of an oncoming male replied to her.

"No, inside, down the pink tube, dear lady."

There was laughter, and Keir, head in air, wondered at such wit. Also, he wondered at the illusion of sex. It had whipped him to anguish over that woman, and now she was

[145]

no more to him than a highly coloured cushion stuffed
with flock.

Chapter Twelve

1

ALREADY Sybil was beginning to think of the things that could be purchased when Keir became a member of the firm, for Sybil—through Keir—was proposing to reconsider her social importance. She was not a snob, but she could appreciate the value of an enlarged income, and the virtues of authority. It presaged more comfort, more security, and a new sense of power in the presence of the world's shop-window.

"I can buy that—if I want to."

It was the "can" that was so supremely satisfying.

She and Keir would be able to furnish the spare bedroom. In fact, "Merrow" opened its small mouth and offered many suggestions.

"I would like a carpet in the passage, please, instead of linoleum, and a really nice tea-service. Yes—I'd love a rose-bowl in the middle of the table. Yes, and it would be awfully jolly if I had a crazy-paving path leading up to my front door. Then, there's my kitchen. There are lots of things I could do with in the kitchen. You might even buy me a refrigerator."

Sybil reproved the small house for making so luxurious a suggestion.

"That's much too expensive. I know the larder does let us down sometimes in hot weather, but a refrigerator!"

Keir's needs were not to be neglected. He spent so little on himself. His wardrobe was very limited, and his stock of underclothing was—to say the least—patchy, and instead of cheap cotton pyjamas— Then—his bicycle: it was growing distinctly decrepit, and a member of the firm of Samson, Hoad & Smith could not trundle to Kingham on a rusty old machine. Probably in the course of a year or two they would be the owners of a small car. Both Keir's new dignity and his responsibilities would necessitate a car. He would be supervising the firm's various jobs and visiting clients—yes, almost like a doctor—and obviously he would have to dress to the part. Mr. Keir Smith could not represent the firm in a pull-over, shabby grey flannel trousers, and a stained soft felt hat.

Some instalments were still owing on Joanna Mary's perambulator, and with those payments wiped off, the pram would become the property of the Smith family. It would be available for subsequent Smiths, and especially so for the small son,—Sybil's dream child. Her passion to produce another baby, repressed for the moment, now reasserted itself.

"I do want a boy, Keir."

"Plenty of time yet, Syb."

"But it will be good for Jo. And if we are going to be quite well off—"

Keir had to explain to her that the position of a junior and unmoneyed partner in a firm was not as simple as it seemed. Normally, he might have to wait twelve months before his share of the year's trading expressed itself in ready cash. He had propounded his problem to Mr. Samson, and Mr. Samson had understood it. In his early days he had had to solve many such problems.

"All right, Keir. Suppose we arrange for you to draw five pounds a week from the firm for the first twelve months? At the end of the year you'll draw the balance. Can you manage on that?"

Of course Keir could manage, but he had to explain to Sybil that for the next fifteen months or so their income would continue to be much as it was. Moreover, when his income as a partner became available, its first charge would be the repayment of the mortgage on "Merrow." He hoped to wipe off the debt in three years.

Sybil was disappointed.

"But can't you leave it a little longer, Keir? It isn't as if we were middle-aged. And your prospects—?"

He said: "I don't like owing money. If anything happened to me—"

She was gently sceptical.

"Why, anyone would think—! Look at the Browns in that new cottage down the lane. They've got three, and he's only a clerk in the Council offices."

"That's Brown's affair, not mine. You never get anywhere, kid, unless you look ahead. We'll wait till the partnership deed is signed and sealed."

"Is that a promise, Keir? You see, a second child never costs as much as the first."

"How?"

"Oh, well—one's bought things, and one knows more."

"Yes, that may be so to begin with, but kids grow up. And if I had a boy, I should want to give him the best chance."

"Well, you'll be able to, won't you? Some day you will have half the business. I don't want to think of Mr. Samson going—but—"

Her calm forecasting of the future surprised him.

"That's not on the cards yet, thank God. And one isn't quite so damned selfish. Besides, I don't know that I shall throw up my hat when I'm left alone with Hoad. He's— slimy."

Sybil defended herself.

"I didn't mean, Keir, that I— I was just thinking of what we might expect. One has to think of these things, hasn't one?"

He said: "When you are building a house, Syb, you have to get the foundations inspected and passed. Sound sense, too."

But to Sybil mere ballast and cement might appear as dull and obvious substances. Necessary, oh, certainly, but wasn't it permissible for one to be a little fanciful? You did not buy seeds to keep them shut up in a cardboard box. You planted them as prospective flowers.

2

Both of them were young and ardent, and life was full of very desirable things and of exciting situations that waited to be possessed or experienced. Keir might be cautious with the caution of a man who wished to make sure that the ground was freehold and properly titled before building a house on it, but he was more than a precise and careful little fellow. His ambition was held on leash. When the chance was actually his, sealed and signed, he would be furiously ready to justify it. He would prove to Samson and he would prove to Hoad, and especially to Hoad, that he was the man of destiny.

He had ideas, but he did not blurt them out in public. He understood that Mr. Samson had had ideas, and that though those ideas might be a little out of date, they had served Mr. Samson's generation. He had no intention of appearing before Mr. Samson as the insurgent and patronizing prig. "Yes, that was all right in your day, but people are different and houses are different." Mr. Samson was still very limber on his feet and would cut across and through the traffic of Kingham High Street like a boy.

If the firm's imagination needed quickening, the change would have to be gradual.

Keir had imagination. He saw the new world still hungry

for houses, and in spite of much sententious prosing about the new world's standardization he had a feeling that the new world craved contrasts. Being so crowded, its urge was to elbow its way out into some little corner of difference, were that corner ever so small. It might rush out into the country rather like cattle who had been stalled all through the winter, and it might disfigure the country in its desire to possess it. It did not mean to disfigure it. It was not yet sufficiently wise as to the aloofness and the otherness of beauty. It might be under the impression that it could descend upon beauty and possess it as it descended upon Brooklands or Hendon, but Keir did believe that the urge towards beauty was there. Bluebells and sweet turf had to be martyred in order that lovely and silent things might yet teach modern man that life is not all waste-paper and tar.

Looking about him at Kingham, he saw the rows of dreadful yellow brick cottages built by the late Victorians, and the "refained" red brick villas of the Edwardians. Little gables, little turrets, pretentious bow windows, much white paint! Certainly some of the new-age building had the flatness and the flimsiness of cardboard, but, on the other hand, much of it was individual and imaginative. There were one or two houses in the Abbey Lands estate that caused Keir qualms of delight. He believed that imagination could express itself in a cottage as satisfyingly as in a villa. It was a question of proportion, of beauty of line, of the right texture and colour in your materials.

People—or some of them—wanted individual houses. The builder's business was to put up a little house or cottage that made people stand and stare and become creatures of desire. A house should be like a comely face, instantly alluring and attractive. And if possible, it should not be crowded up with other faces like a photo of the local "Bowling Club" or of the "Kingham Amateur Dramatic Association."

During the early part of the winter he spent many of his evenings in experimenting in cottage and house designs. He bought a box of chalks and coloured his rough sketches, using blurred browns and soft greens and creams. He showed some of these sketches to Mr. Samson, but he did not produce them to Mr. Hoad. Hoad was all for utility and the obvious, and quick returns.

Mr. Samson, having colour in himself, could appreciate colour objectively, but he retained the impression that beauty cost more money.

"Prices are cut pretty close, Keir."

Keir knew that, but he was convinced that beauty need cost no more or very little more than ugliness. You threw in the imagination and the taste and mixed them with the materials. Besides, he believed that there were people who would be ready to pay a few pounds more for a house that was a little unlike the house next door.

"Have you ever noticed the names people give their cottages—yes, even the ones in a row?"

Mr. Samson had noticed it.

" 'The Rosary'—'Skiddaw'—'Two Oaks.' That sort of thing, Keir."

"Well, isn't that—significant? The houses may be as like as two petrol tins, but the people want to be different."

"Or snobbish?"

"I think there is more in it than that."

Mr. Samson nodded.

"Well, there may be something in it. Private information, my lad,—but I hear there's some land coming on the market. I have one or two friends who are interested. We might develop a small estate of our own. I'm not dead yet."

Keir put his plans away.

"I should say not, sir. I hope there will be a good many years more of your liveness."

"Well, I'm feeling that way myself, Keir," and he

chuckled.

Sybil was beginning to think about her Christmas shopping, for the seasons of the year and their festivals were of serious and happy account to her, and "Merrow" had to eat hot cross buns on Good Friday, and surprise Joanna Mary with an Easter egg. Sybil bought holly; it was brilliantly berried that year; and the electric globe in the sitting-room had a sprig of mistletoe attached to it. Already Sybil was attempting to initiate Joanna into the mysteries of Christmas; she proposed that Joanna should hang out a very small sock.

"I do believe that children should be a little fanciful, Keir."

"Fairies—and all that?"

"Of course. You can't prove to me that there aren't fairies."

"I don't want to disprove your fairies, kid. So far as I'm concerned, Mr. Samson's just like Father Christmas."

Sybil laughed.

"So he is, all white and red. He's a dear."

It happened upon Christmas Eve. Keir and a couple of carpenters were working late in the shop, finishing off a pair of gates for a house on Kingham Hill. Keir had promised to be back at "Merrow" at six to take Sybil out shopping. Her Christmas present had yet to be bought, and the shops were keeping open late.

He and one of the other men were turning out a couple of gates on the big bench in the middle of the shop when the door opened and a head appeared. It belonged to the firm's lorry-driver, who had brought his lorry back into the yard.

"Heard the news?"

"No. What's that?"

"The boss has been killed. Run over by a bus in the High Street."

Keir experienced one of those moments of mental numbness. He stood leaning against the bench and staring at that face in the doorway.

"What do you mean?"

The lorry-driver was very full of the news.

"I came along with my old bus just after it happened. You know how the old man always fancied himself on being fly on his feet. He cut round a tram and the bus caught him. A wheel went over his head."

Keir felt sick. He had a sudden vivid glimpse of that jocund white head and ruddy face. Just pulp! He heard the lorry-driver revelling in detail.

"Reg'lar — squelch."

And suddenly Keir blazed.

"Shut up. Haven't you any decent feeling?"

The man stared at him.

"What the — the matter with you?"

Keir gave a toss of the head as though shaking some horror of blood out of his eyes. He turned and went to the corner of the shed where his coat was hanging, and put it on. He was aware of the silence, conscious of being watched by those other men. He was trembling. The nausea of the thing was still on him.

"Where is he?"

The lorry-driver stood with slouched shoulders, his hands stuffed into his overcoat pockets.

"They took him to the borough mortuary."

Keir moved towards the door, and as he did so, the lorry-driver ceased to be the newsmonger and became man. He stepped in front of Keir.

"I shouldn't if I were you, mate. He ain't exactly—"

Keir looked the man straight in the eyes.

"That's all right, Jack. I know what I'm doing."

He walked round the man and out into the dark yard where the black bulk of the lorry showed against the lighted office window. Hoad would be in there. Had Hoad heard? And suddenly to Keir the damp and muggy night was Hoad. A greasy road, tramlines, the wheels of a bus, Hoad's little smeary smile; God, was one so filthily personal as all that! His right hand made a queer movement as of pushing something away. He found his bike under the iron-roofed shelter by the gate, and he wheeled it out, but he did not attempt to mount it. He walked along the edge of the pavement, pushing the machine along the gutter. He became aware of a glare of light and of movement, Kingham High Street on Christmas Eve. Glare, movement, colour, women, hordes of women. Kingham High Street was one huge shop-window. It was packed with traffic. Turkeys in a fishmonger's shop, rows and rows of dead turkeys. An old fellow dressed as Father Christmas was carrying a Christmas tree along the pavement and advertising somebody's Yuletide Bazaar. Women and girls and children. A small group of dirty and excited children charged past him, and one of them bumped against his leg. Somewhere here old Ruddy Face had had his white head— Good God! Just an incidental mess, with Kingham High Street full of its glare and its crowded preoccupations. A paragraph in the papers. Tragic death of a well-known Kingham resident.

Tragic death—indeed!

For, suddenly, the tragedy of the thing as it affected him, Keir Hardie Smith, became overwhelmingly obvious. In seven days' time that partnership deed would have been signed. Samson, Hoad & Smith. And Hoad was now the god upon whose knees—

"Oh, you swine!"

For the moment the reaction of his rage was self-accusing. Was everything in this world—self? And this damned street with its glare and its noise and its crowds? People jostling each other to get on trams and buses, people herding in front of shop-windows! Red meat in the butchers' shops, a white head pulped and bloody!

He slung his bicycle round a curve of the pavement and escaped into a side street. He remembered that he had promised Sybil that he would be home at six to take her shopping. Sybil's Christmas present! He took to the gutter and walked along it with his head down, wheeling his machine.

He walked all the way to the Abbey Lands estate, and when he reached the white gate of "Merrow," he saw that "Merrow's" front door was open. He was late, and Sybil had Joanna Mary and the pram ready in the passage and was waiting for him, for Joanna Mary could not be left at home.

"Is that you, Keir?"

"Yes."

He was feeling calmer after that solitary walk. It had even occurred to him that Mr. Hoad was a somewhat helpless person out of the office, and that as a supervisor of work and of men he—Keir—might be as necessary to Hoad as Hoad was to him. Why should he spoil Sybil's Christmas? He need not tell her. He decided not to tell her until after Christmas. Yes, and she should have her present.

He wheeled his bicycle up the path.

"Sorry, Syb. I was kept in the shop."

In his own ears his voice sounded cheerfully casual.

"I shan't be a minute."

He put his bicycle away in the shed and, returning to the front door, found Sybil bending over Joanna Mary and the pram, and Keir was penetrated by a pang of sudden compassion. These two simple creatures, the woman and the child, were dependent upon him. He was aware of his wife's slightly flushed and excited face. It was one of her happy and care-free occasions.

"All ready, Keir. I'm going to leave Jo with the Browns for an hour or so. Mrs. Brown said I might."

Keir bent down and gently tweaked his daughter's nose. "Who's Father Christmas? Just you tell me that."

Joanna chuckled at him.

"Da-da."

She was a truly wonderful child.

When Joanna Mary and pram were being inserted into the Browns' narrow hall, Sybil happened to glance at her husband's face. She surprised Keir at a moment when he was not conscious of being looked at, and Keir's face was the face of a man who was very tired. It was curiously shadowy and lined, and Sybil's festive occasion was clouded by a transient shadow.

They were out in the dark lane and walking towards the lights of Kingham. She had slipped a hand under his arm.

"Tired, Keir?"

He rallied himself. Had his cheerfulness appeared too much like painted canvas?

"Just a bit. Had a long day. Do me good to have a little beano."

In Kingham High Street he shepherded Sybil towards a particular window. He happened to be wise as to the desire in the heart of his wife. Besides, she did need that winter coat. The one she was wearing was cheap and rather shabby.

The coat he bought her had a fur collar and cuffs, and though the fur was cony, it reproduced the mode of the moment. He stood and watched Sybil put the coat on and look at herself in a mirror.

"Oh, Keir, it's lovely!"

"It suits you, kid."

The fur at her throat made her face look douce and desirable. She was woman.

"Oh, yes, I'll wear the coat. Could you have the old one sent home?"

"Certainly, madam."

Sybil's eyes seemed to fill with secret and surprised laughter. The saleswoman had called her "madam." But then her husband was—to all intents and purposes—a partner in the firm of Samson, Hoad & Smith.

Out in the street she hugged Keir's arm.

"You are good to me. It's a lovely coat."

Twenty yards down the street they came upon a newsvendor selling a late edition of a local paper. The man carried a placard, and on it was printed: "Local tragedy. Well-known Kingham resident killed."

Keir went suddenly white in the presence of that newssheet. He was aware of Sybil asking him a question.

"I wonder who it is, Keir. Do you know?"

He lied to her.

"No."

"Buy a paper."

He drew her past the placard.

"No need to bother about that rag on a night like this."

Chapter Thirteen

1

KEIR spent Christmas wondering whether his life's opportunity had died with Mr. Samson, and in waiting for some gesture from Mr. Hoad. Surely, the surviving partner would communicate with the potential partner at such a crisis in the firm's career? But when the silence continued, Keir began to question it. What was its significance? Did it mean that all was well?

He felt both restless and inert. There was a pride in him that refused to approach Mr. Hoad either emotionally or with a view to appraising the situation. Hoad was not the kind of a person to whom you betrayed emotion; he was rather like a batrachian sitting in some dim, dark world of his own and waiting for a fly to settle. He would dart out a tongue and suck in the fly or a figure. He was not a man whom you approached soulfully when your spirit was in travail.

Keir felt paralysed and yet painfully sensitive to the things and the people about him. The familiar face of his world had become strange. Even "Merrow" seemed suspicious and unfriendly, a little house that mistrusted its foundations. It asked him awkward questions. "What about me? What about my mortgage? Half a year's interest is due on December 31st. Oh, you have the money put by. But what will Mr. Samson's executors want to do about me?" Why couldn't the wretched little house enjoy its Christmas and leave law and finance till tomorrow?

Moreover, Sybil was so full of her Christmas, her mistletoe, and her holly. They dined in state at one o'clock, almost as a partner in the firm of Samson & Hoad might be expected to dine. Joanna Mary occupied her high chair, into which she could be bolted with a wooden rail. They ate roast beef and Christmas pudding. There were oranges, almonds and raisins, and crackers.

Joanna had to pull crackers with Daddy, her mother assisting. She blinked when the thing went bang, and then gurgled with laughter.

Sybil crowned Joanna Mary with a purple cap.

"Da-da, da-da."

"She wants you to have a cap, Keir."

They all put on caps, and Keir's was a fool's cap. *Absit omen!*

Sybil hunted for mottoes. It was part of the ritual and she loved it. She passed one to Keir. He read it, but to himself:

> "Your eyes are like the twinkling stars,
> My love lies bleeding behind bars."

A voice in him exclaimed: "What — balderdash!" He was trying not to feel that the little domestic festival was a pathetic farce. He pulled another cracker with Joanna Mary and extracted the motto and read it as though it might contain words of esoteric meaning:

> "The rose is red, the sky is blue,
> I'm feeling sad because of you."

He crumpled up the slip of paper and flicked it into the fireplace.

That Christmas dinner remained with him oppressively, suspended within him like his thoughts. He went out dutifully for a walk with Sybil and Joanna Mary and Joanna's pram. They walked to the river and along the towing-path, and everything looked grey to Keir. He was moody with-

[160]

out meaning to be moody. Should he go and see Hoad and get it over? It was no use telling his wife about the tragedy until he knew how it was going to affect them.

He did not go to see Mr. Hoad, but he became filled with a sudden tenderness towards Sybil. Mere self-pity translated itself into compassion. He was responsible for these two creatures, and Sybil was still so flushed with her Christmas. She took simple things to heart. He helped her to put Joanna Mary to bed, and afterwards they sat together in front of the fire.

"It's been a lovely day, Keir, hasn't it?"

She wanted to have her hand held, and he held it.

"Rather."

"Wasn't she funny with the crackers?"

"Yes, she blinked a bit, didn't she?"

"Did you notice my new coat?"

As a matter of fact he had not noticed it, though he had been the donor, but he lied.

"Just suits you, that fur collar."

Sybil rather thought so, too.

He did not know what to do with himself next day, for his suspense was like a meal that had refused to be digested. At eleven o'clock he got out his bicycle and rode to Samson & Hoad's. It was possible that Hoad had reacted to the stress of circumstances and was putting Boxing Day to other uses. He might be in the office, but Keir found the yard gates shut and locked. A closed crisis still confronted him, and he remounted his bicycle and rode home.

That evening, after Joanna Mary had been put to bed, he told Sybil of Mr. Samson's death. At the moment she was rummaging in a drawer for some wool with which to darn a pair of his socks, and suddenly comprehending the bitterness of the mischance, she stood looking ruthfully at her husband. He was sitting in front of the fire and leaning towards it with a significant stillness.

"Keir, was it the news on the placard?"

"Yes."

"Then—you knew?"

"Well, it wasn't exactly the sort of Christmas present—"

"Oh, Keir."

She made a quick movement towards him and sat down on the arm of his chair. She seemed to understand that he did not want to be touched. He was feeling brittle and restive. Her face had an extraordinary gentleness. She just let her hand rest upon his shoulder.

"Keir, you ought to have told me."

"What was the use of spoiling—?"

"But, oh, Keir, your troubles are mine, aren't they? I shouldn't have let you buy that coat."

"Oh, that's all right, kid."

"Poor Mr. Samson. He was such a kind man. So different from—"

"Yes, rather different from the other fellow."

"Have you seen Mr. Hoad yet?"

"No. I wasn't going to rush at the fellow and let him see that it mattered too much."

"But, Keir, he'll want you all the more now, won't he? He won't be able to supervise all the outside work."

"He may want me, kid, but he's the sort of man who'll just try to use me. I shall find that out tomorrow."

2

A young clerk who had been engaged by the firm less than a month ago put his head into the carpenter's shop and addressed Keir.

"Smith, the gov'nor wants you in the office."

Keir left the bench, took off his apron, and put on his coat. If the crisis was upon him, he would go to it, properly dressed, though young Collar & Cuffs had not presented him with any prefix. He crossed the yard, where men were loading bricks into a lorry and, entering the office, found Mr. Hoad at his desk. There was an official sombreness about Mr. Hoad. He had put on a black tie.

"Come in. Shut the door, Smith."

He did not ask Keir to sit down. It was his intention to define and circumscribe the situation. His pince-nez seemed to have slipped slightly down his nose, and his glance was upward and oblique.

"Terrible business this. Shocking. A sign of the times. Mr. Samson, if I may say so, was the kind of man—"

Keir stood still, and Mr. Hoad's fingers fidgeted about the desk.

"It's a most serious blow to the business."

There was a pause, and Keir felt that Mr. Hoad was waiting for him like a black cat, while he was waiting for Mr. Hoad.

"I can quite understand that. Mr. Samson was the business."

Mr. Hoad's eyes blinked. He did not appreciate the tone of the remark, but it gave him his opening.

"Precisely. I thought it only fair, Smith, to let you know at once that under the circumstances I do not feel justified in assuming—any of the commitments that our revered chief—"

Keir was conscious of a flash of inward scorn. Revered chief indeed! Why couldn't the slimy fellow say exactly what was in his mind, instead of sitting there like a black cat denying the other creature a dish of cream?

Keir was abrupt. Hoad should not know how hope trembled in him.

"You mean—about the partnership?"

Mr. Hoad's smile was surreptitious and cajoling.

"Exactly. Under the circumstances and placed as I am —I may find myself short of capital. Mr. Samson's executors may wish to realize his interest. My responsibilities—heavy—rather problematical. Of course, it must be plain to you that had you been in a position to introduce—"

To Keir, Mr. Hoad's voice was like a melancholy and disturbing little draught blowing under a door. He understood, oh, yes, he understood. Mr. Hoad had him. He could produce no capital.

"Yes, you wouldn't get any money with me," and he could have added, "but you might get something more with me," but he didn't.

Mr. Hoad waved deprecating hands.

"We won't put it quite so crudely as that. I want you to recognize my difficulties. I am responsible for the business—now. I may have to go to the bank for a loan. You see, I am being quite frank with you. I'm sorry, but any idea of a partnership must be postponed."

Postponement was an admirable word. Keir moistened his lips and swallowed it.

"Postponed. I see. Then, you may reconsider the idea—later?"

Again Mr. Hoad's smile oozed.

"Oh, certainly. It will depend—of course—on the firm's position financially. If, in a year or two—"

Keir was very sure that he was being fobbed off with a shadowy supposition, but even the shadow was precious to him. And he was helpless, so damnably helpless. The black cat possessed both the milk and the saucer.

"Meanwhile, you wish me—?"

Mr. Hoad's little mean face expressed relief. It became almost bright and cheerful.

"Oh, of course, Keir, of course. I want you to carry on as foreman. I shall want you to overlook some of the outside work."

"I see. The same pay?"

"Just at present I must ask you to meet me—in that way.

I shall have an anxious year or two."

"I see."

Inwardly he felt bitter, but the man in him would not flinch before Hoad.

"All right, I'll do my best for the firm."

"I'm sure you will, Keir. I have every confidence in you. Of course—all this is between ourselves."

"I understand."

In the nature of things he had often addressed Mr. Samson as "sir," but it would never occur to him to accord the "sir" to Hoad, and the little slimy snob in Hoad was half expecting it. He was ready to appreciate the tribute, especially from the lips of Keir. It might help to appease his dislike of Keir and of what he would have described as the shock-headed cockiness of Keir.

"That's all, Smith, I think. We have to attend to business —in spite of this most shocking—event. I should like you to go along and see how they are getting on at that new house in River Lane. Yes, at once, please. I have so much to occupy me here for the moment."

Keir went, and felt himself walking towards some inevitable edge, and on the faces of the other men he discovered that morning suggestions of ironic curiosity. They knew; they were somehow wise as to the secrets of the firm's official life. Mr. Keir Hardie Smith had had his conceit chastened, and they were pleased.

Work had piled up during the Christmas holiday, and as was often the case human nature was apt to be slack after two or three days of relaxation. Keir, as supervisor for the day, had several jobs to overlook in different parts of Kingham, and one particular piece of work caused him to use strong language.

"That's a nice bit of botching. Knock off and get back to the shop. I'll come and do the job myself tomorrow."

At the end of the day he was both late and tired, for

frustration may have a negative effect upon a man. Trifles had irritated him, trifles that normally would have been shed like shavings from a plane. He had a second interview with Mr. Hoad, but it dealt solely with the day's work, progress, material that was needed. It was half past six when he mounted his bicycle and rode home to "Merrow." The evening was dim and stagnant, and he was conscious of the slackness of the muggy December night. There were no stars, no glitter, no keen edge to things. To Keir all was blurred and moist and melancholy.

He dismounted at the little white gate. He stood there a moment holding his bicycle by the handles. He could see a vertical streak of light between the curtains of the living-room, and he was moved to sudden emotion. His throat contracted; his bowels yearned. He was just man poignantly conscious of those simple realities that are like the bread and wine of a sacrament. If he uttered no words to himself, it was because these human essentials had existed before words. Wife, child, home. It was as though he had rediscovered them, or had discovered them as emotional symbols for the first time in his life.

Mystic human trinity in unity! Almost he could understand the feeling of woman for that which is flesh of her flesh. The little, hard, circumscribed ego that was Keir seemed to melt and to encompass those other two in a living flux of love and compassion. The three of them were one, and as he walked up the path towards that slit of light, he saw it as a rift in his own loneliness. He had been cast down and disappointed, but behind those curtains light and warmth and comradeship waited for him. He was glad of Sybil. He found himself yearning towards his mate. She was both poor Sybil and a creature of infinite wealth and potency. He wanted to be with her, near her, to feel consoled and strengthened by the gentle reality of Sybil.

He put his bicycle away in the small shed and went in.

His voice had a poignant cheerfulness.

"Sorry, I'm afraid I'm late."

He was aware of his wife standing by the table and looking across at him. She seemed to flinch just for one moment, and then with a peculiar wise radiance she came and kissed him.

"Tea's ready, Keir."

The pressure of his lips on hers revealed to her many things, that hope had been dashed and that with it he had become more hers. He kissed her as the sharer in all that was his, and her heart felt big.

"You're tired, Keir."

"Just a bit. Had a long day."

His arm remained round her as though he realized the dear reality of her, his need of her.

"Oh, Keir, never mind. It will come again."

"You've guessed?"

"I knew—directly you looked at me."

"That's rather wonderful of you, kid."

"Is it? Not when things matter. Don't you understand that? There's a kind of quickness in one.—The kettle's boiling."

She moved away from him to the fireplace. His eyes followed her, and then he sat down at the table that was laid.

"Jo in bed?"

"Yes."

"Just as well. Yes, I've had one straight in the face, Syb, but there are compensations. If it hurt a bit—there are other things. Rather funny to miss your chance just by seven days."

She was filling the tea-pot.

"So Mr. Hoad—?"

"Oh, just Hoad. I had more than a feeling that he would keep me out. Of course, there are things to be said on his side. The chap hasn't the stuff in him the old boy had. He's frightened and careful and slippery."

He seized the loaf and cut it.

"He wants me to carry on—of course."

Sybil sat down behind her tray.

"But he'll find out, Keir. He'll find out that he can't get on without you, especially now that he's alone."

Keir gave a little laugh.

"Perhaps, perhaps not. I have an idea that he's the sort of man who will use me, but keep me off the ladder. Well, anyway, kid, I've got a good balance on the credit side, yes—you."

Chapter Fourteen

1

MR. SAMSON'S estate devolved upon two sisters, and the greater part of it was immobilized in the firm of Samson & Hoad. The capital value of the business interest might be regarded as influenced by goodwill, and Mr. Hoad came to an arrangement with Mr. Samson's executors. Meanwhile, the executors, faced with death duty and looking round for ready cash, decided to realize certain of Mr. Samson's investments and to call in his mortgages, Keir's among them.

Keir interviewed one of these gentlemen and put his case before him. If they pressed him for the money, they would have to take "Merrow" and dehouse him. Keir was very much worried. The executor was sympathetic. He was sorry, but to clear the estate they needed cash. He advised Keir to arrange for the transference of the mortgage. In all probability one of the many building societies would do his business for him.

Keir interviewed a local agent who acted for "The Rainbow Building Society." It was a big concern and advertised itself extensively by putting to the public the question "Why Pay Rent?" The society accepted "Merrow," and the transfer and repayment to Mr. Samson's executors were arranged; but Keir found that he would have to pay the building society six and a half per cent, thirty-two pounds ten a year, and to Keir a five-pound note was more than petty cash.

But base metal tempered the other metal in him. If he

was to act as the official supervisor of Mr. Hoad's contracts, he would miss no chance of performing the work efficiently. He continued to hope that the gentleman with the pince-nez would be brought to appreciate the commercial value of Keir Hardie Smith. He made allowances for Hoad. The man had the whole business on his shoulders. He had to account to Mr. Samson's executors. If he proposed to possess the business, he would have to accumulate the capital needed to buy out Mr. Samson's sisters.

As Keir put it to Sybil: "The thing is to realize that the other fellow has his worries, just as you have. I'm going to wire in and show him that I'm up to the job. One can't do more than that."

Keir did his work thoroughly and with an efficiency and vigilance that a go-easy world might have described as ruthless. He did it honestly in the sense that he strove to make sure that the men he supervised gave an honest return for the wages they received. His world did not describe him as ruthless. It referred to him in private as a — little boss, or Hoad's spy, or as a — —. It did not like the way in which Keir turned up at eight o'clock and marred the peace of that getting-ready-to-begin period, the casual gossip, the early pipe. He was here, there, everywhere. You never knew when to expect him. He appeared to cultivate the art of the unexpected. A bricklayer's labourer was heard to remark that: "The chap buzzes round you like a — mosquito."

There was no one to warn Keir that he was in conflict with the plain man's natural inertia, or that he was challenging a mass prejudice. He should have been wise as to it, and possibly he was wise, but that which was Keir was Keir. He could be intense, the inevitable individualist, perhaps too much the egoist. He had the essential fire; he was a little Prometheus, whom the great god Demos would wish to see chained to the rock. He was quicker in thought and movement than the average man. He set too hot a pace.

That a sulky atmosphere surrounded him was evident, but Keir was rather too ready to regard it as mere winter fog. The fellows would get used to him and to his authority, and they would be obliged to accept his keenness. Had not Mr. Samson warned him that when success comes to a man and compels him to exercise a little authority over men who regarded him as an equal, he is apt to be grossly unpopular? But there were easy virtues that he lacked. He was too serious and aloof in the presence of his little world's resentment, carrying himself too much like the proverbial schoolmaster. Old Samson had been more of a sea-captain, vigorous in voice and language, but full of Bills and Freds and a kind of jocund heartiness that had made him appear as a man among men. Keir was too damned superior.

One morning he found a Mr. Sparks in the yard talking to a couple of men who had come in with a lorry. Mr. Sparks was a person who had not been seen about the premises in the days of Mr. Samson. He was a trades-union official, a fellow with light blue eyes, a little black moustache, and a prominent and shiny chin. He commanded language, especially so on a platform. He could be suave and he could be truculent. When in conversation with an employer of labour, he would stand with his hands in his trousers pockets, his head thrown back, his face exuding a shimmer of self-confident cleverness. "Yes, I'm up to all your tricks."

As Keir passed by, he nodded.

"Morning, Mr. Smith."

The salutation was ironical, and Keir understood its significance. He paused in the doorway of the carpenter's shop and turned to look back. He saw Mr. Teddy Sparks walking in the direction of the office.

Half an hour later Keir and Mr. Sparks met again in the yard. Keir had been attending to the loading of a lorry and making sure that certain material had been included in the load, when Mr. Sparks emerged from the office. The lorry had cleared the gates, and Keir and the official had the yard to themselves.

Mr. Sparks was in a blithe mood, and feeling facetious.

"Hallo, Napoleon!"

His polished and prominent chin and light blue eyes prompted Keir to throw back the challenge.

"Well, what about you?"

The other man laughed.

"Not one of my household gods. Do you keep a bust of the Emperor on your mantelpiece? My job, old lad, is to see that such busts are busted."

Keir's irony was ocular rather than vocal.

"Is that so?"

Mr. Sparks walked past him, turned, and showed his teeth.

"Do you want the straight tip from me?"

"I don't bet."

"Oh, you're smart, aren't you! But you're too dashed smart on the wrong side of the fence. It's a pity. You and I—"

He became abruptly confidential and ingratiating.

"Look here, old lad, you ought to be one of us. I know a thing or two. I know a thing or two about this firm."

He inclined his head towards the office.

"Where do you think you belong? To the boss in there, or to the chaps who do the job? Where's your loyalty lie? I could tell you a thing or two."

Keir looked at Mr. Sparks's chin as though it fascinated him.

"Supposing I said that I belong to myself?"

Mr. Sparks gave a toss of the head, a trick that he found dramatic and useful when addressing an audience.

"You've said it. Absolutely! Good old Manchester school. Every man for himself, and devil take the hindmost. If that's your creed—"

Keir smiled at him.

"Look here, Sparks, my job is to see that men do the job. Your business is to—"

"Not so quick, old lad. My business is to see that every chap has a job, and that he's not jobbed over or off it. That's just the difference. You're not thinking of the men; you're thinking of yourself."

Keir could not deny himself the obvious retort.

"And you? Completely disinterested, always and everywhere?"

Sparks gave another toss of the head.

"You can cut that out. I'm class-conscious—anyway. I don't rat on my own people. Well, you wait and see."

Keir let the incident pass. A man like Sparks had his own particular preoccupations; he was obliged to light a fire under the pot and make it boil occasionally. And if the men were somewhat sulky, Mr. Hoad was suave. He was very polite to Keir during those first six months, and his suavity even tempered Keir's severity. Keir had been watching two or three men until he had convinced himself either of their incapacity or of their dishonesty in the matter of output, and when he had made up his mind about them, he spoke to Hoad.

"There are one or two chaps who ought to be stood off. Slow-motion artists. I have been watching them for weeks."

"I don't like sacking men, Keir."

"I quite understand, but it's part of my business to keep you wise."

Mr. Hoad equivocated.

"I appreciate that. Why not give them a broad hint? I don't want any bad feeling in the business."

As Keir was going out of the office, his employer called him back.

"Keir, just a moment. You set a pretty high standard.

I'm not quarrelling with that, but one has to remember in these days that labour is always looking for trouble. I'm rather a believer—in conciliation."

Keir understood. Hoad was not Samson.

"I see. But if a man's bluffing and he thinks you are afraid to call his bluff, I don't believe—"

Mr. Hoad fidgeted in his chair.

"Yes, yes, one has to be firm of course. What I mean is, Keir, that, human nature being what it is, one has to indulge in a little winking. I quite understand that—your position— Yes, I appreciate your—loyalty. But a little of the velvet glove, Keir, the velvet glove."

Keir might feel a little contemptuous towards Mr. Hoad and regret the jocund candour of Mr. Samson, but he could and did accuse himself of being prejudiced in his own favour. His integrity and his thoroughness were not disinterested virtues. He knew that his very efficiency was inspired by an ulterior motive. He had to convince that rather gelatinous creature Mr. Hoad that he—Keir—was solid and substantial and still the potential and perhaps the inevitable partner. It irked him, and there were moments when he felt himself posing before a man whom he both disliked and despised.

"Damned sycophant."

He had never accused himself of truckling to old Samson. Moreover, he had some understanding of the men's attitude of passive resistance. They gave themselves, and all that they could deny their employer was a portion of themselves. They subscribed to that futile supposition that by limiting effort they enlarged the potential opportunity. If you did less work, there would be more work for you and for others. He resented their stupidity—as he saw it—even as they resented his strenuousness. He would have said that men like Sparks truckled to the indifferent man, and both flattered and exploited him. Sparks offered to spread a vast feather-bed and to invite the whole world to recline on it.

Keir talked more to his wife. He discovered that Sybil was wiser than he had imagined her to be, and the comradeship between them deepened and enlarged itself. He was surprised to find her more than ready to justify his activities.

She said: "A lot of it's just jealousy, Keir. Most of them would be much rougher than you are—if they were in your place."

The gentle solidity of Sybil could be less gentle than it seemed. In a crisis her instincts might dominate her sentiments.

"All men want as much as they can get. It's natural, isn't it?"

Yet during all those months Keir was conscious of keeping one corner of an eye upon that narrow face and figure in the office. Hoad, with his pince-nez and his finicking fussiness, was Keir's little man of destiny. He may have hated his employer even as some of the men were tempted to hate Keir, for the secret self-regard, the inward strutting pride, of man is so easily offended.

Keir felt himself to be Hoad's superior, and Hoad sat in the seat of authority.

2

Yet, when the firm of Samson & Hoad became Samson, Hoad & Gott, Keir was utterly unprepared for the change. Hoad's very suavity was by its nature surreptitious.

Even some of the employees knew of the event before the rumour of it reached Keir. In fact the news came to him casually across the counter of a shop. He had stopped on his way home to buy a couple of ounces of tobacco.

"I hear young Gott is going into your firm."

Keir's change was lying on the counter, five pennies and a halfpenny, and for the moment he forgot it.

"What's that? Who told you?"

"Oh, gossip."

"Who is he?"

"Why, young Gott. You know Gott's in High Street."

"The caterers?"

"That's it. Old Gott must have done pretty well. I suppose he's buying his son a share in the business.

Keir was walking out of the shop, leaving his change on the counter, and the tobacconist called after him: "Mr. Smith, your change." Keir came back with a little self-conscious smile and collected the coppers. He did not attempt to explain his absent-mindedness, but he did wonder whether the man behind the counter suspected that this piece of news had been like a blow low on the body. Almost it had had the same effect as such a blow. It had knocked the wind out of Keir and made him feel faintly sick and unsteady. His stomach had dropped. He was conscious of a horrid sense of deflation as though some strand within him had snapped.

Young Gott! He had never seen the man. Till a moment ago he had not known of young Gott's existence. The chap's father had built up the leading confectionery and catering business in Kingham. There was a Gott's Restaurant in High Street. Keir could conclude that Gott senior was a man of means, and that Gott junior, somehow preferring bricks and mortar to cake, was being presented with his opportunity.

But Hoad had said nothing, and though Hoad was under no obligation, Keir felt bitter, bitter and mortified. He had no claim upon Hoad other than his effort to safeguard Mr. Hoad's business, and the fact that but for old Samson's death he would have been Hoad's partner. But the fellow might have told him, instead of letting the news reach him through the back door.

He cycled home to "Merrow," and the "Merrow" lane was now dressed on either side with bungalows of all shapes and sizes. The community had spilled over into Keir's quiet corner, and sometimes he wondered what would happen to all these clerks and rentiers if the pound note became waste-paper and other countries refused to supply England with free food. But that was hypothetical, and Keir was in contact with reality. He was not aware of the gentleness of the June evening, or of the sun-splashed trees trailing long shadows. There was no beauty in the day for him. The face of June might have been the face of a harlot, sinister and suborning under the light of some street lamp.

He found Sybil in the garden, tying up a row of Canterbury bells. She was standing in the border with a length of bass between her lips. Joanna Mary, who had been presented with a minute portion of the earth's surface as a safeguard against haphazard and far-flung activities, was busy with a tin bucket and a wooden spade. She was proving herself a very teachable child. She understood that when her mother said: "Jo mustn't hurt poor flowers," her mother was somehow a flower.

Joanna was squatting and patting a small mound of earth with a spade when her father pushed his bicycle through the gate. She stood erect, and on her knees showed two patches of garden soil. She bumped up and down on her fat legs and waved a spade.

"Dada—!"

Dropping her spade, she rushed at him, for she knew that if she could waylay her father at the gate, he would sit her on the saddle of his bicycle and, with an arm round her, wheel her as far as the shed. Keir might be in a black mood, but the edge of it did not reach as far as the face of his small daughter. If he had eaten sour grapes, Joanna Mary's very new teeth were not set on edge.

"Hallo, where's the money for the bus ride?"

Joanna chuckled and embraced his leg.

"I've got penny in purse."

"Oh, have you!"

He lifted her up, and Sybil, bending over the flowers, turned a head to smile at them.

"There's a letter for you, Keir. I left it on the window-sill."

Having humoured Joanna Mary and put his machine away, he went into the house to get his letter. Joanna followed him and stood solemnly waiting upon his pleasure. He found the letter, an oblong business envelope addressed by hand with a penny-halfpenny stamp in the right upper corner. He recognized the handwriting. It was Hoad's.

He opened the letter and read, and as he skimmed the words, he thought: "Yes, Hoad's just the sort of chap who does a dirty job on paper." He was conscious of harsh anger, a bristling, cold resentment, and Joanna Mary, staring up into her father's face, wondered why it looked so funny.

"MY DEAR SMITH,

"I think it right that you should know that the exigencies"—what a Hoad word!—"of the business have obliged me to introduce a partner with capital. Mr. Edward Gott is joining the firm. I am sorry that circumstances should have compelled me to disappoint you in the matter, but I do opine that you will understand my position.

"I shall be glad to see you in the office early tomorrow. Mr. Edward Gott has had two years' experience with a London firm, and he will—of course—take over some of your responsibilities—"

Keir's lips were pale and retracted. He stuffed both letter and envelope into his jacket pocket. Exigencies—opine! He became aware of a small hand grasping a trouser

[178]

leg.

"Dada—I've dug—such a big hole."

He was trembling. He was on the edge of one of those rage-storms that smite a man in moments of bitter mortification. He looked down at the child. She too was elemental, but so different from the elements of his anger. He had a feeling of snatching himself back from some ugly self-betrayal. He picked up Joanna Mary and carried her out to her own particular mud-patch. He inspected the hole that her wooden spade had dug.

"By George, that's a wonderful hole! You didn't do it all yourself."

She nodded emphatically, proudly.

"I did."

It occurred to him to wonder where the fascination lay in the digging of a useless hole. Some infantile urge towards accomplishment, display? And after all—the Pyramids were no more than holes dug upwards into the air.

He laughed.

"Splendid. You'll be able to bury Rose in it"—Rose was a rather hectic doll.

Joanna took him seriously. She was shocked.

"No, no, no bury poor Rose."

Joanna had been put to bed before Keir showed his wife Mr. Hoad's letter. Sybil was looking a little hot and untidy after an hour's work among her flowers, and at such a time she reminded Keir of a pretty and animated child who had been romping with other children. She never suggested the sloven. They had carried two deck-chairs into the shade of the beech tree.

"What do you think of that, Syb?"

If, as his good comrade, he expected her to share in his fears and hopes and worries, to acclaim his triumphs and drink death or disaster to his enemies, he was merely man. He did not know that most women are apt to improve upon

[179]

the opportunity and to regard a man's boyish outbursts as part of the day's foolishness. The romance may have passed from all rages, both sexual and spiritual. But Keir was surprised by her response to that letter. She was more actively angry than he was and anger was rare in her.

"It's—abominable. It's—treachery."

She may have suffered mortifications and disappointments of her own, but in this matter she was with him body and soul. She trembled; she was pale; her very hair was insurgent.

"It's so—mean, after all the work you've put in. Miserable little worm! I'd like to—"

Keir's bitterness was whimsical.

"The gilded youth has the cash, kid. Isn't 'Gott' German for god? The golden god! But he kept me in the dark until he had brought off the deal. I rather thought he was the sort of chap who would use me."

There was a note of pain in his voice.

"I'm sorry, Syb. I thought things were going to be different for all of us."

Impulsively she seized his hand and held it. Hoad's letter was lying on her lap.

"Oh, Keir, there's nothing for you to feel ashamed of. You couldn't help not having the money."

Her eyes and mouth grew poignant.

"If you hadn't married me—"

He was touched to the quick.

"That's made no difference. I shouldn't have been a Gott. Besides, there is a difference. You're something more, Syb. Oh, yes, you are. You've taken it so damned well. I suppose some women—"

"Oh, Keir, what hurts you hurts me."

Chapter Fifteen

1

At eight o'clock Keir went to the office, but the office had not yet opened, and having one or two jobs to overlook, he rode off on the day's round. His first call was at a house that was being built by the firm on Kingham Hill, and as he dismounted, he heard loud laughter coming from the shell of the new building. Putting his bicycle against the hedge, he passed through the temporary gate, and entering the house by what was to be its front door, he surprised the men in conclave. Two of them were smoking pipes, and it was obvious that the occasion was so socially significant that the postponement of the day's work was justified.

Keir looked at the group of men and at his watch.

"About time to get a move on, isn't it?"

He was conscious of receiving ironical glances. The smokers did not put away their pipes, and instantly he was wise as to the situation. The atmosphere of that brick shell was hostile. Rumour had spread. His authority slid upon thin ice.

He did not utter another word. He stood there with his watch in his hand, and no one addressed a remark to him. One of the smokers, a bricklayer, seated on a plank supported by two buckets, knocked out his pipe and, ignoring Keir, issued an invitation.

"What about a little job of work, boys?"

Keir understood. He put his watch away. The men were on the move, but their activities were self-ordained and were not inspired by his presence. He had to move out of the way to let them pass to their various places, and not one of them looked at him. The facetious fellow of the party began to mount a ladder, and as he did so, he tapped the toe of a boot against each rung.

"Put your money on Early Worm, Charlie."

Keir waited until they had distributed themselves about the building, and, returning to the road, mounted his bicycle. As he pedalled off, he heard laughter celebrating his retreat. Someone shouted: "What price the Sergeant Major?" There was more laughter.

Keir rode back to the yard and, going to the office, found that Mr. Hoad had arrived. He had sat down a moment ago at his desk and was adjusting his pince-nez. A clerk was busy with the morning's mail, and when Hoad saw Keir's face, he let fall over his own face the veil of a little, shimmering smile.

"That you, Keir. Come in. Just a moment, Hobbs. I want a few words with Mr. Smith."

The clerk, with a curious glance at Keir, got up and went out. Mr. Hoad's hands began to fiddle with the various objects on his desk; not that any readjustment or rearranging of these articles was needed. Mr. Hoad's uneasy hands sought occupation.

"You had my letter, Keir?"

His air of embarrassed brightness was an offence to Keir. It was so like the man and so like his silly question.

"Oh, yes—I suppose you couldn't let me know earlier."

"If it would have made any difference, Keir, of course I should have notified you."

"Some of the men knew before I did."

"That couldn't be so."

"Couldn't it? I got the news yesterday from the man who sells me my tobacco."

"The leakage wasn't from this office."

Keir felt that he was being inveigled into a futile argument upon a question of procedure that neither concerned him nor continued to be of any importance. Hoad had picked up a box of matches and was rattling it.

"I think I explained in my letter—"

"Yes."

"I'm sorry if you are disappointed, but you remember I warned you. Mr. Gott is bringing the necessary capital into the business. I was finding myself very cramped."

He gave the match-box a last shake and put it down.

"Well, that's the situation, Keir. I can only suggest that you make the best of it. Mr. Edward Gott—"

Keir interrupted him.

"Yes, that's quite plain to me. What interests me is—my position in the future. Am I to understand that I go back to the shop as foreman?"

"Of course, Keir, of course that's open to you. Your position will be just what it was in Mr. Samson's day. Mr. Gott will take on the supervising, though I expect to get about myself now that I shall have a partner. I hope you will stay with us."

His glance lifted to Keir's hat and remained fixed upon it for a moment. Keir had come into the office wearing his hat, and he was still wearing it. The office was not a place where etiquette was elaborated, but Mr. Hoad would have been more pleased if Keir had removed his hat.

"Well—I think that's all, Keir. It's for you to decide. As you know, this firm doesn't have to stand off its regular hands. Employment's steady."

Keir stood staring at the office desk. He smiled very faintly.

"I see. Well—I suppose you will give me a day or two to think it over."

Mr. Hoad's glasses glimmered at him.

"Certainly. Take till the end of the week."

As Keir went out, he met a young man coming towards

[183]

the door of the office. The young man was wearing plus-fours, and stockings of some audacity. He was a good-looking, solid, self-confident youngster and obviously not the type that is given to introspection. He had good teeth, blue eyes, an easy laugh. He was the sort of man who went about with his hands in his pockets and took life as it came.

The young man nodded at Keir.

"Morning."

Keir was not in a mood to respond to the easy friendliness of so cheerful and serene an extrovert. He was full to the lips with a sense of his own frustration.

"Morning."

His response was abrupt. It made him appear sulky, when he was only self-absorbed. The young man smiled and went into the office. He was Mr. Edward Gott, the new member of the firm, known to his intimates as Eddie. He smiled at Mr. Hoad. His facile smile could include even the prim fussiness of the senior partner.

"Morning. Afraid I'm a bit late."

Mr. Hoad had so far rationalized young Gott that he could address him as Edward. Mr. Gott hung up his hat. He had a head of hair that possessed a natural wave that many young women might have envied.

"Who's the chap I met going out?"

"Keir Smith, our foreman carpenter."

"Looks a bit of a Bolshie."

The cataloguing of Keir as a Bolshevik appeared to amuse Mr. Hoad.

"Oh, not quite that, Edward. A little temperamental. Yes, I think that is the right word."

2

The day was strange to Keir. It was as though some

essential and vital process had been arrested in him, and his hands were the hands of a fumbler. He walked slowly across the yard to the door of the carpenter's shop and hesitated before entering it, for into that familiar building he would carry his feeling of frustration and of failure. There were other men working at the benches, and they would watch him hang up his coat and put on an apron and become once more Keir Smith the carpenter. No doubt they would gloat a little over the return of the prodigal, the fellow who had been bucking around seeing that other fellows did their jobs.

He had to compel himself to enter that shed. His assumption of nonchalance was too sharp in the edge. He was conscious of being scrutinized for a moment by those other men. He went to the corner where the coats hung, and as he took off his coat, he was sure that the eyes of the carpenter's shop were levelled upon his back. He faced about sharply and surprised two of the men grinning at each other. The fools!

Well, anyhow he was top dog in this little corner of the world. He spoke brusquely.

"They are waiting for those window frames. Any of them ready?"

The information such as it was, was presented to him. One of the men grumbled at the quality of the wood. It was warped, and the timber-merchant's machines were both sanguinary and obsolete. A firm that sent out deal planed as they planed it ought to be forcibly liquidated.

"The damned muck wastes a chap's time."

Keir took possession of the bench that had been his. He was looking at the same tarred fence and the top of the lilac bush, but old Tower with his mild, bald head was beside him no longer.

"Pass over some of the stuff."

He was back at his bench, but both his hands and his

head were different. Almost he felt incoordinate and clumsy, a botcher, because the soul of him was distraught and disjointed. Even the shavings that littered the floor irritated him. They got under his feet. And in pegging a tenon he split the mortise, for his movements were rough and harsh.

He swore.

"Who sent us this — pulp?"

Someone laughed.

"Some old shake-merchants. I reckon it was growing in Russia this time last year."

Besides, did not Keir know that the tradition of the firm had changed? They were cutting costs. Mr. Hoad was out for economy. If old Samson had been a stout sort of putlog, Mr. Hoad was a lath, and pretty whippy at that.

The day dragged on. It was full of ineptitudes and of exasperations. Even the work came cross-grained to Keir's hands. His head was full of other vexations. He was going back to "Merrow," a "Merrow" that was mortgaged. He was going back to tell Sybil that he had been slapped back into the old pigeonhole. All their plannings together, their dreams, were like the chips and the sawdust under his feet. He was just a man at a bench, and should he decide to quarrel with that bench, some other man would soon occupy it. He had to conform to the crowd complex. There was a boy in him that could have wept and a little dethroned god who raged. He was striking a chisel handle with a mallet, and chips flew. Yes, and in the more up-to-date shops the craftsman's place was taken by the machine, machines that sawed and planed and grooved, even a machine that sandpapered the shorn product. Life itself was a mere mechanism. He had tried to escape from it, and he had failed.

But as he cycled home on that summer evening, he realized himself as one of the crowd. Hundreds of other workers on bikes were streaming through the main streets of
Kingham and distributing themselves into lanes and side
streets. They were the corpuscles in the great organism's
blood stream, and necessity pumped them to their labour
or to their homes. They just circulated, and because Keir
was feeling a little afraid of life and its vicissitudes, he
became conscious of the man in all those other men. He
understood their passions and their dreads, their envies
and their prejudices, their resentment in the presence of
too much success. He supposed that many of them did not
think too deeply, and it was as well, for it seemed to him
that no system of thought could produce the material
Elysium that would mollify the multitude. The less a man
fretted, the more simple his demands, the less conscious
he would be of the frustrations and the failure. Baccy and
beer. Certain of their own intellectuals might curse their
own crowd and accuse them of being stupid swine, but there
may be virtue and wisdom in such stolidity. The inevitable limitations of the crowd community cannot be thrown
down like fences. The circumscribing and ordering of life
become more complex and complete.

The bitterness of the day was chastened for him, because
this fear of the future was upon him, and when man is
afraid, he draws nearer to his fellows. In the Abbey Lands
road he fell in with a neighbour, that Mr. Brown—a clerk
in the Borough Council office, whose three children had
provoked Sybil into quoting him as a prophet. Mr. Brown
was a delicate and round-shouldered man who took life
and his work with a kind of gentle seriousness. He was
black-coated, industrious, and no rebel.

Mr. Brown remarked upon the badness of trade. He

happened to know that a part of Kingham was finding it difficult to pay its rates.

"One's lucky to have a settled job. Yes, and a bit of garden. How are your potatoes doing this year?"

Keir liked this other man. There was a quality of quiet courage in Brown, and Brown had three children. Often Keir had seen that worried look at the back of Brown's eyes. It made him think of a troubled child looking out of a window on a wet day.

"Oh, pretty well. I'm afraid my wife's the gardener."

"Yes, you're one of the lucky ones, Smith, if I may say so. Same here. I married a friend, not a cheap cinema fan. How some chaps manage these days I can't imagine."

Keir was riding on the outside. He felt protective towards Brown.

"Well, they don't. I've seen something of the inside of some of the new homes."

"I suppose you have."

"We have to go into them in the way of work. Silk stockings and a dirty sink. Tinned salmon and the bath all slimy. If a girl loathes housework and can't cook—"

Brown's eyes lit up. He was one of those creatures who found his own mate the core and creator of his world of sentiment.

"Yes, pretty hopeless. Tell you what—I'm jolly grateful to a woman who backs you up. It isn't all jam for a girl. Kids, yes. No joke, but it's worth it—if you've got a philosophy."

They arrived at the gate of Brown's cottage in the lane. He too had a mortgage and a life insurance to keep him thinking.

"So long, old chap. I've got to cut the grass."

Mr. Brown swung himself off his machine, and Keir smiled back at him.

"Always the grass!"

"Yes, always the grass. But after squatting in a chair, yes, it's a contrast."

Keir rode on. He felt that the humanity in the other fellow had warmed him. This other man had worries. Well, of course. One ought to remember such things. It was possible to become too self-centred and to regard oneself as the only fly stuck on the fly-paper. Brown was a wholesome, kindly chap in spite of his three kids, or because of them. He was fond of his wife. He had not let himself go sour.

Keir, dismounting at the gate of "Merrow," found Joanna Mary waiting to waylay him. She had to be lifted up and plumped upon the saddle of his bike. He trundled her as far as the shed.

"Where's mummy?"

Joanna pointed to the end of the garden where Sybil was down among the early potatoes exploring the produce of the first root with a fork. She was counting the tubers. They were not very large, but Sybil was satisfied.

"Oh, Keir—there are thirteen. Not so bad."

He teased her.

"Thirteen! Can't you find another? I don't like thirteen."

She took him seriously. She thrust in the fork, and turning up the soil, she did discover one rather minute tuber like the last small pig in a litter.

"Fourteen!"

Keir's eyes dwelt upon her in a particular way. She was a lovable creature, and he was lucky. Holding Joanna Mary by the hand, he went across and took the fork from Sybil.

"I'll put it away for you. Here, let Jo have No. 14. How many little pigs went to market? What, you don't know, Jo? Your education's been neglected."

He was provoked into posing as a philosopher. The day had been full of bitterness, and at the end of it there was a jest on his lips. He was looking at fourteen young potatoes in the hollow of his wife's apron. He was carrying the fork for her and holding Joanna Mary by the hand. What a picture of domestic devotion! And yet the facile sneer was absent, and if he could smile in the face of his fate, he was somehow more than a little, flippant self-analyst in trousers.

In his wife's eyes he divined the question that she had not asked. "What news?" With Joanna Mary between them he walked with her up the garden path. His face looked smoothed out. He was contriving to transcend the bitterness of the day's happenings.

"I'm back in the shop."

He was aware of her quick, comprehending glance. For an instant her mouth looked poignant. She was wounded for his sake.

"At the old bench, Keir?"

"The one I used to tell you about. With the black fence and the lilac bush to look at."

The set of his head was gaillard.

"I felt quite fumble-fisted. It's just a bit of life. One's not unique, you know.

She said nothing, but when they came to the back door, he met the steadfast fondness of her eyes. She both smiled and yet did not smile. There was more than mere understanding in her eyes. The dear comrade in them cried out to him, applauding and proud and tender: "You're brave. You've taken it—as a man should. If you had been just bitter and hard and angry—I should have felt sad. But you're not. You're bigger than that. Oh, my dear, I love you."

He smiled at his wife.

"Thanks, Syb. It's good to be with someone like you just now."

4

He chose to remain at his bench.

For when he had considered his crisis, he acknowledged that there was no reasonable alternative. He might have marched out upon his dignity and applied for a job elsewhere, but in Kingham such opportunities were limited, and he was tied to Kingham by "Merrow." Possibly there were five or six other firms in Kingham who could employ him, but not as Messrs. Samson, Hoad & Gott employed him.

As for setting up in an odd-job business of his own, he realized that so questionable an independence was beyond his resources. He had obligations and no fluid capital. He could not afford to rent a little shop in a back street and hire labour and put up a board and wait. It was not in him to go touting round Kingham as a little man who could perform cheaply the repairs and redecorations of other little people. He had some knowledge of what that kind of life could offer. For three months you might be worked to the bone, and your profits be less than the wages of an employee in a well-established firm, and for the next three months a drought would prevail, and life be an affair of potatoes and bread and margarine and weak tea.

He submitted and endured.

If there was any bitterness in him, he concealed it. He was once more a man among men, his little brief promise of authority withdrawn, his future much as theirs. Moreover, there was born in him during those difficult days a feeling of fatalism. His chance had perched and flown. It would not return.

He faced the facts calmly and those other men, watching for signs of revolt and for the sulkiness of a conceit that had been chastened, were disappointed. He came and went among them and worked with them as though he had known no other world or dreamed of no other accomplishments. He was the Keir Smith of two years ago, but less aloof and seemingly more cheerful. They divined in him that which a more understanding observer would have described as dignity. Being plain fellows they confessed in the vernacular that Keir had guts.

If life had handed him the medicine, he had drunk it down without a grimace, and in a little while they ceased from exchanging significant glances behind his back. They thought of him as Keir, and not as Mr. Smith. He too, calling them by their Christian names, was received into the fold of their unprovoked goodwill.

Chapter Sixteen

1

So Keir looked out of his window and saw the black fence and the lilac bush, and if he bent forward over the bench and looked obliquely through the glass he could see the door of the office, and perhaps the figure of Hoad or Gott emerging or entering. A particular pane of glass in the window produced in Mr. Hoad's figure characteristic distortions. It made him appear even more long and meagre; it gave him a kink in the middle.

Mr. Hoad was not gaining in popularity. His mean little face, his pince-nez, and his tubular legs were somehow an offence to the men. They called him the "Parsnip," and the word was almost a pictograph, for Mr. Hoad was cultivating parsimony, a carefulness as to costs. He was very polite to the men, and they loathed him for it. Had he dared, he would have cut wages, but, being no swashbuckler, he made a flank attack upon the firm's expenditure. Being too much a coward to initiate an assault upon the material status of his employees, he raided his materials. Messrs. Samson, Hoad & Gott began to use cheap timber, poor paint, castings that were made abroad; and the men grumbled. Mr. Hoad had the soul of a swindler. He was jerry-built himself, and the taint would out.

"Old Sam wouldn't have stood for it."

Keir was at one with the men. Old Samson had put his stout and ruddy self into his work, and the reputation of the firm had been built up on good concrete, and it was with a kind of sardonic interest that Keir observed Mr. Hoad's prevarications. His specifications were imposing. The best timber was budgeted for, but if there was no architect to overlook the job, Mr. Hoad economized. He was a breeze-block man, an importer of cheap, foreign-made doors. If he could put in glass of light weight, he put it in. The paint-shop became known as the "dope hole."

As for Eddie Gott, he was cheerful, easy, go-as-you-please. He was neither very thorough nor very experienced. His fundamental interests lay elsewhere. He drove girls about in a highly coloured and swanky little car and could be seen at "The Ace of Hearts" at five o'clock in the morning eating bacon and eggs after a night of adventure. Yet the men liked him. He symbolized physical success. He was just what so many of them would like to be, a chap with money, a card, a fellow who could dress up and play hell with the girls.

Yes, Eddie was all right. He was not the kind of man who would have scamped his job so far as materials were concerned. He would not have prostituted the paint-pot. But Hoad! A slimy little —, and not so relevantly virile as the vulgar epithet implied. A spot of grease, a louse. And in some curious way Mr. Hoad's stinginess permeated the whole concern and began to suffuse it with unrest and suspicion.

Keir, more sensitive than his fellows, was quick to divine disturbance in the atmosphere. The firm of Samson, Hoad & Gott was still a non-union business. In the old days the men would have said that they knew where they were with old Sam. In a sense they may have preferred his downright solidity to the coruscations of a demagogue like Mr. Sparks. But Hoad was not Samson. He spread suspicion, an elemental mistrust, a feeling of niggardliness and fear. He affected the men in somewhat the same way that a windy officer worried the troops in the trenches.

Keir, listening to fragments of conversation, knew that the firm had become an unhappy ship, not only because the chief was showing himself to be a bad shipmaster, but because his crew distrusted him as a man. Also, it became known that the firm was losing credit and, what was more serious, contracts. If Mr. Hoad had shown himself a successful pirate, much might have been forgiven him, but as one of the workshop wits put it: "He's the sort of chap who ought to be driving a third-rate hearse. What's worse, we're the corpse inside of it."

Their discontent had to sublimate itself. Mr. Samson had said that the British working man was the best in the world, but that he was apt to be an awkward beast if you got him sulky, and Keir, meeting Mr. Sparks outside the yard gates, found the fellow unexpectedly affable.

"Hallo, Keir, how's life these days?"

There was a whimsical invitation in the official eye, but Keir was cautious.

"Might be worse."

Mr. Sparks lit a cigarette.

"Might be much worse.—You take me? There's a bit of a breeze in the air."

He eyed Keir obliquely, for according to rumour Keir might prove to be the firm's one and serious nonconformist, and if so, Keir would be in the minority of one. Mr. Sparks, like all men who are ambitious in their own particular calling, might and did regard Keir's conversion as a *tour de force,* a possible flower in the official buttonhole. He edged up familiarly to the occasion.

"Between you and me—there's a situation."

Keir understood him.

"For you?"

Sparks gave that characteristic flick of the head.

"Now, be fair. I'm just the man's man, that's all. I'm a sort of figurehead. We're not satisfied. Get me? When an employer starts messing a business about—"

Keir watched Mr. Sparks's eyes.

[195]

"You can't tell an employer how he is to run his business, can you?"

"Oh, can't we! We can make things a bit interesting for him. Now, look here, Keir, you must know what sort of stuff you are handling."

"Yes—I know."

"Well—that's not—O. K., is it? The men are fed up with the show. You think that over. You're a straight one. You ought to be with us."

Keir smiled.

"And we can present each other with gold watches and illuminated addresses! As a matter of fact—the old boy was as straight as an oak post."

Keir's smile appeared to spread to the face of the official. Sparks was not a bad chap, and when he was not pushing his program upon the public, he could betray a sense of humour, and in the not very far future Keir was to forgive the other fellow his shiny chin and little black moustache and his air of rather cheap infallibility. Teddie Sparks was human.

"Yes, that's right. Old Sam was so straight and stiff that it was no use trying to put a rope on him. Besides, what you say on a platform and what you think in private—"

He gave Keir a gentle dig with his elbow.

"I've responsibilities to my show. And it isn't always all roses, I can tell you. I have to put in an advert. now and again. This firm's going union."

"Solid?"

Sparks puckered up his eyes at him.

"I'm living in hope."

This was serious news for Keir. He gathered that Sparks has been sounding him, and that if the situation developed and he should prove recalcitrant, he would be a marked man. He could count on no protection from Hoad, for if Mr. Hoad was cornered and compelled to employ none but union labour, he would have no compunction about sacrificing an obstructionist. Keir would find himself extruded like a piece of grit from the machine. He could feel the crisis in the air. It looked at him out of the eyes of the men with whom he worked. One of them, a quiet fellow who was employed in the painter's shop, dropped him a hint, and Keir thanked him.

"Yes, I know, Jack. Everybody is to sign the covenant. You chaps are watching me."

"Well, you're one of us. You can take it from me that what I'd stand for under old Sam I won't stand for under Mr. Slippery."

"There's something in it, Jack."

"There's a damned lot in it. Look at the muck I have to use, stuff that won't stand the weather."

Keir smiled at him.

"Will joining the union alter the paint, Jack?"

"And why shouldn't it? Haven't we a right to get sulky over a swindle?"

Keir could detect an uneasiness in Mr. Hoad. The fellow was worried and for that reason all the more suave, and Keir suspected Mr. Hoad of trying to sound him on the situation. The soul of Keir laughed. He was not deceived by the Hoad mincings and circumlocutions. He guessed that Hoad was capable of using him as a dummy, as an argument, even as a possible ally. He would attempt to set Smith up against Sparks and to parley behind the figure of a recalcitrant Smith. Lastly, the crisis might provide him with an excuse of ridding himself of a man who was too much Samson.

Keir remained grave and aloof in the presence of the Hoad suavities. He was blind to suggestions. He gave no information and asked for none. He gathered that Mr. Eddie Gott was of no combative value in such a crisis. The younger partner would welcome an easy solution, conform, and run away to play.

[197]

Mr. Hoad became more pointed in his questions.

"Have you noticed any—discontent among the men?"

Keir put on an air of surprise.

"I'm not having any trouble in the shop. Isn't discontent a social generalization?"

Hoad gave him a spiteful look.

"There's a very awkward spirit abroad, Keir. Most disturbing. I ascribe it to the loss of all religious feeling."

Keir said: "Quite so."

In a week he knew exactly how he stood. Mr. Sparks had been able to hand Mr. Hoad an ultimatum. The firm would agree to employ union labour and nothing but union labour. Yes, the men were solid.

Mr. Hoad compromised. That is to say—he surrendered. But he took off his pince-nez and polished them.

"You say that every man in the firm is taking his ticket?"

Mr. Sparks was wearing his autocratic manner.

"Every man."

"Even—Smith?"

"Yes, I can vouch for Keir."

Hoad made a little wriggling movement in his chair.

"And supposing that Keir—? He's a foreman, you know— Between ourselves, Mr. Sparks, I rather suspect Smith of having worried the men. I'm all for peace. That's why I am ready to meet you. I don't want a disturber of the peace in my employment, a fellow who is bossy and tactless."

"Oh, Keir's all right. Besides, if he signs on—"

Mr. Sparks loved a suggestion of truculence when he was sure of his opponent's flabbiness. Mr. Hoad had better not interfere with Keir if Keir conformed. And that was that.

After the interview Mr. Sparks strolled, hands in pockets, into the carpenter's shop.

"Hallo, Keir, can I have a word with you?"

Keir left his bench and they went together into a corner

of the yard, and there the official explained the situation. He said of Hoad: "He's as artful as a wagon-load of monkeys. I've got a shrewd suspicion that he has a down on you, old man, but I have him tied up properly. If you come in, he'll have to let you alone."

He offered Keir a cigarette.

"Have one. Yes, there are good employers—and bad; and the worst are the slippery ones. I always got on with old Sam. I had no change out of him, and he had no change out of me."

Keir accepted a cigarette. He understood that he was in a corner between Sparks and Hoad, and of the two men he preferred Sparks.

"Right. Give me till tomorrow."

"I will. Look here, I can be a tactful bloke. I'll just stroll into the shop about ten. If it's yes, just nod at me."

2

The adventure of going home was becoming more and more a crowd affair, and between five and six o'clock Kingham could recall to Keir that phrase: The Solidity of Labour. Hundreds of men and girls streamed through the main streets, and this swarm of bicycles possessed the roadway. It held up the cars, ignored them, or balked them with sullen wilfulness. It might and did cast glances of hostility at the "autos" of the prosperous. It poured north, south, east, and west out of Kingham, knee to knee, and nose to tail. Its sources were various, for during the last few years the purlieus of Kingham had seen the erection of several factories. There were eddies and cross-currents, for coordination was lacking. Operatives who worked in the northern area rode south to their homes, and vice versa.

Keir had made many attempts to detach himself from

this procession and to steer a secret course of his own and avoid the convoy, but circular tours round side streets inevitably had returned him to the multitude. He had conformed, and now he rode with the crowd. He wobbled in and out with it, was carried along by it.

On that evening when the choice of conforming had been thrust upon him, he was saying to his soul: "I want to be free."

But what was freedom? Where was it to be found? Was not the very concept of freedom an illusion so far as it concerned this crowd of clerks and typists, mechanics, labourers, shopmen? There was no escape from the bench or the counter or the stool. Life had become a factory, producing articles for profit rather than for use, and man had become the slave of a system. Were a frenzy for freedom to stampede the crowd, it would find its career stayed on the edge of that bitter sea, starvation.

The socialists might provide minor ameliorations, serve out little savouries from the communal kitchen, but they too were part of the crowd. Keir had talked to men whose socialism was their credo, and he had divined in them a deep uneasiness. They might utter bold words, but in their hearts was the fear of the cataclysm. Your lips might lisp altruism, but of what use were phrases when the foundations began to quake under your feet? Work, work and food for these millions. Eden, the Golden Age! But Adam was still Adam, and no I.L.P. could feed him on tinned altruism and hot air.

Freedom, yes, a relative freedom might be possible for the few, for the masterful, the fortunate, the very skilled, the very determined and courageous. As Keir saw it, there were certain members of the community who would always command more social value. It was inevitable. As for the angelic voices, he mistrusted them. Somewhere, even in a mock social heaven, there would always be a secret golden cake.

He rode homewards with the crowd. It thinned out gradually to a trickle. It ceased when he entered the familiar lane. He rode alone to the little white gate of "Merrow," and at this gate the haunting shapes of Hoad and Sparks seemed to vanish.

He found himself kissing his wife, and as though that kiss was a seal and a symbol. Freedom! The contract of marriage. Had not the old people been wise in suffusing life with sacraments?

Could a man ever free himself from material things? Was not freedom otherwise, inward, secret and spiritual? If you could not escape into your self, and perhaps into some other beloved self, what escape was there?

He was becoming far more dependent upon his wife. He felt more at ease when he brought his problems home and laid them in her lap. He liked to talk things over with her, for in Sybil life had developed a serene solidity, a wholesome and workaday wisdom. The little, sensitive bud had opened and set its fruit. Almost, her more impatient and flippant sisters might have condemned her as the patient little ass upon whom man—the eternal egoist—laid the baggage of his doubts and dilemmas.

"Something to tell you, Syb."

They carried their chairs on to the small lawn, and on the lawn next door Mrs. Challis and her portable wireless set and two men were severally vocal. A year ago the hubbub would have irritated Keir, but on this evening he did not appear to notice the Challis world.

"The firm's going union."

Sybil had brought a basket of peas with her, the last picking from a late sowing, and she shelled them into a bowl. The bowl reposed in her lap. Keir, sitting forward in his chair, and smoking his pipe, watched her busy hands.

"Will it make any difference to your money, Keir?"

"No, I don't think so. One just resents being tied up."

She raised her brown eyes and looked at him just as she looked at Joanna Mary.

"Yes, you like to be master. You're so very proud, you know, Keir."

He smiled at her and accepted her decretal. Her first question had been that of the domestic economist primarily concerned with the fundamentals of housekeeping. She had become a very capable economist, and yet he believed that she could understand his dislike of all coercion. "Merrow" itself was an experiment in individualism, a protest against Paragon Place and too much propinquity.

He said: "It's a question of being able to call your soul your own. You can't when you join a caucus. You have to swallow all the bunk, and shout the class catch-cries. You've got to cheer when some loud-speaker is let loose on a platform and bawls out a lot of stuff that you know to be nonsense. This freedom! The machine has to go on working. We're told we mustn't do this and we mustn't do that, or you are given the tip to slow up the machine. Or we are dragged out on strike when most of us only ask to be left alone. It's all so damned silly."

Her hands shed green peas into the basin. She looked at his dark and rebellious head with an air of benign understanding. Men were such children. They became excited over politics and theories, just like a mob of boys playing football with no referee to decide on the points of the game. They shouted and argued.

"Does it matter very much, Keir?"

"Matter!"

"Well—I mean—there's so much more. Or—I should say there was so much more. Can't one look on a trades union and all that as a sort of workshop? When you put on your coat and come home—"

He gave a toss of the head, and a laugh that was almost

soundless.

"That's just what I've been coming to. After all, life's relative."

"Relative?"

"Oh, that's a word they use a good deal now. If one's pigeonholed as a worker, one need not be pigeonholed as a man. All those chaps who go to London and sit in offices, well—in a sense—they are just as much tied up as we are. We all live under the eternal autocrat—necessity."

She emptied the last pea pod.

"Just as it was in the Bible, Keir. God made Adam—"

He held his pipe at arm's length and looked at it.

"Yes, Jehovah! We've got our Jehovah still, my dear, whether we call ourselves deists, or rationalists, or socialists, or just—scientists. Life's all coercion—in a sense—though we try to cheat ourselves with phrases. We may learn to dodge a few bricks. We can adapt."

His wife smiled at him.

"Did Adam grow green peas—like ours?"

He was quizzed, and he quizzed her in return.

"Could you teach Eve a thing or two about cooking? I guess you could. One shouldn't froth too much. There's too much froth about most of us these days."

Chapter Seventeen

1

IN the latter half of August the Smith family went for a week to Ramsgate. A heat wave had made a sudden appearance, the temperature was eighty-five in the shade, and Joanna Mary was sick in the train. The third-class carriage held its full complement of five a side, and poor Joanna spilled herself over her mother's holiday cretonne frock.

"Oh, my dear! Quick, a handkerchief, Keir."

Keir saw that Sybil was much more sorry for Joanna Mary than for her own frock. Even the heat and the catastrophe could not spoil her temper, and Keir hurried to assist as best he could. On the whole the carriage was sympathetic, though a fat and florid elderly man who was sitting beside Sybil edged off and covered his knees with a newspaper. A motherly person next to Keir reft half the newspaper from her husband's knees and crumpled it into an improvised basin.

"Poor little soul, it's the heat."

Keir had taken Joanna from her mother, and he and the kind person attended to the crisis while Sybil tried to clean her frock. Moreover, Joanna's front needed attention, and the motherly person sacrificed her own handkerchief. Joanna, none the worse, and feeling herself to be the centre of attraction, could yet apologize like a small gentlewoman.

"So sorry. It—would—come. Oh, poor mummy's frock!"

Eventually the improvised basin was ejected from the window, and the two soiled handkerchiefs were wrapped up in a piece of newspaper. Sybil was assuring the motherly person that she would have her handkerchief washed and returned to her if she would give her—Sybil—her address.

"There's no occasion at all, my dear. You're very welcome. You give that frock of yours a sponge directly you get in."

Sybil was flushed and grateful.

"But do give me your address."

"We're going to Ramsgate."

"So are we."

"No. 5 Victoria Terrace."

"Now, isn't that a coincidence! We're going to No. 3."

Joanna, returned to her mother's lap, smiled solemnly across at the motherly person. She approved of the motherly person. She wanted to repay kindness with kindness.

"I've got a bucket and spade. Have you got a bucket and spade?"

"No, my dear, I haven't."

"I'll lend you mine."

The stout lady leaned across and kissed her.

"Now, isn't that sweet?"

At Ramsgate station Keir man-handled their two suitcases. No need to waste money on an outside porter. Joanna insisted on carrying her own impedimenta. The motherly person and her florid husband were taking a taxi. What with the heat and adipose tissue, a taxi was inevitable; besides, they had a nice little greengrocery business in the Essex Road, Islington. They offered the Smiths a lift. It was accepted for Sybil and Joanna and the suitcases, but Keir insisted on walking. He would not crowd them up. But later, when he was unpacking in the No. 3 back bedroom, and Sybil was sponging her frock, he confessed that there was a great deal of kindness in the world, and Sybil agreed with him.

"Yes, there is. I do hope this won't stain."

Joanna was watching her mother.

"It was dirty of me, wasn't it? But it would come."

"Yes, darling, you couldn't help it."

Keir laughed.

"Well, that's rather my view of life."

No. 3 Victoria Terrace asserted that it possessed a view of the sea, and certainly by squeezing yourself against an upper window you could obtain an oblique view of the ocean, just a glistening strip of it stretched between the chimney stacks of Prospect Terrace and the bulk of the Palace Hotel. This was of no great import, for the sea was there; it could not escape, nor could all the children in the world have removed Ramsgate sands. Keir's was the delight of introducing Joanna Mary to the sea. The heat had upset Sybil. She woke with a disastrous headache and decided to stay in bed till lunch on two aspirins and a cup of tea, and Keir had to attend to the toilet and the dressing of Joanna. It was a gorgeous day, with a light breeze to temper the heat, and when Keir and Joanna arrived on the sea front, Joanna stood holding her father's hand and looking at the sea.

"Where does it stop, daddy?"

"Down there."

"No, the other end. Does it go on for ever and ever?"

"Bits of it—right round the world."

"It must have given God a lot of trouble making it."

Keir was amused and touched. Poor God! He was muchly responsible. And from below came a babel of voices, like some multitudinous bird song, joyous and incessant. The sands were stippled with colour. Humanity was sunning itself. The sea was coming in, and hundreds of wooden spades were busy. Keir and Joanna found a sloping way and a series of steps, and when the sands were gained, Joanna bounced up and down on fat and exultant legs.

"Oh, isn't it—lovely!"

The cry might have been her mother's.

Keir and the child found a claim that had not been staked out by other families. The bucket and spade were brought into action. They began with sand pies, but that was a mere kickshaw. Joanna grew ambitious. She wanted a castle, a mound with a moat round it to defy the incoming sea. Other children were building castles, and Keir took off his coat and laid it on the sand; he got busy with the spade. Joanna assisted, scooping up sand with the bucket. Her little face was solemn and flushed and moist.

"It's coming up, daddy. Dig, dig."

Keir threw up a mighty mound, and presently the little swishing waves began to lap the glacis. Keir and Joanna stood on the summit like a couple of Canutes. Man's handiwork crumbled, and when a large section of the mound flopped into the water, Keir picked up Joanna and carried her to safety.

"That's what happens when you try to stop the sea, young woman."

The sturdiness of Joanna was not convinced. She was an optimist; she wanted to begin all over again, but her father was warmer than she was, and he sat on his coat and lit a pipe. Joanna, squatting down beside him, took off her shoes and filled them with sand.

"I've got Ramsgate in my shoes, daddy."

"You won't find Ramsgate very comfortable when you try to walk in them, my dear."

Other children were paddling, and Joanna wanted to be in the fashion; so when Keir had finished his pipe, he took off his socks and shoes and rolled up his grey flannel trousers. Joanna had prepared herself, and, imitating her father, stuffed her white socks into her small shoes.

"Oo—it tickles!"

They played games with the sea, daring Father Neptune to come on and scurrying back when he threatened to come on too thoroughly and souse Joanna's petticoats. Keir enjoyed himself. He had not enjoyed himself so much for a long time. He felt like a kid, with the problematic part of himself pleasantly discarded. He thought how much prettier Joanna's pink feet were than his rather knobbly ones. What a pity it was that life could not stay all pink feet!

At No. 3 poor Sybil's headache continued in spite of aspirin and a half-darkened room, and she decided to remain in bed for the rest of the day. Joanna and her father went down again to the sea, and, since the tide was out, Joanna captured a very small crab. It was put in the bucket with some seaweed and water and carried back to No. 3 Victoria Terrace as Joanna's offering to her mother.

"I've caught you a crab, mummy."

Sybil's headache was better, and she could pretend that the small crustacean was the most marvellous of creatures. It spent the night in the bucket under the wash-hand stand, and next day it was returned to the sea. For Sybil was softhearted even towards crabs, and she explained to Joanna that the crab was but another Joanna, and that the crab's mother would be feeling anxious and distressed, and that the baby crab was homesick.

"We must be kind to crabs, Jo."

Joanna Mary agreed with her mother. The crabling had had a night out and had enjoyed free board and lodging with the Smith family. With great solemnity the bucket was carried at low tide to a shallow pool, and the crab returned to its native element.

Joanna watched it walk away.

"Do you think it will find its mother, mummy?"

Sybil was quite sure that all would be well with the crab world. She believed in being very sure with children. She had often declared to Keir that children should be taught to believe in things. Keir had not asked her to define and catalogue her "things." If Jo continued to believe in her mother, and perhaps in him, she would not grow up a little

[208]

domestic cynic, and that was about as far as his faith could carry him.

2

It might have been said of Keir that he belonged to three different generations. He was his Victorian grandfather, his Edwardian and rebelliously rational father, and his neo-Georgian and contemporary self. Had he been asked to choose between the three, he would have elected to look upon the world of men with the eyes of his comfortably credulous grandfather. His memories of his father and of his father's rather snarling reasonableness were not happy ones, for the elder Smith's world had been founded on too much Huxley and political economy. And Keir's contemporary self was so modern in the shrug of its shoulders. His father had been so very sure that all religion was sacerdotal humbug, and somehow his iconoclasm had satisfied him. Keir, having no religion, would sometimes yearn for a God, for a revelation that would renew the martyrdom of man and give it passionate meaning.

He had come out alone and had walked along the harbour wall. The sun was setting, and he paused to lean against the wall. The holiday crowd was promenading; fishermen were preparing to pack up for the night. His nostrils were full of the smell of the sea. He was not very conscious of all those other people, mothers and fathers, children, young men and girls to whom life was largely the adventure of sex. It was a noisy and a cheerful community. It did not stand on the edge of the unknown and challenge the unknowable to manifest itself.

Keir remembered his small daughter's question.

"Where does it stop, daddy? Does it go on for ever and ever?"

His eyes were whimsical and sad, for like a young child

[209]

he was in a mood to ask just such questions, and there was no father to answer him. What was the thing called life? Had man been just a fortuitous emergence from green slime? And whence the slime? Did anything that man experienced—matter? Eat, drink, and get money, behave like a cheerful, organic creature, laugh and sneer by turns. Cultivate a serene, superior flippancy! Was that the ultimate and only posture, or did man hang on a cross and cry like Christ: "My God, my God, why hast Thou forsaken me?"

And suddenly Keir was afraid of the sea, and of the darkness that was spreading out of the east. A little, chilly wind seemed to paw him with clammy and contemptuous fingers. He turned towards the town and its lights. There was man, man and his dynamo, and his high-tension wires and his pubs and his noise, his shrimp teas and his cinemas. The human show. What could you do but submerge yourself in it, swim with other fish in the behaviorist aquarium?

He walked back to Victoria Terrace. He walked fast, like a man hurrying home on a bitter and bewildering night. He wanted light, even electric light, and drawn curtains, and the faces of those other creatures who were familiar to him.

He found Sybil waiting by a window. She had just put a very tired Joanna Mary to bed.

"Oh, Keir—I was feeling a little lonesome."

"Were you, kid? Well, what about it?"

"Let's go to the pictures."

They went.

3

That was the last Smith holiday before the slump.

As a matter of fact, the weather had long been gloomy in the north, and Lancashire had ceased to think for those soft and sluggish southerners, perhaps because in the old days cotton and cerebration had been the products of slave labour and of a bald-headed complacency. King Coal was weeping sooty tears. The steel industry had become a painted lath. Certainly, gramophones and wireless sets continued to sell, and the output of small motor-cars mounted and mounted, and people were found who would finance dirt-tracks and greyhound-racing.

The depression moved south. Possibly the effects it produced were patchy, and a borough like Kingham was not in the bottom of the trough. Trade statistics made gloomy reading, with exports shedding millions every month. Prices tumbled. The experts commenced the eternal wrangle upon over-production and under-consumption.

Creators of enterprise were worried, labour inclined to be suspicious and sullen. If Mr. Sparks was asked for his views, he put on his platform manner and blubbered his chin.

"It's a vast ramp. They're preparing an attack on wages. Not a penny off the pay, you chaps, or a minute on the day."

Keir found Mr. Sparks's truculence frothy and unconvincing. Rumour had it that the firm was losing contracts. Mr. Hoad might send in ingenious estimates and undercut his competitors, but somehow the Hoad policy was not paying. Though prices were falling, Mr. Hoad's customers may have discovered the poor quality and texture of the firm's product. It became obvious to Keir that work was short, and he could watch the men spinning out their jobs and so assisting in the firm's undoing.

Hoad went about with an air of emaciated apprehension. You could imagine him sitting up like a hungry rat and trying to sleek out his whiskers. But adversity was driving him out of his rat-hole, the office. The pay-sheet and the output did not balance each other. The men were going slow; paint-brushes lingered lovingly; ladders were very much ladders. Mr. Hoad's head with its glimmering glasses would appear unexpectedly in the doorway of the carpenter's shop, apologetically suspicious, and one morning he caught one of the younger men smoking.

Mr. Hoad screamed.

"Put that pipe out."

The voice was a new voice. It had lost all its suavity.

Mr. Hoad was greatly excited. His lower jaw quivered. He looked almost as white as his collar.

"You can't work and smoke. What do I pay wages for?"

He snarled at Keir.

"You're responsible here, Smith. Get a move on, get a move on."

And then, as though his chattering rage had exhausted itself and given place to fear, he banged the door and fled. The offender had removed the pipe, but when the door had closed, he stuck it back in his mouth.

"— little ape."

Keir said nothing, but went on with his work. He was becoming a sceptic in the matter of the spoken word. The opposing factions handed each other words like the pieces of a puzzle that did not fit and were not meant to fit. "Increase production"—"We're not going to be pushed to provide you with profits"—"Wages must come down"—"Smash the capitalist." The silly wrangle both saddened Keir and worried him. He began to believe that man's only education was necessity. Nor was he sorry for Hoad. Hoad was as much in need of education as were the obstructing operatives.

Sometimes he had to cycle past the Labour Exchange in Elm Road. The queue was increasing, trailing along the pavement and spreading into little, sullen groups. Men out of work, men on the dole, old men and louts, decent fellows and social spongers.

Would he ever be in that queue? Hanging about at street corners, sneering at people in cars, suspicious, disgruntled, and growing perhaps cynical and callous. "— the —. Tax 'em to death. What's the use of a Labour Government if it can't skin the swine?" Yes, bitterness, ugly looks, suspicion, sodden boots.

He began to watch and wait for the inevitable hand to glide in and pluck one of the men from the carpenter's shop. One Friday it appeared. He of the pipe had received his ticket and his *congé*. He came in looking white and savage.

"I've been stood off."

There was silence in the shop.

"Hard luck, Alf."

"Hard luck be —. The — little swine has a down on me. It's victimization. I'm going to see Ted Sparks. He'll put it across the blighter."

And then, suddenly, he grabbed a plane and with a sweep of the hand sent it crashing through the window.

"By God, I wish I had a Mills bomb. I'd chuck it through the little — window."

4

Two weeks later six other men were discharged by Messrs. Samson, Hoad & Gott; two painters, a bricklayer and his labourer, a plumber's mate, and another man in the carpenter's shop.

Keir was left with a fellow named Hobbs, one of the quiet sort who was a steady worker. Hobbs had a sense of humour, and a wife and five children, and perhaps because of them his sense of humour ran in harness.

"We're two of the tame ones, Keir. We've got Whipsnade all to ourselves. Yes, it won't be you."

"Why not me?"

Hobbs was planing down the edge of a board. He had thin and hairy arms, and a hollow chest. He paused to clear the plane of a chip.

"Oh, you're a fixture. You cost a bit more than I do, but then I've got no head for shaping a big job. Seen Alf since he was stood off?"

"No."

"Ran into him at the 'Chequers' last night, full of beer and blasting-powder. He was cursing Ted Sparks. There's no sense in that sort of foolery."

Keir agreed. He was discovering that however nicely a trade-union organization might weave its restrictions, it could not compel an employer to hang suspended in a void. Caught in the complexities of material circumstances, Mr. Sparks was as helpless as the men. He had interviewed Hoad and protested against operatives' being discharged, and to satisfy him Mr. Hoad had produced figures, a profit-and-loss account that was incontestable.

"I'm not a charity organization. The work's not there."

It wasn't. Psychologically the community—or that part of the community that provided employment—was in a negative mood. All expenditure was being postponed. Those who had bank balances were sitting on them.

Mr. Hoad was both bitter and pathetic.

"What can I do? What can you do? Go on pushing and you'll have the whole social scheme on its back. Well, smash us. What good's that going to do your people? Oh, yes, I know, that's the idea in some quarters. Make business impossible for the employer and then oust him and take over. But just how much would there be to take over?"

Keir saw the tragedy as Hoad saw it, but from a different angle. While the community was arguing and squabbling about an abstraction known as surplus value, the reality was drifting away. Everybody was so intent on squeezing a sponge that the limitations of a sponge appeared to be forgotten. Meanwhile necessity waited with a spear and a jar of hyssop.

Chapter Eighteen

1

In the autumn conditions were so bad that Mr. Gott senior intervened, and since he had been proposing to build a series of six cottages for some of his employees, he decided that the occasion was propitious. Prices were down; Samson, Hoad & Gott were a skeleton firm in more senses than one, and Mr. Gott had his land, a semi-derelict market-garden on the outskirts of Kingham.

Mr. Gott was a stout little man with a large head and a large face. In appearance he suggested Italy. His temperament was both shrewd and flamboyant, and his hard-headed optimism inflated its cheeks and blew upon the pessimistic Hoad. As for the slump in trade, he chose to regard it as a necessary and nasty emetic which a swollen-headed democracy would be compelled to swallow. A lot of raucous idealism and socialist rot! The community needed a purge.

He would say: "Yes, let 'em get into a thorough good mess. Bad trade! Well, what do you expect? Taking money from the guinea man and passing it to the twopenny man. There's no margin about the twopenny man. Yes, let's all go on strike. No wages for a couple of months. Everything in cold storage. They might begin to think a little and stop squinting down their silly noses. All this penal taxation, and squandermania on social bunk? What's the use of having a gramophone in the parlour if your larder contains three cold potatoes?"

Mr. Gott was a good employer because goodwill is a business asset, but he had no illusions as to the angel in man. A slack sentimentalism encouraged the slacker. He preferred a red-capped communist to the Uriah Heeps of a saccharine socialism. You knew where you were with the complete pirate. "I want your cash. Pass it over." Yes, the Russian idea, the cult of the truculent young man. A corrupt and capable clique coercing the many. It was nothing so new, nothing to get excited about. If that very vain old man Mr. Shaw went to Russia and had his beard buttered, was one to regard it as part of a wonderful new dispensation? Mr. Gott had begun life as somebody's butler. He knew both Goodwood and Epsom. If society was founded upon economics, and the whole of finance rested upon credit, why credit mortal man with all sorts of immortal and transcendent qualities which he did not possess? It was just silly. You might get the sheep to follow you in imaginary Elysian fields, but what would happen when the mirage melted and your flock found itself pastured in the Sahara?

Such was Mr. Gott's attitude towards industry, and it was the attitude of thousands of other Gotts, and though it placed itself on the right-hand side of the Via Media, it was perhaps a more practical posture than that of the gesturing gentlemen of the Left. He had invested "Eddie" and two thousand pounds in the firm of Samson, Hoad & Gott, and when the shares fell, Mr. Gott thought it time to "average." The firm needed a contract to keep its men and its workshops in action, and Mr. Gott would possess six new cottages built at a very reasonable figure.

The work began in October. Labourers were busy cutting foundation trenches in a soil that sustained the ghosts of innumerable cabbages. It was a dreary piece of ground, surrounded by the back gardens and yards of cottage property, that was not far removed from the purlieus of Paragon Place. It had a view of the Kingham gasworks, and when the wind was in a certain direction, it smelt of them.

Keir's participation in the building of this row of cottages did not become out-of-door and active until December. He was kept busy in the shop working upon window and door frames and the skeletons of staircases, but by the middle of December No. 1 cottage was ready for the carpenters. Keir went straight from the comparative warmth of the shop to the raw cold and sizzling bleakness of a north-east wind. It was a particularly unpleasant December, and he had not been tempered to it.

Up among the new timber he worked with a pull-over under his coat, and his collar turned up. His fingers felt as cold as the nails they had to handle. It was a depressing scene, grey sky, drab buildings, the bulk of the gasometers, the squdge of the derelict garden, all the debris that accumulates when building is in progress, puddles, mud, oozy heaps of clay, planks, messes of mortar. The rawness got at his bones. He seemed to be suspended in the sky for every northern draught to blow upon.

The men were sulky and depressed. They had to stodge through much mud. The local wit christened the site "Wypers." Sometimes there would be two or three days of frost, and the bricklaying would be held up. To vary the program it rained. Keir went home with a wet jacket, which was hung to steam in front of the kitchen fire. He could not swear that it was a beautiful world, and that working on a roof in December symbolized the dignity and solace of labour. But there it was. Both Mr. Hoad and Mr. Gott were pushing the job. Costs had to be curtailed, and the men kept busy.

Sybil fed her man well. She even inculcated into Joanna Mary an appreciation of her father's importance as the mainspring of the domestic machine. Sybil did not question the values of marriage. She did not belong to the very young school that appears to regard marriage as the most disgusting and indecent of relationships and, while denouncing the fug and the sordidness of the double bed, is quite

[217]

prepared to go to bed with **any** casual man who appears to be convincingly male.

"Hang up father's coat, Jo."

Jo herself got into the way of feeling Keir's coat and insisting upon his shedding it.

"You're wet, daddy."

Keir would deliver up the sodden garment to Joanna, and the small creature would hang the coat over the back of a chair.

But Sybil was worried about Keir. He came home looking drawn and tired, and there were times when he was irritable. It was as though those cottages in their sea of squelch filled him with nausea. Much of the timber was sodden and pinched the saw. Always you were working at a disadvantage, in the wind or the rain.

"Will you be on that job much longer?"

"Most of the winter, kid."

"I call it silly to build at this time of year."

Keir agreed as to the silliness of the business, but it was both business and necessity and Gott.

"We'd be stood off but for this job. It's the first decent contract the firm's had for six months."

"But you can't get on, can you, in the same way?"

"As a matter of fact, we do and we don't. A chap will slog in to get warm, but there's something in him that grows chilled. And old Gott's a pusher. He's round there most days stimulating us through Hoad."

He laughed.

"And I might have been in the firm, strolling around in an overcoat watching other fellows work! Hoad's almost pathetic."

"Pathetic!" Sybil had no sympathy for Hoad.

"Yes, he'd like to scream at the chaps, and he daren't. He just goes around nibbling at them. He's not the man for a tight occasion like old Sam would have been."

Sybil found fault with Keir's waterproof. It was old, and it had ceased to be proof against the weather, and its collar was greasy and discoloured.

"You must have a new waterproof, father."

"Can't afford it, old girl."

"We've got to afford it."

Sybil had a small hoard saved gradually from the house-keeping. It had been intended for emergencies and Christmas presents, and this was most certainly an emergency. She took Keir out shopping next Saturday evening and bought him a new mackintosh at an outfitter's in the High Street. Almost she treated Keir like a boy. She assured herself that the garment buttoned up properly round his throat and gave adequate protection to his knees. Some of the silly things had too few buttons and flapped open below in a wind.

She made Keir turn round.

"Yes! It's quite a good fit on you. How about the sleeves?"

"Just about right."

She paid for the coat. It was done up in brown paper, and Keir carried it home.

2

On the Tuesday before Christmas a snarling north-easter made work on the roofs of the cottages a bitter affair. Keir had two men with him and he brought them down and put them on the joists and struttings and floors of cottage No. 1. They were more protected here, though the wind made the shell of brickwork cold and draughty.

Mr. Hoad turned up about ten, wearing a muffler and looking pinched and worried. He was annoyed when he saw no one at work on the roof. Old Gott had been rude to him the day before and had said quite plainly that Hoad could not manage his men. He, old Gott, had caught two of them smoking in the temporary shed that was used for cement and tools, and old Gott had exercised sarcasm. "I suppose you count that as skilled labour. Must be a pretty tough job smoking a pipe." Hoad minced through the mud, walking on his toes. He found Keir and the other carpenters at work inside cottage No. 1.

"Why aren't you up on the roof, Smith?"

Keir was feeling cussed and in no mood to be snarled at.

"We've been up. The wind cuts your head off. I thought we'd get on better down here."

Hoad had been dared to exercise authority, and he was angry.

"Damn it, messing about where no one can see you. That roof has to be on by the New Year. Get on with it."

Keir went white.

"It's not safe to put the chaps up there. Your hands get so — cold that you can't hit a nail. I suggest you go up the ladder—"

Hoad squealed. Nostrils and lips nibbled. The cold had pinched up his nose, and his glasses were perched awry.

"I gave you an order. That roof—"

"You can give the order yourself, Mr. Hoad. I'll go up, but you can speak to the men."

His attitude was aggressive. He gave Hoad a look that said: "Damn you, all right—I'll go. I'm up to it—but you —you miserable little bit of chewed string—you wouldn't stay up there five minutes." He took a hammer and a bag of nails and went aloft, leaving Hoad shivering and outraged. Hoad watched Keir's legs ascending the ladder. He was moved to shout at him.

"All right. You'll be put off at the end of the week."

But he did not give Keir notice, for one of the other men was in no better temper than Keir.

"I'm not going up there today, gov'nor, and that's that. It's not safe."

Hoad blinked at him and suddenly became suave.

"Well, perhaps you're right. You'll get on faster under cover. It is rather bleak today."

The man spat. Bleak indeed! Why didn't the little — go up and freeze? And Mr. Hoad, with a conciliatory grin, called up to Keir.

"All right, Smith, carry on down here."

But Keir was angry, and with an anger that was stubborn and recalcitrant. He remained on the roof. He would show Mr. Hoad that he was afraid neither of the wind nor of employers. He hammered nails as though he was hammering heads.

"All right. I'm up. I'll carry on."

He remained on the roof all the morning, and by one o'clock the north-east wind had blown the wilfulness out of him. He was chilled to the marrow; even his stomach felt cold. And suddenly he was scared. What a fool pride was this that let itself posture upon a roof on such a day, because a fellow like Hoad had spoken to him saucily! Supposing he had got himself badly chilled and had to lie up? As he came down the ladder, his hands hardly felt the rungs. His face looked harsh and blue.

In cottage No. 2 the men had a fire burning in a brazier and were sitting around on planks. Keir joined them. One of the carpenters made room for him. A bricklayer's labourer was boiling water for tea.

"You look a bit tucked up, mate!"

"And no wonder. What did you go up there for, Keir?"

"Oh, he just got me cussed."

Keir went close to the brazier and bent over it. He felt that he wanted the heat of the fire in his cold belly and chest. His hands were numb, but hands did not matter.

"Little swine! Did you see the way he gingered it through the mud?"

"Just like a girl with her Saturday-nighters on. He's only

fit for a draper's shop."

The bricklayer's labourer was pouring out tea. He came to Keir.

"Get your mug, mate. You look as though you wanted something hot inside you."

Keir sat on one of the planks near the brazier and drank hot tea and ate the lunch Sybil had put up for him. A part of him was growing more and more attentive to the cold void in his belly. He waited for the hot tea and the food to warm him, but instead of warming him they aroused a kind of nausea. He began to shiver. He did not finish his meal.

All the afternoon his stomach felt heavy as well as cold. His chilled vitals had refused to deal with the food, and about four o'clock he knocked off work and went home. He managed to reach the gate of "Merrow" before the growing nausea overcame him. He was helplessly and incontinently sick in the front garden.

3

Keir spent his Christmas in bed, and the soul of "Merrow" was harrowed and distraught. Sybil and Joanna Mary had transferred themselves to the spare room, and Joanna Mary spoke in whispers. Daddy was very ill, oh—terribly ill. If you listened outside his door, you heard a strange sound, a frightening sound, Keir's panting, avid breathing. He coughed, and between the coughs there were little groans. To Joanna it was a Christmas of strange terror, of hushed gloom, and of the comings and goings of the doctor and of a rather pert young woman in uniform. It seemed to Joanna that her mother's eyes grew as big as saucers, and Joanna's eyes matched her mother's. Mumsy was sitting up at night with daddy, and during the day her mother would lie down for a couple of hours on the bed in the spare room, and Joanna would keep very still.

Once she surprised her mother in tears. Sybil was washing some crockery, and her weeping was silent. She dried cups and saucers and plates, and her eyes were wet. The small soul of Joanna was stricken. She stood and stared at her mother. Her chin began to quiver, and suddenly she caught hold of her mother's dress and pressed her forehead against Sybil's thigh.

"Mumsy mustn't cry."

"Oh, my dear!"

"Daddy's going to get well. I've asked God. So God will make daddy well."

Sybil dried her eyes with the first thing that came to hand, the glass-cloth. She bent down and kissed Joanna.

"Yes, daddy—must—get well."

But for some days both doctor and nurse were doubtful as to the event, and it appeared more than probable that this might be Keir's last Christmas on earth. Neither the nursing nor the medical profession includes teleology in its textbook, and Joanna alone was in conjunction with God. Nevertheless Joanna and her transcendental friend proved themselves potent. Keir came safely through the crisis. He ceased to be smothered by his own juices. His breathing was stilled. For days he had been a bemused, burning abstraction, with a dry tongue and cracked lips, but half-conscious of the individual thing called Keir. Daily he had been aware of Sybil, and a thirst, and the spout of a feeding-cup, and his labouring chest and cracking head. Once more he was man, feeble, at the mercy of his pillows, but able to space out the rhythm of things and to think. He became aware of the radiant but haggard face of his wife. Strange combination! Her eyes were like tired ripe fruit about to fall.

"It's been a near thing, kid, hasn't it?"

"Oh, Keir—"

Almost she broke down, and caught herself, and put herself back upon the pedestal. She wanted to sleep. Her desire for sleep was overpowering.

"It's all right now, Keir."

His eyes dwelt upon her.

"You were here all the time, weren't you?"

"Most of it."

"Funny, you know, Syb, but one night when you were sitting there, you had two faces. Everything seemed double."

She laughed, and her laughter was the tingling of a tense wire.

"The doctor's been awfully good, Keir. He says you may see Jo tonight."

"How's Jo?"

"She's been a perfect angel."

"Like you."

"Oh, Keir, don't be silly. I just—"

"Look here, old girl, what you want is ten hours' sleep. Go and get it. I'm all right."

"Yes, Keir."

"Oh, by the way, heard anything from Hoad?"

Her tired face hardened.

"He's never been near the place, Keir. He just sent a lad one day to ask—"

Keir smiled strangely.

"Little swine!"

But Sybil was able to tell him that several of the men had been to inquire, and so had young Mr. Gott. Yes, people had been extraordinarily kind. Mrs. Brown had offered to come in and do the cooking for her, or to take charge of Joanna Mary. The world was not a bad world, and if Mr. Samson had been alive, matters would have been very different.

Keir made a little restless movement.

"Have you seen about drawing my insurance money?"

No, she hadn't. The finances of "Merrow" had been left in abeyance. Their credit was good, and she had run up bills.

"Yes, I'll see about it, Keir."

"If you want any ready cash, I've three pounds in a tin behind the books. Top shelf."

"No, I can manage, Keir."

He put out a hand, a rather tremulous hand.

"You've been wonderful, Syb. I'll be at work again in a week or two."

Chapter Nineteen

1

NEARLY a month passed before Keir returned to work. Meanwhile "Merrow" had to exist upon Keir's sick benefit and upon his savings, and at the end of this period the savings were *non est*. Dr. Gibson had told Sybil to feed her man well, and Sybil gave Keir meat twice a day and a glass of hot milk in the middle of the morning. The financial problem would right itself when Keir went back to work, though Keir knew from experience that in Mr. Samson's day the business might have been handled very differently. In the case of a valuable employee it had been Mr. Samson's custom to pay during sickness full wages for a month. He had said that it was worth it even from a business point of view. It gave the workman a sense of security, made him feel that he was something more than a mere "hand"; it inspired goodwill, and increased output.

On the Thursday before the Monday when he resumed work, Keir walked into Mr. Hoad's office. They had not met since the morning when Hoad had lost his temper and Keir had carried his up to cool on the roof. Hoad happened to be alone in the office. He looked over the tops of his pince-nez at Keir. If he had any reason for discomfort, he carried it with a veneer of geniality.

"Good morning, Smith. Glad to see you about again."

Keir was exchanging no compliments with Mr. Hoad. The collar of his black overcoat was turned up to his chin, and it emphasized his pallor. He had not removed his hat. There was a kind of dark dignity about him, the austerity of a man who had been ill.

"I suppose the job's open?"

"Of course, Smith, of course. Glad to have you back. How are you feeling about work?"

"I can start on Monday."

"Good. You had better have a week or two in the shop. There are some joinery jobs in."

"Right. I'll clock in on Monday."

That was all that passed between them, though Keir had travelled to the edge of the dark waters and returned from them, and Mr. Hoad was supposed to be a religious man. He did not like Keir, and he had behaved rather ungenerously to Keir, which made him like Keir all the less. Keir was so suggestive of the Samson days and of the firm's heroic period, and the present was proving itself exceedingly prosaic. The press and the prophets were preaching economy, and the public were denying themselves both interior and exterior decorations. The world's front door would last another year, but the firm of Samson, Hoad & Gott might not survive twelve more such months. It could not afford to be sentimental or to indulge in magnanimous gestures. "And after all," as Mr. Hoad reflected, "I have been considerate to the fellow. I have put him under cover for two or three weeks."

On Monday Keir went back to work, and though he had been walking five or six miles a day to get himself fit, he found that first day in the shop a trying business. He was flabby. The place was stuffy and hot. There seemed to be no air in it. He found himself sweating. His muscles had lost their tone, and after an hour's work he felt that his back and legs had gone.

Moreover, the atmosphere was charged with fine dust, and presently he began to cough.

"Let's have the door open, Fred. There's no air in here."

Fred opened the door and looked at the back of Keir's

[227]

neck. It was very thin, like the neck of a man who had been starved.

"You're not quite up to it yet, mate."

"First day—I suppose."

"That's it. When I came back after my operation, I felt like a bit of jelly. Lord—by one o'clock I was all swimmy."

But Keir continued to cough, and the irritation that caused the cough seemed to rouse in him other fretfulness. The place was full of sawdust. The men had not been so thorough with the broom during his absence, and with sudden petulance he got hold of the broom and began to sweep the floor.

"You haven't cleared up the place."

His interference made matters worse. The sawdust, disturbed by the broom, distributed its finer particles through the air and aggravated Keir's cough. He had to go into the yard to escape from the dust. He walked up and down in this cleaner air, and Mr. Hoad, coming out of the office, found Keir taking what appeared to be a morning breather. Hoad did not remark upon it, but his meagre little face was not friendly. This might be Keir's first working day after his illness, but was it necessary for him to stroll about the yard when there was a warm shop to work in and other men who needed supervising?

Keir returned to the shop. The dust had settled, and his cough did not trouble him again that morning, but in the afternoon he was attacked by a spasm of coughing. There might have been hot sand in his windpipe, and again he had to go out into the fresh air. He felt acutely depressed and worried.

The other men exchanged comments.

"It's the dust."

"Well, you can't expect anything else, can you, in a shop like this? He'd be better out of doors."

At the end of the week Keir came to the same conclusion.

[228]

The dust in the shop continued to irritate his chest. To begin with, the cough had been a dry one, but in a few days expectoration was coming up into his throat. He swallowed the stuff. He could not spit in the shop, and by going to the door to spit he would make the other chaps think him fussy. He was worried. Already he was exercising concealment, not only before his fellow workmen and his wife; he was pretending to his secret self that the thing was not serious. It would pass.

Sybil was troubled about him.

"You're still coughing, Keir."

"Oh, just a bit. The dust in the shop sets me off. I'm going to ask Hoad to let me be outside for a month. He can put me on the cottages."

He was not eager to ask a favor of Mr. Hoad, but knowing how utterly vital a working man's health is to him and to those dependent on him, he muzzled his pride and asked to be put back on the cottages.

Hoad looked surprised and slightly suspicious.

"I thought you would be better indoors."

"I think it's the dust. I'm quite fit to take charge again at the cottages."

Mr. Hoad was searching for some ulterior motive. Worry had turned him into a creature of universal and furtive distrust. Was Keir suggesting that the firm's workshops were unhygienic? They were the same as they had been in Mr. Samson's day. Or was this the beginning of other official interference, a hint that would develop into a demand for a dust-exhausting plant? Absurd and profitless expense at a moment when times were so critical.

He thought it best to humour Keir.

"All right. Get back on the cottages."

He observed Keir as he went out of the office. Yes, the fellow looked drawn and delicate, and sickly employees were an embarrassment. Keir and his temperament had

[229]

always harassed Mr. Hoad. He preferred workmen who were more stolid and eupeptic.

2

But though Keir went on out-door work, his cough remained with him. To begin with, he tried to smother it and to ignore it, or to assure himself that it was one of the after-effects of his illness, and that when the warm weather came, it would leave him. It was just a winter cough, and dozens of working men suffered from it. You had only to look at the pavements on a raw morning and notice those disgusting grey-green blobs of sputum.

But Keir was afraid of his cough. He became more and more convinced that the trouble was not a mere affair of the throat or larynx, but that it was deep within him. He noticed that he was short of breath when riding his bicycle up a hill or climbing a ladder. He had no pain in his chest, nothing but a sense of uneasiness, as though some vague and malign thing had settled there and was devouring him. The expectoration continued, and sometimes he would go into the lavatory and peer down at the stuff he had spat into the pan. It looked like glutinous wads of dirty cotton-wool.

At night he would be disturbed by the cough. He would try to fight it back so as not to disturb his wife, but the thing refused to be suppressed.

"You must go and see Dr. Gibson, Keir."

"Oh, nothing to worry about. It will clear up all right when the spring comes."

His appetite grew squeamish. He found himself flushing after meals, and there was a sense of weight under his ribs. He was conscious of the beating of his heart. In fact he was becoming abnormally conscious of himself as a body that was strangely and disturbingly out of health. Almost, he listened at the door of his physical self as though dreading to

[230]

hear some new and frightening disharmony.

His working day became oppressed by an increasing lassitude. He tried to whip himself up to the job, only to find that the old verve was not in him. He tired so quickly, and towards the end of the day he would be dragging himself about those cottages like a very old man. He was pursued by a dread that refused to be disregarded. It followed him to work in the morning; it went home to bed with him at night.

He would say to himself: "It can't be right that I should feel like this."

He went home exhausted. It was as much as he could do to put his bicycle away in the shed. He was sensitive and touchy about himself. He would carry into the cottage a face that was both haggard and falsely cheerful, and sit down in one of the arm-chairs and try to be playful with Joanna Mary.

There was one evening when he surprised his wife looking at his reflection in the mirror over the mantelpiece. He knew that she was looking at him. It was as though she had a secret of her own or had discovered his secret.

He was irritated.

"What's the matter, Syb? What are you staring at?"

She turned away.

"Oh, nothing."

But a moment later he caught her looking at him in the same strange way, and her eyes seemed to express his own secret fear. He saw her flinch. His face had betrayed resentment.

"What's the matter? Anything funny about me?"

She went to the cupboard to take out the tea-things.

"You shouldn't get so tired, Keir, should you?"

"Can't I sit in a chair for five minutes?"

"Of course, dear, if you want to."

Keir kept up the semblance of health for a few more

days, and then one night he woke up in a furious heat. He was sweating. The perspiration was soaking his pyjamas and the sheets, and associated with this physical distress was a sense of impending disaster.

He felt his wife's hand touching him.

"Keir, you're all wet. You're soaked."

"Yes. I woke up like this."

She was out of bed and at the light. She opened a drawer and found a clean pair of pyjamas.

"You must change them. You'll get chilled. And, oh, Keir, you must go and see Dr. Gibson tomorrow."

He struggled out of the wet sleeping-suit. He had begun to shiver.

"All right, kid. I will."

3

It happened to be one of those rare and halcyon days in spring when Keir went to see his doctor. Dr. Gibson lived in Church Street in a Queen Anne house whose red brick was the colour of a softly tinted autumn leaf. On a green gate a brass plate bore the words: "Surgery. Hours: 9–10, 6–7." A bricked path led to the surgery door, and at the end of a path a very old plum tree was in flower. Keir could not help noticing this mass of white blossom, and its beauty and its significance caused him a sudden spasm of pain. The sky was very blue above the flowering branches, and somewhere a blackbird was singing, and the voice of the bird was like the voice of his own lost, passionate youth.

He rang the surgery bell. A maid opened the door. She looked old and faded and sad, and so unlike that tree. She showed Keir into the waiting-room. There were five other people sitting silently on kitchen chairs.

They were strangers to Keir, and he had to wait for some forty minutes before his turn arrived. The waiting-room

had one big window looking upon a back yard and the doors
of a stable, and in the yard a chauffeur was washing a car.
The man had a thick, red neck, and muscular forearms,
and Keir sat and watched him and envied him his health
and his strength. Two women were bending towards each
other and talking in whispers, and though he was aware of
their voices, he paid no attention to what they said. The
walls of the room had been distempered a pale green, and
the colour seemed to tint the faces of the waiting patients.
One of the men appeared to have trouble with his breathing, and every now and again he would draw in a deep
breath and let it out with a long sigh. There was infinite
melancholy in this sound of distressful deflation.

Keir looked at his watch. Four of the other patients had
come and gone, and the man who sighed was with the doctor. Keir felt his suspense like a length of tightly coiled wire
in his belly. He got up and walked round the room. He
stood at the window and watched the chauffeur polishing
the radiator of the car. The man had the stump of a cigarette stuck between his lips.

The breathless patient came out of the consulting-room.
He did not look at Keir, but took his hat from a peg and
went out.

"Next."

Keir heard the doctor's voice, and with a curious jerk of
the head as though the summons had startled him, he passed
through into the inner room. Dr. Gibson was sitting at a
desk jotting down some details in a case-book. Keir had
closed the door and was sitting down in the patient's chair
before the doctor turned his eyes on him.

"What—you—Smith?"

"Yes, sir."

"I hoped I had settled you, my lad. What's the trouble?"

"A cough."

"Oh! How long have you had it?"

[233]

"It came on when I went back to work."

Keir was aware of the doctor observing him intently. Dr. Gibson's eyes were pale blue and they seemed to stare, but their stare was intelligent.

"Let's have your wrist."

Keir's heart began to beat hard and fast while the doctor was feeling his pulse. He felt curiously tense and breathless.

"Any expectoration?"

"Yes."

"What's it like?"

"White, woolly stuff, sir. And last night—I woke up wet through."

The quality of the doctor's stare seemed to change. It was as though he divined this other man's distress and, in divining it, discovered pity.

"Have you lost weight, Smith?"

"I don't know, sir. I think I'm thinner. I can't manage the work as I did."

Dr. Gibson pushed back his chair.

"Right. I'll have a look at you. Yes, I want you stripped to the waist. Put that blanket over you."

Keir removed coat and vest, collar, tie, and shirt and fastened his braces round his middle.

"Come and sit by the window. That's it. Now, breathe."

Keir's chest rose and fell. He looked at the window, whose lower panes were filled with frosted glass. His eyes were anxious.

"Any pain?"

"No, sir."

Dr. Gibson began to palpate and percuss his chest, and the touch of the doctor's hands had a peculiar and soothing effect upon him. He raised his head higher. He looked through the unfrosted upper panes of the window and saw blue sky and the edge of a white cloud. His heart had ceased to beat so loudly.

Dr. Gibson reached for the stethoscope on his desk. He listened to Keir's breathing, and his face came close to Keir's, and Keir's eyes remained fixed on the edge of the white cloud. He was conscious of a quickening of his suspense. The doctor kept moving the mouth of the instrument from one place to another, but presently his attention seemed to concentrate itself on a point a little below Keir's right collar-bone. And something in Keir began to tremble. He was sure that the doctor had discovered a whisper of doom, some crepitant confession of fate under that patch of skin.

"Take a deep breath."

Keir breathed deeply, and Gibson's intent and listening face seemed the face of his fate.

"Now cough, and draw a deep breath."

Keir was trying not to tremble, for suddenly he had felt cold. The examination was over, and the doctor had passed behind Keir's chair. He sat down at his desk, and there was silence while he made a note in his case-book. To Keir the silence was like the holding of breath under water while the whole of your body craved desperately for air. If there was anything wrong, why didn't Gibson tell him?

"You can dress, Smith."

Keir struggled into his shirt.

"I shall want a specimen of your sputum. I'll give you a bottle to spit into."

Keir stood buttoning his shirt, and his fingers fumbled.

"Is there anything in my chest, sir?"

Gibson looked him straight in the face.

"Yes; I'm afraid there is."

And suddenly Keir understood. The shadow that had been pursuing him became a reality, a solid and menacing presence standing close to him in the room. He fastened his braces and put on his collar and tie. He felt cold, and his throat stiffened with a kind of anguish.

"You may as well tell me the truth, doctor. I've got to face it."

Gibson answered him very gently.

"I'm afraid it's phthisis, Smith. When your sputum has been examined and reported on, I shall— Hold up, man. Sit down. Put your head between your knees."

For Keir's world had gone black. He clutched at the chair and sat down in it. He felt the doctor's hands pressing his head between his knees.

"I'm sorry, sir. Just a bit faint."

"Stay like that, Smith. I'll get you something to drink."

A minute later Keir was sitting upright in the chair, and holding a medicine glass in his hand. His face was ghastly, but he managed to smile.

"Better now, sir. I'll take my medicine— I suppose there's some hope?—You see—I've got a wife and kid."

The doctor took the empty glass from him.

"I know, Smith. It's an early case. There is always hope for an early case. Just sit there for a while, my lad. There's no hurry."

Chapter Twenty

1

KEIR managed to walk back to "Merrow." He saw the little white house and the big beech tree against the tranquil blue of the evening sky, and here too a blackbird was singing. A gate, a path, that familiar green door, and yet Keir's small world had become strangely unreal. Both his hands and his belly felt cold.

Sybil had been waiting, and watching for him through the window. She would not let herself hurry or allow that the occasion contained any element of distress. Keir had walked home, and if a man could walk nearly two miles at the end of a day's work, nothing very serious could be the matter. She went to the front door, opened it, and stood to meet him.

But when she saw his face and particularly his eyes, her hope and her courage seemed to cling together for comfort. He smiled at her as a man smiles to cover up some deathly pain. Almost his eyes appealed to her like the eyes of some shamefully wounded creature. He was beyond mere self-pity. It was as though he came humbly to this comrade, conscious of himself as a creature of bankruptcy and disaster, the bread-winner who was broken. Almost he seemed to fear secret reproaches.

She winced. She seemed to press her hands to her courage as she might have pressed them to her breasts.

"You've been, Keir?"

How futile the question sounded! Again he smiled at her, that wounded, defensive smile.

"Yes. Not very good news, kid."

He saw a shocked fear possess her face. It passed, just as though she had put up a hand and brushed it away. Her eyes grew deep and tender.

"Oh, my dear!"

She put an arm round him. They stood in the little passage, just inside the door, and suddenly he hid his face in her bosom. His hands rested on her shoulders.

"Kid—I'm sorry. You won't be angry with me, Syb?"

She trembled. She folded her arms over his head and pressed it to her.

"Keir! My dear, tell me—"

He broke down. He spoke brokenly.

"It's my chest.—You oughtn't to have married me. I'm no more good."

She was both agonized and exalted.

"My dear, my dear, don't— You mustn't—say—I married you because I loved you, and I'm loving you— Oh, my dear!"

And suddenly he began to cough, and in the thick of the spasm he threw his head back and to one side and thrust her off. His face looked all twisted.

"Keep away, Syb. Mustn't cough in your face. I've got death in me."

She stood back against the wall, her shoulders pressing against it.

"I'm not afraid—"

He was leaning against the opposite wall, his face averted.

"The doctor says we mustn't sleep together. It's like that, Syb."

And then they looked at each other across the passage and were silent, for there was a sound of some small mechanism being trundled along the garden path. Joanna Mary was the possessor of a toy wheelbarrow in which she collected stones and weeds, and Jo had been busy in the back garden.

[238]

Sybil's eyes questioned Keir's. He nodded. He had ceased to cough.

"All right, mother. She needn't—"

Joanna and her barrow appeared. She stood there looking in at her mother and father. She wished her labours to be appreciated.

"I've got all these stones, daddy."

Keir played up.

"So you have. What's the idea?"

"That nasty hole in the path where the water gets."

"Going to fill it up?"

"Yes."

"That's splendid."

She trundled her barrow on up the path, and Keir, feeling that her intervention had somehow restored him to a sense of reality, followed her along the path and watched her empty her load into the pot-hole. Her sturdy legs straddled the occasion, and he, with a little whimsical smile, spread the stones with his foot and trod them in.

"We could do with another load, Jo."

She regarded her handiwork with stubborn solemnity. She had expected the load to fill up the cavity, and it hadn't.

"I must find more stones, daddy."

"Yes, you'll have to."

She set off for the back garden with her barrow.

Keir went into the house and sat down by the fire. He could hear Sybil busy in the spare bedroom, and presently she came in with sheets and blankets and hung them to air before the fire. Keir drew his chair aside so that there was room for the bed-clothes. He felt much more calm and sure of himself now, and a little ashamed of the scene in the passage. There could be too much anguish in such emotion; both of them had been rent by it, and both of them were glad of each other's calmness.

Sybil stood by one of the chairs on which she had hung

the clothes. Her right hand lay along her cheek. Once more she was the solid little mother of the house confronting feral fate.

"Did Dr. Gibson say—?"

Keir's eyes remained fixed on the fire.

"He is having my sputum examined. That's the proof of the pudding. But I think he is pretty sure."

She drew a deep breath.

"You won't be able to go to work. Of course—you mustn't go to work. Will they send you somewhere?"

Keir nodded.

"A sanatorium. I've got a good chance—he thinks—but that's not what's worrying me, Syb. You and Jo have got to live."

She moved to his side and laid a hand gently on his shoulder.

"That's just what you mustn't do, Keir, worry. We'll manage somehow. Other people have to manage."

The window was open, and from the path between gate and house came the sound of Joanna's small barrow, and the rattle of stones as she emptied her second load on to the path.

2

The bacteriological examination of Keir's sputum proved positive. The bacillus of tubercle showed under the microscope as little rods stained red; but when Dr. Gibson broke the news to Keir, Keir took it calmly. He had not expected a reprieve.

He sat holding his hat. His eyes seemed to be looking into the future.

"What's to be done about it, sir?"

Dr. Gibson told him that he must go into a sanatorium, one of the County Council sanatoriums, and as soon as possible. Unfortunately the accommodation was inadequate, and there was always a waiting list, but he would try to get Keir into "Pinehill" at the earliest possible date. Meanwhile Keir must live in the air, sleep with his window open, take as much good and simple food as he could eat, and prepare to fight the disease.

"Your own body has to do it, Smith. It's a battle between your own tissues and the bug. It may sound a rotten thing to say, but try to keep cheerful."

Keir twiddled his hat.

"Couldn't I do a little light work, sir?"

"No."

"We've got to live. One's insurance money won't keep three people. Then—I have a mortgage on my house."

The doctor understood.

"It's pretty hard on you. Why not ask the mortgagees to grant you a moratorium? If they are decent people, they might be willing to do without their interest for a year."

"It's a building society."

"Well, try them. Even a society may have a conscience."

"How long will it be before the sanatorium can take me?"

"It might be six months. I'll do all I can to get you in earlier."

To Keir it seemed a rather hopeless business, but the doctor had urged upon him the essential sanity of hope. He must fight, and he was ready to fight, for he had others to fight for. He went back to "Merrow" and, looking into the eyes of his wife, told her the whole truth.

"It's up to us, Syb. We're both alone in the world. We have no one to help us."

Sybil was strangely calm.

"How much money shall we have?"

"Fifteen shillings or so a week."

She was sitting at the table and she tapped it with the fingers of one hand as though it was a calculating machine.

Fifteen shillings, and food and coal, and rates and clothes and cleaning materials, and the interest on the mortgage! Her eyebrows drew closer together. She confronted her crisis, and not for herself alone, but for the three of them. Like many working women she was capable of supreme courage and self-negation in the presence of such a tragedy.

She said: "I shall have to do something, Keir."

He was watching her anxiously.

"Do something?"

"Yes, work. I can get housework at seven and sixpence a day. Say five days a week; that's nearly forty shillings."

"What, and carry on here?"

"Well, lots of women do it. I'm strong. I've got a bike. If you have to stay at home, Keir, you can look after Jo."

He was touched to the quick. He looked on the edge of breaking down.

"Syb—you're—well, what can I say? You're more to me now—"

She flushed and caught her breath.

"Oh, Keir—I don't mind what I do. I don't really. I just want you to get well."

A few tears showed, but they were tears of compassion and of courage.

"We might let the house, but I couldn't bear it. I love every bit of it, Keir. A woman does, you know, when she's made that way. Besides, where should we go? And you've got the garden here, and even when you go to the sanatorium, I can manage."

He got up and, bending, kissed the top of his wife's head.

"You're a marvel, Syb. I did the best thing I ever did when I married you. But perhaps, my dear, it wasn't the best for you."

She caught one of his hands and held it.

"Oh, yes, it was, Keir, it was—it was. I've been so happy."

He knew a moment of shame, for he was thinking of the

Challis woman.

"You've got a heart in you, Syb. That's better than being just clever. My dear, you're worth two of me."

"Oh, no, Keir, I'm not."

So "Merrow" prepared itself to stand a siege, and the weather was kind to Keir, for this particular spring proved to be quite un-English in the hours of sunlight that it gave to the home counties. Keir had a long chair in the garden, and under instructions from his doctor he indulged in sun bathing. He had been running a temperature at night, but after two or three weeks' rest and fresh air his temperature fell, and his cough and expectoration became less troublesome.

Sybil mounted her bicycle and rode off to call on Mrs. Lugard of Darvels. The Lugards had been in Spain, but were back in England, and Mrs. Lugard, one of those big, fair, out-of-doors women who always had to have a dog near her, had often been kind to Sybil. She had been sorry to lose the girl, and when Sybil poured out her troubles and explained her needs, Mary Lugard was able and ready to help her.

"But can you manage double work, and heavy work, my dear?"

Oh, yes, Sybil could manage it, and would Mrs. Lugard recommend her to her friends?

"You want five days a week?"

"Yes, if I can get them."

"Well, I'll take you for two. I have had nothing but trouble since you and Parsons left me. Cook is still with us. I am giving a help seven and six and her food. Will that do?"

"Oh, yes. And thank you."

There was no lack of employment in Kingham for such a woman as Sybil, and within a week Mrs. Lugard had found her work for the three other days. She recommended her to friends and explained both Sybil's courage and her need.

"She's a good girl and a plucky one."

These ladies treated Sybil very kindly.

Joanna was the one person to whom the new régime seemed strange.

"Why isn't daddy going to work, mummy?"

"Daddy's not well, dear. The doctor has told him to rest. You must not worry daddy."

Joanna looked affronted.

"Of course—I shan't worry daddy"—and she didn't. She was a child of early ripeness in the matter of understanding, a little creature of curious and sensitive sagacity. When Keir slept after lunch in a chair in the garden, she either held aloof or remained the little quietist. She did not challenge her father to play games with her. If he walked in the garden, she too walked like a sympathetic spirit, holding his hand. She even indulged in some elementary gardening of her own. She filled her barrow with weeds, though Keir had sometimes to tell her which were weeds and which were plants.

Almost, his job became the woman's job. He made his own bed and did light work about the house. When Sybil came home, she would find everything washed up, the kettle boiling, and the table laid for supper.

Keir did a good deal of reading. Mr. Lugard came to see him and brought him books.

"Ever read any of the new school, Keir?"

"No, sir."

"Well, here is a selection. I should like your views on the stuff—as a working man."

Keir read a number of contemporary novels, and the impression he got from them was one of excessive dreariness. He gathered that marriage was the most indecent and disgusting of all relationships, that all husbands had fat hands and slimy voices and sinned in secret. Young Intelligentsia had gone back to nakedness and nature. It met its desire casually in the street and went off at once to satisfy it behind a hedge. Even the hedge might be considered an insult to nature, a sort of false Victorian figment. As for the making of money, it was a base function relegated to dull and foolish and obfuscated persons called fathers. You despised them, and your scorn allowed you to sponge on the old gentlemen. You analysed the universe and your small self with a kind of cold, facetious glee. You confessed everything, even the state of your toe-nails. You were an expert in the inspecting of latrines.

Mr. Lugard had little humorous wrinkles round his eyes. The new cleverness amused him. It out-butchered the butcher. And when he sat with Keir in Keir's garden he listened to what Keir had to say, and in the main he agreed with it.

"Just like a lot of naughty children showing off."

Mr. Lugard smiled.

"Yes—I think that describes it. Universal exhibitionism, revolt and ruin in the nursery. These young things do take their breeches down, Keir."

Keir laughed. He was able to laugh that spring.

"I suppose it's amusing to begin with, sir, but surely one gets tired of going about with the tail of one's shirt hanging out. Besides, there's something to be said for braces and buttons."

"Exactly. That's what we old fusters think. A universal looseness parading as freedom isn't quite convincing. And they are so depressing, these bright young things. They know everything and nothing. They are so old and withered."

Keir said: "Isn't it just the pose of a clique? What strikes me about the people who write these books is that they know so little about the real people, people like us. Most of the world has work to do, and that keeps it—rational.

We haven't time to trouble about being clever."

Keir had other visitors, Mr. Sparks among them, a Mr. Sparks who left his platform manner outside Keir's gate, but who could not refrain from agitating. What were the doctors doing? As for the lack of accommodation in the sanatorium—it was a social scandal. But of course when the Socialist Party obtained a clear majority, it would remedy the omissions of the rich. It would be the privilege of property to pay.

Keir found Ted Sparks rather tiring. He was so profligately positive in spite of gluts and trade depression and the necessities of man's human nature. He lacked sense of proportion. He paraded all the stock phrases as though they were performing mice, and Keir, during those weeks of idleness, was busy feeling and thinking. He had begun to understand that right feeling might be more important than a lot of soft and pulpy cerebrating. Life was both relative and unexpected. It was neither a cabbage patch nor a card index. He was seeing life more as a flux, a trammel of tendencies, and not as a rigid system in which social man was listed and pigeonholed.

Mr. Hoad he saw not at all, though Mr. Hoad did send his clerk to express sympathy and to discover whether Keir could be regarded as a more or less permanent absentee. When Sybil heard of the incident, she gathered up her indignation and went to interview the firm's chief.

"I suppose, when my husband is cured his place will be open to him?"

Mr. Sparks had tackled Mr. Hoad on that very question, and Mr. Hoad was ready to promise anything for which he could not be immediately called to account.

"Oh, certainly, Mrs. Smith. If your husband is discharged from the sanatorium in good health, we shall hope to see him back here."

The prevarication was there, ready for use if necessary.

Sybil carried the news back to Keir.

"I've seen Mr. Hoad. He promised that your place should be kept open."

Keir smiled at her gently, for Sybil was still very unsophisticated in her faith in the world of Hoad.

3

But Keir's chief concern was his wife. In a sense he and Sybil were physically sundered from each other, and yet—both spiritually and emotionally—they were nearer together.

Sybil was up at six in the morning, and she gave him a hot breakfast before she went off to her work, and she came back tired and with the bleached look of a woman who had lost blood. Keir noticed that her hands were redder and rougher, but her sweet temper did not appear to suffer. He made a point of having supper ready for her. He was teaching himself to cook.

Afterwards, when they had washed up, he made her sit down and put her feet up.

He read the paper to her, but too much reading and talking made him cough, and he was obliged to resort to the thing he loathed—his sputum flask. Always he felt surreptitious when using it. He would go out of doors or to his bedroom, and yet Sybil, because she loved him, saw nothing loathsome in that bottle.

"I met Dr. Gibson today, Keir."

"Any news?"

"He thinks you will get your notice next week."

Both of them were dreading his sojourn at "Pinehill." They had become so very necessary to each other since Keir's illness, but they spoke brightly to each other of "Pinehill." It was a house of hope, and Sybil, with her sanguine nature, would not admit defeat.

"I shall be able to manage all right, Keir. Mrs. Brown is going to take Jo while I'm at work."

"It will be a bit lonely for you, kid."

"There will be the visiting-days. I'll bring Jo with me. You know—I do feel, Keir, that you are going to get quite well."

He looked at her with deep and serious eyes.

"I want to get well. I've good reasons. Some men haven't, and that's a pity."

Chapter Twenty-one

I

KEIR received an official notice to report at "Pinehill." Meanwhile, the building society had refused to postpone the payment of interest on his mortgage, and Keir could not blame them. They might advertise themselves as dispensers of social service, but the financial system of such a concern could not be expected to adapt itself to the minor fluctuations of individual misfortune.

"It's rather rough on you, Syb."

"Keir, you're not to worry."

She packed his suitcase for him, one of the suitcases that had gone with them on that almost mythical holiday to Ramsgate. She saw that his poor pyjamas were in order, and his shirts as they should be. She shed a few tears over that packing. She was taking a day off and going to "Pinehill," rather like a young mother taking her boy to school. The Lugards were lending them their car for the afternoon, and in the car Keir found a parcel of books with a little note from Mr. Lugard. "No hurry for the return of these, Keir. The very best of luck to you."

Joanna Mary was to be left at the Browns'. They dropped her there from the car, and Keir got out and led his small daughter in by the hand. He did not kiss her good-bye, but bent down and held her face between his hands and looked long and intently at her.

"Be good to mother, Jo."

Joanna's face puckered up, and Mrs. Brown, who had some understanding of the human emotions, infantile and otherwise, picked Joanna up and carried her inside. She let Joanna Mary have her howl and, sitting on the sofa with the child, comforted her.

Joanna, wounded in her small soul, asked Mrs. Brown a question.

"Why didn't daddy kiss me?"

Mrs. Brown, being a mother, knew how poignant and posing the questions of a child can be, and that sometimes it is best to tell the truth.

"Your daddy's not well, dear. He was afraid to kiss you because—it might make you not well."

"He'll come back soon, Mrs. Brown, won't he, and quite well?"

"Of course, dear."

Sybil and Keir held hands in the car. It was high summer, a day of alternate sunlight and shadow, and to Keir, England had never looked more beautiful, and in this beauty Sybil shared. She sat close to her husband, her hand holding his with confident and consoling firmness. She might not be the Sybil of their earlier days, the mere bloom of her youth had passed; she was stouter and more solid, and her face was the face of a woman who worked. Her hands, too, were those of a working woman, and today she was wearing cotton gloves. But there were other beauties, an essential and succouring sameness, the magnanimous mood of her maturity, compassion, courage, a touching and wise simplicity.

They passed over heathlands and through pinewoods. "Isn't it lovely, Keir? 'Pinehill' is like this, isn't it?"

"They say so."

Her feeling was that no one—especially Keir—could die in such country, and perhaps he divined her feeling and answered it intuitively.

"Oh, yes, I'll get well in country like this."

She pressed her arm against his.

"I'm so glad you married me, Keir."

He felt a little choking in his throat.

"My dear—I've had the luck."

He sat and absorbed her and her significance. What was the matter with marriage if marriage could be like this? What did those raw and rancorous young high-brows know of the lives of the obscure and the simple? Superior people, supercilious people! Chuck away all compassion and loyalty and self-restraint and let raw sex be let loose like a young wench in gaudy pyjamas! As if this other comradeship could not transcend sex! And yet—! Oh, yes, he had been one of the restless fools. He had come very near to throwing his most precious possession into the flesh-pot. What would Mrs. Challis have done with a consumptive husband? Packed him up in a bandbox and sent him to hell?

He felt the pressure of his wife's arm.

"Keir, that must be it. The big red building on the hill."

There was a poignant note in her voice. It was as though the red building on the hill was a mausoleum for the living. She was to leave Keir there and go back alone.

"Yes, it looks like it. All pinewoods."

And suddenly he put an arm round her and held her close.

"Don't worry, Syb. I'll get well all right. I've got to get well."

2

Of Keir's six months at "Pinehill" no full record need be rendered.

It was his first experience of communal life as it may be lived in such an institution. He was put to bed and kept there for a while, and his bed spent most of its days in a kind of sunny glasshouse like a big veranda. The doctors presented him with an artificial pneumothorax, which in common parlance means that his right lung periodically was

[251]

deflated and made to rest. To begin with he had some trouble with his food, and his diet had to be adjusted, but at the end of the first month he was putting on weight and he had ceased to cough.

There were twenty other beds in his particular department, and twenty other personalities to be explored and suffered. Keir, as a separatist, did not take too easily to life in public, a perpetual proximity to people from whom it was impossible to escape. He felt rather like a beast in a stall and quite unprotected from other beasts' ruminatings and restlessnesses, but as the days passed, he became more accustomed to all this publicity.

He discovered the virtues of acceptance.

He accepted his neighbours, old Mr. Burk with the beard, who sucked his teeth and persisted in reading aloud from the daily paper, and whose profile was that of a goat. He found it more easy to accept the boy on his right, who seemed to lie in one long blue-eyed dream, and who smiled vaguely whenever anyone spoke to him.

He accepted the doctors and the nurses and his diet, and the various human noises at night. He realized that if you fretted life, life fretted you in return.

Moreover, if he hung on a cross, all those others hung on crosses with him, and in a little while he discovered the courage of those who were crucified. It was a patient and sometimes a cheerful community. "Pinehill" did not encourage long faces. It could be very much alive in that anteroom which opened both ways, to the world of the living and the world of the dead.

There were the visiting-days when he looked into the eyes of his wife, and Joanna sat on his bed.

"Why do they keep you in bed, daddy?"

"Because I've been naughty, young woman. But next week I'm going to be good."

His first glance at his wife would be one of anxious affection. How was she bearing the strain? Was she overworking? His grip of her hand was comradely.

"How are things, Syb?"

"I'm managing splendidly. Do I look ill?"

She didn't, and his eyes dwelt on her dearly.

"You're a marvel. They are letting me get up next week. I've put on eight pounds."

She looked flushed and happy.

"Oh—I've brought you some more books, Keir, from Mr. Lugard. He let us have the car. People couldn't be kinder."

He smiled up at his wife.

"Same here."

His promotion from being a patient was in every sense a kind of resurrection. He left his bed and walked, and walking had never seemed more wonderful. He could potter out into the "Pinehill" garden and sit in the sun and read. But he had not quite the same desire to read. Life itself was a book, reopened and recovered, and his eyes saw the world and its beauty as though they had been re-created for him. The gardens of "Pinehill" were extensive and well kept. He liked to go into the vegetable garden, where men were at work, and into the orchard. The fruits of the earth! Work! In a little while he too would be at work, and labour to him seemed lovely, for in it man expressed himself for his own sake and the sake of others.

He sat and watched a gardener scything grass. The swish of the steel blade and the swing of the shoulders fascinated him. Here was rhythm.

There were the pinewoods and their stillness and their solace. Thousands of dark tree-trunks making a mystery. Bracken played like green foam. He had glimpses of the purpling heather, and the rose mist of the willow-herb, and golden ragwort.

He carried his sputum flask in his pocket.

The foul thing remained there.

[253]

He did not need it.

He made friends. He sat and strolled and talked to other men and women and heard of their struggles and their sorrows and their endurings. On the whole, human nature showed up very well to him. It had courage, kindness.

And once a fortnight he looked into the eyes of his wife.

"Some day I'll make all this up to you, Syb."

"Oh, Keir—I'm just giving what I want to give. That's all."

3

Summer became autumn, and the apples were colouring in the orchard, and Keir was placed among the elect, those in whom the disease appeared to have been arrested. He was permitted to do a little light work out of doors. He was one of those who could say: "Yes, I'm going home. I'm one of the lucky ones." And he was one of the few.

For, in spite of all man's cleverness and scheming, there was more promise of death than of life in this house of the afflicted, and in looking upon the faces of those others who were doomed to die Keir realized how relative was man's control of the forces of nature. He might know so much of the appearances and so little of the ultimate inwardness of things. It was like watching a swallow skimming the surface of a pool, or the leaping of a fish from the deep water. There was no why and wherefore. Things just happened.

Yet, he would have said that certain happenings gave him a sense of security. Sybil's fortnightly visits were like the phases of a friendly planet whose steadfast circuit persuaded man that something was sure, something was stable. If Sybil had worries of her own, she did not bring them with her to "Pinehill." Keir did not know that all the electric bulbs at "Merrow" had successively gone on strike and that new ones had had to be purchased, or that the kitchen kettle had sprung a leak, or that the lavatory cistern was always overflowing. He did not know that another man had been making love to his wife and making it so persistently that Sybil had appealed to the police, and a large sergeant had shadowed the swashbuckler and, catching him sidling in at the gate of "Merrow," had given the gentleman a bad scaring. Keir never did know this, nor that Sybil sometimes went to bed so tired that she felt just able to peel off her stockings. She came to "Pinehill" on those fortnightly Fridays wearing a coquettish hat and an air of "All's well with the world." And the hat was not the only thing that was comely.

Keir was proud of his wife, of the appearance she made, and of the standard she set. Often he compared her to the other women who visited the place, and the comparison was all to Sybil's credit. The day was her love parade, and it owed nothing to the cinema and sensationalism. It entailed a considerable amount of preparation. Mrs. Smith had her hair waved; she manicured her hands and put polish on her rather work-worn finger-nails, and if her presence brought with it a suggestion of emotional perfume, her man was pleased.

His eyes showed it.

"You do look nice, Syb."

"Do I?"

For she was one of those women who understand that a prosaic and perfunctory dowdiness can provoke infidelity in the male. She could indulge in a little secret laugh at the woman who boasted: "I—never—powder my nose." Sybil and most of the world might have retorted: "So I see. What a pity!"

She could tell Keir that she had paid the interest on the mortgage. She had every right to be proud of the money she was earning and the way she was handling it.

"Oh, Keir, I'm so glad we didn't sell the house."

So was he, for he had every reason to suppose that he

[255]

would take up his life where he had left it. He might work short hours for the first six months. He would be a man with a scar in his lung, but, as Mr. Lugard had said to him: "The doctors tell me that lots of us have P.T. and recover without knowing the danger we have been in."

"Yes, I'm glad we didn't sell the house. You're rather fond of it, Syb."

"I love it."

During those six months at "Pinehill," Keir as a realist made other observations upon life. Occasionally he would argue with an excitable little patient whose political views were extreme, and who would point to "Pinehill" as an example of communal methods, but though superficially this crowd of consumptives might be regarded as a communal crowd, the illusion vanished when you studied individuals.

There were the doctors, and one or two of the doctors were more beloved and more successful than their confréres. There were the nurses, and there was variation in nursing-skill and in temperament. There were the patients. Keir could watch the community grading itself, separating into little cliques and classes. When there was a concert or a whist drive, certain individuals appeared to take control. The inevitable unlikeness leaked out even in such an institution as this.

Moreover, there were the grumblers, the flabby folk, and also the spongers. The opportunities for offering to share in other people's property were limited at "Pinehill," but the disposition showed itself, especially after visiting-days. Certain individuals would cadge books and other minor possessions; they tried to borrow small sums of money.

Keir was one of those who was approached by the "Pinehill" spongers. His wife came to the place looking decently dressed, and Keir somehow had the look of a careful fellow. They spun tales to him, but Keir was hard-hearted.

[256]

"Nothing doing. I'm just as hard up as you are."

One of these enterprising parasites was unmasked as the most ingenious and pathetic of begging-letter writers. He was a solitary old scoundrel with a red nose, and he wrote as the father of a family. His children were starving at home. The recipients returned these letters with inquiries to the superintendent, and the ingenious gentleman was put in the pound as a liar.

Winter came, and the garden and orchards were put to sleep, but the pinewoods remained green, and the bracken turned the colour of rust. Keir walked each day, sometimes alone, sometimes with one or two other patients who were ripening for discharge. There had been no recrudescence of the cough, and he was feeling himself to be a fit man. He had been put down for discharge early in December. He would be home for Christmas.

As the date of his liberation drew near, he became aware of an increasing excitement. He was going back to life and work and his own little corner of the world. He was very tired of communalism.

He spoke to the doctor who had been in charge of him.

"I'm grateful to you, sir, for all you have done for me. I suppose I shall be able to go back to work?"

The doctor gave him sound advice. Keir was not yet out of the wood, and his return to a working life would be on probation.

"Let's see, you are a carpenter, Smith."

"Yes. I can get out of doors, sir, a good deal."

"It would be better for you—if you could. It is most important that you should take things easy for a while. Feel your way. Don't go and tear yourself to pieces."

Keir wrote a letter to Mr. Hoad. He said that he was to be discharged in December, and that he hoped to be back at work soon after his return. Mr. Hoad replied, and his letter was nicely vague. He said that he was very glad to hear that the disease had been arrested, and the result reflected great credit upon "Pinehill." And Keir, full of the eagerness and excitement of a man reprieved, did not read between the lines of Mr. Hoad's letter or appreciate its potential prevarications.

The great day arrived on December 5th. Keir was in a holiday mood. He shaved himself a little more carefully, and with a soiled handkerchief added polish to his shoes. He had said good-bye to everybody an hour before the Lugard car arrived. He was gay, almost facetious.

"I shall have my apron on next week."

A small and kindly crowd saw Sybil and Keir drive off. Handkerchiefs were waved, though some of the leave-takers looked sad. Their turn might never come.

"You ought to have an old shoe on the car, Mrs. Smith."

Sybil laughed.

"You'd better ask my husband."

"It wouldn't be out of place," said Keir.

Never had he felt so happy. He held his wife's hand, and she snuggled up against him. She was as happy as he was. She had played her part; she was bringing her man home.

"Oh, Keir—I'm so—"

He kissed her. It was the first time that he had kissed her for months.

"No danger now, Syb. My God—I feel as though a shadow has gone. I was cut off."

She returned his kiss with ardour.

"Oh—I have wanted you, Keir. Sometimes—"

"Yes—"

"I've cried myself to sleep. I felt so lonely."

They collected Joanna Mary from the Browns', and Joanna sat in her father's lap and looked at him with solemn eyes.

"Daddy's grown quite fat."

And Keir kissed the child.

[258]

"That's a nice thing to say about your father."

It was December, and the beech tree had shed its leaves and they had blown about the garden. Sybil apologized for the garden. She had been too busy to tidy it up and tuck it up for the winter, but to Keir the little place had no blemishes. It was his. He did not have to share it with other people, and, having lived in public for six months, he was prejudiced in favour of personal property and gates that could be marked "Private."

The Lugards' chauffeur carried in Keir's suitcase. Had Keir been in a position to write "Esquire" after his name, the chauffeur would have expected a tip. Gentlemen had their uses.

"Glad to be back home, I expect."

"You bet."

Sybil had hurried in to put a match to the fire, and when Keir and Joanna Mary entered that familiar room, the flames were climbing through the coal. Joanna bumped up and down on her stout legs and shook her hair at her father.

"Mrs. Brown says I've been a very good girl."

Keir's eyes lit up.

"That's right. Nothing like blowing your own trumpet."

Sybil pushed an arm-chair forward.

"Sit down, father. You had better keep your overcoat on till the fire's warmed the room up."

She hurried away to take off her things and lay the tea, and Joanna leaned against her father's knees and made conversation. She asked Keir the most unexpected of questions.

"What is a harlot, daddy?"

Keir was taken aback. He prevaricated.

"Something you need not know about, young woman. But who taught you that word?"

"I heard Mrs. Brown say that the lady who lives next door, the lady with the yellow head, was no better than a harlot."

[259]

Joanna wondered why her father looked so strangely serious. And then her mother came into the room with the tea-tray, and Joanna saw her father look at her mother, and his face had a curious brightness.

"Same old tea-pot, Syb. That's splendid."

Chapter Twenty-two

1

ON the Saturday morning Keir walked into Kingham. He wanted to see Mr. Hoad about his return to work, and to arrange that he should work as much as possible out of doors. Kingham looked much as usual in spite of a trade slump; its shops were preparing for Christmas. Its streets seemed more full of loafers, and negligible young women, and loutish boys whom no one was eager to employ. Keir had to pass the Labour Exchange. It trailed from its door a long queue of shabby and apathetic men, and neighbouring doorways and shop fronts and street corners were decorated with them. Keir saw Mr. William Block with his back against the wall, staring with sodden brutishness at nothing. This depressed and bitter crowd sent a little shiver through Keir's vitals. The workless and the worthless! There were men who would always be worthless, and workless men who would become worthless. He was glad to get away from the crowd.

The familiar gates of Samson, Hoad & Gott had been repainted a vivid green, for the elder Gott had suggested to Hoad that it was not wise to look shabby when you were feeling down at the heels. Keir happened upon two or three of the old hands in the yard, and it seemed to him that they looked at him askance.

"Hallo, Smith, out of hospital?"

Obviously so, and yet in the eyes of these men Keir discovered unfriendliness, suspicion. It was as though they were prejudiced against him and yet were a little ashamed of this prejudice. It made them gruff and casual, and Keir wondered.

"The gov'nor in?"

"Yes. You'll find him in the office."

Keir walked in without knocking. He saw Hoad sitting at his desk. Hoad's profile became full face, and instantly Keir knew that his employer was not pleased to see him. He was welcomed with a little embarrassed smirk.

"You—Smith! Out of hospital. Sit down. When did you come out?"

"Three days ago."

"How are you feeling?"

"Quite fit."

They were alone together, but Keir did not sit down. He stood with his back to the office window and facing the official desk. Obviously, Mr. Hoad was not pleased to see him. He kept darting little uneasy glances at Keir, glances that appeared to pick pieces of fluff off Keir's person and deposit them on the floor. He fidgeted; almost he squirmed, and his fussy unrest infected Keir with an equal uneasiness.

"I thought I would drop in and see about taking on."

Hoad blinked behind his pince-nez. He removed the glasses, polished them, and laid them on the desk. Possibly he did not wish to see Keir's face too clearly.

"I'm glad you have called, Smith. I was going to write to you. Now you are here, we had better come to an understanding."

Keir remained mute. What was the fellow at?

"I'm sorry, but we have had to fill up your place."

So that was it. He was to be a subordinate.

"You mean—you have another foreman?"

"Yes."

"Well—I suppose you couldn't wait. You expect me to come back as a—"

His lips closed, for he saw that Hoad's courage had

[262]

twisted itself into an effort to say something that might be unpleasant.

"I'm sorry, Smith, but we can't take you back."

"Can't take me back?"

"No. I may as well tell you at once—that the choice isn't mine—so to speak. It has been forced upon me."

"How?"

"The other men don't want you in the shop."

Keir went white, but his eyes were angry.

"Why?"

"Surely—you understand that a man who has had con‐sumption may be regarded by his fellow workmen—?"

"I don't believe it."

Mr. Hoad snapped at him.

"Believe it or not, it's a fact. I'm not in the habit of lying. Two or three of the men told me very plainly that they would down tools if you were put back. And after all—there is reason in it. It may sound rather hard on you, but look at it from the other fellow's point of view."

"You mean—they look on me—as a sort of leper?"

"Well, in a sense—"

"But—I'm well. I'm not coughing. I'm not infectious."

Hoad shrugged his narrow shoulders.

"It may be ignorance, but it's understandable. Besides, how can one be sure that you have a clean bill of health? Isn't it natural that a man might shirk being at the same bench with you?"

Keir's face was a tragic mask. The anger had gone from it.

"But I could have an out-door job."

"Impossible, and you know it. Business is business, Smith. How can an employer make distinctions and keep a chap in cotton-wool? Besides, there would be the same feeling—among the others. I know it is hard on you, Smith. It's your misfortune."

Keir was almost humble, for the thing had shocked him.

[263]

He was to be one of the workless, a figure in that queue, a dole-monger.

"What am I to do?"

Hoad saw that he had the upper hand.

"Well—I would suggest that you try and get some kind of out-door job, gardening, or driving a car or a van."

"One of your lorries?"

"My dear Smith—I can't sack a man to put you in. Go and see the Labour Exchange people."

Keir walked out of the office and across the yard and out into the street. He was not very conscious of his surroundings. He just walked blindly out into the unknown with a feeling of cold fear in his stomach. His face looked pinched. He was conscious of one solitary urge, to get back home to his wife and a fire and to share with Sybil the terrible reality. He felt weak and sick.

He did not doubt Hoad's word, and in his bitterness certain of the class-cries in which Mr. Sparks indulged came vividly to his mind: "The Solidarity of Labour"—"The Great Brotherhood of the Workers"—"Service not Profit." And his fellow-workers had been the first people to push him into the street, to treat him like a creature that was unclean.

When Keir opened the door of "Merrow," he found his wife at work in the kitchen. Joanna was building a house of toy bricks on the floor. Keir stood a moment looking at his wife and child, and his face was tragic.

"Just a moment, Syb."

He went to their bedroom, and she followed him. She had divined some disaster.

"What's happened, Keir?"

"Shut the door— I've been sacked."

"Sacked!—Oh, Keir—!"

"Yes, it's true. The other chaps won't work with me. They are afraid of me— I'm—I'm—tainted."

[264]

He was trembling. And suddenly his knees seemed to give way under him. He sat down on the bed.

2

So Keir joined the queue outside the Kingham Labour Exchange, and Sybil continued to go out to work.

It was a new experience to Keir, loafing in a shabby street with shabby men, for many of whom there was no room in the world. Nor did his soul belong to the crowd or surrender itself to the crowd's mood. He was more self-conscious than class-conscious, and if he belonged to any class, it was that of the individualist and the artist. The shoddiness and the ugliness of the scene repelled him. His inclination was to hold aloof, and if he had wounds, not to lick them in public. He spoke to very few of his fellow unemployed, and only when he was spoken to.

He ran into Mr. William Block, and Mr. Block struck an attitude and guffawed.

"Morning, Mr. Smiff—fancy us seeing you here!"

Keir moved away, and again Mr. Block guffawed, and Keir could hear him telling his immediate neighbours that the little — over there had got it in the guts, and a damned good thing too. — little bit of swollen tripe.

Many of the men were bitter and full of sordid cynicism. Some of them snarled when a class-car passed. Their hands seemed to finger imaginary bricks.

"Splash the mud over us, that's all they do."

"The — swine—with money."

Some of the men were more bewildered than bitter. Others displayed an apathy that suggested resignation or patience. There were many decent fellows in the crowd, and mostly they were the silent ones. As usual, the worthless element was more vocal.

One of these quiet men said to Keir: "It's nobody's fault
—really. It just happens. I've done a bit of thinking in my
time. Where would we be if we did what the Reds want us
to do? Loot the shops and smash the police and turn the
whole show upside down. There wouldn't be any dole. In
a month or two there wouldn't be anything but a lot of
starving fools. If you smash the machine, and the machine
won't work, where are you? We can't all live on boiled
spuds."

Keir did not remain long with the crowd. A firm at Esher
were asking for a carpenter, and one of the clerks, who was
a friend of the Browns, had been watching out for Keir,
and Keir was sent to secure the job. He had decided on
reticence. He was seen by Mr. Lamb, of Ellison & Lamb,
a youngish man who did not trouble to ask too many questions. Ellison & Lamb were a non-union firm, and Keir
was ready to tear up his card.

"How long were you in your last place?"

"Nearly ten years."

"Why were you stood off?"

"I had to go to hospital, and they took on another man.
I'm quite fit now. I've had all-round experience."

"Let's see, you said your old firm was Samson & Hoad?"

"Yes."

Mr. Lamb smiled. He knew Hoad by reputation and had
been undercut by him.

"Yes, they're on the cheap. We'll try you for a month,
Smith. Trade-union rates, though we're not union. We have
one or two houses going up. Out-of-door. Is that O.K.?"

"It will suit me very well, sir."

Keir had to cycle five miles to his work and five miles
back again in the evening. He took his midday meal with
him, and the men made themselves tea. Ellison & Lamb
was a fairly happy house, a firm of some tradition, and the
men were more of the old country type. Keir felt cheered.

He would show the firm what sort of work he could do. He tore into it.

The spirit was willing, but the flesh was not the flesh of a year ago. For nine months or so he had been loafing; he was out of condition, and a working day is a working day. He got most terribly tired. He arrived home in the evening in a state of exhaustion, but he was determined to hide it from Sybil.

"Oh, I'm getting on fine. It's just a question of climbing back to it. One's rusted up a bit, kid."

Sometimes he was so tired at night that two or three hours would pass before he could fall asleep. He and Sybil were sleeping together again, and he would lie very still in the bed so as not to disturb or to betray his wakefulness. Sybil was a facile sleeper. She went off quickly.

He lay awake and worried. Sometimes he would feel bitter against his own body. Would the thing fail him just when he was struggling back to his opportunity? Oh, no, it was merely a matter of time and of patience. He had always been a wiry chap. The habit of work had to be recovered, his slack muscles tuned up.

Keir did not realize it then, but he was confronting the tragic problem of the man in whom tuberculosis of the lung has been arrested. He had rushed back into the working world to compete with fit men. He was under tension. He was trying to keep step with men who had not to trouble about the pace or the length of the day's march, and if his heart laboured and his breath failed him, he had to surrender or endure. He could not fall out. A second breakdown would be fatal.

At the end of six weeks his cough returned.

The weather was cold and foggy, and his rides to and fro were made in the raw dawn and the equally raw evening. He tried to persuade himself that the cough was due to the fog. He even lied to his wife about it.

[267]

"Too many cigarettes, kid."

Sybil was not convinced.

"You had better go and see the doctor."

He made a pretence of going, but he did not go near Dr. Gibson's surgery. He was afraid to go there. He hung on to the desperate illusion that his cough was a temporary trouble. When the weather improved, it would disappear. He bought himself a bottle of cough mixture at a cash chemist's and dosed himself with it secretly.

The cough continued. His fellow workmen noticed it, and the drawn and worried face of the man who coughed.

"You've got a regular graveyard bark, Smithie."

"Oh—I don't know. Too many cigarettes."

The old and too familiar symptoms began to recur, malaise, breathlessness, expectoration, that feeling of a secret and devouring fever in his chest; yet, with a kind of passionate obstinacy, he concealed things and carried on. He went back to the spare bedroom, pretending that his fear of disturbing Sybil made him cough. He repossessed himself of his sputum flask and used it secretly, though he dared not use it while at work, for it would betray him to his fellow-men.

His mood was one of dogged fatalism. What was the use of surrendering, of becoming a poor sick parasite? If he was destined to die, he would die in harness, or fight till his fate overbore him. His face had a ravaged look, and sometimes his eyes were like the eyes of a hunted creature. He was afraid of his fellow-men, afraid of being driven from the pack out into the wilderness. He became suspicious. He was being watched. He was sure that the other men whispered behind his back.

"He's consumptive. He ought not to be working with us. He's infectious."

He felt himself living in an atmosphere of hostility. He exaggerated trivialities, attached a sinister significance to

[268]

casual words.

The Martyrdom of Man!

Years ago he had read that book and had thought it fantastic and gloomy, but now it was a sort of Adam's Bible.

Sybil was not deceived. She, too, bore her secret anguish, an increasing fear; and one morning when Keir had gone to work, she left Joanna with Mrs. Brown and cycled into Kingham and caught Dr. Gibson before the surgery had closed.

"Doctor, what do you think of my husband?"

"Your husband? Why, I haven't seen him. Nothing wrong, I hope?"

And Sybil understood the secret and wilful courage of Keir.

"He said he had been to see you."

"No."

"The cough's come back, but I know how it is. He lost his old job, and he doesn't want to lose the new one."

The doctor looked grave.

"Tell him to come along, yes—at once. No use shilly-shallying. I'm sorry, Mrs. Smith."

Kind words cut her to the quick. She got herself out of the surgery before her emotion made a public exhibition of itself. Almost she was angry with Keir. She choked back her urge to weep, and wheeling her bicycle into a quiet street, she mounted and rode slowly homewards. A grown woman on a bike—blubbering! How silly! She managed to suppress her emotion. But that very evening she would take Keir to see the doctor. It was inevitable.

3

She expected Keir home about six o'clock, and in her anxiety she left the front window open so that she could hear the sound of the gate. Joanna was at the Browns' and would be collected when she and Keir returned from the doctor's. Tea was laid, and Sybil had her hat on. She was determined to persuade Keir to go with her and see Dr. Gibson after tea.

Just before six she heard the opening and closing of the gate. She went to the window. She had heard footsteps, but the steps had ceased, and in the silence she heard a strange sound, a kind of wet spasm. There was a curious anguish in it.

"Keir, is that you?"

There was some sort of smothered reply, and stricken with fear, she hurried into the passage, switched on the light, and opened the front door. A figure appeared to be groping its way towards her and the light. And then she saw— Keir's mouth and chin were all red; his collar and coat were drenched with the same redness. She saw blood gushing from his mouth in a strange, terrifying, and uncontrollable flux.

"Oh—my dear—!"

Breathless, smothering, he managed to gasp out a few words.

"Happened—just as I reached—gate.—Don't be frightened —Syb."

"Oh, my dear."

Somehow she got him in and to the bed in the spare room. She snatched a basin, a towel. Her own hands were all red, but this horror of hæmorrhage, though it appalled her, roused no repulsion. She held his head.

"I'll go to the Browns' and get Mr. Brown to fetch the doctor—"

His eyes were imploring.

"Not—yet— Stay—till it stops, Syb. Don't leave me."

Chapter Twenty-three

1

KEIR lay in bed and looked at the window. The window was wide open, and the green cretonne curtains kept up a gentle movement. He could see the grey trunk and the lower branches of the beech tree, and very soon all the buds of the great tree would be growing big and golden. He could hear Joanna Mary's wheelbarrow rattling up the path, and the sudden voice of Sybil: "Don't make a noise near the house, dear. Daddy may be asleep."

He wanted to call to them and tell them that he was not sleeping and that he was not worried by the sound of the barrow, but he was not allowed to speak save in whispers. There was to be no excitement, no sudden movement, no talking. He could lie there and think and look at his own useless hands, spread palms-upward on the quilt. There was nothing for him to do but think, to lie there and confront a perfectly hopeless future.

"We shall have to get you back into the sanatorium, Smith."

What was the use? As a worker and a bread-winner he was done for. He had tried to recover his place in the world, to live and labour with normal men, and he had broken down, yes, hopelessly so. Probably he would die, and though he wanted to live, he was not sure that he wanted to live as a poor, pottering parasite, an incubus, a man who had ceased to be man.

His wife came into the room. She stood at the foot of the bed and looked at him with gentle solicitude. She was

[271]

extraordinarily gentle and patient and courageous. She was not one of those women who betray resentment in the face of such a crisis or who allow their worries to escape into fretful self-expression.

"It is time for your warm milk, Keir."

He smiled at her wistfully. He was so very grateful to her because she looked at him without any suspicion of reproach. His own self-reproaches were sufficiently bitter.

"Yes, Syb."

He was submissive, and to Sybil his submission was infinitely pathetic, he—a man who had always been so intense and active. She had loved him for his pride, and now she loved him more poignantly because he was broken and consenting. She went and passed a hand over his pillow and then laid it on his forehead. She had a cool, soft hand.

"You're much better, Keir."

"Oh, yes—I'm better."

She brought the milk in a feeding-cup and supported his head while he drank. His poor neck looked so thin. His weakness wrung her heart. She had made arrangements to go out to work again for three days during each week, but she had not told him yet. She was waiting until he was a little stronger.

"Drink it all, dear."

"Must I?"

"Yes."

He emptied the cup. He was so like a sick child. She lowered his head to the pillows and let her hand rest for a moment on his shoulder.

"Would you like a book?"

"Yes, Syb."

She brought him one of Mr. Lugard's books, and with a last careful glance round the room she left him, closing the door very gently. But Keir did not read his book. He was absurdly weak, and even the holding of a book soon tired

[272]

him. He preferred to lie and listen to his wife's movements, and the coming and going of Joanna in the garden. He had said to Sybil: "Don't stop the kid. I like to hear her about."

He lay and meditated. What would happen to these two if he passed out? What would happen to them if he went on living for a number of years, as a sort of human derelict? Drifting,—drifting. Was there any other kind of work that he could do? If only he had been one of those fellows who could write books, popular books which sold well and made money. Robert Louis Stevenson. But that man had been a genius as well as a very valiant soul. He lay and thought and thought, his fingers grasping the edge of the quilt as though even that soft substance gave him a sense of solidity. What could he do? He was a working man, and without the strength of his body he could do nothing.

He was aware of the scuffling of small feet. A pair of hands and a face appeared at the window.

"Hallo, daddy."

"Hallo, kid."

Jo smiled at him.

"I'm getting more stones for the path."

"Are you? That's splendid."

Stones for the path! If only he had the healthy body of his child? But what if she had inherited from him that delicacy of tissue that might make her vulnerable to the disease? He closed his eyes and tried to think of other things.

2

Keir was allowed to get up.

There was a tremor in the air, a breath of spring, and Keir was told that he might lie out in the garden, provided he kept himself well covered. He might even walk a little, and all this carefulness moved him to a kind of whimsical wonder, a twinge of self-scorn. This business of keeping people alive! Dr. Gibson struck him as being so egregiously and professionally cheerful, but then—it was part of a physician's job to suggest cheerfulness.

"I hope to get you re-admitted next month, Smith."

And Keir was provoked into asking that inevitable question.

"After all, what is the use, doctor?"

Gibson could not let such pessimism pass. Like all professional men he had to subscribe to the particular professional pragmatism. In this war between cells you could not countenance surrender.

"You mustn't talk like that, Smith. You must will yourself to get well."

Keir smiled up at him. Gibson was a beefy, thick-set person with a fine capacity for enjoying life.

"I'm thinking of the afterwards, sir."

"How?"

"Supposing they give me another six months' treatment and send me out patched up—what's the use of it? I've had my lesson. I know now that I can't go back to the old job. I can't keep up with fit men, and the industrial system doesn't legislate for crocks."

"My dear chap—there's always an alternative."

"I have tried to think of something. What is there that I can do? Be honest, doctor. I might be capable of doing a few hours' light work—but a full day—no. As a wage-earner I'm done for."

Gibson fell back on platitudes.

"Well, look here—sufficient unto the day is the worry thereof. What you have to do is to keep your tail up and get well. Afterwards—you can begin to explore."

Keir looked at his thin, white hands.

"Pity I can't write books, doctor. The diary of a down-and-out."

"Well, it's better than nothing. Man's an ingenious devil, and you've got brains. I know an old lady who helps to keep herself by decorating boxes and things with sealing-wax. She's a marvel at it. It's just an idea—that's all."

Keir nodded.

"I know. Some sort of makeshift. Turning out little cabinets for birds' eggs, or converting cigar-boxes into letter-files. Or I might specialize on wireless sets."

Dr. Gibson was not very sensitive to irony.

"Exactly. That's the idea. Things have a marvellous way of turning up trumps."

Sybil was going out to work on four days a week, but her twenty-eight to thirty shillings—added to Keir's insurance money—left them very little margin. More often than not the balance was on the wrong side, for there was the interest on the mortgage to be met quarterly, and the rates on "Merrow" were seventeen pounds a year. Moreover, Dr. Gibson had impressed upon her how necessary it was that Keir should be well and properly fed; plenty of fresh eggs and milk. And the family wardrobe had been falling into disrepair. Keir began to suspect his wife of stinting herself at meals, and he charged her with indulging in unselfish but false economy.

"You aren't eating enough, Syb."

She assured him that she was provided with a very good dinner at the houses where she worked.

"I get all I want, Keir."

He did not believe her. He guessed that she was keeping all the small financial worries from him, and that their budget could not be easy to balance. In fact, Sybil was at her wits' end trying to accumulate a little money to meet the rates, and the gas and electric light bills. She was scanning the house for some piece of furniture that might be regarded as superfluous and upon which money could be raised. The victim offered itself in the person of the Chester-

[275]

field sofa. Sybil had always been rather proud of that sofa, but it did crowd the room, and why cling to a sofa, when you had two arm-chairs to sit in?

She spoke to Keir on the subject.

"I'm thinking of getting rid of the sofa. It does crowd us up—rather."

Keir was not deceived. Sybil and that sofa were somehow associated in his mind, and to reprieve the piece he suggested that Sybil should sell his bookcase.

"But you must have a bookcase for your books, Keir."

"Not much use to us, are they? You can get rid of most of the books too, if you like."

Sybil would not hear of it. The sofa was the predestined victim, and Sybil interviewed a gentleman who purchased second-hand furniture. He came to view the sofa and offered her about a third of the price they had paid for the thing when it was new. Sybil was angry and explored the pockets of other purchasers; she managed to raise the price by three and sixpence, and the sofa departed from "Merrow." It was the first hostage to fate.

The incident produced a strange bitterness in Keir. Because he was down and out, someone else was getting a bargain at Sybil's expense. Yes, in all probability other pieces of furniture would follow the sofa into exile. He and Sybil had housed themselves for health, and now that he was a sick man and unable to earn anything, they were over-housed and over-rated. Common sense suggested that they should sell the bungalow, pay off the mortgage, and move into cheaper quarters.

A return to Paragon Place, or some back street that was equally crowded and drab and noisy?

No, that was beyond the bounds of his pride. But for his rotten body there would have been no selling of sofas. He began to feel bitter towards his own body. What was it but a wretched incubus a crocked machine fit only for the scrap heap. If it was disposed of, Sybil would be free, and in many ways better off.

She might marry again!

Sybil came back one April evening and found no Keir. Joanna Mary was giving a doll a ride in the barrow, and suddenly Sybil felt anxious.

"Where's daddy?"

"Daddy's gone for a walk. He said he would go only just a little way."

Keir had not been out of the garden since his hæmorrhage, but Dr. Gibson had given him permission to take short walks. Obviously, Keir was only doing what the doctor had said he might do, and yet Sybil was attacked by a sense of some impending calamity. She ran out into the lane to see if Keir was anywhere in sight. She walked as far as the Browns' villa, thinking that he might have called on the Browns.

Keir was half a mile away. He had gone down to the river and was sitting on the bank, just above the water. He should not have been sitting on the damp grass, but when a man is confronting death, such trivialities are of small account. There was much water coming down, but it was a windless day and the river ran with a swift stealth. As to its colour, it seemed all sorts of colours to Keir, brown and black and green and silver and flecked with white and with blue. Its surface showed streaks and eddies and little glassy swirls. It was so silent. It just slid past him between its very green banks on a soft April day.

He stared at it and he thought: "It would be so easy. It would wash out everything. There would be no more hope and no more heartache. It would set her free."

He took off his hat and layed it on the bank. He stood up and sat down again. It occurred to him that he ought to lash his feet together with his handkerchief. He took out his handkerchief and rolled it into a rope, and then he remembered that Sybil had given him six handkerchiefs as a Christmas present and that this was one of them. He unfolded it, smoothed it out, and put the thing back in his pocket.

A reaction swept over him. What a beautiful world it was, and he wanted to go on living in it. He wanted to be loved. No, not death, but the faces and hands of his loved ones. He was overwhelmed with sudden loneliness. He got up and walked rapidly along the towing-path and up a lane that led away from the river. He walked so fast that he was out of breath, but he did not notice it. He was going home. He wanted to go on living and being loved.

When he came to the gate of "Merrow," he found his wife waiting for him there, and suddenly he was ashamed, for it seemed to him that she knew how he had been tempted.

"Just had a bit of a walk, Syb."

Her eyes reproached him, for he looked exhausted.

"You shouldn't do it, Keir. You've tired yourself out."

"A chap must do something."

He followed her into the house. They were alone together in that familiar little room, and suddenly his manhood failed him. He sat down on the arm of one of the chairs. He broke down and wept.

"I'm no more use. I'd be better dead."

She was shocked and alarmed. She tried to comfort him.

"My dear, you mustn't say such things."

"But they're true."

"No, no. When you get to the sanatorium—"

"What's the use of my going there? They just feed you up and send you out again. I shall never be able to work.

It would be the same old business over again. I'm no good for anything; I shall never be any good."

She held his head on her shoulder, and she was afraid. Her courage had endured for months, but she too was near breaking-point. She wanted help— She felt that she must do something. But what? Her man was drowning in the deeps of his despair. Yes, she must do something.

She stood up. An idea had come to her.

"I'm going to see Mrs. Lugard, Keir."

"What can she do? They've been jolly good—but—"

Sybil's face was set.

"Gentlefolk sometimes know things we don't. They hear of things we don't hear of, Keir. Promise me you'll stay here —quietly. Oh, my dear,—I'm so—so frightened. Promise."

His courage recovered itself at her cry.

"Yes. Sorry, Syb. Damned snivelling kid. I'm all right now, I'll put Jo to bed."

She looked at him poignantly.

"I'll go now. I'm trusting you, Keir. I'm trusting you."

Chapter Twenty-four

1

SYBIL went to the back door of Darvels, and the door was opened to her by that supreme domestic authority—cook. Jane had been with the Lugards an impossible number of years. She was pre-war in all her characteristics and her prejudices, in her cap and her skirts and the dressing of her hair.

"Oh, Jane, I'm in such trouble. Is—she—in?"

She—was Mrs. Mary Lugard, and if the household spoke of her with brevity, it was not with disrespect. Mrs. Lugard was staying in Somerset with a sister, but He—was at home. Cook had just finished serving His dinner.

"Come in, my dear. What is it?"

"Keir. He's feeling so hopeless about himself."

"Poor lad— I always did tell you he was the serious sort."

"I wonder if He would see me, Jane."

Cook was sure that He would. She had sent Him in a perfect savoury, and he had eaten it all, and he was in the library with his coffee and his pipe. She would go and ask Him. And if Sybil felt like a cup of cocoa—

"No, Jane—I couldn't. I don't feel like cocoa. Do say I am so sorry to worry him—at this time of the day—but that he may be able to give me some advice. He has travelled so much, and he knows so much."

Cook went forth upon the adventure. She found Mr. Lugard well down in his chair, wearing his horn-rimmed glasses, and looking perhaps much wiser than he felt.

"What is it, Jane?"

"Mrs. Smith, sir. She's in great trouble about her husband. She came to see Mrs. Lugard."

"Husband worse?"

"From what Sybil says, sir, he's feeling hopeless about himself. She's wondering if you'd see her."

Mr. Lugard put down his book.

"Of course, Jane. Send her in."

Mr. Richard Lugard was a man of multifarious interests and of some experience. In his university days he had been an enthusiastic supporter of East End missions, travelling down regularly to Poplar to box and play billiards with the Cockney lads. Each year he had gone to camp with them, but with London, and especially the East End of London, becoming more greasy and swarthy and Mediterranean, Mr. Lugard had reformed himself. That is to say he had lost his sense of high endeavour. He had come to loathe "Uplift" and to associate it with priggery and the new education. He preferred dogs and gardens and the bucolic mind and an attitude to life that was rather that of Gaffer Brown when some bright young graduate in glasses proposed to teach the old fool how to suck eggs. The world was becoming so deucedly clever.

But Mr. Lugard's interests were various. He liked to read about the buccaneers and that old plundering blackguard—Morgan. He liked adventure, whether it was in science of sociology, or big business, or the floating of some new process. He read all the serious journals, while remaining a man who could play absurd games with a puppy.

When Sybil was shown in, he instantly rose and with an air of simplicity shook hands with her. He had such mellow manners that no one noticed that he had any manners.

"Sit down and tell me all about it, Sybil."

Sybil burst into tears, and somehow she did not feel foolish in Mr. Lugard's presence.

"Oh—I'm so—so worried, sir."

"Well, tell me all about it. And there's no hurry. I'm sorry Mrs. Lugard isn't at home."

Sybil recovered herself. Very simply she put Keir's case to Mr. Lugard, explaining it from Keir's point of view as well as from her own. She was aware of Mr. Lugard stretching out a hand and rummaging among the books and periodicals on the table beside his chair. He listened to her, and while he listened, he opened a particular pamphlet and kept glancing at it, while remaining attentive to Sybil. It was as though she was describing a journey while he followed it all on a map.

He said: "Silly of me. I ought to have thought of it before. Ever heard of Papworth, Sybil?"

Sybil had not, nor had Mr. Lugard till a couple of months ago, but the life of the consumptive colony had so interested him that he had driven down to Papworth and explored it. He had made the acquaintance of Papworth's creator and had discovered in him one of those Elizabethan types that suggested Drake and Raleigh, a Grenville or a Sidney, a temperament colourful, creative, and touched with imagination.

"What is it, sir?"

Mr. Lugard explained Papworth and the aims and ideals of Papworth.

"You see, Sybil, it is not like an ordinary sanatorium. The idea is that consumptives should be able to live and work and have their own people about them. It's not just a place to be ill in."

"You mean, sir, that if Keir got well he could stay and live and work there?"

"Yes, that's the idea."

"And Jo and I could join him?"

"Yes."

She had become flushed and excited.

"But that's wonderful. Why didn't anybody think of it

[282]

before? That's what's killing my man, sir, the awful feeling that he is no use, and that he'll never be any use. The awful feeling too that other men won't work with him."

Mr. Lugard smiled.

"Yes, that's the tragedy; but the man who founded Papworth isn't a mere doctor. He had vision, understanding, courage."

"Perhaps he felt what we feel, sir."

"Yes, probably."

"Would it be possible for Keir to go to Papworth?"

"Certainly."

"Then—there's hope, sir. Oh, you don't know what hope means. But of course—you do. Perhaps you would come and see Keir."

"I'll come tomorrow morning."

"And if— How does one manage—?"

"I'll go down to Papworth myself and see what can be done."

Sybil could have kissed his hands.

"I don't know—really—why you should be so kind, sir."

"Oh, that's nothing, my dear child. Life's a dreadful sort of failure if it doesn't teach one to be kind."

2

There was hope in Keir's eyes and in his heart. There was new hope in him as he shaved himself and tied his best tie, for as a man he knew Mr. Lugard was not one of those flamboyant and impulsive people to whom everything that is new is marvellous and final. Mr. Lugard had given Sybil some literature on Papworth Village Settlement for Keir to read, and Keir had read all there was to read before falling asleep.

At the breakfast table he showed to his wife the face of a

[283]

man who had ceased to despair.

"Funny we should not have heard of it before, Syb."

"Yes—I wonder why Dr. Gibson didn't tell us about it."

The omission was due to ignorance, that curious professional ignorance which may be the product of cliquism and complacency. The professional god, like most other deities, is a jealous god and averts his eyes from all that may be described as heretical and falsely miraculous. Later, when Keir spoke to Dr. Gibson of that unique community, Dr. Gibson looked mildly offended. "Papworth—Papworth, never heard of the place." His tone suggested that the thing smelt of charlatany, or that the enterprise could be dismissed as a fad, and perhaps a fashionable fad. Was it orthodox? Had its creator qualified as a medical practitioner, or was he one of those offensive people who dare to walk in advance of the professional experts, and who capture a bishop or two, and a duchess and a cabinet minister, and who advertise some flagrant and successful hocus-pocus?

Keir, sitting in the April sunlight with Mr. Lugard, asked some of the questions that Dr. Gibson might have asked.

"Is it quite all right, sir? I mean—is it run by doctors, responsible people?"

Mr. Lugard was gently amused. He was able to reassure Keir. He could understand the scepticism of a man who had plumbed the deeps of despair.

"There are hundreds of men working at Papworth, many of them men who had given up all hope of ever working again. I have seen them."

"What sort of men?"

"Men of all kinds, Keir. Schoolmasters, shop-assistants, labourers, ex-policemen, clerks."

"There are workshops?"

"Yes, they make furniture and leather goods and many other things. Just imagine, a village in which every worker has been a consumptive, a village in which every man can live a more or less normal life. He hasn't to compete with men who have not been handicapped by the disease."

Keir asked many other questions. What happened to a patient when he was first admitted? Sanatorium treatment. Oh, yes, and supposing the disease was arrested? The patient was allowed to work? At work—perhaps—for which he had been trained? Yes. He was—so to speak—on probation. His day's work was carefully graded. He was kept under observation and examined at regular intervals. And supposing he made good? He would be earning quite good money; he could become the occupant of one of the Papworth cottages. His wife and child could join him. He would be the possessor of a home.

Keir said: "It seems too good to be true. It's the thing, sir, that a chap like me has been praying for. It means—hope."

And then he looked rather sadly at the small white building with the green door. He and Sybil had been so proud of "Merrow." It was associated with early memories of their marriage and with dreams of success.

"I suppose one ought not to get sentimental about bricks and mortar, sir."

"But one does, Keir."

"It will mean selling this place."

"Why not let it?"

"I take it that if I go to Papworth, I might be there six months or a year before the wife and child could join me?"

"Yes, I believe that would be so."

Keir looked thoughtful.

"Well—I've got to go through with it. I suppose it would be better if Sybil stayed on here. We should have to pay the interest on the mortgage, but we shouldn't have to pay for storing the furniture. And I shall be off her hands. She'll have to go on working, poor kid."

Mr. Lugard had something to say upon the subject.

"I don't think your wife is pitying herself, Keir. And that is rather rare in these days, and a virtue to be saluted. The people who face things out for themselves are almost unique."

"I know what you mean, sir. Always expecting someone else to carry their burdens for them when the weight begins to chafe them just a little. State cadgers."

"I see a good deal of other cadging, Keir. I have quite a number of so-called friends who—because I have no children and am considered to possess some spare cash,—seem to think that I ought to pay for their children's education. I don't. Well, what about Papworth? The decision is with you."

"Of course—if they will take me, sir."

"Then, I'll motor down tomorrow and see what I can do."

3

Mr. Lugard did not tell Keir that he had been so inspired by the significance of Papworth that he had sent the institution a substantial donation. He drove down next day by way of Baldock and Royston. It was a morning of sudden rain and sudden sunlight, a blue day, wet and glittering. At Papworth the avenue of lime trees leading up to the old white house with its huge Ionic portico were purpling their leaf buds. Mr. Lugard was shown into the library, on the left of the hall where orderlies were laying the tables for dinner. He had sent up his card to Sir Pendrill Varrier Jones.

Sir Pendrill came down to him in the library.

"You may remember me—perhaps. You allowed me to explore your village last month."

Sir Pendrill remembered everybody. He was one of those

[286]

men of action who give no appearance of hurry. If he had the head of a Welsh bard, he had the manners of a courtier, and the wisdom of a gentle autocrat.

"We are always glad to see our friends."

Mr. Lugard explained that he had come to Papworth on business, if the placing of a patient could be regarded as business.

"A case I am interested in—a rather pathetic case."

Sir Pendrill took Mr. Lugard upstairs to his sitting-room, and on the stairs he was heard to say that all such cases were pathetic, but that Papworth did not exaggerate their pathos. Moreover, Papworth was not the melancholy place that the over-sentimental might take it to be. It cultivated courage and cheerfulness.

Mr. Lugard stood a moment and looked out of Sir Pendrill's windows at the grass and the old trees. The place had atmosphere. It was English, and so quietly English.

He said: "It seems to me that it was extraordinarily wise of you to settle in a place that was—dressed. One expected a sort of municipal building scheme."

Sir Pendrill was lighting a pipe.

"We may be new—oh, very new—but—"

Mr. Lugard smiled at him. He was more and more sure that Sir Pendrill had the head of a poet and that his epic had not been written on paper.

Sir Pendrill gave Mr. Lugard lunch, and having discussed Keir's case, they talked of other things. Mr. Lugard, who loathed noise, was surprised by the tranquillity of the big white building. It housed the settlement's hospital; there were scores of patients in its wards, and yet no sounds seemed to penetrate to the director's room.

"You are amazingly quiet here."

"You think so?"

There was a little whimsical glint behind the question, and Sir Pendrill looked towards one of the windows.

[287]

"I sleep over there. When you have a community like this on your shoulders—"

"Yes—I can understand— All the problems climb the stairs to this room. You mean you sleep in a tent?"

"I'm not quite so primitive as that. I have a bungalow away there among the trees."

"Your retreat? Yes, I should gather that it's necessary."

Mr. Lugard's humanity felt at home with the large and tranquil humanity of this other man.

"How did you come to start this scheme?"

Sir Pendrill smiled at him.

"I—? Oh—it would be more correct to say that it started me. I saw the tragedy of these broken lives. Something became inevitable. It began with a shelter in a back garden."

"But you had the vision."

Sir Pendrill relit his pipe and let the challenge pass.

Mr. Lugard walked through the village before he left. It was the most amazing village in England, and he could imagine Keir working here and going home to one of the red brick cottages. He thought to himself: "We tired and flippant people need something like this, something that is so utterly worth while." He was in a happy mood. He had good news for Keir. Papworth would take Keir in immediately.

That evening, after dinner, he was driven to "Merrow," and he broke the good news to Keir and Sybil.

"You can be admitted next week."

Keir's face looked all smoothed out. He had begun to hope.

Chapter Twenty-five

1

MOST patients arrive at Papworth via Cambridge, the settlement bus meeting them at Cambridge station, but Keir and Sybil and one shabby suitcase travelled to Papworth in the Lugard car.

Keir found saying good-bye to Joanna and to "Merrow" a heart-in-the-throat affair. He was like an emigrant setting out for a new continent. If he survived the struggle in the wilds, he would have to make a home there for these other two. He supposed that he would never see "Merrow" again, for if he died at Papworth, most certainly he would not revisit the scenes of his youth; and if he lived at Papworth, he would go on living there.

His face looked stark as he walked out of the gate. No, he was not betraying any emotion. He held Joanna firmly by the hand; she was to spend the day with the Browns. He did not look back at the small white bungalow or the beech tree. He spoke almost jocosely to the Lugard chauffeur, who had become very much a friend.

"First-class tickets to Papworth, Fred, and no punctures."

"I've got new tires on, Keir."

"What I want, old man, is a new inner tube."

Joanna was left at the Browns', but Keir surrendered that emotional crisis to his wife. His eyes said: "Take her in, Syb; I can't bear it," and Joanna, suddenly wet and woeful, was carried in by her mother. Sybil returned to the car with a face that was asking not to be looked at too closely. Fred, the chauffeur, tucked them both up in the back seats of the limousine just as he tucked up Mr. and Mrs. Lugard.

They sat close together, holding hands. Sometimes one or other made a desultory remark, but mostly they were silent. Outer London displayed to them innumerable new building estates with row upon row of mass-production houses. Notice-boards announced to the world that it could own its own house for the sum of £695.

"Just like one of your drapery shops, Syb. One and eleven pence three farthings."

Sybil wanted to know who lived or who was going to live in all these thousands of houses, and Keir could not tell her. He surveyed them with the eye of the expert.

"Lot of trash, most of it. I wonder what the repair bill will be ten years hence."

His own repair bill was a gamble with death, and the green of the young year seemed to him strange and tantalizing. Open country now, though it was scarred by the new concrete highways. He sat and held his wife's hand and dreaded the moment when he would have to relinquish it. He had begun to realize how much he depended upon this other human creature.

They passed through the broad street of Baldock and came to the chalkland, great grassy undulations under a thin blue sky. There was a sadness in the landscape, and to Keir's mood it appeared too large and unfriendly, like the sea when you are feeling too much alone with yourself. This downland had none of the wooded richness, the secrecy, of the hills above Shere.

"Rather bare, Syb."

"Yes."

"I like my world a bit more shut in. You can see too far here."

He hoped that Papworth did not live among these grey-green hills, and when they turned north at the Royston crossroads and came to gentler country, he was glad. Elm trees and hedges, and meadows, a wood here and there; consoling, closed-in country. But they were approaching Papworth, and he held his wife's hand a little more firmly.

"Nearly there, Syb."

She understood him. Her fingers closed on his.

Then, quite suddenly, they came to the valley where Papworth lies. The village begins as a few new cottages standing in their gardens beside the road. Trees rise up, old sheltering trees. There is a sudden glimpse of the white solidity of Papworth Hall. The valley fills with a feeling of humanity, houses and buildings where people live and work. The sun shone out. The grass was sheeted with it and flecked with shadows.

Keir's face brightened.

"I did not think it was like this. I thought it would look like—'Pinehill'—or a bit of new suburb."

"It's just a village, Keir."

"Just as though it had grown here."

Which it had.

Both of them were a little over-awed by the height and massiveness of the hall's Ionic portico. It was the gateway of Keir's new world, and he felt rather like a small boy being taken to school for the first time by his mother.

"I suppose we ought to come here?"

Fred, the chauffeur, had collected considerable information with regard to the Papworth routine.

"Yes, it's quite O.K. You aren't calling on the Prince of Wales! The hospital and the offices are in the hall."

He rang the bell, and a nurse appeared, and, like many nurses, she had much to do and was a little abrupt and pragmatical. Was one of them a patient? Oh, the man. Was he expected? Yes. Well, they had better wait in the library. She would tell the matron that there was a patient for admission.

She showed them into the library and disappeared.

Cloistered together in that big room with its shelves of books, they felt like two rabbits shut up in a hutch. Papworth had a multitude of jobs to do and other matters to memorize, and Keir strolled up and down looking at the literature. Sybil sat down at the long table. There was silence. Both of them felt restless, creatures of suspense. The place was strange to them, and in a little while they would be separated.

Keir went and stood at the window. It looked across the gravelled space to the avenue of limes. Very soon the trees would be in leaf.

"Seems very quiet here, Syb."

"Yes—you wouldn't think—"

"I wonder if we've come at the wrong time? A place like this has to have its time-table."

"Don't worry, dear."

And then the door opened, and to them appeared Miss Borne, the matron, solid, rosy, the Dea Mater of Papworth in her dark brown uniform. The room became different. It felt warmed by the human presence of this woman with her blue eyes and her wise and capable kindness. She sat down and so did they. She smiled upon them; she asked questions. She was instantly their friend.

"I hope we haven't come at the wrong time?"

Miss Borne looked at Sybil, and Sybil looked at Miss Borne. There was something about this solid and steadfast woman that made people feel that life was more secure.

"No, my dear."

Her kindness was the kindness of a woman who was responsible for a multitude of daily details. She had a lap into which other people cast their troubles.

"You have been in a sanatorium before?"

"Yes."

"My husband tried to work too soon—and too hard."

"There are many cases like that."

[292]

She observed them both with her wise blue eyes.

"You two would like just a moment together. Then—your husband—will have to—"

Sybil understood. Her eyes thanked this other woman.

For a few seconds they clung together alone in that big room. Their leave-taking was almost silent, as silent as it was poignant.

"Take care of yourself, Syb. I'll be all right here."

"Oh, my dear."

"Now, don't you worry. I'll write tomorrow. You've been a wonderful wife to me, dear."

"Oh, Keir—you must—"

"Of course. I'll get well. I've got to get well."

2

The life of Papworth began on the top floor of Papworth Hall. It was like a storage tank from which the inmates flowed gradually to the lower floors and so out to the chalets and yet farther to the workshops and the hostels, if fate was kind. Keir, as a new patient under observation, ascended to that upper floor. His bed was in a corner of the ward, but so placed that he could look out of one of the Georgian windows at the parklike grounds of the hall. This world was growing green.

A great lawn spread to thickets of trees and flowering shrubs, and between two of these thickets a broad grass way led upwards. At the end of this green vista were walnut trees. Birds sang.

The ward was full. Papworth was always full.

Keir was tired after the long drive and the stress of the day's emotions. He lay there with closed eyes, thinking of so many things. He was alone and yet not alone. He had exchanged a few words and a smile with his neighbours, and these other men let him lie in peace, for there is a quick sense of comradeship among the sick, a more sensitive comprehending of the other fellow's necessities. This new chap did not want to be worried.

The ward remained very quiet. It read or worked out crossword puzzles, or just lay and dreamed. Occasionally it coughed. There were patients in it who were content to lie in peace and be thankful when the little flame of life was not blown slantwise by the draught of their disease.

There was a sudden stirring in the ward, a rustling of papers, a sense of movement in the beds. The presence was there, that presence which was Papworth. It stood for a moment in the doorway, it was both deliberate and dramatic; it crossed the ward to Keir's bed. Keir was lying with his eyes closed, but seemed to divine the presence. He opened his eyes and saw a big man, with his large, pale face and his mane of very black hair.

The doctor?

Sir Pendrill smiled at Keir. There was no flexion of that strong figure. Sir Pendrill carried himself like some senator leading the procession up the Sacred Way. Life had dignity, poise, rhythm. If he was a little unusual, it was the unusualness of a personality conscious of imaginative purpose and of power. There was a gentleness about this vivid person, a serenity of understanding.

"I am afraid I have spoilt your sleep."

Keir lay and gazed. His smile was like the smile of a child. Something seemed to flow to him from the presence. It was so consoling, so calm. It had interposed between man and death.

"I wasn't asleep, sir."

"Just—thinking?"

"Yes, just thinking, sir."

Sir Pendrill's fingers rested on Keir's wrist.

"Mr. Lugard's case. Well, just get settled down. You have

had a longish journey. We shan't worry you till tomorrow."

He passed on to the other patients, and Keir was aware of the brightening of those other faces. This man with the massive head brought a new vitality into the ward. He was human; he understood.

"How's the latest puzzle going, Macey?"

"It's a bit of a twister, sir."

"You're looking better."

"I'm feeling champion, sir."

The presence passed out, leaving behind it in the ward a curious vibration in the air. Keir, still ignorant of the visitor's identity, turned to his left-hand neighbour, a Northampton shoe-operative named Briggs.

"Who was that? The doctor in charge?"

Briggs looked tolerantly at Keir as though a newcomer had to be forgiven for being a consummate greenhorn.

"That? Haven't you seen Jones before? We call him Father."

"Sir Varrier Jones? The man who made Papworth?"

"Sure."

Keir lay and looked at the ceiling. He heard a voice say: "The one and only Jones. Wish we saw him oftener."

Someone replied: "Why, the Old Man's got the whole blinking show on his shoulders. He's P.M. and Managing Director and Chief Advertising Agent. If you cut him up into little bits, you wouldn't make him go round every day."

Yet another voice closed the discussion.

"He gives us all the time he can. He has given us all we've got. It makes me feel better to be near a man who's started a job like this."

Keir felt strangely calmed. His next-door neighbour had passed him a magazine, and he thanked Mr. Briggs and pretended to read it, but presently he closed his eyes. He wanted to think. In the darkness he seemed nearer to all those things that were dear to him, and in this ward he felt

like a stranger in a strange land. His sentence would be a
life sentence, if the doctors were able to reprieve him. He
would live and work here— So that had been Sir Pendrill
Varrier Jones, the man who had begun his great work with
one patient and a hut in a back garden. The tragedy of the
one had made him comprehend the tragedy of the many.
A dark, lionlike head crowned with imagination and with
pity. But what a strange thing that one man should set out
to make money, while another gave himself to the remaking
of men!

Keir opened his eyes suddenly and turned to Mr. Briggs.
Mr. Briggs was a lean, swarthy person with a sharp nose and
one of those lower lips that associate itself with pithy and
forcible language. He had his spectacles on his nose.

"What about work here?"

Mr. Briggs looked at Keir over the tops of his spectacles.

"You're an early worm, you are! Yes, there's plenty of
work here."

"Employment for a carpenter?"

Mr. Briggs's lower lip protruded.

"I should say so. You wait till you see the cabinet and
furniture shop. Reg'lar hive of industry, and all up to date.
Then there are the fowl-houses and chalets, and what not.
I'm going into leather."

"Leather?"

Keir was very ignorant, and Mr. Briggs enlightened him
further.

"The turnover here last year was round about seventy
thousand pounds. They make some of the best leather goods
in the kingdom. Suitcases, attaché cases, trunks, bags. Yes,
all started by the one and only Jones. He's a bit of a marvel.
He's got vision, my lad, vision."

Keir was examined next day by Dr. Stott. It was a very thorough examination, and Keir, feeling like a man on the edge of a precipice, watched the doctor's face for signs of hope. Would they be able to snatch him from the dark abyss or was it too late? Dr. Stott was sitting on the edge of Keir's bed and jotting down some notes on the case-sheet.

Keir did not want to be a nuisance; he did not want to appear afraid, but that question quivered on his lips.

"Has it spread, doctor?"

Dr. Stott looked at Keir kindly through his glasses. He had gone carefully into the history of the case.

"Just that right lung. Eat and sleep, my lad, and try not to worry."

Keir smiled faintly. Was his case more desperate than he had feared, and was the doctor being kind to him? He asked no more questions. He watched Dr. Stott dealing with the other patients and tried to decide whether the doctor's manner was equally kind and brisk and impartial. Dr. Stott was jocular with Mr. Briggs.

"I am going to mark you for downstairs."

Mr. Briggs's sallow face went quite pink.

"That's the stuff to give me, sir. I'll soon be among the leather goods."

Dr. Stott laughed. He approved of such spirit.

Later Miss Borne came to Keir's bed, and Keir, looking up into her rosy, solid, and reassuring face, wanted to ask her a question. His eyes were hungry, and Miss Borne had lived for years with such eyes. She understood the secret hopes and the secret anguish.

"Matron, may I write home?"

"Of course."

"What—what may I say?"

Miss Borne had had many such poignant questions asked

her. They were asked at times by men and women to whom it was impossible to hold out hope. But in Keir's case the problem was not quite so pathetic. She had spoken to Dr. Stott concerning him.

"Tell your wife we are quite pleased with you."

"Then—the doctor—thinks—?"

"You are still an early case."

Keir seemed to draw a deep breath. His head sank back on the pillow. He smiled at Miss Borne.

"Thank you, Matron."

Chapter Twenty-six

1

THE morning sun poured into the ward, and all the world was green.

In the bed next to Keir a new patient, a lad with a thin, flushed face, had been coughing incessantly, and his distress had worried Keir. He was moved both to pity and to impatience. This other man's suffering was so much his, a distraction and a reminder, a discord in the song of hope.

The coughing had ceased. It was replaced by another sound, a sound that made Keir look sharply at his neighbour. The new kid was blubbing, and though he had buried his face in the pillow, the sound could not be smothered.

Keir was moved. Had he not suffered that anguish of hopelessness when the heart of man dissolves into despair? He stretched out a hand, but he was not near enough to touch the lad.

"Kid, don't take on like that."

The other's shoulders shook.

"I'm done for. I'll never get better."

Miss Borne and the doctor came into the ward, and Miss Borne's blue eyes were quick to see that tragic, weeping child. She went instantly to the lad's bed. She was consoling, kind, firm. She sat on a chair beside him, and spoke to him like some mother and nurse.

Dr. Stott had left her the occasion. She was the woman for it. He went to Keir's bed and with that little quiet smile of his looked at Keir as though he was concealing a gift behind his back. "Now, then, let's have another look at you." A fortnight had passed since Keir's admission, and he would have said that the life-clock within him was ticking more strongly. Dr. Stott looked and listened. Keir's chart was showing open water, and the weather was fair.

"I'll mark you for downstairs."

Keir's face flushed up just as Mr. Briggs's had done. He was suddenly more conscious of the sun and of that green world beyond the windows. He was a little breathless.

"I'm glad, doctor."

"Don't get excited. Take it easy."

Dr. Stott smiled and passed on, and Keir, full of his own secret exultation, remembered the lad in the next bed. He was lying quite still now and watching Miss Borne, who had joined the doctor. He watched her as though her solid wholesomeness symbolized life and hope.

Keir spoke to him.

"Cheer up, kid. You'll be going downstairs soon."

The lad turned and smiled at him.

"Isn't she a marvel! Sorry I was such a—"

"Don't you worry. We all of us go through that."

So Keir, promoted downwards, which is the right kind of promotion at Papworth, found himself and his bed in a sunny ground-floor ward with the green grass at his feet, and the trees full of the sunlight. In the little lake at the bottom of the lawn two swans were busy rearing a family, and Father Swan patrolled the purlieus and advanced menacingly upon all intruders. Dr. Stott was the only person who could deal with him. Dr. Stott's laboratory stood near the lake, and Dr. Stott's comings and goings could not be left at the mercy of so feathered and fussy a father.

Keir's world had enlarged itself. No longer did it seem bounded by four walls. He was out in the air by day; he was part of the spring, of the green insurgence of the year. The thorns and the laburnums were in flower. Birds sang, and in his letters to Sybil there was an echo of this singing.

He felt at ease with his neighbours, and in a hospital neighbours are like the poor, always in evidence. On his right hand he had an old fellow who was known as Dad, or William the Silent. Dad had been a night-watchman in a London warehouse, sleeping by day and keeping himself company at night, and his tongue had rusted up. Report had it that he became conversational only in the company of a cat, the warehouse cat having been his sole companion.

On Keir's right lay Jannis, the dark, sallow, sensitive Jannis, with brown eyes that looked black. His had been a desperate case, and even Miss Borne had felt gloomy about him, but Jannis had refused to die. He had a wife and child parked somewhere in a London suburb. He had made up his mind that they were to join him at Papworth, nor was his sanguine courage the illusion of the consumptive. He was doing well; he would do better.

"Hallo, been deflated?"

Yes, Keir had had the needle. His lung tissue had been put to rest. He and Jannis were much alike in temperament. They swapped books and ideas and opinions, and shared a kindred philosophy.

Jannis told Keir his story.

"We had been married just a year, and our kid had come when the trouble started. I was a clerk in an insurance office. I had to go to a 'san,' and my wife got a job as a waitress in a tea-shop. We had to sell our furniture, the precious furniture we had bought only a year ago. Worried? You bet I was, but I did quite well at the 'san.' They sent me out at the end of six months, and I went back feeling full of beans. Well—I got a facer. The company wouldn't take me back. Against their regulations—or something. I tell you I felt down and out. One of the unemployables. I got a half-time job as a kind of cheap tout for a firm who worked on the instalment system. It was the middle of winter. I may say that my underclothing and my boots weren't exactly O.K.

[301]

And my meals—rather the bun and glass of milk business. In three months I was down again. I tell you I felt like going off the Embankment. A parson in town told me of this place, and here I am."

His case was so like Keir's. Half the cases in Papworth were like the cases of Jannis and Smith.

"What's your wife doing?"

"Oh, just carrying on. Keeping the kid and herself, and paying for the storing of the furniture left to us."

"Mine's doing just the same. Some women have some stuff in them."

"By George, haven't they! That's why I mean to fight for it."

And Jannis laughed.

"If there's somebody waiting, it makes a difference. Ask Father William. He's wanting to go back to the warehouse cat."

Jannis explained that his wife could visit him only once in six weeks. Yes, the train-fare was the problem, and the lady who managed the tea-shop was a holy terror, spent a small income on beauty culture and cut wages to the bone. When a woman did drive a hard bargain, she drove it harder than a man.

"I tell you, Smithie, I'll like to go and break up that tea-shop. No, Stella doesn't grouse. She makes a joke of the thing, but I know she lives in terror of losing the job. Life's such a scramble these days."

Keir was more fortunate, for once a month the Lugard car was put at Sybil's service, and Joanna Mary was boarded out for the day with the kindly Browns. The drive was a long one, some hundred and fifty miles, with outer London to be negotiated, too long a drive for Joanna. At least, Sybil thought so. Joanna had a rather delicate tummy, and Sybil had grown nervous about the child. She dreaded lest Jo should have inherited her father's delicacy of tissue.

When visiting-day came, Keir shaved himself very carefully and was quite fussy about his hair. The other men were gently amused. Keir might be preparing to receive his best girl instead of a wife. But Jannis understood. When you were up against things, sumptuous flappers ceased to interest you.

Sybil mingled breathlessness with dignity. The reunion was so much in public, but Jannis turned a considerate back on them, and Father William took cover behind a newspaper.

"Oh, Keir—"

Keir had no words for her, only eyes and hands. She sat and held his hands and gazed at him.

"Keir, you—do—look better."

"I—am—better."

"You look fatter."

"Well—I've put on eight and a half pounds. I'm behaving like a model case."

He looked searchingly at his wife. Was she doing too much? Would her strength and her courage stand the strain?

"How are things, Syb?"

"Oh—I'm quite all right, Keir."

"Eating properly?"

"Yes."

She produced something from her lap. Keir had noticed the offering, but he had not remarked on it.

"Oh, Jo sent you these. She picked them herself."

"Out of the garden?"

"Yes."

Keir put the flowers to his face.

"We'll have to have a garden here, Syb. You and Jo can't get on without a garden. You tell Jo that."

There was a race between Keir and Jannis as to who should be the first to be promoted publicly and officially to trousers, and Keir won the race by a fortnight. His condition had been less serious than Jannis's, and, being a manual worker, he had more stamina than the clerk. He was absurdly proud of his new state. He was eager to do things, to be allowed to help, as all Papworth helped when it was able. Never had he been so pleased to be on his own feet. The world of nature had been a kind of tapestry hung about his bed, a two-dimensional world, but now it was a world of three dimensions. It had depth for him. It could be explored and penetrated.

He said to himself: "I'm up, yes, up," but if his tail was more erect, he did not parade with arrogance before Jannis and Father William.

"You'll soon be shedding pyjamas, old man."

He said this gently to Jannis. Such things could not be said to William the Silent, for "Dad" was not making progress. In fact he was slipping back, and never again would the warehouse cat rub against his legs. William knew it; his neighbours knew it, but the illusion of life was not shattered.

Keir asked when he would be allowed to work.

"I'm fit for something now, Matron."

She was the wise autocrat.

"You wait a week or so and feel your feet. Go and play billiards for half an hour and see how you feel."

Keir could not play the game, but another patient offered to give him a lesson, and after Keir had walked round and round the table for ten minutes and tried pot-shots at everything and nothing, his urge towards activity deserted him. He was so shaky that the cue was his master.

"I think I'll have to sit down for a while."

He sat down in the doorway and was content to look at the grass and the trees while the other fellow practised breaks. Miss Borne had been quite right. The spirit might be willing, but the flesh was weak. He would have to go gently. And Miss Borne, happening upon him there, saw that he had discovered his limitations.

"You will go and lie down after dinner, Smith."

"Yes, Matron."

At the end of another week, after light exercise and potterings about the grounds, he felt that he would soon be fit for work, and work would have a significance and a usefulness. He would be active; helping. By some people it was held that Papworth is an experiment in socialism. It is not. The more intelligent of the inmates become wise as to the significance of this community. It signifies service, that service which the socialists preach while confining its practice to a clique. Papworth is communal to a point, and utterly individual beyond that point. Individual effort matters. Men have to help to save themselves.

Keir had not yet been down into the village, where other men who had passed through the crisis were at work. In theory there was equality, or equality of opportunity, here, yet Papworth produced the same inevitable social pattern that refuses to be dyed a universal red. It was both a blending and a contrast of colours. Some of the patients who passed out into Papworth's working world became managers and foremen or skilled hands; others were content to remain mere hammerers of nails. The individual flowered according to his faculties.

Keir the convalescent somehow avoided that working world. It lay there in the valley below him, its roofs showing amid the trees. It tantalized him. It was the world towards which the hope within him yearned, but he was so desperately afraid of hoping for too much and too prematurely. He had not forgotten that other relapse. And so he kept to the hill upon which the white hall stood, and if he wandered down the avenue of limes, he did not go beyond the gate. A voice within him said: "So far and no farther. Possess your soul in patience."

He made many friends. He visited the other patients in their chalets. Soon he might be promoted to a chalet. He was looking forward to being the possessor of one of those little huts where he could gather his possessions round him and be alone sometimes with himself. He discovered many other men who felt about it just as he did. He noticed their books and photographs, simple things that satisfied the individual instinct and suggested the apartness of a home.

As a laconic, one-eyed patient put it: "A chap likes to be by himself sometimes. If you snore at night, no one's got a grievance. My little wooden hut does me proud."

Keir was strolling one summer evening along one of the paths, and he paused to look at a very old oak tree that must have stood upon this hill before Papworth Hall had come into being. He was conscious of a presence. He turned and saw the creator of Papworth walking towards him over the grass. Sir Pendrill was passing from his bungalow among the trees to the big white building where he worked. But for a moment the one and only Jones was away in another world, and Keir found himself looking at the face of a man who dreamed.

Keir had a feeling that he wished to efface himself, to stand aside and suffer this other man to pass without thrusting his own presence upon him. Sir Pendrill had much to carry in that big head and upon those broad shoulders. He was responsible for a whole community. He was Atlas bearing his own particular world. But Sir Pendrill saw Keir and came out of his abstraction to speak to him. He smiled at Keir.

"I hear you are doing well, Smith. That's splendid."

Keir flushed up like a sensitive boy.

"Yes, sir."

There were many things that Keir could have said to Sir Pendrill. He could have poured his heart out in gratitude to this other man, but he was shy. And all that he did say was: "You must have a wonderful memory, sir." Sir Pendrill smiled at him as though he divined something of Keir's feeling.

"Not quite so good as it was, Smith."

He passed on. But Keir stood and looked again at the oak tree. Who had planted it? But did it matter? Sir Pendrill had planted a tree here whose roots went deep into the warm earth of humanity.

3

Keir took his first walk in the village. He followed the meadow road from the Hall which brought him to the big building where chicken-houses, sheds, chalets, and garden-houses were manufactured. This big building was open to the south, and in it scores of men were at work, assembling the sections. Towards the main road stood the timber-store, with the machine-shop next to it, so that the raw material was brought in, machined, and passed to the assembling-shed. It was all very efficient and workmanlike.

Keir's bowels yearned in him. He smelled again the smell of timber and of sawdust, perfumes that impregnated his whole working consciousness. He went in and touched some of the timber, the deals and battens, and it was like touching the hand of a friend. In the machine-shop he bent down and scooped up some sawdust into his palm and held the stuff to his nostrils. By George, how good it was, like the smell of the warm soil after rain to the worker upon the land! He slipped that little pile of white dust into his pocket so that most significant and reassuring perfume should remain with him.

All this new and clean white wood, how lovely it was! He examined some of the houses and sheds that were being assembled. He spoke to a tall thin man who was working at a bench fitting a section of a building into a jig.

"You seem pretty well organized here."

"Yes, it's all a system."

"Was this your job before you came here?"

The man looked amused.

"No, I was in the City Police."

Keir laughed.

"Nailing timber instead of nailing narks! You look pretty well on it."

"I am. I have my wife and two kids in one of the cottages. My eldest won a scholarship at Cambridge."

"That's pretty good. Must make a difference having your kids with you."

"I should say so. It's like this: if you ever feel you are a bit finished, you can concentrate on the kids, watch 'em grow up and make good. I'm lucky. My kids have never been any trouble to me. Well, you see, my missus is one of the old sort. She likes being at home."

Keir made his way out to the main road and discovered the village shop. The manager of the shop was an ex-consumptive. Keir went in and bought a packet of chocolate to send to Joanna Mary. He saw a little tea-garden under the trees next the shop, for the use of the colonists and their friends. He wandered up the field road past the new men's hostel and the women's hostel towards the church, and in the meadow he sighted tennis courts. Even this most popular of games was provided for at Papworth. On the brow of the hill stood the nurses' hostel, Miss Borne's pet pride; and in the deep green valley beyond, an old farmstead spread its roofs.

Keir wandered back to the main road. There was so

much more to be explored, the new and handsome village hall in which picture-shows and dances were given and in which the colony met as a community. Nearly opposite it was another hostel for men, and the furniture factory. Keir had been told that he might visit the factory. Patients who hoped to be able to work were encouraged to consider and select an occupation, unless, of course, a man's previous training marked him out for some particular job. Keir, making his way into the building, chanced upon Mr. Jarrett, the manager.

"What do you want, my lad?"

Keir explained himself and his purpose. He was a trained craftsman. Yes, he had done cabinet work.

"All right, have a look round."

The factory fascinated Keir. The very latest machinery had been installed in the machine-room for sawing and planing and rebating. There was even a queer machine for sand-papering the wood, a machine that dealt with and extracted its own dust. From the machine-room the timber passed to the fitting-room, where a number of men were assembling the various articles. Beyond it lay the finishing-room and the show- and store-room where the products were exhibited, and Keir was astonished at the finish and the quality of the work. He examined beautiful walnut and mahogany specimen pieces, sideboards, bureaus, bookcases. His eyes lit up.

Near the packing department he fell in again with Mr. Jarrett, and Mr. Jarrett, who had an eye for a man and for business, nailed Keir.

"Ever done any veneering?"

Yes, Keir had. It had been a hobby of his, and he had the hands for it.

"We have one first-class chap. He was a farm labourer before he came here. We could do with another."

"I'd like to try."

"Well, you go and get passed fit as soon as you can. There's good money to be made here."

Keir wandered out again and on up the main road. He found himself scrutinizing the Papworth cottages set in their gardens on the banks above the road. Some of them were detached, others semi-detached, neat little red buildings amid trees and flowers. Someone had told him that a Papworth cottage could be rented for seven and six or nine and six a week.

He stood and looked at the garden of a particular cottage. It was full of summer flowers, snapdragons, and marigolds, clarkia and lavatera, phloxes and sweet peas. A young woman in a light blue linen dress was at work in it, and he thought: "It might be Sybil, and Jo with her wheelbarrow. Please God, I'm going to get well."

Chapter Twenty-seven

1

SYBIL had trials of her own, and had she been asked to select the sin against the Holy Ghost, she would have identified it with meanness, especially that meanness that walks hand in hand with self-indulgence. She could cope with a Mr. Brown who showed signs of becoming sentimental and silly about her, for Mr. Brown was a sensitive creature and easily put out of countenance. Mrs. Lugard had recommended her as housemaid-help to two middle-aged suburban ladies with pink and brassy faces, the Misses Twine. The Misses Twine still saw themselves as girls. They were dressy, bridgy, golfy, slangy women who drove about in an electric blue car and spent money freely. They were the kind of women who talk in theatres and during concerts and found the world full of impatience and were full of a loud self-satisfaction.

Mrs. Lugard had said: "I don't know them very well, Sybil, but they are supposed to be good sorts."

The Misses Twine may have gained that reputation because they were so good to themselves and to numbers of casual and vicarious men. They called their house "Westward Ho," and it was always prepared with little drinks and cigarettes and large chairs. It was a kind of club for the adventitious male. The Misses Twine were known familiarly as Billy and Tilly.

Sybil soon discovered that the cook and the housemaid at Westward Ho had other views upon the subject. The cook was the sixth cook the Misses Twine had engaged in the space of two years, and she was ripe for the harvest. She was a rather stout and decent body who liked to stay put, if life would allow her to be static.

The Misses Twine locked up the store-cupboard and the little corner cupboard in the drawing-room that contained numberless bottles for the preparing of cocktails. The kitchen was run on severely economic lines. Billy Twine always checked the tradesmen's books. People were so ready to do you.

But cook did like her cup of coffee in the middle of the morning. She did not see why she should not have her cup of coffee when Alice could carry to her housemaid's pantry all those cocktail glasses to be washed. Gin and bitters and benedictine and vermouth and créme de menthe and what not! Cook ordered her own special coffee. She and Alice and Sybil sat down to cups of coffee at eleven a.m. They began their working day at seven a.m., and sometimes it did not end till eleven in the evening. The Misses Twine dined many men. They breakfasted at nine-thirty or later, unless, of course, they had to be on the first tee at Worplesdon or St. George's Hill at ten-thirty.

Miss Billy discovered the coffee. There was a row about the coffee. To her sister Miss Billy spoke of "those three females guzzling in the middle of the morning." The drawing-room of "Westward Ho" became full of stridencies. Cook had been told that she could pay for her own coffee.

Cook went up and packed her trunk. Alice followed her. They had the impertinence to use the Twine telephone and to ring up a taxi.

Cook, who was quite a good-tempered person, was heard to say: "I have had enough of these two old balls of string."

They departed on the bosom of a final storm. The Misses Twine denied them their wages. They were leaving without proper notice, dishonouring their contract. No, not a penny! The Misses Twine were the injured parties.

Sybil, left cleaning silver in the pantry, heard those two

distant and discordant voices uttering maledictions. The lower orders were impossible. They were sponging, peculating, insolent slackers. "It's the dole, my dear." But Miss Billy came in to Sybil; she cooed to Sybil. It was really very awkward. Miss Twine would say nothing about this dastardly desertion, but would Sybil assist them until further help could be obtained?

Sybil explained that she was responsible for a bungalow and a child, and that she had other houses to go to. Miss Twine was sweetly persistent. Surely Sybil would consider them. She could abandon her other patronesses in such a crisis. Of course, the other people would understand.

Sybil offered Miss Twine an additional day, one of her own days, but she could not disappoint her other ladies.

"Couldn't you come in for the week-end? We have visitors. It is so very awkward."

Sybil had planned to go down to Papworth that Saturday.

"I'm sorry, Miss Twine, but I am going to see my husband."

Miss Twine looked pained. Selfish, unaccommodating creature! Could not Sybil put off the visit for a week?

Sybil refused, and Miss Twine went off to send telegrams and to visit the local registry office. Really, life could be very exasperating. Eddie Black and Teddie Toogood had been coming down for the week-end, to play mixed foursomes at St. George's Hill. Oh, these women!

But that was not the end of the story. Sybil gave the Misses Twine two days a week, and at the end of the third week Miss Tilly missed a green jade necklace. There was a tremendous pother about that necklace, and Sybil had been the only other person in the house. The registry office had been unable to provide service.

Billy said to Tilly: "It must be Smith. I shouldn't have thought it of the woman."

They went about with shut-up and accusing faces. It was

obvious to Sybil that they suspected her.

"I suppose she pinches things for that wretched husband of hers."

Miss Billy Twine had an unpleasant laugh.

"Not for husbands, my dear."

But Sybil had suffered sufficiently from the suspicious faces of the ladies, and then, on the very day when she was preparing her ultimatum, she found the necklace. It had slipped into the deep crevice at the back of a Chesterfield sofa.

Sybil ran up to Miss Tilly's bedroom. Miss Tilly was resting.

"I've found the necklace, miss."

"Where?"

"At the back of the sofa."

Miss Tilly was sceptical, polite, and rather abrupt.

"That must be a relief to you, Smith."

Sybil stood and stared at Miss Tilly Twine. Then she went downstairs, put on her things, and walked out of the house. The mean, suspicious beasts! She was owed fifteen shillings for two days' work, and she never received the money.

Tilly said to Billy: "Well, she was lucky to get off, and she knows it. I suppose she grew windy about the thing. I had suggested having the police in."

And that was that.

2

But at Papworth Sybil forgot the Misses Twine, and even if she had not forgotten them, she would not have resurrected the ladies for the troubling of Keir. The Lugards and their car were absent in Scotland, and Sybil had had to travel by train. She had pawned her best electroplated spoons to provide her railway fare, for the loss of

[314]

those fifteen shillings had run her short. She had left Kingham at an unconscionable hour in the morning, and she
would return to Kingham about midnight. Meanwhile she
sat with Keir under the trees in the tea-garden next the
village shop, and the shadows flickered over her face and
her blue frock.

Keir thought her looking rather thin and tired, but he
had good news to give her. He had been like a man floun-
dering in a marsh, and gradually, in his struggle with the
sucking slime, he had felt the ground growing firm under
his feet.

"Dr. Stott overhauled me yesterday. Everything's quiet
inside."

He had insisted on Sybil having eggs for her tea. As a
patient he was entitled to a little pocket-money, and he had
saved up his pennies to pay for that tea.

"Oh—Keir—!"

That was all she could say. She clutched his hand. They
shared a moment of exquisite emotion.

"Have some jam, Syb."

"I've only just finished my eggs."

"You must have some jam. It's real good stuff, straw-
berry."

He pushed the dish towards her and watched her help
herself.

"No, more than that. Tuck into it."

"It's real fruit."

"Yes, none of your turnip and aniline dye. You're looking a little on the thin side, Syb."

"Oh—I'm all right."

"Sure?"

"Yes."

"Look here, we've got to talk about things, Syb. I asked
Dr. Stott's advice. He told me that if I keep on as I am, I
may be able to do light work in three months. There's a job

ready for me in the furniture shop. But—"

He watched his wife's face.

"It's a life's job. I mean, Syb, that if I stay here and work at easy pressure and don't have to rush it with men who—"

She looked him straight in the eyes.

"Of course, Keir, I understand."

"It would mean—that you and Jo—"

She helped herself to more jam. She knew that it pleased him to see her enjoying the jam.

"Can we get a cottage here, Keir?"

He seemed to breathe more easily.

"Yes, in time. Then—you won't mind?"

"I think it's a lovely place."

"We have concerts and picture-shows and dances. And there's a tennis club, and a gardening club. The flower show is—"

His wife smiled at him.

"Your idea of jam, Keir?"

"No; but some women have queer ideas about the country. It would worry me to feel—"

"You needn't worry, Keir. Don't you know that I—"

"I know you're about the best pal a man ever had."

"Oh, Keir."

"It's God's truth. But, look here, we shall have to do something about 'Merrow.' Wouldn't it be easier for you in rooms until I have made a home here?"

"We could store the furniture."

"Yes, and you would have a little money in hand. The place should fetch more than the mortgage."

"May I think it over, Keir? Lodgings, you know—"

"I do know. It's only that I want to save you worry and work."

"I shan't worry so long as you are getting better. And they do rook you in lodgings, Keir, and there is always trouble about cooking."

[316]

"Well, do just what you like. I want to have a stroll and show you some of the cottages. There's a school here for Jo to go to. No, not a single kid in Papworth has developed consumption. They are a healthy crowd."

His wife's face lit up.

"Not one?"

"Not one."

Keir showed his wife over the settlement, and though Sybil was impressed by the largeness of the village hall, she was chiefly interested in the Papworth cottages. She preferred those higher up the hill, standing well about the ancient Ermyn Street, with their gardens backing upon a meadow. From the garden you could look across at the white hall and its trees and a crowd of little chalets that had the appearance of a flock of chicken-houses.

Sybil hung over fences and gates and admired the flowers.

"What is the rent, Keir?"

"About seven and six and nine and six a week, rates included."

"Think what we paid at Paragon Place! And if you are able to work—?"

Keir knew that his wife was doing sums in her head. He recognized that domestic and contriving expression.

"I might earn nine or ten bob a day. You see, we are not allowed to do an eight-hour day. Six is the limit, and the idea is quite sound."

"Nearly three pounds a week."

"That's about it."

Sybil nodded her head.

"I could manage very well on that. We could even put a little money by. Holidays, you know. Do they have holidays at Papworth?"

"Rather. Just like anybody else."

Sybil gazed longingly at the cottages. Her desire was to explore the interior of one of these hypothetical homes, and her desire was satisfied. A woman, emerging from behind a row of sweet peas, came face to face with Sybil, and friendly glances were exchanged.

Said Sybil: "Please don't think us rude for looking over your fence like this—but your garden's a picture."

The gardener was pleased. Had she not taken a prize for her sweet peas at last year's Papworth flower show!

"Lovely things, aren't they?"

"I've never seen better. Yes, my husband is a patient here. We hope to have a cottage some day. They look such nice cottages."

Sybil's hint was naïve and appealing.

"Would you like to look over one?"

"I'd love to."

"Well, come inside."

"May I—really? It is kind of you. Do come, Keir. You ought to see it too."

3

Keir attained to his chalet, and with it he was given a little light work in the garden for the sake of exercise and as a physical test. He weeded, and picked fruit, and for two months he received no pay for his work. He did not expect to be paid for it. He regarded it as part of his treatment, exercise in the open air for the benefit of the body and soul. He was glad of the work. His hands were in contact with the soil, and if he still kept that pinch of sawdust in his pocket, that too was elemental and good. He was coming to understand the spirit of Papworth, the large and beneficent wisdom that lifted a man up and set him on his feet and watched over him. "Friend, help to heal thyself." If Papworth set you a task, there was reason in its pragmatism, gentle exercise for heart and head.

Yet Keir found one or two men who grumbled, men who

were so steeped in the modern cult of doing as little as possible for as much as they could get that when a wise management found them occupation, they resented it. They groused; they loafed. They were being exploited. They were doing work for Papworth, and Papworth was not paying them anything for it. Yes, they were being exploited.

Keir had an argument with one of these gentlemen in a corner of the walled garden where they were weeding an onion bed. The gentleman said that Papworth—like all institutions—was run by a lot of — toffs. Oh, yes, hadn't Keir seen the toffs who came down in swank cars and patronized the place? It was like a — zoo, and the patients were just so many animals in cages for the toffs to stare at. Making a chap work, using him, and not giving him a — penny for it. Fourpence a day pocket-money! The sanguinary ramp ought to be exposed.

Keir grew hot. He felt contempt for this awkward, stupid beast who was being given his chance to live, and who would have regarded God with suspicion if God had set him to gather fruit in Eden.

"Well—why don't you clear out? There's nothing to stop you from going?"

The fellow took Keir literally. He said that he would see Jones and have it out with him. He seemed to regard Sir Pendrill as the eternal boss. And if he did not get any satisfaction out of Jones, he would write to the *Daily Wail* and show the place up.

Keir let fly.

"One doesn't expect gratitude from people, but one does ask for sense. You get housed and fed and doctored and a chance to live, and you think you're exploited. What the devil do you think they get out of a chap like you? What does society get out of a chap like you?"

The man flared.

"You mind your — business. Who asked you—?"

"Oh, shut up," said Keir; "some of you fellows make me sick. You don't know a weed from an onion. Aren't you getting your chance here? Where else would you get it? Why should a man like Sir Pendrill trouble—? Oh, yes, just because he's big, and you don't understand that sort of thing. Some of you never will understand it."

Keir was told that he was one of the blighters who sucked up to the toffs. "After a soft job, are you?" But Keir had said his say. You might lay into an ass of this order for ever and ever, and he would just bray at you. Keir removed himself to the other end of the onion bed and worked alone and in peace.

He loved his little chalet. It was individual, and somehow his, and it was so pleasant to blow out the candle at night and to know you were alone. No chatter, no fool noises, for Keir's neighbours in the adjoining chalets loved peace as much as he did. Sickness and suffering soften and civilize man unless he is made of that poor pulp which turns sour and rotten. If there was any quality of fineness in a character, it was tempered here.

Sometimes the wind made a murmuring in the eaves of the little building. Doors and windows were open and let in the stars. Keir did quite a lot of star-gazing. The Great Bear and Orion were part of his new world.

Keir was resting on his bed one afternoon after tea when Jannis appeared. Jannis was up and allowed light exercise, but his face was still the colour of fine vellum. He sat down on the top step of Keir's chalet.

Keir had just been reading a letter from Sybil. It contained a singular piece of news. Messrs. Samson, Hoad & Gott had called their creditors together.

"You're looking pretty cheerful, K. Good news?"

Keir raised himself on one elbow.

"I suppose it shouldn't be, but it is. My old firm have gone smash."

[320]

"And you're bucked about it?"

"Well—I suppose it's human nature, but the man who spoilt my best chance in life has gone smash with it."

"You're a good hater, Keir."

"I am. Hasn't one the right to hate the mean things and to love the good things? Don't let's humbug ourselves about universal love."

Jannis stroked the back of his very black and sleek head. It was a characteristic gesture of his.

"Well—I don't know. I felt rather like blowing up my old company when they shut me out in the cold, but there are all the other fellows to remember."

"Yes, that's true, the other fellows and their wives."

Chapter Twenty-eight

1

PROBABLY Dr. Stott would have said that it is very necessary to study a patient's temperament as well as his simpler physical reactions, though in that very complex creature—man—the balance may be turned by a rose leaf. Dr. Stott was responsible for the Papworth children, and he liked to observe them in a state of nature, splashing in an open-air swimming-pool. The young animal exhibited itself revealingly to the expert's eye. It might be well fleshed and vital and active, or sensitive and shy and needing a delicate touch. Sensitive tissue might imply a sensitive spirit. Dr. Stott read his Keir both as a body and as a man. He saw in Keir a worker who was yearning to use his hands. Keir belonged to that particular type, the lean, intense, and somewhat separative people in whom the passion to do and to create is dominant. He would never be the cheerful loafer, the gentleman of the pub and the street corner, ingeniously otiose, and active only under the eye of the foreman or the boss.

"I am going to have you 'boarded,' Smith. I think you are one of the men who are better working."

"When will it be, sir?"

"Next week. But I want to impress upon you the need for caution. Don't rush at your job like a dog let off the chain."

Keir smiled at him.

"Oh, I've learnt wisdom, sir. I've had my lesson."

Keir was "boarded" in the library, that same room in which he and Sybil had said good-bye to each other, and the spirit of his wife seemed with him. The examination was very thorough, and an hour or so later Keir heard the verdict. It was announced to him by Dr. Stott.

"We are going to try you in the furniture shop. I had a talk with Mr. Jarrett about you. Two hours a day for a fortnight—as an experiment. If you pass that test, we'll make you a four-and-a-half-hour man."

So once again Keir went to work. He was to retain his chalet until he had taken his place on the pay-roll as a four-and-a-half-hour man. Then he would be transferred to one of the sanatorium block chalets. He walked down the avenue of lime trees on a sunny September morning and he was as nervous and as excited as a lad up for his first examination. The adventure of living and working was once more his. He was a man, not a poor derelict, a human hulk rotting in some back street.

He reported to Mr. Jarrett.

"Hallo. I was expecting you, my lad. Two hours' light work. Right you are. I've got a job for you."

He led Keir to a bench and showed him the face of a drawer that was to be veneered with walnut. Keir could try his hands on that, and if he needed any help or advice, Mason would give it him. Mason was the shop's expert, a dark, quiet lad, a little god in his own craft, but not a jealous god.

"I would rather try on my own, if I may?"

"That's the spirit."

Mr. Jarrett left him to work out his own salvation and to settle himself in with his neighbours. The atmosphere of the workshop was cheerful and friendly. A new man was not regarded as an interloper, but as a useful member of the community who would assist in making Papworth and himself financially self-supporting. That was the crux of the whole problem. A community such as Papworth could not crucify itself on the cross of ca' canny.

Keir was nervous. He was so afraid of bungling that first job. He dreaded lest his hands should have lost their cunning. In the old days he had had the touch for such work. He would have made a very capable surgeon. And this film of wood that had to be cut and glued to the face of the drawer could so easily fool a man whose hands trembled, and Keir's hands did tremble.

Someone came and watched him, and Keir wished the fellow would go away. He did go away. It was Mason, the expert; and Mason, being a sensitive lad, saw that Keir was best left alone.

Keir's hands trembled. This would not do! If he got this film of wood kinked or crooked, both he and Mr. Jarrett would be able to say that he had made an unholy mess of the job. But how absurd this panic! He could feel his heart beating hard and fast. He paused. He leaned against the bench and then went for a stroll down the shop. He watched a big, fair man placidly assembling an oak bedside cabinet.

The man smiled at Keir.

"A Christmas present for Jerry."

And Keir laughed, and with his laughter the spirit of his fear seemed to depart like some exorcized demon. Laughter was good. Man was the only living creature who could laugh. He felt that his hands had become steady and sure. He went back to his bench. He smiled at that oblong panel of veneer. He thought of one of those cottages, and of Sybil and Joanna Mary.

His hands dealt deftly with the film of walnut. It spread itself and sat down and adhered to the face of the drawer like a young skin without wrinkles. The crisis was over. Keir stood and contemplated his handiwork, and the panic mood of half an hour ago. That a man should be afraid of a piece of wood! Well, had he not read of authors being afraid of their pens, and of eminent pianists perspiring as they sat down on a platform and placed their fingers on the

[324]

keys? If you did not fear to mar the exquisite quality of your craft, you would never make a craftsman.

Mr. Jarrett, walking through the shop, stopped at Keir's bench and examined the face of the drawer.

"That's not so bad, lad."

"You'll pass it?"

"I should say so."

Mr. Jarrett was a Yorkshireman, and laconic, but Keir could judge by the quality of the finished articles in the showroom that Mr. Jarrett did not pass dud work. Keir's hands had made good.

2

For a fortnight Keir worked two hours a day in the furniture shop, and at the end of the fourteen days Dr. Stott re-examined him. The verdict was wholly in Keir's favour. There was not a moist sound to be heard in his chest, and the disease appeared to have been arrested. He had put on weight, and he was eating and sleeping well.

"You managed the two hours—comfortably?"

"Quite, sir."

"I'll mark you up as a four-and-a-half-hour man. I'm very pleased with you, Smith."

Keir was buttoning up his shirt. He had something to say to Dr. Stott.

"I'm very glad, sir. Of course, you know that what makes all the difference here—is—that one isn't worried."

"Yes, we do know that, Smith. That's part of our philosophy."

"I think it is the worry that helps to kill many men, sir. Black fear, a horrible sense of insecurity, the feeling that when you have been patched up, you will be pushed out into the world again to sink or swim."

"Most of them sink."

Keir nodded. He had been up to the lips in that hopeless sea.

"Which means, sir, that man does not live on a bottle of medicine. Mind is at the back of everything, your mind, my mind, Sir Pendrill's mind."

"Mind—plus something else."

"Yes—I know. Compassion."

So Keir was given his bench in the cabinet shop, and became a four-and-a-half-hour man. Mr. Jarrett experimented with Keir; he assigned him some simple cabinet work, and when he was sure of the craftsman in Keir, he put him on to the more delicate and intricate work. The shop had received an order for a suite of dining-room furniture in walnut: sideboard, table, six chairs, and a bookcase bureau. Keir was promoted to be Mason's assistant and understudy in the veneering. It was a ticklish job covering a large surface like that of a sideboard, and sometimes the "shop" would pause to watch Mason and Keir handling those delicate sheets, but both Mason and Keir were so much part of their work that they were quite unconscious of being watched. Both of them were dark, intense, slim-built men. Sometimes when bending together over the work, their heads seemed to touch.

Keir had no eyes for the clock, but sometimes he listened to the clock within himself. It ticked rhythmically and steadily, and little by little his confidence returned. Papworth had given a new temper to his mainspring, and it showed no signs of failing. At the end of his four and a half hours he was a little tired, but happily so, and for the remainder of the day he could rest and read or walk. He took a daily tramp of three miles. It was autumn and the trees were changing colour, and in this golden world he found a new beauty and a new consolation. It was autumn, and winter was coming, but he could count upon the spring.

Keir had to vacate his chalet. He was to undergo his test as a six-hour man and live in one of the hostels. He moved into what was known as the Old Hostel, a single-storied building on the west of the main road. The hostel contained a dining-room, a billiard-room, a games-room, two- and one-bed cubicles, and lavatories, and to Keir was assigned a bed in one of the two-bed cubicles. These little rooms were very simply furnished. Each bed was covered with a blue bedspread. The hostel humorist had suggested that each cubicle should have a white line down the centre of the floor, and that no occupant should park any of his possessions in the other fellow's territory.

Keir shared his cubicle with a young man named Broster, who worked in the trunk shop, and Broster was the colony's special fellow-my-lad. Though he wore grey flannel trousers and a pull-over, these articles had an otherness that was Broster. Charlie Broster had one of those honey-coloured heads that appear to require infinite attention, and when Keir was dressed and ready for breakfast, Broster was still buttering his locks. A cheerful and casual and noisy young man, he whistled like a bird in the spring or burst into sudden song, and his voice was not as sleek as his head. He would be one of the last to leave the billiard or games room in the evening, and most certainly he was the last to leave his bed in the morning. A hostel—by the nature of things and character of its construction—is not padded against noise, and Broster was a noisy young devil.

"Hallo, Smithie, shall I kiss you good night?"

Keir, tucked up and trying to go to sleep, appreciated neither Broster's facetiousness nor his loitering.

"Get into bed, my lad, and have done with it."

But Broster was always so very much awake, save in the workshop, and he wanted to lie in bed with the light on and read the paper. He made an extraordinary amount of noise crumpling and turning the pages of the paper.

He was the most cheerfully complacent young man, so thick-skinned with self-sufficiency that no hints penetrated. No one could criticize Broster—for to himself Broster was quite above criticism. On Saturday afternoons he would rush off to Cambridge and delight the girls. It was said that at Cambridge he posed as a member of the University, that he had purchased a second-hand cap and gown, and kept them at a friend's house and in them paraded the streets of Cambridge.

Also, Broster snored. He had suffered from adenoids as a child, and he snored—as he did everything else—with a breezy abandonment. Keir had discovered that when men are gathered in a close community, individual whimsies have to be suppressed. Tolerance and good temper became essential virtues. He could not heave a book at Broster because he snored. Broster's snoring was as inevitable as his coloured jersey, his buttered head, and his casual conceit.

He bore with Broster's physical attributes for a month, largely because the hostel was full of such good fellowship, but he found it less easy to bear with Broster's philosophy. The fascinating of the feminine world may demand high finance, and Lothario valued himself at no mean figure.

Broster never had enough money. The world of Papworth did not reward him for his labours as he expected to be rewarded. Youth is so full of itself, so conscious of its infinite beauty and charm, that it expects society to press overflowing coffers upon it.

"Jones must be making a pretty penny out of us."

Both of them were lying in bed, and Keir, who wanted to go to sleep, was terse with his stable-companion.

"How much do you think he makes out of you?"

"They pay me a miserable thirty-six bob a week."

"Probably they make a loss on it."

This was absurd, and Mr. Broster said so.

"Haven't you heard of surplus value, Smithie, the surplus labour creates and never gets? The capitalist pinches it."

As a working economist Keir had delved deeper than young Broster, and as a practical man he had found that the socialist theories split upon the rock of human nature, the inevitable frivolities and laziness of man.

"What's your surplus, Broster?"

"That's just what I should like to know."

"So should I."

"My argument is that a show like this ought to produce all the figures to the men: costs, profits—and what becomes of the profits."

"And supposing your activities didn't show a profit?"

Broster was too serenely sure of his social value.

"Don't be silly, Smithie. Do you think my six hours a day aren't worth more than thirty-six bob?"

Keir turned over and prepared for sleep.

"Quite possibly they're not. Switch the light off, my lad. The debate's closed."

The paternal eyes of Papworth were not blind, and Charlie Broster's Saturday and Sunday pilgrimages to Cambridge were known to headquarters. The fatherly and responsible world spoke kindly but firmly to Broster by the mouth of one of the settlement doctors. He was warned against burning his torch as a fit man could burn it, but the youth in him was restive. They were treating him like a kid. Papworth wasn't a penal colony, and if a fellow could not have a bit of beano once a week, well—he might as well join the Church of England. All this moral tosh about the wisdom of continence! That sort of stuff was dead.

Keir was treated to Charlie's rhetoric. He could have told the lad that when a doctor gives you good advice for nothing, you might be the recipient of surplus value that

[329]

was worth reflection, but he was tired of Charlie Broster. Youth could be so shallow and smart and heartless, the eternal Narcissus, and Keir, hearing from Jannis that he—Jannis—was moving into the New Hostel, managed to get himself transferred. He and the clerk set up house together happily in a rather superior sort of cubicle. Their moods and habits did not clash. They had outlived their crudities.

Keir did not see the end of Charlie Broster. All that he heard was that poor Butter-head had suffered a relapse and had been returned to hospital. His own surplus value had become a minus quantity.

One of the older men who still used the vernacular spoke of Broster as a "Poor, — young fool." Keir did not think of the lad quite in that way. To him Broster was typical of youth, and especially so of modern youth. It resented discipline. It had been told so cleverly by the bright young men who wrote books that the superstition of self-restraint is as obsolete as the sacraments.

Young Broster died during the winter. He passed away, just as youth's hot faith in its own cleverness passes away. The old fool—and the young fool! But if the old fool has reached sixty, his folly must be allowed some survival value. Keir's desire was to become one of the staid, sentimental industrious old fools.

Chapter Twenty-nine

1

As Keir read deeper and deeper into the pages of Papworth, he realized that it was not only a notable experiment in practical compassion, but also an essay on common sense. The wisdom and the vision that had made Papworth possible were reinforced by the plain common sense of the community. Men accepted that which had been self-evident for centuries, those human realities that a raucous and strutting idealism has attempted to ignore. A large and flabby Mrs. Slop ladling out treacle to her horde of pets, and brimstone to all the other children, was no goddess here. Her elevation of organized pilfering into a profession of faith may be nothing but an appeal to those very instincts in man which the Old Humbug pretends to deplore: to obtain power through preaching self-pity and a pilgrimage to the shrine of St. Plunder!

Keir and Jannis, discussing life's realities in their cubicle, were agreed that life might be a rough business, but that men could not escape it by becoming sheep. As for the sheep community—you had to accept the sheep-dog and the shepherd. Common sense was at one with science in assuming that men differed. They differed in their hereditary outfit, in physical capacity, mental possibilities, and above all in character. One man might be of more value to the community than another. Why did one citizen become an expert surgeon, while his neighbour hacked holes in a road?

"Just privilege, just opportunity?"

Jannis had a sense of humour.

"So much of the modern cant, Keir, is just saving the faces of the unsuccessful. I suppose some people would say that we belong to the unsuccessful, but I'm damned if we do."

Keir laughed.

"Well, we seem to have held up the offensive of the T.B. bug. And we both have jobs that cannot be left to the casual and cheerful fool."

Their tails were up, and an erect tail is to be encouraged in a community such as Papworth's not because Papworth ever indulged in dog-fights, but because courage and character and common sense are the blood and the bones and the brain of any community. Had not the one and only Jones set them the example? "To the bench, my merry men. Buckle to. Live and laugh and labour, and play. A community of talkers ends in tosh. Up, up, those who have the brains and the character and the skill. Let's to our benches, all of us! And if some show more wisdom and skill and character than others, let us not snarl at them. The victor is worth his laurel crown. The Greeks knew that more than two thousand years ago. They ceased to be Greeks when they forgot it."

Papworth graded itself, and on the whole the common sense of the community accepted this grading. Papworth had a "Head," and it respected that head. It accepted managers and foremen and its skilled craftsmen. It accepted the common sense of capacity and the logic of the pay-sheet. For, as Jannis put it: "If a workshop reduces its capacity to the level of the least efficient worker, its standard of living is bound to get down among the sawdust. This isn't charity; it's common sense."

Keir became a six-hour-a-day man. He had ceased to be Mason's understudy; he was Mason's co-partner and comrade. By arranging their work together, by emulation and mutual help, they found that they could increase their out-

[332]

put. Papworth benefited; so did their fellow-workers; so did they.

"What we want here is capital, capital and yet more capital."

Papworth hungered for capital. It lusted to expand. It needed capital for cottages, capital for hospital accommodation, capital for plant and raw material.

Keir pinned a big C up over his bed. C stood for cottage, and Jannis chipped him about that C, declaring that it stood for covetousness.

"Which commandment was it, old lad? Thou shalt not covet thy neighbour's wife, thou shalt not covet thy neighbour's car, nor his house, nor his War Loan, nor anything that is his. But that's not the creed of the day. Covet anything that the other fellow has that you haven't and tax him till he can't afford it."

"C stands for capitalist and cottage, Jannis."

"We shall never be Rockefellers, Keir, but we can attain to a cottage. I hear there are another six to go up."

"And the waiting list?"

"A dozen applicants—at least—and we come seventh and eighth."

"That means our waiting for another batch to be built."

"There may be vacancies. But that means that some poor beggar has gone back to the sick-list. Get thee behind me, Satan! But I do wish some nice old lady would leave the show a whacking legacy ear-marked for the erection of cottage property. If people only knew—"

For that was Papworth's problem, the problem which has energized all progressive communities that are building up instead of squandering, to produce its product, sell its product, and maintain a margin that could be used for the further benefit of the community. The colony had to carry its sick and its children, and its citizens were not men who could be worked at full pressure. But the quality of the work was admirable. It sold. The yearly turnover was increasing. Those who presided over the community's figures could say the settlement was paying its way; but for the expanding of hospital accommodation and the erection of houses for workers it still needed help from the outer world.

That help was provided. It flowed in quietly and generously, and yet Sir Pendrill, looking out from the windows of his enterprise, saw further than the roofs and the fields of Papworth. Papworth was like a theatre outside whose doors long queues waited. His urge was towards the creation of a theatre many times enlarged, over whose doors could be written: "Enter all ye who are sick and suffering and without hope."

2

Sybil came to Papworth on a Saturday, and a friend of Keir's in the "shop," hearing that Keir's wife had to travel to and fro from Kingham in the day, offered to put Sybil up for the week-end. The Theobalds had a cottage a hundred yards or so beyond the estate office, and Keir was grateful for their kindness. He would pay. Joanna Mary was to spend the week-end with the Browns.

Winter had come, and on the Saturday afternoon Keir and Sybil went out and walked. It was a day of frost and of stillness, with a clear sky and a westering sun that showed up the bare branches of the trees. Smoke climbed straight from cottage chimneys. The hedgerows had a sparkle in them, and the frost still lay in the shadows.

A vital day. Keir was head in air. The tang of the day was on his lips, and health in his heels. He was walking faster than he knew, and his wife noticed it and was glad.

"Look at that smoke, Syb; it's quite blue."

She looked at his alert and freshened face.

"So it is. You can walk, Keir, now."

He glanced at her with a sudden smile.

"Going too fast for you?"

"No."

They had come to a lane. It led to a wood in which the oak trees caught the winter sunlight. Their trunks were a greenish gold. There was a field-gate here and they leaned upon it, and suddenly Keir kissed his wife. It was a lover's kiss. Her dear, cold face had for him an exquisite softness.

"Man wasn't made to live alone, Syb."

She leaned against him.

"Keir, I wish I hadn't to go back."

"So do I, kid. It's just a question of waiting."

"What a pity one can't move 'Merrow' here!"

"Yes, if we could!"

She looked at the oak trees sheeted in the winter sunlight.

"Keir—I've had an idea."

"What?"

"I've been thinking that I might be able to get work at Cambridge. Jo and I could go into lodgings. I should be so much nearer. I could come over every week-end."

He held her closer.

"Syb, that's a great idea. I'll ask somebody about it. We have visitors from Cambridge. There's Lady Isherwood, Professor Isherwood's wife. She's on the general committee."

Keir appealed to Papworth's Dea Mater, Miss Borne, and Miss Borne's capacity for helping people was eminently practical. In her the community symbolized its supreme and kindly common sense. She found jobs for patients and sometimes paid for them out of her own pocket. A consumptive and bedridden girl was provided with drawing-lessons. A journalist handed his last articles to Miss Borne, who passed them to the editor of the Papworth magazine. Miss Borne's ambition included the building of a rest-house and home for retired nurses.

[335]

She listened to Keir, an eager and rather apologetic Keir.

"I don't want to waste your time, Matron."

Miss Borne was one of those busy but unflurried people who appear to have time for everything.

"What is it, Smith?"

"It's about my wife. She is wondering whether she could get work in Cambridge, so as to be nearer. Of course, we are hoping—in time—for a cottage."

"What kind of work?"

"Housework. She and the child could live in lodgings, and she could go out for the day. I'm able to help her now, but she is one of those who like work."

Miss Borne smiled her tight little shrewd smile.

"How refreshing, Smith! It shouldn't be very difficult, I think. I'll ask some of our Cambridge friends when they come over to visit us."

Within a fortnight the business was arranged. A firm of estate agents at Kingham found an immediate purchaser for "Merrow." The little place was sold at a profit, and Sybil, having consulted Mrs. Lugard, opened a joint account at the Westminster Bank. She and Keir had a credit of ninety-five pounds, three shillings, and fourpence. She was given a pass-book and a cheque-book. She arranged for the moving and the storing of the furniture, and on one December morning she said good-bye to the white bungalow and the beech tree.

She shed a few tears over it, tears that Joanna Mary seemed to understand.

"Can't they put it on wheels, mummy? I've seen awful big lorries as large as a house."

"It's somebody else's house, dear, now."

"You haven't sold my wheelbarrow, mummy, have you?"

"Oh, no, dear. It's with the furniture. You'll want your wheelbarrow when we move into a new cottage."

"Shall I see daddy at Cambridge?"

"You'll go over with me and see him. Of course. Oh, here's Mrs. Brown. She is coming to see us off at the station."

One of Papworth's Cambridge friends not only had found Sybil four days' work a week, but had arranged lodgings for her in Mill Lane, in a cottage occupied by a college cook and his wife. Mill Lane, a tortuous little street, burrowed its way down to the river. Sybil's bedroom window looked towards the river and the "Backs," and she could see the tops of the great elm trees.

She and Joanna Mary arrived on a Friday, and on the Saturday they went over to Papworth. Keir was waiting at the bus-halt, and Joanna, snatched by her father from the step, flung her arms round Keir's neck.

"Oh, daddy."

He kissed the child almost with fierceness. He was getting something back from life, and to feel is to live.

"The Theobalds are giving us tea, Syb."

He walked through the village holding Joanna by the hand. He met friends and acquaintances, and some of them stopped and were introduced to Miss Smith. Joanna looked up at them with characteristic solemnity. It was an occasion, and she was conscious of it and of being somehow a little person of importance. Also, she was wearing a new hat and coat and shoes.

"I'm coming to live here soon."

The various new friends smiled at her. Papworth was pleased to see its children.

3

To Sybil, Cambridge was so very different from Kingham. Certainly, there were the same buses and motor-coaches and cars, the same crowded haste in the grey streets. Never had she seen so many bicycles or so many young men or so many solemn buildings. In her simplicity she divined a tradition here that still shuffled about the college courts like a very old man with cobwebs in his hair. Gentle cobwebs, gossamer, dust motes flickering in the sunlight. Sleek grass, old trees, the sound of bells, top-hatted porters at college gates, gowns, the organ-playing in King's College Chapel. And Woolworth's, and the International Stores, and the cinemas, and at night the eyes of young men searching the faces of the women.

Joanna Mary settled down quite happily in Mill Lane. Mrs. Bland's children were out in the world, and the college cook's wife treated Joanna like a grandchild. Sometimes Joanna would walk a little way with her mother when Sybil went out to work, but Sybil was nervous about the traffic on the child's account, and she would not let Joanna come beyond a point where a road had to be crossed. There were so many bicycles, motor and foot-pedal, so many cars.

Sybil was working as housemaid-help in three different houses, one a doctor's, the other two belonging to dons. The doctor lived near Corpus College, but the dons' houses were as widely apart as the mental make-up of their occupants. Professor Tinsley, a disciple of Einstein's, lived in a terrace house not far from the Botanical Gardens. Mr. Fortescue, a humanist and a classicist of the classicists, preferred one of the houses beyond the "Backs." Even though the new world regarded Tennyson as an obsolete and succulent platitudinarian, Mr. Fortescue still thought in terms of immemorial elms.

Sybil preferred the Fortescue house to work in. It was easy and unhurried, and rather untidy and unpunctual, and full of books and odd furniture and pipes and a smell of nicotine and literature. Sybil thought it a nice, friendly, good-natured house, and though its haphazard dreaminess gave her more work, she did not mind. Professor Tinsley's house was very different. It had the cold, clean efficiency of a laboratory. Professor Tinsley did not smoke. He was pale of face and eye, and he dieted himself. His wife made Sybil think of a pot of refrigerated cream. The lady had a red and polished tip to her nose, and belonged to many learned societies. She was an authority upon sociology and eugenics.

Yet Cambridge produced in Sybil a curious restlessness. Much of Cambridge was ugly, some of it was beautiful, and if Sybil could love Clare Bridge and the Great Court of Trinity and King's Chapel and the "Backs," she also loved other things. There were the shops. Her life had been very full of unselfish dullness, and there was in this university town a perfume of youth. It was as though Sybil was infected by this youthfulness. It was like some subtle essence impregnating her. She could not or did not analyse her restlessness. There were days when she felt as though something strange was going to happen. Her face had a flush. Something sang in her. Youth, youth!

In Mill Lane she sometimes met a young man, an undergrad. He was tall and slim and freckled, with blue eyes that looked at her with a gaillard shyness. Perhaps he had books under his arm. Often she met him without a hat, and his fair hair had a waviness. Almost it was the colour of honey. She felt a little strange thrill when she saw this young man in front of her. She never looked at him as they passed each other, but she was very conscious of his nearness.

He looked at Sybil.

For Sybil was still a comely person, and if her hands were somewhat roughened, her neck was cream. She was full of bosom, and sleek of shoulder, and her short-sighted brown eyes had the allure of their wildness. She might seem tame, but in her—as in most women—was the wish to be desired, and the urge to give to the desirer when the fruit has the ripeness of youth. The thing confused her, and, feeling so strangely confused, she fled past youth with sudden, inward colour. She was troubled. How absurd! To be put out of

[339]

countenance by a casual boy in grey flannel trousers and with freckles and honey-coloured hair!

She remembered that occasion when Keir—

But she loved Keir and Joanna Mary, and yet there was in her a kind of virginal tumult, a consciousness of youth and of youth's poignant and eager glances.

One evening, coming home late from the Fortescues', she met the lad in a dark curve of the lane. The pavement was very narrow. He moved off it to let her pass.

He spoke to her.

"Good evening. It seems silly, doesn't it, when we pass each other so often—"

She was frightened, alarmed by the sudden surge of sex, for there was something in her soft ripeness that provoked him, and she knew it.

"Yes, of course. But one passes so many people—"

She was breathless. She paused for a moment, shrinking against the wall. He laughed softly, soundlessly.

"But one doesn't notice many of them."

He was almost as shy as she was.

"My name's Hammond. I'm at King's."

She did not tell him her name. She wanted to fly from him, but for the moment something held her.

"I say—you couldn't come out—some evening? One doesn't often get the chance to talk to—"

She blurted out her protest.

"Oh—I couldn't. I have to put my small girl to bed, and every night I tell her a story."

"A fairy story?"

"Yes."

"I see. But—I suppose— I didn't quite imagine— It does matter, does it?"

"Oh, yes."

She gave him a slanting and poignant glance in the dusk, and fled. He did not follow her. He stood looking after her.

He smiled. The provocation of her wildness remained with him. Perhaps—tomorrow? He strolled on, with the long, easy lope of youth. Tomorrow! But Sybil, in strange distress, was almost running to the door of that very small house where Joanna Mary would be waiting to be put to bed. She was glad of Joanna Mary. She opened the door, and from the half-lit interior of the house a voice came to her instantly.

"Is that you, Mrs. Smith?"

"Yes."

"Thank heaven—you've come. I thought of sending for you. The blessed one got out into the lane—"

Sybil forgot all about youth and its turbulence.

"She's not—?"

"Just bruised. A wretched brat of a boy on a bike knocked her over. I've put her to bed. But she's been crying for you."

Sybil rushed upstairs.

Keir never heard of Joanna Mary's adventure in the lane. The child was not badly hurt, but Sybil was full of self-accusation and remorse. To Keir's wife life moved in mysterious ways. She believed in God, a God who appeared in your secret garden and called you by name. "Sybil—Sybil, art thou not a mother and a wife?" Her sensitive simplicity fell upon its knees.

Henceforward she avoided Mill Lane. She walked an extra and virtuous mile in order to reach the Fortescue house. Only once did she meet young Hammond, and she found that the insurgence of sex had vanished. She smiled, gave him a casual little nod, and passed on.

But she wanted to be with Keir. If man was not made to live alone, neither was woman. She wanted that cottage, and a garden, and all those things that make a woman such as Sybil feel secure.

"Will it be much longer, Keir?"

"Tired of Cambridge, Syb?"

"I'm tired of being alone."

He was as innocent as most husbands who, though youth and its urges may have vexed them, regard the woman in the house as stable as a piece of furniture.

"It's all my fault, Syb."

"Oh, no, dear."

"Well, as a matter of fact—I think there is something in the air. Jannis heard a rumour that we have been left a legacy."

"We?"

"I mean—Papworth. And some of it is to go on cottages."

Chapter Thirty

1

JANNIS, that dark creature, had his whimsical moods, for a man's moods are so much Nature's. Though no longer a babe within his mother's body, he is still the child shut up in the womb of Mother Mystery, and Jannis was a black Celt. That is why he and Sir Pendrill, high priest and disciple, could see in the silver sickle of the moon a reaping-hook or the edge of eternity. A robin's song was not just a robin's song, but the whole of autumn, pungent, red of leaf, faintly macabre. He was a child of the planets. He cast horoscopes, but his own nativity he dared not explore.

He cast Keir's horoscope.

"You are fortunate, my child. Struggle—suffering—and then a blue, serene sea."

Keir had grown very fond of his room-mate, this dark, delicate creature whose eyes looked black. He became accustomed to Jannis's moments of gentle melancholy.

"There is always some bogy, old man. When *homo sapiens* grows so educated that ghosts cease to function, man turns to and creates a bogy out of himself."

Keir understood; he understood this truth only too well. He had a feeling that Jannis was afraid of the darkness, and especially of a grey and grizzly winter dusk. He would come in looking pale and hunted and make straight for the hostel fire. In these moments of vague fear he was a sociable creature who hurried to warm himself with his fellow-men. He stretched out his hands to life's blaze. He became gay, tragically gay.

[343]

Sometimes when they had turned out the light in their cubicle, they would lie and talk for a while, and out of the darkness Jannis's voice would philosophize.

"When we have got our cottages, old man, and the flesh of our flesh near us, what then?"

"You are always looking too far ahead, Jannis."

"It's my fate. But there's always an edge, isn't there, an edge where the sunlight ends and the shadow begins?"

"Well, keep in the sunlight."

There was silence between them for a moment, and then —out of the mouth of Jannis flowed the very words that were always haunting Keir.

"Fear, fear of the tomorrow, that's our shadow here, old man. Tomorrow may be the edge of a shadow. There is no day for us but today."

"One has to live in the present?"

"Utterly and absolutely."

"Well, after all, isn't that the secret of living? I look into the eyes of my wife today, I play with my child today. What is tomorrow?"

"Yes, but man's urge has always been tomorrow. We're not static creatures; like everything else, we flow."

"If tomorrow means fear, let's cut it out."

A little gentle laugh came from the other bed.

"I can't—somehow. Is it that I'm too much of a beastly little egoist? No, it's not what might happen to me, but what might happen to those others. You just go out into the darkness; they stay behind—with what? An empty grate? At the mercy of the world? That's my shadow, old man. That's why I clutch at today."

Keir understood.

"I suppose the war was rather like that. We missed the war, Jannis. The only thing is to carry on. There will always be fear of some sort. They give us all they can here."

Jannis sighed.

"I wish they could give us God."

The bitter cry of man crucified. "My God, my God, why hast Thou forsaken me?"

For under the edge of the shadow of death man may hide his head in the cloak of fatalism or look yearningly at the stars. Keir understood what his room-mate was feeling, for he too had wandered alone in the dark places. He could have cried with Goethe: "More light, more light!"

Immortality, survival, or faith in some beneficent Intelligence? Was man blown out like a candle, and had he to fear every gust from the unknown? There might be no tomorrow, nothing but today, and if today failed you, was that the end?

But to Keir during those winter months there came a kind of clarity of inward vision. He groped, even as the winter sun groped its way through the clouds, but each day the planet rose higher on the horizon. Hope swelled in him with the gradual burgeoning of the spring. Blackbirds sang again. The earth was growing green.

Someone gave him a book of Samuel Butler's, and he devoured it. Chance, or cunning? Had man emerged from the slime as a mere jumble of fortuitous circumstances? Had he just happened out of nothing, to become again nothing? Had all the world's visionaries been mere mouthing fools?

One spring day, leaning over a field-gate and looking at bluebells in a wood, he seemed to hear a mysterious sound as of bells. Perfume and vague laughter, sunlight playing in and out of the young green leaves. The bronze buds of the oaks were swelling, and suddenly this painted screen of the sense world seemed to become diaphanous. It was as though he could look through it and catch glimpses of a beyondness. A field-gate, a wood, flowers, both real and strangely unreal. What comprehended it? Consciousness? Why consciousness? And if consciousness had come out of the slime and manifested in its awareness of beauty, was there not an infinite significance in this consciousness? A lamp had been lit. Man carried it about inside him, and the light had become so familiar that man had ceased to appreciate its significance.

Keir thought: "If I see beauty—there is beauty. If I feel good things in me—the good exists. If I feel shame—then, there are things that are shameful. Realities, the realities of my conscious self. The gate, flowers, trees, the inward movements of my psyche. Realities. A dream within a dream in which God is apprehended."

He was conscious of a curious exultation, of a sudden tranquillity. It was as though the painted world of the senses had ceased to be opaque. He had a feeling that he had passed through it. It was like water or some mysterious, vapoury atmosphere. He had transcended his senses.—Other dimensions! Well—why not?

He told Jannis of his experience.

"Go down to that gate, old man, and look at the trees and the flowers. I got away there—into somewhere else."

Jannis laughed.

"Lob's Wood?"

"I got caught up in the mystery of my own consciousness."

That Keir the carpenter should end in mysticism was—after all—but the heritage of the craftsman, for in every passionate craftsman lurks the potential mystic. That which caresses the clay or moulds the marble divines the soul of some other creator. Jannis went down to Keir's wood, and though he did not see what Keir saw, he returned wondering and consoled.

"Everything was still, old man, and then a little wind came and the bluebells trembled ever so little."

"Did you hear them ringing?"

"That's a whimsy."

"Is it? Why should it be? After all, an electric light would seem pretty whimsical to Pharaoh. I have a new light inside me, Jannis. It shines beyond words. I have asked for a miracle, and a voice said to me down there: 'Isn't man himself a miracle? Consider your own consciousness.'"

The flame in Jannis was more wayward. It seemed to tremble on the edge of the darkness of fatalism.

"Oh, man, if one really had proof—! If one knew that tomorrow was a door!"

"Why shouldn't it be? Our three-dimensional world may be just a box."

"I wonder what Sir Pendrill thinks about it."

Said Keir: "A man who could conceive and create a place like this must have faith in something. I mean—he can't be the chance product of primeval slime. There's a sort of profound common sense in faith. That's how I have begun to feel about it, and I'm different for feeling about it in that way."

"There's all the difference in the world. It means there's a significance in things."

"Yes, it means that hope goes on."

3

It was at the Papworth flower show that Keir told Sybil the news. He was to become a colonized man and draw a craftsman's pay. They were moving with Joanna Mary through a world of sweet peas and dahlias, monstrous turnips and gigantic vegetable marrows, marrows that would have made more than a load for Joanna Mary's wheelbarrow.

"We shall want our furniture this winter, Syb."

He was aware of the quick lift of her head, and of the lighting up of her face.

"Oh, Keir! Cottages?"

She was as quick as ever in her enthusiasms.

"Yes, six of them. They have started on the foundations. One of them is to be ours."

"When will it be ready?"

"I expect we shall be able to get in some time after Christmas. It will depend on the weather."

Papworth built its own cottages, with the help of fit men as bricklayers and labourers, and Keir took Sybil and Jo to look at the site. It lay at the top of the hill, sheltered by trees, and stacks of flettons and mounds of ballast showed that the business of building was under way. In fact a couple of bricklayers were at work on the very cottage that would be Keir's, though the wall was no higher than the wall of Romulus when Remus leaped over it.

Keir had an inspiration.

"You ought to lay a brick for luck, Syb."

She was in love with the idea, and when the matter was explained to the bricklayers, they tumbled to it. Sybil was given a brick and a trowel, and some mortar was held ready on a shovel.

"What do I do?"

One of the bricklayers gave her a demonstration, but she spilt half the mortar from the trowel. The second attempt was more successful.

"Give it a tap, missis, for luck. Yes, with the handle of the trowel."

And then Joanna Mary insisted upon laying a brick. The bricklayer wanted to support and guide her hands, but Joanna was all for independence.

"I can do it myself."

The brick had to be relaid after her back was turned.

During the late summer and autumn when the day's work was over, Keir and Jannis would stroll up together to watch the cottages growing. The Smiths and the Jannises were to occupy two semi-detached cottages. They would be next-door neighbours. As a Papworth citizen the craftsman in Keir was on the alert. He was interested in the quality of the bricks and the soundness of the timber, and in the spacing of joists and rafters, but some of the settlement carpenters were at work, and Papworth was building for itself. Keir knew all the tricks of the trade, and especially the tricks of the timber-merchant who would unload his warped and twisted battens and his damaged matchboard on the innocent and the careless.

But Papworth and the presiding spirit of Papworth insisted upon thoroughness, and it could not suffer itself and its work to be let down by a pawky commercialism. It did not believe in the text of "Fool the other fellow if you can. Prepare to be found out on occasions, and keep an expert liar on the premises. And always remain: Your obedient servants." Keir knew that all the timber that was delivered at the work for storing was checked and inspected. It had to be sound stuff, for Papworth gave quality.

In the village there were still to be seen some of the earlier products when Papworth and its workers were learning their craft. It was rather a crude product, and when Keir compared the beautiful pieces that were being turned out now with the clumsy and poorly finished articles of the earlier years, he understood Papworth's pride.

"Do your best, and then go one better."

The soundness of such a creed comforted him. It cheered the craftsman in him. He had heard Jannis expatiate upon some of the secret triumphs of the estate office and try to imitate Mr. Rice's tight and humorous smile. Someone had ordered chicken-houses—quite a number of chicken-houses—from a certain firm and had been badly let down by them. At the time of delivery the work had not even been put in hand. An angry gentleman had wired to Papworth.

"Please quote the earliest date when you can supply"—so and so.

Papworth had wired back: "Ten days."

The houses had been built and delivered in ten days, and the angry gentleman, somewhat appeased, had passed on the information to the defaulting firm.

"You have been badly licked by a colony of ex-soldiers and consumptives."

Jannis was amused at the way Keir appointed himself amateur supervisor of the cottage property. He would get up on a step-ladder and examine the lathing of a ceiling, and go up into the roof and look at the joists and the tile battens.

"Lob's Wood, old man. Found any bluebells?"

Keir retorted.

"It's all O.K. What about your ledgers, Jannis? No blots?"

"Facetious fellow!"

"It's better to be conscious of your craft—than of your class, old lad. That's what's wrong with a part of the old country. It's been so full of rabid and silly class-consciousness that it forgot all about its craft. I'd put a few of the financiers down coal-mines for a month and set a few miners figuring out costs. Both parties would be the wiser for knowing that there was something different and difficult in the other fellow's job."

4

The elms were turning yellow, and on those still autumnal days any sudden movement of the air would bring a shower of gold to earth. Keir began to talk of spending Christmas in the new cottage, and then—because of a certain sound in the night and a look by day in the eyes of his friend—he ceased to talk about the future.

Jannis's cough had returned. It was little more than a clearing of the throat, and to Keir it was obvious that Jannis was trying to conceal it and the thing's significance even from himself. The edge of the shadow was there, more definitely there, but the clerk would not admit it. If he cast little, fearful glances behind him, they were but momentary glances. He preserved an air of gaiety, but Keir knew that the heart of his friend was afraid.

He noticed that Jannis became breathless when walking up the easy slope to the new cottages. He persisted in visiting those cottages, for tomorrow still mattered intensely, and he would not surrender his tomorrow. He talked to Keir about what he and his wife intended doing in the cottage and the garden. They were going to grow the finest sweet peas in Papworth. He meant to build a wireless set of his own and get Paris, and Milan, and Berlin. Yes, Mary Jannis was making arrangements for their furniture to be moved from the warehouse.

"Wasn't it a good thing we managed to save most of the furniture, old man?"

Keir, looking at his friend with eyes that could not be deceived, felt the pity and the pathos of it. Was Jannis just pretending, or did he know?

But if Jannis knew that one of them was to be taken and the other left, was it necessary for him as a friend to draw Jannis's attention to what might be both tragic and obvious to his friend? At Papworth there were men who kept up the illusion of living to the very last, men of the temper and courage of Robert Louis, who, with a smother of blood upon them, could gasp out the words: "If this is death, it might be worse." Keir had a feeling that Jannis was only too

[351]

conscious of the closing shadows, and that like a man chosen to lead a forlorn hope, he made himself smile in the face of the enemy.

How futile to blurt out the obvious: "You're coughing again, old man. You ought to report to the doctors."

One night, coming in rather late to the cubicle after a game of billiards, Keir surprised his room-mate sitting up in bed with a thermometer in his mouth. Jannis, like a self-conscious boy caught smoking a cigarette, and with the glass tube held between his teeth, mumbled out something about influenza. His eyes looked pleadingly at Keir.

Keir began to undress, as though clinical thermometers were of no significance. He was aware of Jannis removing the instrument, and holding it up to the light to discover where the mercury stood on the scale. There was silence. Jannis was wiping the thermometer with a handkerchief, and Keir had a feeling that his friend was frightened.

Keir sat down and took off his boots.

"Haven't kept you awake, Jannis, have I?"

Jannis was lying on his back, staring at the ceiling. His figure had a tense stillness.

"No, old man. I thought I had a bit of a temperature. Halliday in the office has been down with flu. I expect I've caught it."

"Much of a temperature?"

Jannis lied, and Keir knew that he was lying.

"Just over ninety-nine, that's all. I shall be all right tomorrow."

Keir said: "Oughtn't you to report, old man, and lie up for a day or two?"

Jannis lay and stared at the ceiling as though a large black spider was poised up there and ready to drop on him.

"Oh, no, it's nothing. I hate making a fuss. So long as you are not worrying about—"

"No, I'm not worrying."

"There is plenty of fresh air in here."

But that night Jannis's cough was more troublesome. It filled the small room with a sense of distress and of foreboding. It kept Keir awake for a time, and he knew that Jannis must be awake, but neither he nor the clerk spoke to each other during the night. If it was his friend's wish to pretend that all was well with his world, Keir felt that he must stand by to help in supporting the crumbling pillars of that world.

His friend's tomorrow was growing dim.

Chapter Thirty-one

1

PAPWORTH kept Christmas, and if the settlement was—according to the very clever people—a colony of incurable sentimentalists, no one in Papworth complained. If Sir Pendrill willed it—and Sir Pendrill was a Welshman—that a prodigious Christmas tree should be planted and decorated in the village hall, it was done and done dramatically. Keir was one of those who helped to decorate the tree, and if some slobbering English idiot murmured that "The show was for the kids," Keir was happy to find himself on the side of the idiots.

For this Christmas was to be for him unlike any other Christmas. It was not mere beef and beer. If it celebrated the birth of the carpenter who was to be crucified, the ever recurring martyrdom of man, it was also a new birth, a piece of symbolism, compassionate humanity gathered together and lighting Christmas candles. Keir's childhood had lacked the Christmas spirit. His sneering, strenuous, pallid father had scorned such sob-stuff, the fool with a white beard and a red flannel dressing-gown. Keir came to this Christmas rather as a wise and gentle child to whom the wonder of life had been restored. He was one with the Kings, and the Shepherds, and the Wise Men. He was tired of raucous demagogues preaching social plunder.

There were visitors, Sybil and Joanna Mary and other men's wives and children. There were the nurses, and Miss Borne, and the doctors, and friends from Cambridge, and Sir Pendrill—who might have worn a black velvet cloak and a trunk hose. One of the departmental managers dressed himself up as Father Christmas. The Papworth musical society sang carols.

Keir held his small daughter's hand.

"Ever seen a tree like that, Jo?"

Joanna had not. It was an immense tree that went up to the roof and twinkled and glittered.

Sybil looked flushed and happy. She had been to see the new cottage, where the plaster was drying off. They were to occupy that cottage at the end of January.

"I wish I was a kid, Keir."

He smiled at her with whimsical benevolence.

"Aren't you one?—I rather think you'll always be one."

"I'm getting quite middle-aged, Keir."

"Rot."

She had been glancing over the faces of the Christmas crowd for the face of Keir's friend.

"Where's Mr. Jannis?"

"Oh, he ought to be here—somewhere. He's one of the world's kids."

Jannis wasn't to be seen, and yet Keir knew that the clerk had put on his party mood and suit for this show, a new blue shirt with a blue collar and tie. What had happened to Jannis? Keir wanted his friend to be part of his particular party. There might be no more Christmas shows for Jannis in this three-dimensional world.

Keir was circling the glittering, green spruce, holding Joanna by the hand, when his eyes were drawn to one of the oak doors at the end of the hall. He saw Jannis standing there looking like a ghost, some pale thing that had blown in for a moment out of the winter night and would return to the mists in the meadows. Keir was transfixed by the apparition of his friend. He stood still and stared at Jannis, feeling that Jannis was seeing something more than a crowd of men, women, and children. The clerk seemed to hang there—crucified—though his arms were not nailed to the limbs of a cross.

Suddenly Jannis turned and went out, and Keir guessed the truth. This man who knew that he had to die could not bear to look upon this children's show. It was too tantalizing, too warm and well lit, too full of poignant associations. Jannis had gone out into the darkness.

Keir became aware of his small daughter pressing against his thigh. She was gazing up at his face.

"What's the matter, daddy?"

"Nothing, Jo."

"You looked so funny."

He glanced again towards the door where his friend had been standing.

"I thought I saw a ghost, Jo."

"Ghosts! There aren't such things as ghosts."

"Oh, aren't there, my dear, aren't there!"

2

Keir did not see Jannis again till late in the evening when all the visitors had gone and the candles had been quenched on the Christmas tree. Keir found the clerk sitting alone over one of the hostel fires. He had drawn his chair close to the curb and was leaning over the fire as though both the body and the soul of him felt cold.

Keir was touched by the lonely figure of his friend. As he closed the door, Jannis half-turned and looked at him. There was heart-break in the clerk's eyes, a kind of deprecating mute anguish.

Keir sat down on another chair and spread his hands to the fire. He felt that there was nothing that he could say to his friend, to the poor, chilled man-thing who was trying to warm himself before going out into the last darkness. He knew that it was not death that could be so bitter, but the parting of those human contacts, the dread of what might happen to the people who were left behind.

Jannis spoke. His lips began to tremble some seconds before the words came. He did not look at Keir, but gazed at the fire, and his voice was the voice of a man who was very tired.

"Have they all gone home?"

"Yes."

"I'm glad Mary and the kid couldn't come. I don't think I could have gone through with it, old man."

Keir felt himself voiceless.

"You know you ought to report to the doctors, Jannis."

"What's the use? I know I'm done for."

He rose from his chair, spreading his arms like a man drawing in all the breath that his lungs could contain. To sleep—oh, to sleep and forget!"

"Let's go to bed, Smithie. Where's everybody?"

"There's a whist drive on at the old hostel."

"Oh, let's go to bed, old man. I'm—I'm glad you saw your people. Come on."

Keir said nothing. He rose and, slipping a hand under Jannis's arm, went out with him into the corridor.

They undressed in silence. Jannis was the first in bed, and Keir turned out the light and slipped in between the sheets.

"Good night, Jannis."

"Good night."

But Keir did not feel like sleeping. Not a sound came from the other bed, yet Keir was sure that Jannis was as wakeful as he was. He felt the darkness to be charged with his friend's dry anguish. Other men came to bed. The neighbouring cubicles received their occupants. Cheerful voices sounded in the corridors, but presently all was still. The December night was misty and windless, and in Keir's bluebell wood there would not be so much as the crackle of a dead leaf. He lay wakeful, and troubled for Jannis's sake, though his own day had been full of simple, happy things, that brilliant tree, Joanna's flushed face, the tranquil eyes of his wife. And yet how near was the edge of the eternal shadow! He had been fortunate; he was healed; he could hope. But this other man!

And suddenly he heard a sound coming from the neighbouring bed, a sound of secret, hopeless weeping. He was shocked, profoundly moved. This other man's anguish might have been his anguish.

Keir left his bed. He knew that his overcoat was hanging on the cubicle door, and he groped for it and put it on.

"Jannis, old man—"

The clerk's sobbing broke out like the sobbing of a child.

"I didn't know you were awake. How damned silly of me, snivelling like this!"

"Jannis, you mustn't say that. You've been so full of courage."

Keir was feeling for a chair. This smothering agony in the darkness made him tremble.

"It's no use, old man. I'm done for. I've known it for some time, and seeing all those kids and the women—it upset me. I know my number's up. They'll never come here. I shan't want that cottage."

Keir found the chair. He placed it beside Jannis's bed and sat down.

"Jannis, I know how you are feeling. Here's a hand. Hold on."

In the darkness his friend's hand felt for his, found it, and was grasped.

"If I could sleep, old man! It's such hell lying awake and thinking and worrying. What's to happen to them?— Where's my handkerchief?"

Keir found it for him under his pillow.

"I'm so sorry, old man, so sorry."

Keir sat there for a long time holding his friend's hand. He had buttoned up his overcoat and turned up the collar, for the room was cold, and yet he knew that he could bear it for a little while. "Could ye not watch with me one hour?" Jannis's hand lay very still in his. There was silence. And presently Keir knew that his friend had fallen asleep. This human contact had soothed him. Keir waited for a while and then gently withdrew his hand. There was no movement, no protest. Jannis was breathing quietly, and Keir stood up and, slipping off his coat, went back to bed.

3

The green of the leaf on an evening in May.

Keir was building a rustic arch for climbing roses in the new garden. Had he been honest with himself, he would have confessed that he had no great liking for rustic arches, but Sybil desired it, and so—a rustic arch there had to be. A three-inch French nail struck slantingly on the head flew off like a bright splinter from the larch pole and lost itself in the grass. Keir smiled. He supposed that he would have to look for that nail, for there was a shortage of nails, and the day was the Sabbath.

He stood for a moment with the hammer in his hand. He was very conscious of the green world, the elms, the golden oaks, the meadows, the thorn trees coming into blossom. At the other end of the garden his wife was planting out snapdragons. He saw her blue apron and intent brown head. Joanna too was busy with her barrow, occupied as in the "Merrow" days in collecting stones for the path.

Keir looked over the village. He could see the white brow of the Hall, and the great trees about Sir Pendrill's rest-house, and the roofs of the workshops and the cottages.

Life had a simplicity here, and Keir had come to believe in the beauty and the beneficence of simple things. They were like the warm sunlight on your skin, the smell of the soil after rain, the moon shining upon mown hay.

In the cities man talked too much. He was like water fretting against a wall.

And Keir thought: "It is better to do things than to talk and read about them. The hammer in my hand is better than the pen of the daily scribbler. The man who made this place ought to be happy."

A NOTE ON THE TYPE IN WHICH THIS BOOK IS SET

John Baskerville (1706–75), of Birmingham, England, a writing-master, with a special renown for cutting inscriptions in stone, began experimenting about 1750 with punch-cutting and making typographical material. It was not until 1757 that he published his first work, a Virgil in royal quarto, with great-primer letters. This was followed by his famous editions of Milton, the Bible, the Book of Common Prayer, and several Latin classic authors. His types, at first criticized as unnecessarily slender, delicate, and feminine, in time were recognized as both distinct and elegant, and both his types and his printing were greatly admired. Printers, however, preferred the stronger types of Caslon, and Baskerville before his death repented of having attempted the business of printing. For four years after his death his widow continued to conduct his business. She then sold all his punches and matrices to the Société Littéraire-typographique, which used some of the types for the sumptuous Kehl edition of Voltaire's works in seventy volumes. The text of this book was set in Baskerville. The punches for this face were cut under the supervision of George W. Jones, an eminent English printer. Linotype Baskerville is a facsimile cutting from type cast from the original matrices of a face designed by John Baskerville. The original face was the forerunner of the "modern" group of type faces.

COMPOSED, PRINTED, AND BOUND BY
H. WOLFF ESTATE, NEW YORK.
THE PAPER WAS MADE BY
TICONDEROGA PAPER CO.,
TICONDEROGA,
NEW YORK